MAKING A TINDERBOX

Book One in The Tinderbox Tales

EMMA STERNER-RADLEY

Heartsome Publishing

DEDICATION

Dedicated to my family – for always letting me daydream and thereby building an author.

CONTENTS

ACKNOWLEDGMENTS

Firstly, I have to thank marshmallows and black coffee for getting me through the times when writing and editing was no fun. No really.

Thanks to my family for always being supportive even though I am not in Sweden helping you or basically being of any kind of use to you. Mamma, pappa, Anna, Torbjörn, Oscar, Victor, Ester. You are so understanding and I am proud to be your daughter, sister, sister-in-law and aunt. I cannot thank you enough. Now, do us all a favour and just skim over the erotic parts of this book. Especially chapter 24 – skip that one. Or at least tell me you did.

Also, huge thanks to the person who pushes me to fulfil my dreams. The woman who encourages me, worries about me and makes my life unmeasurably better just by being in it, my darling wife. Amanda – without you I never would have gotten to where I am now. I will spend the rest of our lives together trying to repay you. You're my miracle.

A very special thank you to my utterly brilliant editor, Jessica Hatch, who improved this book immeasurably with her great insights and expertise at what a manuscript needs. All without ever tampering with my voice or my way of telling a story. After her, the keen eye and steady hand of the heroic Cheri Fuller found any remaining bumps and smudges.

A set of unpaid heroes helped out too. Shannon Mcclure, Aurelie Gilbert, Miira Ikiviita and Pilar Ortega all read the un-edited draft and asked the sort of questions that I needed to clarify and improve the little (but oh so important) stuff.

Any mistakes that remain are solely mine. This book needed you all – thank you.

A special shout out to Frances Craig for reading my first novel a few years back and despite its awfulness – encouraging me and telling me that my descriptions of made-up settings were great. I hope you'll like the ones in this book too.

Lastly I'd like to thank, as always, the woman who was so instrumental in shaping my personality and creativity. My moral compass and sounding board.
Malin Sterner
1973-2011
I wish you could have seen this. Jag saknar dig.

INTRODUCTION

Hello reader. Whether you're a fantasy buff or just opened this book to get to the romance – Welcome to a parallel world! Or a new planet, if you prefer. It's called the Orb and has a civilisation which is set in a time and space similar to when the industrial revolution began in Europe. (1760 to around 1820 for those of you who slept in history class – hey, no judgement here. I personally can't remember a single math class.)

Some things have been borrowed from later in the 1800s, some things are utterly fictional and some things I hope have been borrowed from our future – like the increased diversity and more open-minded values. However, the people of the Orb are still people, so they have found other ways to hate and fear those are different. Read on to see what I mean.

This book, while being stand alone and completely free of cliff hangers, is the first book in a series called The Tinderbox Tales. This book will focus on the continent of Arclid which has many traits borrowed from Great Britain. Other parts of the Orb will be slightly similar to other countries and continents in our world. Now, Arclid is the name of a real place in our world. If you know of that place, you'll understand why it was funny to name a whole continent after it. In this book there are many such Easter eggs. Not only for people who know about British geography, but also for history buffs. You do not need to know any of these things to enjoy the book, however.

It is generally accepted as gospel that those who read lesfic (books for women who love women) tend to not read or enjoy the fantasy genre. Most lesfic readers seem to want contemporary romance books. If you are one of these unsure readers – I'd urge you not to worry. You can just read this story for the romance, the humour, and the suspense, without worrying about all the world-building stuff. If you however like fantasy – there will be a short glossary and a map at the end of the book.

With that, I leave you to your reading. If you have questions or comments please see my author bio for ways to contact me.

And of course, reviews are gold dust for writers as it helps us sell our books and keeps us writing. So if you have the time and inclination, please review.

Oh, and by the way... the good news is that white ravens do exist in our world too. The bad news is that sugar pumpkins do not.

CHAPTER 1
WINTER WEDDING

Lady Elisandrine Falk was ushered into the room, and the door was shut behind her with a loud bang. A heartbeat of silence, and then there was a click.

Was that the door being locked? Have they actually locked me in?

She put her hands on her hips and sighed. Oh well. There were worse gilded cages than this one. A silver clock on the wall chimed, and out of it popped an intricate clockwork bird. It nodded its head as it chirped.

Its cheerful telling of the time mocked her. The bird appeared to be the only nod to anything modern around here. From what she had seen in the carriage over and in her short march up to her room, this remote castle and its tiny neighbouring village seemed stuck in the past. Not a factory to be seen and not a hint of steam to be detected. It was all trees, fields, and this old-fashioned castle, which was much smaller than the one she was used to. It was all beautiful, picturesque, and utterly wasted on her.

Elisandrine surveyed the room, taking in the majestic but sparsely decorated stone walls. Centurian marble, known for the pink striation in the white stone, she decided. Just as in Highmere, the royal capitol she used to call home. Her interest in architecture and buildings was one of the few things she remembered sharing with her father. She wished he were here now. He would have put a stop to this infernal wedding.

She walked over to the lavish bed and sat down, facing the window. She was relieved that it was a single bed.

So, this is not where I will be living with my husband. Unless he will call me into his room when he wants to consummate the marriage.

Like that would ever happen. She laughed to herself. No, she would be out of this castle and this dull relic of a village long before that. Prince Macray would have to find some other woman to warm his bed and attend royal gatherings on his arm.

She had been content as a lady-in-waiting to her highness, so why had the Queen gotten it into her head to marry Elisandrine off to her younger brother? Not only did Prince Macray lack moral fibre, common decency, and a chin — he was also under-developed in the sense of humour department. No, thank you.

Lady Elisandrine Falk had never planned to marry, but if she had to, it surely wouldn't be him. She wished she were a commoner. Then she could choose whatever partner she wanted, position and gender be damned. Sadly, she was Noble-born, meaning she was to be married off to a man and bred like a prize mare.

Or so they told her.

So, she stared out the tall stained-glass window. In the distance, she could just make out the little village of Ground Hollow, which bordered Silver Hollow Castle. She wondered how high the drop down was. Could she escape if she didn't find a safer way out of this ridiculous marriage proposal in the coming months?

She sighed again, taking in the lonely room. For lack of anything better to do, she went over to one of the room's bookshelves. She ran her slender fingers over the spines, trying to find a tome to take her mind off her current situation. Perhaps a book with some inspiration on how to escape a marriage. Or how to escape a castle.

Hours later, she was so engrossed in a book about Noble marriages throughout history, with an interesting chapter about wives poisoning their husbands, that she hardly heard the knock at the door. At first Elisandrine wondered if it was one of the guards that had been assigned to her, Corinna.

No. I am not likely to get that lucky again.

She had managed to get Corinna into her room, and her bed, for some fun a short while ago. Afterwards, the guard had sadly become paranoid and assumed Elisandrine's motive for the bedplay was to be freed.

While that would have been welcome indeed, it hadn't been her motive. Distraction, comfort, and the treat of a beautiful woman in the handsome royal uniform — that was what Elise had seen, wanted, and subsequently got.

No, the knock on her door was unlikely to be Corinna coming back for more, so Elisandrine turned to glare at the offending door.

"I hear you knocking and I would let you in, stranger," she called. "But someone has locked the door from the outside, so I am afraid it is not up to me."

She knew she shouldn't be facetious to whomever was on the other side of the door, but she couldn't help it. She didn't do well with being locked up.

There was an unlocking click and the door opened,

revealing Prince Macray. He stopped in the doorway, adjusting the cravat at the collar of his dress uniform.

A cravat? I really have stepped back into history. Will he expect me to wear a corset and a big bustle, too? Gods forbid.

Macray cleared his throat. "Lady Elisandrine. I apologise for that the guards locked you in. My sister ordered them, and me, to ensure you did not get lost. It seems they took that order a little too far."

She kept her face stony. "I would say so, yes." There was no point in telling him that one of the guards had... seen to her needs before locking her up again. It would only muddle things.

The prince took a step into the room and closed the door behind him.

"Elise. May I call you Elise? I know my sister does."

Your sister is the Queen and my one true mistress. She is as impressive and imperial as her title commands. She does whatever she likes, however she likes. You are a boring, chinless milk-toad without any true power. So, no, please refrain.

Elisandrine buried her thoughts and simply said, "You are to be my husband, they tell me. I expect you can call me what-ever you wish."

To her surprise, he gave a pained sigh. "Yes. I suppose so."

He slumped against the wall. His skin, a pale pink, looked perfectly at home against the pink-streaked marble. Only his shrugging shoulders in the burgundy uniform made him unable to blend into the background.

For the first time, he piqued Elise's curiosity.

"You... seem unhappy, your Majesty."

"I am as unhappy as you are about this match." He must have seen the look on her face, because he rolled his eyes. "Oh, do not even try to deny it. You look at me like I just sneezed all over your face. You do not wish to marry me, and I do not wish to marry you. Nevertheless, marry we must."

4

This changed everything. He didn't want the wedding to go through either?

"Your Highness," she began hesitantly. "I am not following you here. My mother —and your sister the Queen — can marry me off to anyone they want. But you, you are a royal prince. Next in line to the throne. Surely, you can have any woman of Noble birth to be your wife?"

He gave a mirthless laugh. "Yes, I can. But as I do not want any of you, I did not care which one I was matched up with. It is all a breeding program for keeping the throne and to make sure the Noble bloodlines continue, anyway."

Elise raised her eyebrows but hummed her agreement. That much was true, but no one ever spoke of it so candidly.

He looked at her, as if assessing her. "I suppose we should make pretty little royal brats of various colourings. Your black hair mixed with my blonde. Your oak-coloured skin mixed with my... hmm, what is a lighter wood colour?" He tapped his finger against his chin. Then his face lit up. "Ah yes, *birch-coloured* skin. Your yellowish eyes mixed with my dark blue. Your striking beauty mixed with my clear features. I guess that was why my sister chose you. Either that or she secretly wanted to bed you and assumed I would have the same taste."

Elise stared him down defiantly. "And do you?"

He sniffed. "I am not certain. You are highly attractive, anyone with eyes can see that. But I hate the permanence of you. If you were forbidden fruit, I might desire you endlessly. However, as I have to have you and only you for the rest of my life, I find you as appealing as healthy bread."

Elise stepped into his personal space and snarled. "Then feel free to keep that doubtless diseased breadknife between your legs out of my loaf."

Macray sniggered. "Ah, there is the famous fiery temper of Elisandrine Falk. No wonder my sister calls you 'fire-starter.' Do not take it so personally. I told you, I enjoy variety. I want a new lover in my bed every night. I cannot stand being forced to have only one thing. There is so much restriction in the royal life. The one thing I was allowed some choice and variety in was what lovers I took. Now, that is all over. No more fair milkmaids or rough stable hands to keep me entertained."

He paused to sigh. "You know what our culture makes of affairs outside of wedlock. The shame would be too big. Now it is only you. Forever. And you do not even like me. So excuse me if I refrain from pretending to be thrilled about being shackled to you."

She took a deep breath to calm herself, clasping her hands behind her back. "You are right. There is no point in pretending. It is better that we both know how we feel. I am as uninterested in you as you are in me. It is not personal for me either. I simply saw myself with another type of partner."

"What type might that be?" he asked, his tone showing little else than boredom.

"The type that has a little more in the chest section and a different configuration between the legs."

His eyebrows shot up his forehead. "You want only women? No men at all?"

She put her hands on her hips. She had seen this reaction before.

"Does that surprise you?"

He shrugged. "Perhaps a little. Nevertheless, you know the rules as well as I do. Nobility can, like the commoners, sleep with anyone they want. But when we pair off for life, it has to be someone of the opposite gender so that we can procreate."

She groaned. "I know. But perhaps I am not content to merely procreate. Maybe I want freedom to choose? Possibly see if I can marry for love one day in the distant future?"

He scoffed. "I am certain you do. And I wish to live alone and bed whomever I want when I take the fancy. However, that is not our lives. Those are not our options. We are not allowed options, Lady Elisandrine."

"What happened to calling me Elise?"

He looked at her dejectedly. "What does it matter?"

His depressed air was contagious, and in a rare instant, she felt her fighting spirit flicker. "I suppose it matters very little."

"Try not at all. Anyway, I came to bid you welcome to the castle and to inform you that we are scheduled for a winter wedding."

He turned and walked out without a further glance in her direction.

Winter would take over Arclid in about three months. Elise had hoped for at least half a year before the ceremony, but now it seemed she would have only half of that. She knew little about the world outside of the circle of Nobles or what she would need to live there. She didn't even know how to get herself out of this wedding, out of the Noble set, and out into the real world where she could build her own life.

There were so many questions and no answers. And time was running out.

The door slammed closed behind the prince, seeming to seal Elise in as indubitably as her fate had been sealed.

CHAPTER 2

THE FARM, THE APOTHECARY, AND THE WOMAN AT THE WINDOW

Farmwork. Nessa Clay was sick to death of farmwork. Thank the gods this was her last season. She ran her hand over her neck, feeling a sheen of sweat and grime on it.

I'll never understand why I can sweat like this when it's this chilly outside.

She stretched. Every muscle in her body complained about overuse. Still, she knew this meant the sweetest sleep waited for her tonight. The deep, reviving sleep of those who had utterly exhausted themselves physically.

She was of two minds at how she felt about harvest season being over. Part of her was glad since her body could now rest and she could leave her parents' farm to start her own life. The other part would miss the simple joys of working her body tired and the safety of the little farm and her kind parents. The safety of Ground Hollow, in short. The village might be dull, but it was sheltered and cosy. She would miss that nearly as much as she would her parents.

"Nessa, would you like some water?"

She turned and found her mother handing her a dented tin cup. She emptied it in two long gulps. It hurt her throat going down, too cold. Everything here was too much. Too much cold, too much heat, too much work, too much boredom, too much... of everything being the same day in and day out.

"Thank you."

Her mother took the cup back. "It's the least I can do. Thank you for staying another few seasons to help me and your father. Now that we know the sugar pumpkins are taking to the soil, we should be fine for the upcoming years."

Nessa nodded. "I know. I didn't mind. I'm sure I'll have plenty of years on my own out there in the big world. It was nice to spend a handful more seasons helping out here at home and making sure the new crop took."

"You're so thoughtful, heartling. Most young men and women have started their lives by your age. I'm sure it was hard to see your friends start families or travel away from our little village."

Nessa smiled as warmly as she could at Carryanne Clay's worried eyes, which were framed by wrinkles as much created by the harsh winds on the fields as age. She surveyed her mother's face and knew that she would look much the same as she got older. She had inherited her mother's pale skin, grey eyes, high cheekbones, and almond-coloured hair. Other than having her father's slightly upturned nose and wide smile, she would look like the woman in front of her one day. She found that she was happy about that.

She reached out to caress her mother's cheek. "I'm twenty-five years old. Not an old crone. As I said, I have plenty of future ahead of me."

"Yes, of course. Have you decided what you will do?" Carryanne asked in sensible, clipped tones.

"I plan to darken your door for a little longer. Maybe rest a little before I leave for Nightport."

Her mother grimaced. "So, you are going to the big, bad city after all?"

Nessa pretended not to notice her mother's disapproval. She walked into their house of wooden slats and mud-covered walls. Carryanne followed close behind.

It was warmer inside, but not by much. Nessa wasn't going to miss the draughty houses of Ground Hollow.

"I think so, yes. I don't remember all that much from our visits to Nightport when I was little, but I remember enough to know I want to see it again. Everything was so big and so different even back then. And now…"

She stopped, searching for words that explained the obvious, ones that wouldn't be insulting to life in their small farming village. She knew her mother must have heard the news coming from Nightport and other cities in the last five years or so.

The world was changing rapidly, but it was only changing in the cities, leaving rural areas behind. The cities had factories, steam power, gas light, new worldviews. Ground Hollow, with its twelve farms and handful of houses, was the same as it had been the last one hundred years. Generation after generation farmed and shipped their goods out on the manmade canal that ran alongside the village. As far as Nessa knew, the only thing that had changed during the past century was that they had gotten a clock instead of a sundial for their church and an apothecary had opened.

"Today… everything happens in the cities, Mum. Nightport is always changing. Growing. The future is being created in the cities, and I want to see it. Our little village is nice, but nothing ever happens here. That is exactly as some people want it. But I… need change, I guess. Fresh views to clean the dust off my eyes."

Carryanne rubbed her brow. "But Nightport has beggars, pleasure sellers, and thieves. Not to mention the gambling halls. Or the drink and strange mind-altering powders. Nothing there is safe."

Nessa gave her mother a pointed look. "I've had a lifetime of safe. Don't you think it's time I saw more of the world? Grew? Got to know myself?"

Her mother sighed. "Fine. Just be careful. And make sure you find yourself a good occupation. I won't have you be one of them there strays that blow into the city and then starve on the streets. If you can't make ends meet, come back here and start over when we have fed you up again."

Nessa barely managed to stop herself from rolling her eyes. Her father had said about the same thing this morning, even using the same expression of feeding her up again. Her parents really needed to divvy up who was going to say what after their whispered late-night chats about her future.

Nessa tried for a reassuring smile. "Of course."

"Good. Stay and rest as long as you can. I would prefer if you weren't travelling until the worst of winter has gone. Maybe until spring."

Nessa hesitated. "Mother, I shouldn't wait that long. It's more than half a year until spring. And it's not all that cold yet. I'll rest a few days, but then I should leave before it *does* become cold. Besides, if I don't go soon, I'll probably lose my nerve and stay."

Her mother looked like she was about to argue, but then the fighting spirit died away, leaving only sadness in her grey eyes.

"Fine, but don't complain to me if there's a cold snap and you freeze your toes off on the road to Nightport! You are fully grown and make your own mistakes. More water?"

"Yes, please."

Nessa watched her mother go back out to the pump to refill the cup.

Melancholy hit her full force. She was sure that both her father and mother had hoped that she would say that she didn't know what to do. That she would stay another year here at home to figure it out.

But they would have to watch her leave the nest soon. Arclid was a big continent, and she had seen so little of it. She hadn't seen the highlands or the midlands, and she hadn't even explored much of the lowlands where their village and Nightport were located. Not to mention that she hadn't crossed the vast seas to any of the other three even bigger continents. That had to be remedied. Even if the prospect scared her.

Just as soon as she had rested enough to stop her muscles from reminding her how bountiful their harvest had been this year. And packed. And made exact plans for where she was going and what she was going to live off.

And... plucked up the courage to actually go.

Nessa was now feeling much better despite her aching muscles. She had eaten a bowl of freshly picked winterberries, bathed, and put on clean clothes.

Now she was walking into the centre of the village to visit Layden, her best friend since they were schooled together as children. After apprenticing in Nightport, he had returned to Ground Hollow and settled down with his wife, Isobel. Together they had opened the village's first apothecary.

She passed the Halstons, the family of three who lived three farms down from her parents. They smiled at her, and Roi Halston looked like he was about to engage her in conversation. Nessa felt her heart begin to pound and hurried her steps away while berating herself for her panic.

Keep moving. Get a grip, woman. You are too old to be this shy. You have known these people all your life.

But then, that was the problem, wasn't it? They knew her and would pry. Ask questions and judge her actions, decisions, and even her appearance. Right? She didn't turn around to see if the Halstons had found her rude. She was almost at the apothecary anyway.

She stopped outside it and looked up at the newly painted sign above Layden's and Isobel's shop. Pride swelled in her chest. Layden had a head for learning, a deep-rooted wish to help, and a work ethic that nearly rivalled the one she had been brought up to have. Sadly, they also shared the lack of drive and ambition. That was why it had taken marrying Isobel for the apothecary to open and be run successfully.

Nessa walked in and was greeted by the couple's little daughter, Hanne, who came tottering over with her thumb in her mouth.

Crouching down to the girl's height, Nessa smiled at her. At least children never made her feel shy.

"Hello, little honeycomb. Are you manning the shop today? Where are your parents?"

She knew that Hanne couldn't speak properly yet but hoped the girl would point in the right direction. Or that her parents would overhear the questions. The latter happened, and Isobel came out from the adjacent room.

"Nessa? Good afternoon."

Nessa smiled, even though she knew that the woman in front of her wouldn't return it.

"Hello, Isobel. How are you?"

Isobel put a hand on Hanne's shoulder. "I'm fine and so is my family. You?"

"Well enough. I'm glad that harvest is over. It was a big one this year, and it took its toll on all of us."

Isobel gave a sharp nod. Everything about her was as distant and terse as always.

I've got to figure out why this woman doesn't like me before I leave. Otherwise I'll always wonder.

Layden came out to join them. If his wife had been cold at the sight of Nessa, he was all the warmer. He came over to hug his old friend as tightly as usual. Nessa's mood heightened at his familiar smell of strange herbs and old books. His wire-rimmed spectacles were covered in a fine dusting of something white, and there was traces of the same substance on his clothes and hands. Against his dark brown skin, the little white bits of powder looked like stars in the night sky.

"Have you been mixing up powders or are you actually growing dusty with age?" Nessa teased.

"What?" He looked down at himself. "Oh, right. Yes, that's a new powder I'm trying to perfect. If I get it right, it should cure stomach ailments."

Hanne sneezed. Isobel looked at Nessa like it was her fault. "Yes. My husband is very busy and him bringing traces of dangerous powders out here isn't good for Hanne."

Layden held up a hand. "It's all right, my cherished. I'll take a walk with Nessa. The wind will blow this dust off me in no time and clear out my lungs. I shall be back soon."

Isobel made a face as if she'd eaten month-old fish, but then gave another sharp nod. Layden gave her a kiss on the lips and Hanne a kiss on the head. Then he walked outside.

Nessa followed him after waving goodbye to Isobel and Hanne.

"Layden? Don't you want a coat or a cloak? This autumn wind is cold, you know."

"No, Miss Responsible. No need for that, it will only be a brief walk."

She shrugged and put her hands in her pockets. "Suit yourself."

They walked in companionable silence for a while. Soon the buildings of the village square were behind them and they were alone on the long path. The crunching of their feet on the gravel, the wind through the crops on the surrounding fields, and the birdsong from high up in the trees were the only sounds she could hear.

Three levels of sound. One sound below her, one at her height, and one above her. She had never thought about that before. She turned to Layden, wanting to mention it to him but wasn't sure if he would think her strange. She looked back ahead of them. They should simply walk, enjoy the quiet break from work. Nessa led the way as she had through most of their friendship. She walked them towards the castle, passing more farms and fields where everything was quiet on the surface, while the hard work carried on somewhere out of sight. It always had and always would.

Nessa looked at her childhood friend. "So, little Hanne is growing like a barn-weed. She'll outgrow both you and Isobel in no time."

Layden beamed. "Yes, she's growing strong and healthy. And she's a happy, easy-going child who listens to her parents. Much as I was."

"She seems to take after you quite a bit. Isobel is many things, but I wouldn't say she's easy-going."

"Don't be unkind, Nessa. Isobel is a lovely woman to most people. She just struggles with you," he said, the last sentence nearly inaudible.

Nessa stopped abruptly. They had never broached this conversation, even though it had been hanging in the air between them. She hadn't dared to complicate things. Now, however, they had stumbled into it, and Nessa would seize the opportunity. She carried on walking and said, "I know. I don't know why, though. I supposed that it was because you and I were such close friends. Does she worry that I'll try to steal her husband?"

Layden sniggered while adjusting his spectacles. "No, she knows you have no interest in me. In fact, that is the root of the issue: your lack of romantic interest."

The castle appeared on their right side now. It was the only beautiful thing in Ground Hollow, unless you counted the fields and the trees. Nessa didn't. She was bored stiff of them. The castle was different. She had never been inside it but often as a child tried to peer through the large cracks in the high stonewalls surrounding the castle.

Nessa focused on the imposing structure to keep herself from getting tongue-tied. Her nerves weren't made for open and honest conversations. She had assumed Isobel was jealous of her friendship with her husband and left it at that. But if she was leaving soon, she should know why Isobel had spent the last four years being cold towards her.

"What does that mean?" Nessa asked with feigned nonchalance.

"It means that she is not worried about your interest in me, but in your disinterest in her."

That took Nessa's gaze away from the castle and back to Layden. "What?"

He sighed. "She feels slighted because she was madly in love with you when we were younger. But you always ignored her."

Nessa scrutinised him, trying to tell if he was joking or being ridiculous. "Don't be silly. People don't fall in love with me. You know me, I'm an awkward workhorse without conversational skills. Half a nose-length from being ugly, as well."

Layden snorted as he adjusted his spectacles. "Nonsense. Besides, you always think no one could fall in love with you."

"Because it's true. Anyway, Isobel wasn't even schooled

with us. She lived in Little Hollow. She told me once."

"Yes, but she often came on the canal boats to Ground Hollow with her mother to trade. Don't you remember playing cradle ball in the square and often being interrupted by a ragged girl in a dirty dress? It wasn't to see me that she would pester us. She was there for you. From the age of thirteen years, she was mad about you. She says that you were the most lovable person she had ever met. Kind, steadfast, and smart."

Nessa chewed her lower lip, uncertainty making her bite a little too hard. Her memory could barely conjure up the image that he was painting. Had that girl truly been the pragmatic Little Hollow woman who swooped into Layden's life four years ago and wed him?

Well, drag me behind a marrow-oxen. I never even guessed.

Still shaken and unsure of what to say at this revelation, Nessa gazed back to the castle for a safe place to look. That was when she spotted something in the top window of the south wing. The window opened, and a young woman leaned out. Nessa squinted to see clearer. The woman wore a pale lilac dress, and her hair was a cascade of black waves down over her shoulders.

"You there! Yes, you two. There's no one else here, is there? Are you from Ground Hollow? I have some questions about the village," the woman in the window shouted.

Nessa shut her mouth, which was hanging open.

Who in the name of the gods is this?

"Y-yes, we are. Ask away, milady," she said in a nervous stutter.

"Not like this. I am not going to stand here and shout. Someone in the castle will hear if they have not already done so. We need another plan. Could you scale the wall and climb up to my window, do you think? I would come down to you, but I am not allowed to leave the castle."

Nessa looked at the window, which must have been at least

three floors up. Her gaze moved to the row of large, sculpted stone roses that decorated that part of the castle. If her feet got purchase on them, she could climb along them to the window. She'd always liked climbing, be it trees or walls. She was built for it, strong and nimble.

She heard Layden give a feeble sneeze. "I think I have had quite enough fresh air. I should be getting back to my warm apothecary and continue mixing my powder. You stay here and shout with the bride-to-be. Just don't let her get you into trouble. Or break your neck."

Nessa looked over at him. "The bride-to-be?"

He rolled his eyes. "Yes, Miss Clueless. That loud woman is Lady Elisandrine Falk. She's been taken from her position at court to Silver Hollow Castle to marry Prince Macray. Gods, Nessa, didn't you hear the commotion at the crack of dawn? Most of Ground Hollow was here when the royal carriage dropped her off. Not that she noticed that we were all there. She seemed too busy pouting under her ridiculously wide-brimmed hat. Anyway, I'll see you later."

He turned and started to walk back before she had time to answer. Another shout was heard from the castle, distracting her from saying goodbye.

"Well? Do you think you can manage it? Say, right before the stroke of midnight?"

Nessa looked at the woman in the window as she considered the unusual request. The breeze was blowing the dark hair in front of her face, almost obscuring what looked like uncommonly pretty features. Not that the lady's looks mattered, of course. No, it wasn't that which was keeping her rapt attention. Nessa had never spoken to a Noble before. As far as she knew, Nobles only talked to you if they wanted you to do manual labour for them or sneak into their bed for the night.

There was something intriguing about this stranger. Including the fact that she was a stranger, something rare in

Ground Hollow. Nessa liked her posh, precise, and pleasant way of speaking. Not to mention her brazen way of approaching a stranger without seeming nervous.

Be honest. It doesn't hurt that she seems to be absolutely stunning, does it?

There was a strange tingle running through Nessa. She needed to know more about this Lady Falk.

Pensively, she scratched the back of her neck. It was absurd to trespass into the castle grounds to then climb a wall and speak with an engaged woman at night. A Noble woman, at that. It was not done. What was worse, it was a huge risk. Which was the number one thing that Nessa tended to avoid. But this was her future princess, who clearly wanted to know about the village that neighboured her new home. That was harmless enough, was it not? Nessa had a duty to obey her future princess.

Besides, if the lady wasn't allowed to leave, if she was kept in the castle against her will? Well, that sounded like she needed help. That trumped her own addiction to safety and any sense of propriety.

Nessa cleared her throat. "O-of course, milady. Or your Highness. Or Majesty. Um. Whatever. I shall return and attempt to c-climb up right before midnight."

"Oh, 'milady' will do. Splendid. Thank you ever so much! I must go, I think I hear footsteps in the corridors."

With a bang, the window was closed and the princess-to-be was gone.

Nessa scratched the back of her neck again. On a normal day, finding out that Isobel had been terse with her because she felt like a spurned lover would have been the oddest occurrence. But what just happened with the lady in the window pretty much overshadowed it. There were so many questions. It was worrying, but it carried a thrill. As Nessa began the walk back, she knew she wanted more of that.

CHAPTER 3
MEANWHILE, IN SILVER HOLLOW CASTLE

Elisandrine watched the villager with the clear voice and the endearing stutter stride away. Her long, light brown braid bounced against her back in a pleasing way. Elise sighed. She hadn't heard footsteps like she said, she simply wanted to finish the conversation quickly.

"That was quite possibly a thoroughly bad idea," she whispered to herself.

She'd taken to doing that throughout the day, a sure sign that she needed human interaction. Elisandrine knew she wasn't very good at being alone and she was starting to feel the tugging need to speak to someone. Someone who wasn't her reluctant husband-to-be. Too bad the lovely guardswoman wouldn't return to her room. Or her bed.

She giggled softly, enjoying the adrenaline that rushed through her at the memory, but her mirth faded quickly.

Her need to talk to someone, in combination with her need to know more about the village she found herself in, had driven her to shout out the window. That wasn't very ladylike, of course. But something told her that even though the door was open, any attempt to leave the castle without a chaperone would be stopped.

Elise ran her fingers through her thick waves of hair, trying to make it lay neatly over her shoulders. She couldn't see the woman with the braid any longer, so she turned her gaze back to her prison cell of a room. It was a pretty room; she wondered what the woman with the braid would make of it. She and the male villager with her hadn't been the first Elisandrine had spotted beyond the walls today, but they had been the only ones who looked like they might have time to stop and talk to her. She wondered how hard life in this village was. It must be quite hard to explain the haggard faces and quick marches of the few people she had seen pass throughout the day.

Since her late teens, she had been at the Queen's court in Highmere, the capital of Arclid, located in the centre of the midlands. There had been no village there, only the vast city and the lands owned by the Crown surrounding it. The life she had led had probably been worlds away from the ones these villagers had.

She looked at the book she had abandoned in the reading chair between the shelves. So far, the book hadn't given her any inspiration for escape. She decided that there probably wasn't any solution other than to run away. She could think of no scheme or political move to nullify the engagement. Not unless her current circumstances changed. For example, the Queen might want to marry off her brother to a princess from one of the other continents to make an ally. Or maybe Macray would contract a disease that made him unable to marry. She shunned that last thought. No matter how desperate she was not to marry, she shouldn't wish sickness upon anyone. Seeing her father die from red pox had taught her that much.

She would have to leave her old world behind and take the risk of going on the run. Possibly the risk of exposure or starvation, too, as she had nowhere to go and no occupation to sustain her. Or she would have to wait and hope that circumstances changed. After all, they were scheduled for a winter wedding. She had about three months until the shroud of winter was over them.

The problem was that Elisandrine Falk was very bad indeed at waiting and doing nothing. Time ticked on. She groaned, flicked her hair over her shoulders, and went back to her book.

～

It was about a quarter of an hour before midnight. Elise had spent the rest of the day reading and pacing her room, with the exception for a pair of hours spent in the dining room having supper with Prince Macray.

It had been a silent and sombre affair with far too many courses, causing a constant wait for a new bowl full of opulent ingredients with unnecessary spices. All to show off.

I am not going to miss drawn-out and barely edible Noble suppers.

Having been raised to eat slow with ladylike bites, and the lack of any conversation, had made the meal drag on even more. Elise had no appetite for food or conversation with Macray.

Back in her chamber, she found herself considering praying to gods, which she didn't believe in, that she would be spared a lifetime of suppers with him. She let out a long breath. At least midnight was nearing now. Elisandrine paced the floor, hoping that the villager with the braid and the voice as clear as icy spring water was going to show up.

She couldn't imagine why she would. Why would anyone take the time and risk of climbing the walls around the castle

— and then up the actual castle walls — only to speak to a woman they didn't know?

Oh! Unless the villagers assume that any request coming from Silver Hollow Castle is a royal decree?

What if the woman took it as a command and then hurt herself while climbing? It would all be Elise's fault. She pinched her wrist and cursed herself.

There was a noise outside her window. She hurried over and saw that the line of stone roses that led up the walls between all the windows had something new on it. A woman.

The light of the full moon gave Elise a good view of the climber. She found herself smiling at the bravery — or possibly foolishness? — that the villager was showing. She settled for bravery. The woman had some sort of hook that she appeared to wedge between the blocks of marble while her other hand held on to the stone roses. Elise assumed her feet were on the roses, too.

Her stomach churned. How could she have endangered this woman's life just because she didn't want to risk being discovered outside by the guards? She wanted to shout to the woman to turn back and get to safety, but she was almost up to Elisandrine's window now, so there seemed little point. Instead, Elise unlatched the window and reached out her hands, waiting for the villager to be in reach. When she was, Elise grabbed on and used her feeble muscles to try to pull the woman in through the window.

Luckily, the villager seemed to have the strength that Elisandrine lacked and so took on the brunt of the work. With one last pull, the woman was in the room. They stared at each other for a moment, then Elise ended the silence with an emphatic, "ow."

CHAPTER 4

LATE-NIGHT VISITOR

Nessa stared at Lady Falk. "Did you just say 'ow?' Did I hurt you when I came in?"

The lady grimaced. "Well, yes and no. You *did*. However, you *are still* doing it as well."

"Pardon?"

The lady spoke in plainer terms. "You are on my foot."

Nessa looked down so fast that she nearly twisted her neck. Her brown boot was perched on top of a pretty, heeled, white shoe. She pulled her foot back immediately.

"I'm so terribly sorry, milady."

Lady Falk laughed. "That is quite all right. Bruised toes are a small price to pay for this visit, considering you risked your life for it."

Nessa shrugged, convinced her cheeks were reddening. Why did she always have to blush? It was even worse than the stutter. "Don't worry about that, m-milady. I enjoy climbing and it was a n-nice moonlit night for it."

"I am relieved to hear it. Would you mind closing the window? Unlike you, I have no outerwear on."

"Of course," Nessa said. She latched the window before

placing her climbing hook in the pocket of her beloved leather coat.

She caught Lady Falk looking at her. "Oh, but now you will be too warm. You should remove your coat. You can place it on the window there, if you like?"

"Y-yes, milady." Nessa placed the coat on the window sill and turned back to her host. "So, milady wished to ask some questions about Ground Hollow? Welcome, by the way; our village is proud to have such a prestigious guest."

Lady Falk grimaced again, as if she smelled something sour. "Guest? I will be a resident soon. Perhaps you do not know this, but I am to wed Prince Macray this winter."

Nessa gave a little bow. She wasn't sure if she should say that she already knew that or not, so she avoided it. "Then we will be even more glad to have you as our princess, milady."

"Well, that will make one of us."

"Pardon?"

Lady Falk waved the question away. "Oh, nothing. What is your name?"

"It's Nessa Clay, milady."

"I see. Good evening, Nessa Clay. Pretty name. So much better than the long monstrosity of Lady Elisandrine Falk. Not to be improved by changing 'lady' for the longer 'princess'. That will take some getting used to."

The lady pensively looked up at the ceiling. Nessa took the chance to brave a closer look at her. The cascades of wavy black tresses she had spotted earlier framed a well-proportioned face. Lady Falk had deep-set, shining, light brown eyes that Nessa couldn't stop staring at. They were so light that they were almost yellow.

Golden, they're actually the colour of gold. I've never seen anything like them.

Nessa's gaze wandered to smooth skin which was a little darker than her own, even with her tan from working in the fields. Lady Falk was a tad taller than her, but had a slighter frame. There was kohl around her eyes and a reddish tint to her generous mouth, a colour which surely couldn't be created by the gods alone.

She wore the same long, pale lilac dress as earlier. It had an abundance of delicate lace all leading to a waist strapped in by a wide purple belt and an unusally low neckline revealing some of a petite bosom. Nessa's heart skipped a beat.

She quickly focused back up to those golden eyes, waiting for the lady to speak. It was only then that she realised that her taking stock of what her the princess-to-be looked like hadn't gone unnoticed. On those reddish lips was a smile which was far too knowing and amused for Nessa to be comfortable.

"Do I look as you had expected? Your prince seems to think I am attractive. Even if he is not actually attracted to me."

"What?" Nessa blurted out.

Lady Falk's smile grew. "Are you shocked that he said that I was attractive or that he is not attracted to me?"

Nessa swallowed. "Milady, it is not my place to have an opinion on either."

Her ladyship looked disappointed. "I see. Well, never mind all that. I need to know more about your village. I already know that it is beautiful but archaic, as all of Arclid's countryside, from what I have heard. But what else? How big is it? How far is it to the nearest town? I come from the midlands and know little of the lowlands. All I know is that we are several days ride away from Highmere. Surely there is a big town or a city closer to here? A lowland city?"

Nessa blinked at the barrage of questions. Her uncertainty regarding the reasons behind these queries made her hesitant about how to answer. There seemed to be more to this than the lady getting to know her new home. In the end, Nessa began babbling and hoped that the answers the would-be princess wanted were somewhere to be found in her stream of words.

"Ground Hollow is a s-small village indeed. To the east you have Little Hollow which, as the name tells you, is a smaller village than ours. To the north, you have large amounts of forest and through it, the road up to the midlands. West is more f-forest and a mass of villages much like Ground Hollow. Or so I'm told. South is towards the city of Nightport and then the sea. Nightport is known as a somewhat rough city but a busy, expanding one, too. It's the biggest city in the lowlands. As far as I know."

"Ah. Yes, I have heard of it. I believe there is a harbour there with ships that go to all the other continents. Do I detect some warmth in your voice when you talk about it? Do you hail from Nightport?"

Nessa puffed out her chest. Imagine little old her being mistaken for a Nightport native. "No, I'd have a much different accent if I was. I was born and raised here. But I plan to travel to Nightport soon and make it my home."

Lady Falk's eyes widened, and she took a step closer to Nessa. "Really? Are you travelling with someone? Do you have occupation and accommodation waiting in the city?"

Nessa looked down, rubbing the back of her neck. "I'm travelling alone. And no, I'm afraid I have neither. I know it's foolish to leave for the city when I am so ill-prepared. But, um, I have waited to leave for a long time, so I feel like I have to go soon or I'll implode. Besides, I have friends who have travelled there and made a good life for themselves, even if they only brought a handful of coins. It can be done."

Lady Falk clasped her hands in front of her and beamed. "Well, bring me along as a travelling companion, and I can promise you more than a handful of coins. I have a purse chockfull of golds and silvers to add to the party."

27

Nessa gaped at her. *She didn't just suggest what I think she did, did she?*

"Milady, I don't —"

"Please, call me Elisandrine. Or perhaps even Elise, as my friends do. If we are to travel together, you cannot keep calling me 'milady.' Unless you want to, I suppose."

Lady Falk, or Elisandrine as Nessa was now trying to think of her, was scouring the room, clearly looking for something.

Nessa blinked. "I-I… I don't know what to say. Are you serious?"

"Deadly serious. I am a good travelling companion. I never complain about long journeys, I am adventurous, I do not mind paying for food and board for us both. Oh, and I sing."

Nessa knew she was staring open-mouthed at the woman in front of her, but what else could she do?

"You… sing?" she croaked.

Elisandrine appeared to have found what she was looking for. She was crouched down in front of the bed, taking items out of a large chest and placing them on the floor. Nessa saw her place a golden hair clip, two books, a piece of extravagant jewellery, and what looked like an ornate coin purse into a satchel.

"Yes, I sing, and if you do wish to travel with me, I will gladly sing to entertain you. Best to my knowledge, I do not snore or smell unpleasant. I am willing to learn to cook and clean. Perhaps even mend… well, whatever it is that one mends. Furthermore, I am not at all picky about where we end up. I simply need to be out of here."

Nessa didn't know where to start. "But milady… I… um… Are you packing? I don't understand. You live in this beautiful castle, and you said yourself that you are to wed the prince this winter."

Elisandrine opened a box and took out a wide-brimmed hat with some sort of feathers on top. She pursed her lips as she stared at it, shook her head, and then promptly put in back in the box. "Yes. I also said that he does not want to wed me, and the gods know I do not wish to marry him. The Queen will never let me get out of what she seems to think is an excellent match, so I plan to escape."

She glanced up at Nessa for a moment. "I only asked you here to pump you for information. If you, however, happen to be leaving for the nearest city soon, well, it seems like a golden opportunity for me to escape now, while no one expects me to. Closer to the wedding, I am sure they will up the guards to keep an eye on me. Presently, no one will expect me to take off as soon as I arrived," she said, tucking a small but full glass bottle between her books.

"No. Me included," Nessa muttered.

Elisandrine stopped packing and looked up at her again, wide-eyed and blinking her long, black lashes.

"Oh, I am so sorry! Do you not wish to travel with me? You seemed so friendly and you sounded so sad about traveling alone that I assumed that you would be amenable. Is that my Noble blood making me presumptuous again? Were you only being polite?"

There was insecurity in those wide, golden eyes now. The skin-crawling sensation of letting people down overtook Nessa.

"No, no. I would be honoured to travel with you. It's just that I…" She trailed off.

Elisandrine tilted her head. "That you what?"

Nessa pulled at her earlobe. "Firstly, it's not safe to walk at night. That means you'd have to spend the night in my parents' home. I'm afraid it's humble, draughty, and sometimes has field mice in the eaves. Secondly, I won't be travelling in the way you are accustomed. Like most farms in Ground Hollow, we don't have a horse. Only an old ox to pull the plough and the boat along the canal. Therefore, I'm going to walk to Nightport. Which is about a day's walk."

"Fine by me," Elise interjected with a smile

Nessa held up a finger. "Hang on. I'm afraid I hadn't finished, milady. I was going to say that when I get there, I'll have to live in the most meagre of circumstances until I find employment. Rent the cheapest room I can find and take any job that'll buy me rent and bread."

Elisandrine picked up the coin purse from the satchel. "Not anymore. This will not sustain us for more than a few weeks, but it will get us decent accommodation until we find jobs."

Gathering her courage, Nessa crouched down next to the lady on the floor. "May I?"

"Of course," Elisandrine said, handing her the purse.

It was heavy. Very heavy. They could buy quite a bit of land in Ground Hollow with that sort of coin. Especially if the purse had golds and silvers in it, not just coppers. She wasn't sure what it would buy them in Nightport, but it was sure to make their stay much more comfortable.

Nessa cleared her throat. "Well, that should serve you very well no matter where you decide to stay. But milady —"

"Elisandrine. Or Elise."

"Right, yes, Elisandrine. I've just met you. And you have just met me... Are you certain you wish to travel with me? And under such complicated circumstances?"

"Yes, I am sure. I do not mind taking risks. Besides, strangers have never bothered me. It is the people you allow close to you that scar you. Wait, what do you mean by complicated circumstances?"

Nessa stood again. "W-well, I assume that if you escape the castle and your planned marriage, people will start s-searching for you and try to take you back."

"Oh yes, they most certainly will. Not for long, though. I shall not be the first person who escaped a royal marriage. Remember the Queen's aunt being left at the altar? They searched for the groom-to-be for a full two weeks. Then someone more eager to take his place stepped in. As there is no love, political alliances, or riches involved in this match, all they need is someone compatible to mate." Elise closed the satchel and stood up before continuing. "Someone will surely take my place in days. Besides, my mother will be ashamed that I did not fulfil my duty. She will try to cover up that I ever existed and probably aim to put my awful cousin in my place at Macray's side."

Nessa gaped at her. Could a mother be that callous?

"I know what I am doing," Elise concluded. "I have given this a great deal of thought, even if it may not seem that way. I need to leave, but as I have limited knowledge of the world outside of Noble circles, I need a guide. And crash boom bang, here you are. It is clearly fated to be this way." She smoothed her dress down and leisurely adjusted her hair.

"I see. I'm amazed at how easily you make decisions. It's taken me many years to decide to leave my safe home," Nessa said shyly.

"That is simply my nature. Besides, when you are not allowed to make many decisions about your own life, you learn to not dither when you finally get a choice. I need to move quick or this gilded cage will snap shut around me forever."

Nessa chewed the inside of her cheek. "Pardon, milady, but... what about when we get to Nightport and have found accommodation?"

"What do you mean?"

"Well, what happens then? Do we part ways?" Nessa asked.

Elise smiled warmly, crinkling the corners of her eyes. "Oh my, you really do fret about everything. I do not believe we can decide on that now. Perhaps we will hate each other after travelling together. Or maybe we will be friends for life. We will have to decide on paths when we reach the fork in the road."

The platitude was one Nessa had heard her father say many times, but it didn't calm her. Perhaps Elisandrine was comfortable with making life-altering plans at the drop of a coin, but she wasn't. She looked at her feet, thinking hard to catch up to the other woman. How could she refuse the offer? Lady Falk was, according to every law of society, her superior. She also needed coin, and Elisandrine had that. Moreover, it might be nice to travel with someone so interesting. Someone who was brave and had the drive she herself lacked.

She raised her head to look Elisandrine in the eye and say that she would like to travel with her, only to see that the lady had already put her satchel over her shoulder and was peering down the window.

"You know," she said to Nessa, "I have never climbed a wall. Do you think I will fall?"

Nessa swallowed down a chuckle and caught up with the lady. "Not if I help you. Besides, I suggest we don't go down the way I came up. It would be far easier to tie some form of rope here and then lower ourselves with that."

Elise stared at her with knitted brows and her kohl-lined eyes wide.

Nessa tried to be more specific. "You hold on to the rope, or whatever we can use as one, and sort of walk your way down the wall. I'll go first and show you."

But before they could go, there were footsteps, and then a knock on the door. As the women stood stock still, Nessa's heart began thudding so hard that she heard it rush in her ears.

"Hide under the bed," Elisandrine whispered after a pause.

Nessa hesitated. Perhaps it would be better to try to climb down again? If she was caught in here, what would they do to her?

"Now!" Elise hissed.

Nessa obeyed and shimmied under the lavish bed covered in silks. She was just barely in when Elisandrine kicked her newly-packed satchel under there as well. Nessa grabbed and hugged it tight.

She watched Elisandrine's feet as she walked over to the door and opened it. More light spilled into the room as she heard Elise say, "Macray, what an honour to see you again tonight."

She saw Elisandrine's white heeled shoes walk back into the room, followed by a pair of big, blood-red leather boots.

"It might be an honour, but if so, it is an inconvenient one, I fear," Prince Macray drawled.

The prince's voice sounded smug and laced with amusement. Nessa's heart pounded even harder. If it continued to pick up, she worried about passing out.

Elise gave a tittering laugh. "I am sure I do not know what you mean."

"Oh, come now. I heard voices from in here."

"I was talking to myself," Elisandrine said. Nessa was impressed with how calm she sounded.

"No, no, future wife of mine. Two distinctly different voices. Both female. Now, where could you have hidden her? Who is she?"

Nessa held her breath as the prince opened the large chest that Elisandrine had just packed from. Then he strode over to the bed and bent down. An ornate watch fell out of his uniform jacket's pocket and dangled in front of Nessa's eyes. She had never actually seen one and marvelled at its beauty and technology. Peasants like her had to get the time from the crowing of a rooster, the setting sun, or the village clock tower. Soon the dangling timepiece was replaced by a face with squinting eyes.

"Well, hello there. Welcome to Silver Hollow Castle," Prince Macray said with a toothy grin.

CHAPTER 5

PRINCE MACRAY INTERVENES

Elisandrine felt an equal amount of fear and annoyance. Of course he would find Nessa and ruin it all. He mustn't know that she was going to escape. She had to disguise Nessa as something other than a travel guide.

"She is my lover," Elise blurted out.

Prince Macray chuckled. "What?"

She put her hands on her hips. "I told you. I prefer women."

He laughed again. "I never doubted that. In fact, I am willing to wager that you prefer lovers that are smaller than you so you can boss them around. However, what I do doubt is that you could have found someone to seduce after only a day in the area. Especially as my guards inform me you have not left the castle."

Elise kept her face as neutral as she could.

Ah, so the lovely guardswoman has not confessed her indiscretion, then.

Out of the corner of her eye, Elise saw Nessa scramble out from under the bed. She was happy to see that she didn't bring the satchel with her, but its shoulder strap stuck out. Macray couldn't be allowed to see the bag. It had the Falk house emblem on it and all her valuables in it. It would be obvious to him that she was leaving. Or he would think that Nessa was stealing it and throw her in the dungeons. The last thing she wanted to do was reward this woman's kindness by getting her locked up for life.

Elisandrine saw Macray turn to evaluate Nessa. She took the chance to stare right into Nessa's eyes and nod her head in the direction of the bag, hoping that Nessa would get the hint and push the strap under the bed with her foot.

Nessa stared at her in confusion for a while and then her brow smoothed as she gave a tiny nod.

She got it. Thank the gods.

Nessa took what looked like a nervous leap forward and placed her arm around Elise's waist. No. She hadn't understood. She had thought that Elise wanted her to do something else; back up her lie.

"Yes, Your Highness. She did have time to seduce someone. I-I saw her arrive in her carriage this morning and was instantly smitten. I spoke with her through her window this a-afternoon and affirmed that she was, um, wanting a romantic tryst. So, I scaled the w-walls and now I'm... here. Your Majesty."

Elisandrine wanted to scream. It was a sweet lie, and she could see that lying didn't come easy to her new friend. She could also tell that Nessa wasn't sure about the arm she had draped around her waist. The hand was barely touching her side, and even through her layered dress, she could feel the increasing warmth of the palm.

Exceedingly endearing. She merely wished that Nessa spent less time being lovely and more time hiding satchel straps.

Luckily, Macray was facing them now, and not the bed.

Perhaps he wouldn't see the long strap sticking out. Perhaps it was only to Elise that it seemed so obvious, laying there and poking out like a dog amongst cows.

She tried to breathe calmly and keep Macray's attention on them. She put her hand over Nessa's, pushing it closer to her body, making it grip her properly. Then she turned her head, placing her face a hair's breadth away from Nessa's. She brushed the tip of her nose with her own, finishing the performance by giving Nessa the most amorous and flirty smile she could. Nessa's cheeks grew crimson, and even in her panic, Elise noted how adorable she was when she blushed. She squeezed the hand at her waist, unsure if she did it to reassure Nessa or herself.

"No," Prince Macray said.

Elisandrine's head snapped towards him. "No? What do you mean 'no'?"

He grinned. "This was too easy to get you to confess to. And the two of you are acting far too shady. There is something bigger going on here than passion of the flesh."

He looked so pleased with himself for his surmise that Elise itched to wipe the smug condescension off his face. There was only one way to catch him off-guard.

She straightened to her full height and let go of Nessa's hand. With a couple of careful steps back, Nessa pulled away, and Elise advanced towards Macray. Drawing his full attention away from the anxious Nessa. "Fine. Yes. There is something else going on. I am leaving, and Nessa here will be my guide."

She heard Nessa gasp and wished that she hadn't involved the innocent woman in this mess.

Macray looked taken aback for a moment. The lower part of his chinless face wobbled as if he was about to cry. Luckily, it turned out to only be shock and passed in an instant. He looked up, features collected once more. "I see. Well, do not let me keep you."

Elise stared at him. "What?"

"Well, I do not want you here, do I? If you disappear, my sister will have to find a new wife for me. It will delay the inevitable a few more weeks if I am lucky. Perhaps that winter wedding can be moved until next spring."

Elise had a sneaking suspicion that it wasn't just the extra time as a bachelor that made him want her to leave so much. She was willing to wager that there was some wounded pride at her rejection.

Or perhaps you are only assuming that because you are full of yourself.

She suppressed the unpleasant thought and latched on to what was important. "If you want me to leave, will you help us?"

His eyebrows shot up his forehead. "Help you?"

"Yes, we planned to escape through the window, but it seems dangerous. Considering that the only physical activity I am used to is bedding women, I will probably get myself killed. Can you sneak us out through a less perilous exit?"

He recoiled and began to shake his head before he stopped and groaned. "I suppose that is the gentlemanly thing to do. I have a passageway leading from my bedroom out to the back of the castle. Beyond that is a part of the wall which has cracks that make it easy to climb."

Elise saw Nessa roll her eyes and assumed that the secret passageway into Prince Macray's bedroom was well-known in the village. Elisandrine looked at Prince Macray and saw pride in his regal eyes.

"You wanton little sleep-around," she said with a purr.

He sniffed, looking offended.

She rushed to clarify. "Not that I am one to talk. In the upcoming days, you will probably hear a confession from a guard about being lured into my bed. Corinna was the first name. What was her surname again? Stinn? Sten? Stein! Yes, that was it. Please do not punish her. She did nothing wrong. In fact, she did everything… just right," Elise said, smirking.

The offended look on the prince's face dissipated. "I see. It is nice to not be the only — how was it you put it? — 'wanton little sleep-around' in the castle."

Elisandrine quirked an eyebrow to go with her smirk. "Likewise. Still, I shall leave before I become more competition than company. Congratulations on that clever passageway of yours."

Macray took a bow. One highly sexual creature acknowledging a compliment from another. "Thank you. Oh, and I will let Guard Stein know of your praise and relinquish any punishment. After all, showing our guests a good time should not mean you are penalised."

They smiled knowingly at each other. Finally, something she could appreciate about the man she almost married.

Nessa cleared her throat. "It's not for me to say, I know. But perhaps we should make some haste? Before one of the patrolling guards or staff find us? I have no acceptable reason to be here."

Her terse tone snapped Elise out of her reverie. "Yes, of course. Please lead the way, Your Majesty."

Macray nodded and strode out of the room while checking his pocket watch.

Elisandrine picked up the long strap of the satchel and put it over her shoulder. She saw Nessa fetch her worn leather coat and a thick shawl that Elise had left on the bed. Nessa gave her the shawl and said, "I'll let you borrow some warmer and more comfortable clothes when we get to my parents' farm."

Elise smiled at her. She knew next to nothing about this woman, but someone who played along with her lover ruse and worried about her comfort this much would surely be a good travel companion. Fate had served her well.

CHAPTER 6
SAYING FAREWELL

Nessa was glad to say farewell to Prince Macray at the end of his secret passageway. He was her prince and in that was not only royalty but the steward of Arclid's lowlands.

But that didn't mean that Nessa had to like him. He had seduced far too many villagers and left them heartbroken when he moved on. A night or two of passion and physical comfort was one thing. Breaking promises of a lifetime as a royal courtesan was another.

Elisandrine didn't seem to like him either. Nessa wondered if she, too, could see the callousness under the toothy smile and handsome uniform. Or perhaps the distrust of the royals, that Nessa had heard was so ingrained in all of Arclid, was even stronger in the people from the midlands? Or perhaps it was a Noble trait?

Her thoughts turned to Elisandrine in general. She was such a force of nature and left Nessa quite out of breath. Especially when she had brushed their noses. And when she had squeezed Nessa's hand on her waist. That waist was so thin, and her hand was so cold. Nessa wanted to get a full meal and a few hours of physical activity into the Noble woman to warm her.

Warming Elise made inappropriate thoughts start to form. So, Nessa focused on her departure instead, which had been pushed forward. She would have to say goodbye to her parents and friends in the morning and leave for Nightport soon after. Maybe it was better that way? The days of waiting she had planned would only be torturous. More time where her parents would grump at her and tell her she should stay in Ground Hollow. Perhaps a quick, clean break was best? Maybe meeting Elisandrine had indeed been fate, as the other woman claimed.

"So, what will be our next move, travel guide of mine?" Elisandrine asked.

She was looking at Nessa with a smile and her hands on her hips. Nessa wondered if she would look as driven tomorrow, after a meagre breakfast and a day's walk to Nightport.

"Our next move will be getting over this wall," Nessa said, looking up at it. She spotted cracks that could be used for foot- and handholds. Macray had been truthful. The top of the wall had crumbled away. Either by an act of nature or an act of a wanton prince. It shouldn't be too hard to climb, not even for Elisandrine.

"That does not look too hard. Give me a leg up, and I will try to climb it," Elise said, having clearly reached the same conclusion as Nessa.

She helped Elise up. After a few near misses, the Lady lowered herself down on the other side of the wall. Nessa followed, grateful that she didn't have to attempt it in high-heeled shoes. She said a silent prayer to the gods that Elisandrine would have the same shoe size as her so that she could wear her second pair of boots on their trip.

Nessa stole another look at Elisandrine when she had her feet back on the ground. She remembered what Prince Macray had said about Elisandrine wanting smaller lovers that she could boss around. Sure, Elisandrine was taller than her, but she wasn't bigger. Nessa had lean, strong muscles from farm work and curves, which Layden had assured her had caught the eye of quite a few men and women in the village. She was not smaller than Lady Falk, and she wasn't about to be bossed around.

Elisandrine brushed down her dress and turned to face Nessa. "Well, here we are. What do we do next? I doubt we need to run, Macray will ensure no guards go to my room to check on me. Did you say that we could only make our way to the city when it becomes light?"

"Yes. The roads to Nightport aren't safe after dark. Especially not as we get closer to the city. We will have to spend the night on my parents' farm."

Elisandrine adjusted the satchel on her shoulder. "All right. Lead the way."

Nessa thought for a moment. "Would you mind if we stopped off somewhere first?"

"Probably not. However, that depends on where we are stopping."

"The apothecary. My oldest friend owns it. He is the man you saw me with this afternoon. I would like to say goodbye to him tonight as we'll have to leave first thing in the morning."

"Of course. We shall go there first, then. So. He is a friend? I would have guessed a lover."

Nessa started. "Really?"

"Yes. There was such an intimacy in how you walked and how you looked at each other. But perhaps that was the distance playing tricks on me."

"Yes. It was. I have never held any romantic feelings for Layden. And he's a married man."

Elise smirked. "That does not mean that he holds no romantic feelings towards you."

"I'd rather not speak of this, milady," Nessa said, allowing her tone to grow stern to show that she meant it. She began to walk towards Ground Hollow's little town square. Elisandrine immediately followed. "Of course. I apologise, I tend to speak far too freely. It got me into masses of trouble at court. Although, secretly, I think the Queen enjoyed it," she said.

"Was that why she wanted you as a sister-in-law?"

They walked in silence for a few heartbeats.

"Hmm. I had not thought of it that way. I saw my marriage as a banishment because I caused mischief. Either by speaking out of turn or by losing my temper, which I tend to do even more than speaking inappropriately. It never occurred to me that the Queen was trying to make me... family."

"I should say that she likes you a great deal if she was willing to let you marry her brother."

Elisandrine hummed softly, a strange look on her face. Then the silence returned.

A swarm of lux beetles flew in around them. They both stopped to watch the sky turn into a festival of yellow and green lights. Mating season made the lightning bugs glow their brightest and fly low and slow.

One flew a little too close to Elise and brushed her hair. She laughed, and Nessa started at the sound of it. For some reason, she had expected Elisandrine's laugh to be a girlish giggle. Even though she guessed that Lady Falk was close to her own age, she felt like a headstrong and flirtatious lady of court should giggle. Like in books. Not give the heartfelt, loud, laughter that escaped Elisandrine's lips right now.

Nessa tried to hear that wholehearted, sweet laugh past the sudden pounding of her pulse in her ears. The woman in front of her wasn't some inaccessible creature from a different world. Not an elegant painting of a princess-to-be. Elise was simply a woman of flesh and blood. She was real. Kind, young, ready for a new life, entertained by the pretty beetles, and as lonely as she herself was. Nessa had the disconcerting sensation of feeling like she knew Elise's heart and mind. Just for a fleeting moment. She noticed that she was staring, her mouth opened enough to make it dry.

Nessa averted her eyes as she asked, "Are you ready to walk on?"

"What? Oh. Yes, I suppose so. I have never seen lux beetles so close up. I have been inside, watching them do their dances in a garden or swarming down a road. I thought they would be disgusting, like bugs usually are, but they are surprisingly lovely."

Nessa held out her hand to one, nearly catching it before it flitted away to court another lux. "Lovely? Yes, I guess they are. They light up evenings like these and remind you of how incredible nature can be. How it can surprise you with its own simple form of magic."

This time, Nessa caught Elisandrine looking at *her*. Studying her. Nessa cleared her throat and began walking again. Soon Elisandrine was walking next to her, so close that their shoulders brushed, sending jolts through Nessa every time it happened.

"So, how did you come to know this friend of yours?" Elise asked.

"Layden? We were schooled together."

Elisandrine's brow furrowed, as if she was trying to remember something. "Commoners are usually schooled form the age of… hmm… eight to eighteen, yes?"

"Yes. You can study further, but you have to travel to one of the cities to do so. And find a way to pay for your studies or a patron who will pay for you. Or a master to apprentice with."

"I see," Elise said. She walked closer to Nessa now, making their shoulders touch even more. Sometimes their hands brushed past each other, fingers touching ever so slightly.

43

Sparks seemed to form where their skin connected. Nessa didn't move away even though something akin to panic mixed with attraction was building in her stomach.

The moonlight was glinting off Elise's black hair as she asked, "Did you enjoy your schooling?"

"Yes. I love to read, so I took the chance to read any book I could. Even the dull ones," Nessa admitted.

"I like to read as well. Although I never had to bother with dull books. There were enough books for me to only pick out the interesting ones in Silverton. I wish I could say the same for the other students."

"What? That they picked interesting books?"

Elise laughed. "No, that they were interesting. I do not know how well-informed you are about Noble children and how we are schooled?"

"I'm not informed at all. I've been told you are meant to have better teachers than us. But that's all I know."

Nessa swung her arm a little wider than before and her little finger accidentally brushed the back of Elise's hand for a prolonged, heart-stopping moment. The other woman made no show of having noticed.

"Well, yes. Noble children have the best scholars available in the land. Sadly, what they had in intelligence and experience, they often lacked in kindness and teaching ability. Despite that, I could put up with them. The people I despised were the other students. I wanted to throttle them daily. We were a small group, only fourteen when we started at the age of six. By the age of seventeen there was only eleven of us left."

Nessa stared at her. "You mean you killed three of them off?"

Elise's face contorted into anger. "What? Gods no! What do you think I am, woman? I mean that the red pox hit the Noble circles and took lives."

Nessa felt like all the blood drained from her face. "Oh, right. Of course. I sincerely apologise, milady."

Elise rubbed her forehead. "It is not your fault. Excuse my outburst. I suppose the mental strain of the day is making me tired."

The chill of the night was making Elise shiver a little. Nessa pondered offering up her coat but hesitated. Would a creature this dainty and beautiful want to wear her worn, dirty leather coat? "That's understandable. You've made a lot of decisions today."

"Yes, and being held captive is not restful; it wears on your nerves. I certainly do not recommend it. What is even worse is putting up with Macray…" Elisandrine gave a theatrical yawn which made Nessa laugh.

They kept walking; Nessa could see Ground Hollow Square in front of them now. A field owl hooted in the distance while Nessa scrambled for something to say.

Just make conversation. Pretend you know her and that she likes you. Pretend that you are not an insecure, boorish farm girl.

"Do you mind if I ask why you hated the other students?" Nessa asked.

Elisandrine shrugged. "They were obnoxious. A few were lovely, but most of them were raised to be competitive, aggressive, and arrogant. Not only did they believe they were better than all the commoners in the land, they also believed that they were better than each other. Every day was a battle of who had the most perfect clothes and were the best at their studies. It is hard to make friends when you are all constantly trying to beat each other."

"That sounds horrible."

Elisandrine turned to her, lightning fast. "Oh, listen to me complain. You must have had it so much worse than me. I assume you had no sunberry juice break every two hours. Or handcrafted seats and desks to fit your individual sitting style?"

45

Nessa chuckled. "No. We had things like a ration on the amount of oil our lights could burn in winter. So many dark mornings and afternoons were spent squinting by a barely lit lamp."

Elise's eyes widened, glinting in the moonlight. "Really?"

"Yes. Although I have to admit that I liked most of the children I was schooled with. With the exception of a handful of bullies, of course."

She looked up and saw the sign of the apothecary in the distance. "There's Layden's apothecary. He and his family live above it. I'll go knock on the door and hope that we don't wake his little daughter. If we do, Isobel will kill me."

Nessa put her hands in her pockets and picked up the walking pace, eager to get to the apothecary and get this over with.

Elise came up behind her. "Isobel?"

"Layden's wife. She doesn't like me. Well, he says she did once, but she certainly doesn't anymore."

"Ah, did you step on her toes, too?" Elise teased.

"No, nor did I climb a garden wall and then the walls of a castle for her. You know, I never asked why you couldn't sneak me into the castle some other way."

Elise was next to her again now. "No. You just climbed up there because I asked you to. And because you could. I knew then that I liked you."

"Because I follow orders blindly?" Nessa faced the door to the apothecary, purposefully not meeting Elisandrine's eye.

"No, because someone needed help and you assessed the situation, saw that you could help, and then simply did it. It shows courage and kindness."

Nessa wasn't sure what to say. "Thank you," she finally mumbled.

Elisandrine stopped and looked from the apothecary back

to Nessa. "You are most welcome. Should I wait for you out here?"

"No, the night winds are too cold. Especially with only a shawl over that dress. Come with me. It will be fun to see Layden's face when I show up with an actual Noble in tow."

Elisandrine quirked an eyebrow at her but then smiled. Nessa smiled back before knocking on the door, praying to the gods that Layden wouldn't mock her for blushing.

It took a while before someone answered. Nessa pulled her coat closed against the cold, considering buttoning it up now that she wasn't lending it to Elise.

Layden finally opened the door, looked behind him into the dark building and then stepped out. He was wearing only a pair of short britches and his spectacles. In his hand was a candle he had used to light his way. She saw him put his free arm around his naked, broad chest with a look of embarrassment. His dark skin was covered in goosebumps.

Nessa frowned. "Why don't you ever wear a coat?"

"I would start with why he is not wearing a shirt. Or socks," Elisandrine murmured behind her.

"I was in bed, Nessa! Then I had to rush out here to see what fool was knocking at my door far past the stroke of midnight, nearly waking my wife and daughter."

Nessa winced. "Ah, right. I'm sorry. I didn't mean to wake you. I guess we won't be invited in then. Well, I won't keep you standing out here in the cold for too long. I just had to say goodbye tonight as we are leaving tomorrow."

For the first time, Layden looked past Nessa and over to Elisandrine. His eyes grew wide and his mouth fell open. He snapped it shut and looked back to Nessa, whispering, "What in the name of the gods is she doing here?"

"Listening to you not realising that I can hear you," Elisandrine answered.

Nessa smiled. She took off her coat and hung it over Layden's broad shoulders.

"I climbed up to her window like she asked. Then we spoke. We decided to head for Nightport together in the morning."

Layden looked like he was about to swallow his tongue. "But she's —"

Elisandrine stepped forward. "Meant to marry the prince, yes. I do not want to. So, I am going with your friend to the city instead. I have the coin and the nerve to do just about anything, while she has the knowledge and cautiousness to make sure that the 'anything' does not get us killed. We need to start early in the morning in case they are searching for me and because we have a long day of travel ahead of us. So, you should say your farewell to Nessa tonight."

Nessa opened her mouth to add something but realised that this pretty much summed things up.

Layden looked at Elisandrine and gave an awkward little bow. Then he turned back to his old friend, wrapped her coat closer around him and peered at her. "With respect, Nessa, are you sure this is a good idea? Travelling with someone who will be chased and who is... so different from you?"

Nessa looked him in the eye, willing his scepticism to disappear before it melted her resolve. "No. Probably not. But it does seem to be moving things along. And I need to move along. Before I lose my nerve and end up staying here, taking over the farm one day."

He sighed. "Yes. I know. I'm just going to miss you. I'm going to miss you so much."

She got up on her tiptoes and put her arms around his neck, pulling him down to her in a close hug while avoiding the flame of the candle.

He hugged back and whispered, "Please be careful."

"I will," she whispered back.

She stepped away from him. "Say goodbye to Isobel and Hanne for me. Oh, come now, don't look like such an abandoned lamb. You studied in Nightport, you know it's only a day's travel away. I will be back to see you and my parents soon."

He frowned. "I know. Please, make it very soon."

"Of course. Now give me my coat back and go get some sleep. No doubt you'll have to make some important dusts to cover yourself in tomorrow morning."

He glared at her as he gave her back the coat. Then he gave Nessa a quick kiss on the cheek. He turned to bow in Elisandrine's direction again and then he hurried back inside, shielding the flickering candle with his hand.

When the door closed behind him, Nessa blew out a breath and faced Elisandrine.

"Right, that's done then. Now we just have to go home to my parents and tell them that I'm bringing a Noble, who was almost a princess, into the house. Without any warning and with an explanation that hardly sounds likely even to me." She gave a faintly nauseous grin. "This should be fun."

Elisandrine smiled reassuringly. "Lead the way."

CHAPTER 7
THEIR FIRST NIGHT

Elise looked at the humble house before her. She was squinting through the moonlight to better see the telltale architectural design of the roof, wondering if Nessa's family knew, as she did, why it had that particular appearance. Her eyes drifted to the worn wood and lack of windows. The design of the house probably wasn't in the fore-front of these people's minds.

Nessa knocked. Then they waited a while in silence. Guilt at waking the Clays grew in Elise's belly.

The door opened, revealing a woman who must have been around fifty years old. Maybe younger, it was hard to tell with the lines on her face and her sleepy expression. She looked a lot like Nessa, but with a few grey hairs.

Gently, Nessa placed a hand at the small of Elise's back. "This is my mother, Carryanne Clay. Mother, this is Lady Elisandrine Falk. Can we come in?"

Carryanne Clay peered at them both, appearing unsure if she was dreaming; then she shook herself and replied, "Oh. Yes. Of course. Come in."

Nessa walked in, and Elise followed. The room was dark

but for the low burning lamp that Carryanne was carrying. She closed the door and turned to her daughter. "I thought you said you would be having a couple of ales with Layden? And then spending the night on their sofa?"

Elise saw Nessa grimace. "Well, that wasn't *exactly* true, Mother. I went to see Elisandrine here."

Elise thought fast. No mother would want their only child gallivanting out with a woman who they just met, especially not one who would be hunted by royal guards. She considered making up a lie, perhaps saying they met at Layden's and that he could vouch for her.

Then she looked at Nessa and the older woman who looked so much like her. She had a feeling these were not people who made up convenient lies. Nor who looked on idly when the lies eventually broke and the truth spilled out. They were the kind who spoke the truth whenever possible, at least if Nessa's uncomfortable lying to Macray had been anything to judge by. So Elise stood silently, preparing to explain that she was not going to lead Carryanne's daughter astray.

A man walked in from another room of the small, dark house. "Nessa? Carryanne? Is everything all right?"

"That's my father, Jon Clay," Nessa said quietly.

Her father turned out to be a tall man with broad shoulders that hunched forward a bit. He was nearly handsome in a rugged way, but Carryanne was certainly the more attractive parent, Elise decided, right before scolding herself for being so shallow.

"Our daughter was just going to start explaining why she isn't at Layden's but standing here at the stroke of one with a lady in company instead," Carryanne replied.

For a moment, Jon merely gaped at Elisandrine. Discomfort rushed through her, making her adjust her footing in a fidgety way that her mother hated. She heard the echoes in her head. *Stand still. Like a lady. Do not move about like a frightened child.*

Nessa held up her hands. "I'm sorry to bring company, especially someone Noble, to our house without warning you. I'm also sorry for the late hour and for lying to you. I just didn't want you to worry because I was breaking into a castle to free a fair maiden."

Clearly her parents did not appreciate the jokey tone. They only stared at her and Elise sympathised with Nessa so much it ached.

She saw Nessa's chest move as she took a deep breath. Then Nessa told them everything that had happened, from when Elise had shouted out from the window to when they just knocked on the door. When she finished, her parents stared at her with what looked like worry. Or was it scepticism?

Turning from Nessa to Elise, Jon bowed low.

"Welcome to our home, humble as it may be. Had we known we would have such an important guest, we would have cleaned up, made repairs, and had the best of our food to offer you, milady."

Elise bowed back, even though that was not custom. "And if you had, the mood would probably have been more formal and we would all have been tense and nervous. I prefer this. Thank you for the welcome. I apologise for waking you." She smiled as warmly as she could while pulling her shawl tighter against the icy wind that blew right through the house.

The tall man noticed her actions. "Sorry about the cold. The roof is meant to be an attractive feature, but those little peaks it has leave barely visible crevices where the cold winds creep in. No matter how we try to seal it, it's never enough. When we get the time, we will have to build a regular, boring roof. Like the ones my grandparents had. Not this attempt at fancy style that we all had to rebuild in when I was a child."

"New Dawning," Elise said.

He blinked at her. "Pardon?"

"The style of building. It was called New Dawning and was meant to make houses here look different than the ones on the other continents. It was invented by the royal architects of Highmere, my father being one of them, about forty years ago. He told me all about it. The special, peaked roofs were meant to be attractive, yes. They were also meant to allow for small amounts of air to come in to make up for the lack of too expensive windows. My father always said that he wished there would have been enough capital for windows and making the houses out of less flammable materials instead."

Jon smiled. Was that a friendly smile or an impressed one? His face was so hard to read.

"Milady is very kind. I'm sure that the building style you mentioned is what my father, who built this house, was aiming for. But he went a little overboard with the pretty peaks of the roof, and it lets in more air than it should. To counteract that, he covered the walls, though. These old planks might be worse for wear, but in here they are at least covered in good old mud, straw, and stoneflour. Making sturdy building clay."

"So your house is lined with clay and your name is Clay. What a coincidence." Elise heard how vapid that sounded the second she said it. She groaned inwardly and hoped that the Clays neither thought her a moron nor that she was making jokes at their expense.

Nessa chuckled. "No clay and mud jokes, please. Both me and dad have grown up with those."

"Trust me, having heard them ever since you fell for a boy named Clay and decided to take his name is no fun either," Carryanne muttered.

Elise smiled at them, as charmingly as she could. Was there anything she could do to make them like her? Usually she flirted, but even she knew it was a bad idea here and now.

Nessa's face grew serious. "I know you probably have a lot

53

to say to me. And that you won't want to talk in front of Elisandrine. So why don't I take her to my room and let her find some travelling clothes for tomorrow. Then I'll come back down here to talk to you?"

I was right about the complete honesty, then.

"That's probably best," Carryanne said.

Nessa turned to Elise and gave her a wan smile. "My room is up that ladder, in the loft. Don't worry, that part of the roof has been sealed the most. The wind isn't too bad there."

Nessa went to the ladder and began to climb. Elise nodded at both Carryanne and Jon and then followed her up.

The so-called room was a small, open area in the eaves of the roof. There was barely enough room for a bed, a dresser, and an upturned wooden crate, which held a lantern and a rusty old tinderbox. The ceiling was low, making them both hunch over not to hit their heads.

Nessa's shoulders were drawn up, and she was biting her lower lip. "I know, it's not much. But it will do for one night and be good practise for you; you have to get used to roughing it. And sharing a bed. Sleeping close for warmth is important as the cold season is coming." She paused to use the tinderbox to light the candle in the lantern. The warm light of it lit up her face as she continued speaking. "Layden has a sofa for guests, but I'm afraid we don't. We could make the frame of it, but you know how expensive padding is. Well, no, I suppose you don't. Anyway, as you can tell, this house has no room for a sofa anyway."

Elise held up a hand to stop her. "It is perfectly adequate, sharing a bed will not be a problem. Thank you. Just be aware that I tend to steal the covers."

Nessa breathed out, her shoulders dropping as she smiled. "Really? Well, I assume that a woman like you has only shared a bed with lovers. You tend to be more careful when you sleep next to someone you aren't... intimate with."

"I will have you know that I have shared beds platonically before!"

"Oh, my mistake then. When could that possibly have happened to you? Commoners have to do it a lot, but why would a Noble woman have to share a bed?"

"My cousin Grandella. She used to visit once a year, and she was afraid of the dark. So, without asking me, mother put her in my bed with me. Like I was some sort of glorified cuddly toy."

Nessa pressed her lips together, seemingly crushing a grin. Or a laugh? "Well, unlike your mother, I will offer you a choice. The choice of being *my* glorified cuddly toy tonight or sleeping on the floor downstairs. Or, if you feel very strongly about it, I'll sleep on the floor downstairs."

"Cuddly toy it is, then. However, note that I stole the covers from Grandella, too. Your lack of physical intimacy with me does not render you immune to my cover-stealing ways."

"I suppose I'll simply have to steal them back then, mila-dy," Nessa said with a wink.

Elise was reaching for a flirty comeback, sadly this turned out to be one of those rare occasions when none came to her. She wondered why. She usually flirted with such ease.

Luckily, Nessa changed the topic. "In that dresser you will find all my clean clothes. Meaning everything but what I'm wearing right now and the shirt I spilled porridge on this morning. There's not much, but see if you can find something that could fit you and that you can move around in. I have a second pair of boots downstairs, hopefully they will fit you," she said, a line forming between her eyebrows.

Elise waved her worry away. "If not, I shall simply have to spend a day in these stupid shoes or your ill-fitting boots. Not the end of the world. I will simply buy a pair that fits in Nightport later. And thank you, I am sure I will find some clothes. Although the trousers might be a little too short for me."

Nessa snapped her fingers. "Oh yes, I thought about that. In the top drawer of the dresser you'll find a pair of grey trousers. They're a little too long for me and I meant to hem them but never got around to it. They'll probably fit you best."

"Grey trousers. Top drawer. I will find them. You go down and face your parents. Let me know if they want me to sign a contract that I will not eat you alive."

She winked at Nessa, regretting that she wasn't as good at it as Nessa had been. *Why have I never learned how to wink without closing both my eyes? Flirting is supposed to be my forte, and this shy villager is outdoing me.*

Nessa groaned. "Right, yes. I'm going. Wish me luck."

"Good luck," Elise dutifully said.

As Nessa climbed down the ladder, Elise went over to the dresser. The top drawer had three pairs of soft, worn trousers. She picked out the grey ones and threw them on the bed. She decided she would sleep in her dress and wear her new outfit clean and ready tomorrow.

That was when she heard angry whispers. Or maybe worried whispers was a better description.

She could make out the words "making you leave too soon" and later "you know nothing about her." It sounded like Nessa countered every point but she couldn't be sure. She ventured closer to the ladder and heard Nessa growl, "I'm a grown woman, I'll do what I think best. She can be of use to me, and I can be of use to her. It makes good sense to travel together. Her coin will keep me a lot safer than travelling alone will. Plus, I'll have company. You've both said that you didn't want me to be alone."

That seemed to quiet her parents. Elise heard sniffling and wondered if it was Nessa's mother or father who was crying. Maybe it was both. With an aching stab in her heart she realised that her mother had shown nothing but relief when she left home.

"Come here," she heard Nessa say. Clearly the time for whispering was gone.

Elise heard bodies thumping together and assumed that tight, loving hugs were taking place between the Clays. Nessa's family truly loved her. Elise had to acknowledge the ugly jealousy in her chest, but tried to bury it deep. She focused on picking out one of Nessa's linen shirts and a vest. She picked two that were both grey, thinking they would match the trousers even if they were a darker shade.

She wondered if there was a place where she could scrub off the kohl around her eyes and the paint on her lips. Preferably with some water and a cloth. She'd like to wash her body, too, maybe even have a bath. But she didn't want to ask for too much and come off as the spoiled lady.

Nessa came up the ladder. Her eyes were red, and she was clearly sniffing back a crying fit. Elise had to fight the urge to hold her. Or apologise. Or both.

"Hello again. How did it go?"

Nessa shrugged. "It went. They're not happy. But then if they were to be happy, I'd have to stay here for the rest of my life."

"I am terribly sorry."

Nessa sniffed. "It couldn't be helped. They'll get over it when they realise that I won't be killed as soon as I step outside of Ground Hollow. Anyway, how are you getting along?"

"I found some clothes. I was wondering if there is a place where I can get some water to wash my face?"

"Not indoors, I'm afraid. Outside and to the left, there's a water pump. Then if you go past that, you'll see the privy. I'm sorry that the toilet is not in the house, like I hear it is in city houses. And that there is no bath. Ground Hollow has a small wash house in the square, but it closes at sundown." Nessa paused to wipe her eyes. "You go clean up and prepare for sleep. I'll go through my underthings and find you something to wear tomorrow."

Elise took an abrupt step back, almost hitting her head on the low ceiling. How could she forget small clothes? "Oh, right. Thank you."

Nessa shrugged. "That's fine. I assumed you'd not want to root through my underthings."

A jolt of excitement hit Elise as her mind supplied her with an approximation of Nessa in said underthings. There were very obvious curves there, and strong, lean muscles to keep the curves in place. Her body was bound to be as attractive as her face was. Elise scolded herself for the thoughts. Nessa was to be her travel companion. One who was sad at the thought of leaving her family early.

Because of you. You selfish, shallow brat.

Elise decided to use the inside of her dress to rub the makeup off and hurried out to the pump and then the privy.

When she came back, there was a neat pile of woollen socks, an undershirt, and a pair of nether coverings stacked on top of the grey clothes Elise had picked out. The nether coverings were not like the pair Elise was wearing now, which were made of flimsy material and about half a finger's length down her thighs. These would almost go all the way down to her knees. They were thick, too, like the nether coverings Elise wore during her monthly bleed. It occurred to Elise that maybe Nessa didn't have several pairs for different times of the month. This really was a whole new world.

"Everything look acceptable?" Nessa asked.

"Perfect. Although, I am not as blessed with round parts as you are, so it will not fit me as nicely." Even Elise could hear how embassassingly whiny her voice sounded.

"Well, we commoners are constantly told that Noble ladies

are prettier because you are thinner. So, don't envy me my curves."

Elise found her eyes drawn to Nessa's chest. "I really would not believe everything you are told, Nessa Clay," she said with a purr.

She saw Nessa blush again; it was an intoxicating sight. But she wanted Nessa relaxed and comfortable, so she exchanged her smirk for a friendly, open expression. "Your turn to get ready. I will put my borrowed clothes on top of the dresser and get under the covers to start warming the bed."

Nessa left, and Elise got onto the thin mattress. She made herself as cosy as she could with the rough covers and thin pillow, but couldn't find sleep. Not until Nessa snuck in closely behind her, pushing Elise almost to the end of the narrow bed.

"Sleep well, milady," she whispered, and Elise felt the soft darkness of sleep come over her.

CHAPTER 8
AN END THAT IS A BEGINNING

Their rooster Bicksley crowed, and Nessa stirred out of sleep as usual.

Only, this morning, there was a weight on top of her. A solid yet sumptuously soft weight.

As she opened an eye, Nessa found that Elise was draped over her so that she was almost on top of her. She tried not to laugh at how her travel companion was cuddled into her. Having shared a bed with friends often throughout her life, she knew that you slept lightly so that you didn't encroach too much on their personal space. You made an attempt to ensure it didn't get awkward. Evidently, Elisandrine's sleepovers with her cousin had not prepared her very well for platonic bed sharing. Nessa heard noises downstairs as her mother lit the fire and put a pot of water over it for their morning tea.

Elisandrine clearly heard it, too, on some subconscious level, as she nuzzled into Nessa's hair and groaned in annoyance at being disturbed.

Nessa wanted to get up. Her arm, which was pinned under Elisandrine, was tingling painfully and she was growing stiff. Nevertheless, she didn't want to wake the beauty perched on top of her. Partly because Elisandrine's trust was so sweet and partly because it felt nice to be cuddled so close on the chilly morning. However, it was starting to feel a little too nice. Especially when Elisandrine fidgeted, brushing warm skin against Nessa and letting her left leg nestle in between Nessa's.

"Uh, good morning, milady," Nessa said in a panic.

She tried to shimmy away but realised that she'd push her bed companion down on the floor if she did. She was trapped.

Elisandrine groaned again and drowsily muttered, "Just a little longer. I am not getting up quite yet." Her hand bunched in the nightshirt Nessa was wearing and pulled it taut against Nessa's torso. Nessa looked at it, worried it might tear. Then Elise's grumpiness seemed to pass, and she let go of the shirt. She crawled on top of Nessa completely, snuggled down against her neck, and fell back asleep. Her breaths came in slow against Nessa's skin, making it rise in goosebumps.

No, no, no. Wake up, you annoying, adorable woman!

"Milady," Nessa said pleadingly. "It's time to wake up. Time for some tea and porridge. We have our trip ahead of us today, remember?"

Elisandrine yawned and stretched a little. Then she lifted her head so that they were face to face. As Elise's eyes blinked open, Nessa could see every long, dark lash and even a little sleep grit in the corner of Elise's right eye. Those eyes shone like the sun, making Nessa's heart race. She was so dangerously close. Their breaths mingled between their mouths.

As she gradually woke up, Elise relaxed features slowly morphed into confusion and then mild panic. "Oh gods! I am awfully sorry. Wait, I will get off you."

Nessa tried not to laugh. For someone normally so flirty and relaxed, Elisandrine was taking this very seriously. "It's all right. You kept me very warm, and for that, I thank you. Just carefully slide off me so you don't fall off the mattress."

Elisandrine nodded without making eye contact. She got

off Nessa and stood shivering in that ridiculous lacy dress. She suddenly seemed younger than she was, a maiden caught doing something forbidden.

Nessa made her voice soft. "You're freezing. Get back under the covers. I'll bring you a wet cloth to clean yourself up, then you should get into my clothes and come down for tea."

Nessa didn't wait for agreement, knowing that Elise needed space. She fetched two cloths from the drawer and headed down and out. One cloth she soaked out by the pump and quickly washed herself with, quite used to the morning cold and being half-dressed outside. The other she soaked and rung out to take in for Elisandrine.

When she was up the ladder, she realised the flaw in her plan. She now needed to get fully undressed to put her clothes on. Meanwhile, Elisandrine needed to be naked to wash up and put on her clothes.

They blinked at each other for a moment.

Slowly and reluctantly, Elisandrine spoke. "Well, I presume we shall see each other undressed if we travel and live together for a while. We might as well just turn our backs to each other and get the first time over with now."

"Yes, you're right," Nessa said, with greater conviction than she felt. This was ridiculous. It was only showing a little skin. She was used to skinny-dipping in the canal with the other villagers all the time. Not to mention going to the public bath in town. She wasn't shy about her body. Why did getting changed in close proximity to someone matter so much to her right now? Why were her palms getting sweaty?

Control yourself, woman. You're making a spectacle of yourself.

They turned their backs and got on with what they had to do. Nessa only had to turn once, to pick up the socks that she had managed to put out of reach on the dresser. She caught a glimpse of Elisandrine's sandy brown shoulder blade and a thin arm. Nessa let her eyes linger longer than she should, then snapped her head back and closed her eyes for good measure. Until she realised that she needed them open to put her socks on.

You idiot.

She hurried up, barely getting her clothes on properly. Soon she was dressed and on her way down to have some tea and porridge. "Take your time, milady. I'll be downstairs."

Elisandrine just gave a hesitant hum as a reply.

Let's hope the whole trip isn't this uncomfortable, Nessa thought as she trooped down the ladder.

Two hours later Nessa and Elisandrine were preparing to leave. Their bellies were filled with leaf tea and porridge, and each had a satchel slung over her shoulder.

Elisandrine was outside, trying on Nessa's spare boots. Leaving Nessa alone inside, faced with two teary-eyed parents. There were no words left to say. She had promised them letters when she could and visits back to Ground Hollow once or twice a month. She had told them she loved them and that she would be careful. What else could she do?

Wordlessly, she pulled them both towards her for another hug. It was their third this morning, and it felt just as desperate and heart-breaking as the others had.

Elisandrine walked in wearing the worn, old boots. "They do not give my toes much wiggle room, but they fit."

Nessa sniffed. "Good. Glad to hear it."

"Thank you for lending them, and your clothes, to me. And thank you, Mr and Mrs Clay, for your hospitality and breakfast."

"Of course, milady," her father replied, bowing deeply to their guest.

Nessa adjusted her satchel. "Are you ready? We should get going."

Elise stood to the side. "Yes, lead the way."

Out of nowhere, her mother thrust a sugar pumpkin into Nessa's hand. "For the road."

"Mother, I've packed food and drink for the walk."

"Still, you can't have too much sustenance."

Her mother's voice allowed no arguments, so Nessa accepted the sugar pumpkin. She could barely hold it in one hand. They would have to eat it right away so she didn't have to carry it around for long.

"Thank you. Right, we better go before we all start crying again. I'll be back to see you both soon."

Her father grabbed her arm. "Remember to be careful. Watch out for the royal guards, and if they find you —"

"I shall simply agree to go with them, and Nessa will be free to travel on," Elisandrine interrupted. "They will not bother with her, you have my word."

Nessa could see the worry in her father's eyes as he gave a reluctant nod.

"Give my love to Layden and his family if you run into them. Farewell for now," Nessa said and headed for the path leading out to the big road.

She heard Elisandrine's steps behind her and picked up the pace. She wanted to leave before she fell for her parents' silent pleas to stay. She had stayed too many years already. It was time to start her own life.

She heard her parents close the front door behind them and wasn't sure if she was relieved or scared.

Both, she thought as her heart drummed against her chest. *You're both.*

CHAPTER 9

TRAVELLING

Elisandrine walked along without watching her step. She was too busy wondering how to break the tense mood. And the grating silence. It clearly wasn't the time for a long heart-to-heart. Nessa needed time to digest leaving her family and her home, a much bigger ordeal than it had been for her when she was shipped off to court as a teenager.

Then Elise saw the sugar pumpkin in Nessa's hand.

"How exactly are we going to eat that thing? I do not recall ever having had one. Well, other than as a sauce poured over cakes."

Nessa looked back at her and then down at the sugar pumpkin. "I have a knife in my pocket. We cut slices and eat it like that. It's sweet and a little mealy. Very filling. Healthy, too. At least that's what Layden tells me. I'd like us to eat it soon so I don't have to carry it."

"We can try it anytime you like. I am quite curious. Besides, in all honesty, I did not have that much of my porridge this morning. I am afraid my spoiled Noble breakfasts were a little sweeter and less hearty."

A slow tug of the corners of Nessa's mouth soon bloomed into that wide smile of hers. Elise was relieved to see it again.

"All right then," Nessa said. She pulled the knife from her pocket, unfolded it, and cut into the fruit.

The air filled with a sweet, pleasant scent that Elise instantly recognised. "That fruit… smells like you?"

Nessa's cheeks pinked slightly. "Uh. You noticed that?"

"Yes. I have a keen sense of smell and I enjoy analysing scents," Elise admitted.

"I see. Well, my mother makes an oil from the juice of sugar pumpkins and pressed dammon nuts. It's good to keep your hands and lips from becoming chapped when you are out in the cold all day. The pleasant smell is a welcome side effect."

"It is simply marvellous. That smell was all over your bed, and all over me, this morning. To be honest, I was wondering if you just woke up smelling like that every day. I was envying you something rotten! I am glad to find that it is something that comes from a bottle," Elisandrine said.

Nessa handed her a thin slice of the fruit. "Well, jar to be exact. I have a glass jar of the oil in my satchel."

"Careful, I might end up stealing it from you." Elise smirked before bunching up her sliver of sugar pumpkin and popping it into her mouth. The sweet, soft fruit had as nice a taste as it did smell, and she moaned appreciatively.

Swallowing her own mouthful, Nessa chuckled. "You know what? I'm willing to bet you want me to keep the oil so that I continue to smell nice. No one likes a travelling companion who smells like a farm. I'm sure you'll ask to borrow some as soon as we get to Nightport, though."

"Correct on all counts, Nessa Clay."

Nessa grinned and handed her another piece of the fruit, this time a whole wedge. Their fingers brushed, spreading oily, warm sugar pumpkin juice over both their fingertips. At the languid touch, Nessa sucked in a quick breath, swiftly looking down at the ground. Her fingers stayed in place, though, seeming braver than she was. It set off an intense spark of desire in Elise.

She is so sweet and innocent under that capable, strong exterior. Such a heady and tempting mixture of traits.

Elise was just about to brush over Nessa's slightly calloused fingertips again, the skin there always so sensitive that it made any touch intimate, but Nessa smiled shyly and drew her focus back to eating her own wedge of fruit, so Elise decided against the flirtation. Nessa had been through an ordeal when they left her home; now was not the time to try for some bedplay.

Elise concentrated on enjoying the walk and the fruit.

It was so comfortable being around Nessa. She was torn between wanting to keep this easy friendship and finding out if the friendship could grow if an amorous element was added. There was no doubt that Elise was physically attracted to this woman. There were those stunning curves that she stared at last night. And that warm skin, with such a healthy glow, that she had woken up to this morning.

She watched Nessa out of the corner of her eye now, trying to pinpoint what else it was that attracted her. Soft, shiny hair in that braid which frequently allowed a strand or two to escape and caress Nessa's cheeks. She moved slowly but determinedly, an air of strength and calm about her that called to Elise. And that beautiful, broad smile... it did things to Elisandrine that made her feel like a young maiden in the first throes of infatuation. Not that she wasn't young anymore, she was only twenty-three. But she hadn't felt this pull to someone for years.

Still, she knew her thoughts turned to the sexual far too easily and that had ruined many a friendship. She wanted this one to last. It felt incredibly important somehow.

Nessa interrupted her train of thought. "Would you mind if I asked you some questions, milady?"

"Only if you keep calling me 'milady' instead of my name."

Nessa looked down at her feet. "Ah, right. My apologies. I wanted to ask about the Royals. We've seen a lot of Prince Macray since his castle is on the outskirts of Ground Hollow. But we haven't encountered his sister, the Queen. As I now have a former lady at court with me, can I ask about her?"

Elise tried to catch Nessa's eye, but the other woman kept looking at her feet as she walked. "Nessa, there is no need to be so cautious. I will not have you beheaded for treason. Ask away."

"It's not treason or anti-monarchy in any way. I'm just afraid the question might show my ignorance. But here goes. I've seen drawings of the Queen and staggered at her handsome dresses and jewels. Most all, though... I love the strange make-up she wears. It's like a mask, isn't it? The old king had it, too. Why does she wear that? And why doesn't the Prince?"

Elise loosened her ponytail. She wasn't used to having her hair up. "The Queen wears the royal make-up mainly because it is tradition. The blue, grey, and white paint in the shape of a mask over her eyes is a sign of her status, like the crown she wears. It also shows that the monarch is more than an individual, she or he is an institution. One that has always had blue, grey, and white on her, or his, face."

Nessa brushed a few strands of escaped hair behind her ear. "I see. Thank you. Sorry if that was a dumb question."

"No, not at all! I wager a lot of people do not know. The royal make-up goes back eleven generations, I believe. Macray could paint his face, too, but I suspect he worries that it would stains others' cheeks during a kiss. Not to mention during more intimate things." She gave Nessa a meaningful look.

"I see. I wish he would wear the royal make-up, too. It looks majestic and..." Nessa hesitated. "...and it demands respect."

"Yes, and it would improve his chinless face. However, the Queen says it gets horribly hot and itchy as the day wears on. So maybe he simply does not like it. Or maybe he chooses to not wear it because every royalty-hating revolution we have had has used the make-up as a symbol for the dated and ridiculous nature of our monarchy. Anyway, did you have other questions?"

Nessa put her hands in her pockets. "Are you certain I'm not bothering you?"

Elise touched Nessa's elbow, making the other woman jump at what was meant to be a reassuring touch.

"Sorry. Yes, I am utterly certain, Nessa. It is refreshing to speak to someone who does not know all of this by heart. And anyway, I prefer chatter to silence. So, just ask!"

Nessa was quiet for a moment as the pair went over a short rise in the path. "The other Noble children you were taught with seem a lot like Prince Macray to me; selfish and arrogant. Pardon me if this is rude, but... why aren't you like that?"

"No, that is not rude. It is a nice compliment. Hmm..." Elise looked down at her feet on the gravel path. "I assume it started with my grandmother. She was an incredibly kind woman. She saw me playing with a friend one day. We were laughing at a common boy who walked past us with holes in his clothes. She sent my friend home and took me into the house. She sat me down and described to me what life was like for a commoner and how cruel it was of me to mock him for not having the luck I had been born with."

Elisandrine kept watching her feet; it was easier to talk about this if she didn't have to face Nessa.

"Grandmother started talking to me about the way Nobles were and especially about our cruelty. She hated that we were indoctrinated with it and said that was not how she raised my father and not how she hoped he was raising me. The truth was that, while I adored my father, I saw very little of him. But yes, he always said he wanted me to be kinder."

"Then I owe thanks to your grandmother and father for you being more open and nice than Nobles have a reputation for?"

"Well yes. Them and, of course, these," Elise said, pointing towards her eyes.

Nessa frowned. "Your eyes? What do they have to do with anything?"

Elise took a deep breath. Explaining this always made Nobles sound horrible.

"Have you never thought about eye colour and our society? No? Well, your eyes are a light grey, yes?"

"Yes, exactly like my mother's," Nessa said proudly.

Elise nodded, watching Nessa from the corner of her eye. "And your father and Layden both had light hazel eyes I noticed."

"Yes, I suppose they do," Nessa agreed after a while.

"Prince Macray and the rest of the Royal family have dark blue eyes. All of my family have dark brown eyes. In fact, all Nobles have dark eyes of some colour. I, however, have light brown eyes. So light they are almost yellow."

She was about to add that the Noble children had called them yellow like "urine or stinky pus". She stopped herself. After all these years, it still hurt too much.

Nessa was frowning at her. "Wait. So your eyes are light and Nobles usually have darker eyes, how has that made you different as a person? Why has that made you nicer than the others?"

Elise hoped Nessa would connect the dots without her having to explain it, but her friendly features stayed in a confused frown.

"Nobles are meant to have dark eyes. If you have light eyes, people start to whisper that you are not altogether Noble. That you have commoner blood somewhere, and I am ashamed to say that they see that as a horrible flaw. It does not help that we came from faraway Silverton instead of Highmere, nor that my skin is a little lighter than that of my parents." Elise cleared her throat. "That is merely a trick of the blood, by the way. I look like my father otherwise, so I know I am his child. That did not matter to the other Nobles, though. I was bullied throughout my childhood, and even adults looked at me with an upturned nose. Being judged makes you less likely to judge, I suppose."

Elisandrine stopped walking, pretending to gaze at a tree that was shedding its leaves. Out of the corner of her eye, she saw Nessa stop, too. She felt compelled to carry on speaking.

"My mother was thrilled that my father's work as a royal architect made us move to Highmere, where most of the Nobles live, and that this, in turn, made the Queen spot me and take me in as a lady of court. Without that, my mother claimed it would be nigh impossible to wed off a light-eyed daughter. Luckily, the Queen found my eye colour a funny, exotic quirk. Otherwise, who knows where I would have ended up."

Nessa reached out and placed her hand on Elise's shoulder. The touch was tentative and feather light. Elise barely felt it through the wool coat she had borrowed.

"For what it's worth, I neither see your eyes as a 'funny quirk' nor something to bully you for. To me, they seem a very fetching shade of gold. In fact, they look almost the colour of the sunshine. Warm and striking. Who wouldn't be drawn to eyes like those?"

Elise took the hand resting so lightly on her shoulder. "I bet you say that to all the ladies," she said with a smirk.

Nessa laughed shyly and put her hand back down by her side. "Actually, no. I am far too shy to flirt with anyone. Of any gender. Or even without a gender."

Elise groaned at the ease of Nessa's statement. "I am so jealous of you commoners for your open-mindedness. When a Noble does not feel like either gender, or feels like both, their parents force them to choose one. Usually one that fits their body best. All in the name of procreating and extending the Noble bloodlines. Everything is about keeping Noble blood pure in our world. Yours seems so much more natural and full."

Nessa shrugged as she began walking again. "I guess that is one way of seeing it. I see it as we can't afford to bother with what gender or sexual preferences someone has. It's the same with eye colour, I suppose. We are too busy surviving. Keeping our farms filled with produce or animals. Finding work in the new factories in the cities. Or being long-suffering servants to you Nobles." She smiled apologetically at Elise. "We fight, too, but then it's usually over land, coin, or love. Our lives are hard enough without trying to bother about things that people say they are or what they do in the bedroom. Or their colouring."

Elise let that sink in before hurrying up to walk next to Nessa, and saying, "I am sure I will change my mind if I end up starving on the streets. But right now, I can promise you that I would rather be fighting for survival while being free to be who I am and who I want to be with than be locked in an archaic world with a silver spoon in my mouth."

Nessa searched her face. "And who are you and who do you want to be with? If you don't mind me asking?"

Elise paused mid-stride. She couldn't remember anyone ever extending her the courtesy of asking that.

"Who am I? A woman. One who likes to be free, to be able to speak her mind and have fun. One who wants to stand on her own two feet. A sexual woman who enjoys bedplay for fun, not for relationships or for love. Who do I want to be with?" She smirked. "Well, I do not see myself ever settling down. But I want to bed women. That much is sure. Men are all right, but I do not find them attractive. I know that is rare, but that is me. And I am done apologising and explaining."

Nessa laughed. "Duly noted."

"What about you?"

Elise watched Nessa as she looked at the cloudless sky above them. She could hear birdsong and the noise of their feet on the sandy gravel path as time ticked on.

"Let's see. Well, I'm a woman, too. But after that, you and I differ. I am equally attracted to all people. Gender, or lack thereof, doesn't matter to me. Although, as I say, my shyness around most people has left me with limited romantic experience. I've had three serious relationships, though. The longest with a man called Henrico. I thought I would live my whole life with him, but it wasn't to be. Anyway, unlike you, I prefer monogamous relationships and true, deep-felt love. No fucki… I mean, bedplay for the fun of it."

Ah. Of course. She wants a steady, trustworthy partner for life, Elise thought. *Someone who is kind but sober. Dependable, virtuous, and sweet – like her. Well, that rules me out. Shame.*

Elise got close enough to give Nessa's shoulder a friendly bump. "Well, I am glad you are not shy around me at least."

Nessa scoffed. "You don't give me a chance to be shy! You blew into my life like a whirlwind. Just decided that we were going to travel together and be friends. All I could do was nod and tag along."

Elise felt coldness gathering in the pit of her stomach. "Ah. I see. Are you saying that I forced you to be my friend? Have I overstepped and pushed you into this?"

Nessa stopped, looking at Elise with wide eyes. "No! Not at all. I had time to decide if I wanted to let myself be swept up in your whirlwind. And I chose to jump in headfirst. It's strange, I never do that. But your open and simple way of being, it gave me momentum. I feel braver and calmer around you."

The coldness in Elise's stomach slowly dissipated. "I see. Good. Tell me if I ever assume too much or push you in any way. I tend to just act without thinking, and I would hate to lose my new best friend because of it."

Nessa tilted her head. "Best friend?"

Elise swallowed. "Yes. I know I do not know you very well, but right now you are the only person who knows where I am. You have a great deal of control over my future." She hesitated for a moment. "You listened to me talk about my light eyes and made me feel a bit better about them. You lent me your bed and your clothes. Oh, and you are going to share that sugar pumpkin oil. Sounds like a best friend to me," Elise concluded.

Nessa chuckled. "All right then. Best friends, it is. And you can have some oil, but not too much! It has to last me a while."

Elise interlocked her arm with Nessa's. "Of course. Now, tell me all about the ladies of Nightport and how I can get them all into my bed."

Something flashed in Nessa's eyes. Something serious. Before Elise had time to figure out what it was, it had passed. Now there was only a reproaching look. "All of them? That sounds crowded. And like you'll need some sort of cream after the first hour."

"Not at the same time, silly. One, maybe two, women at a time. That way I can keep the variety as I sample all that Nightport has to offer."

Nessa smiled, biting her lip a little. "Sounds like I could get sucked into your vortex of lovers by mistake."

"No, no, no. You do not like frivolous bedplay and you are my friend, you are thereby safe. You shall remain untouched by these hands, Nessa Clay. I swear it," she declaimed dramatically.

She had expected Nessa to laugh, but instead she hummed and walked on, eyes trained fixedly at the road ahead.

Is she judging me for wanting those women? Did she not see that it was a joke? Was she even listening to me or is she focusing on getting to the city? Perhaps I am chatting too much, like I always do.

Elise tried to shake the discomfort and confusion and focus on the nice day. Something that would have been easier if the boots hadn't started hurting like a hundred biting field mice. Elise gritted her teeth and kept up with Nessa's pace.

CHAPTER 10
ENCOUNTERS ON THE ROAD

Based on Layden's descriptions of the road to Nightport, Nessa gathered that they were getting close now. That was a relief, considering her own failed attempt at flirting with Elise a while ago. The joke about getting sucked up in the vortex of lovers had been meant as a flirtation. A possible invitation to... well, she wasn't sure what. Either way, it had been the last time she would try that. The mood had been strained ever since.

She shook her head. *No, not the mood. It's YOU who have been strained and uncomfortable. She must pity you. Stupid! All she wants is a lover for the night and you don't do that sort of thing. Besides, she is miles out of your league. No wonder she shot you down. If that was what she did? Maybe I flirted wrong, I was never very good at this stuff. Ah, gods curse it.*

They needed something to distract them. And she needed more to eat. She wished they hadn't eaten all their provisions, but the walking and constant talking and made them both hungry. Especially Elisandrine, who had forgone her ladylike way of eating to wolf down her portions with impressive vigour. Nessa supposed that was what happened when you weren't used to moving and then found yourself walking a full day.

She saw her travelling companion wince. "Nessa? I know I said I do not complain on long journeys and that was a reason for you to travel with me. Nevertheless, my feet truly hurt."

"I'm not surprised," Nessa said. "You are neither used to this long of a walk nor my boots. We should stop a while to let you take them off and rub your feet a little. I could do with some water, anyway."

Elise immediately hobbled over to a large rock by a tree. She leaned against it while unlacing her boots. "Thank you. My feet feel as bad as when I danced in high heels for three nights in a row."

Nessa scrunched up her nose. "That sounds horrible. Why would you do that?"

Elisandrine rolled her eyes. "Engagement season. That is what the Nobles call it when their children reach twenty years and their parents feel they are ready to be auctioned off for marrying. Atrocious. Anyway, I escaped the weddings but still had to go to the parties, smile and pretend that we were not all part of glorified meat market."

"My, you really have no love for Noble life, do you?'

"I have a love for luxurious beds, huge shelves with books, and fine meals. But that is about as far as it goes," Elise admitted.

She was rubbing her right foot while trying to balance on her left. Even with leaning against the rock, it looked precarious.

"Why don't you sit down before you fall down? I don't mind if you get grass stains on my clothes," Nessa said.

Elisandrine slumped to the ground and gave her a grateful, tired smile. "Yet another joy of being out of Noble circles: no one has a panic attack if there are stains."

Nessa sat next to her and opened the water canteen to take

a long drink. She swallowed and said, "I think we are getting close. The road has broadened, and we have seen a few more people passing. Soon, we should see the walls and towers of Nightport."

"Nightport has walls?" Elisandrine asked.

Nessa handed her the canteen. "Yes. Don't the cities of the midlands have walls?"

"Neither Highmere nor Silverton, where I was born, has walls. Silverton is surrounded by a lake. Highmere, well, I suppose it does not need them. There are a great deal of guards patrolling the city limits. Besides, the knowledge of what would happen to anyone who committed crimes in the capitol is far more efficient than walls."

Elisandrine returned the canteen, and Nessa packed it back into the satchel.

"So you were born in… Silverton? Where is that?"

Elise tilted her head. "I am surprised you do not know. You seem so well-schooled?"

Nessa scuffed her toe on the ground. "I hated the teacher who taught us about the continents so I rarely went to those classes. I preferred to read books in the broom closet."

Elise smiled. "I see. It is a northern city located almost at the border of the highlands. Unlike Highmere, it consists of more tradesmen, markets, and factories than courtrooms, palaces, and parks. Much like Nightport, I guess."

"There are certainly no palaces in Nightport. I remember visiting as a child. It seemed so downtrodden then, relying on harbour commerce and crime, I guess." Nessa closed her eyes to enjoy the warm, buttery sunshine for a moment as she spoke. "Layden and others who have been there lately say that steam power and the factories have changed the city. There is more work now. Which of course means fewer people turning to crime, the city being able to afford repairs and lights. Oh, and more houses being built. That in combination with the steady flow of ships coming in with cargo to trade means Nightport is growing like a barn-weed."

"That is good for us."

"It certainly is," Nessa agreed. "How are those feet of yours?"

Elisandrine looked embarrassed. "Horribly sore. I have spotted what I believe to be blisters in several places, and my heels are bleeding where the boots have chafed."

"I'm sorry. We could have travelled by cart but my parents need our ox on the farm and we can't afford a horse, so horse-back was out of the question."

Elise rubbed her toes. "Please do not apologise. Not your fault at all. I should have made the chinless prince give me a horse. He would have if I had pointed out that it meant getting rid of me faster."

Nessa chuckled. "Well, we can at least clean the blood off your heels and bandage them up."

Nessa double-checked that she had the set of bandages her father always made her pack, even if she had only been out for a short hike with Layden. She located her spare pair of socks, took one out, and poured water on it.

As she used it to wipe away the blood from her compan-ion's heels, she heard two sounds. One was Elisandrine whim-pering with pain. That stung her heart, but it was the other that truly troubled her. They had spoken of horses – and she could hear at least two such creatures coming towards them now. It didn't sound like people leisurely travelling to Night-port. It sounded like someone hurrying towards them.

Nessa didn't waste any time. She picked up Elisandrine's boots and socks and threw them into the wooded area behind the rock.

"Riders! Come on. Quick, behind the rock," Nessa whispered.

Elisandrine looked like she was about to argue, but at the

look on Nessa's face, she clearly decided against it. She followed Nessa behind the rock.

Nessa's heartbeat grew faster as the hoof beats slowed.

"We are almost at the city now. Anything?" a gruff voice called out.

"Nothing I can see. Still naught at all," someone else replied.

There was some snuffling as the horses champed their bits.

Nessa could feel Elisandrine's shallow breath against her neck as she crouched over her, huddling close to make them small as possible. Elise was sitting in fetal position on the ground, holding on to Nessa for dear life. Time seemed to pass treacle slow. Just as Nessa's legs felt like they would give out from under her, the riders decided it was time to move on.

Finally, she heard the sound of hooves tapering off. Nessa straightened her stiff knees and gazed down the road after the travellers. They were definitely Royal guards. The Royal crest was emblazoned on the back of the men's uniforms, and their horses were fitted out in blue, grey, and white regalia.

Nessa couldn't be sure that they had come for them, of course. But why else would they ride from the direction of Ground Hollow towards Nightport in such haste? They had to have come for Elisandrine. Suddenly Nessa felt as if there were eyes staring at them from behind every tree and bush. She swallowed hard.

"Were those Royal guards?" Elise asked. Her breaths came in pants, and her right hand clutched Nessa's upper arm painfully tight.

"Yes. We can't be sure they've come for you. As you pointed out, they shouldn't be chasing you, but I'm not taking any risks."

Elise let go of her arm and gave a shy smile. "Right. So, that was some quick thinking. Thank you. Now we have to figure out where my shoes and socks went."

"Well, yes. Still, that's better than being dragged back to the castle, right?"

Nessa knew that she had needlessly snapped at Elisandrine, but she couldn't help it. She hadn't been this frightened in a long time. Not even last night, when the prince caught them in Elisandrine's chamber.

Gods. Had that only been last night?

Elisandrine's brows knitted. "Of course. Please do not think me ungrateful. It is merely that my feet are getting cold."

She gave an apologetic smile, which hit Nessa like a slap to the face. "I understand, I really do. I'm sorry about being so sharp. I'm not... used to being hunted."

"No, of course. I am sorry to have put you in this situation. All you have done is try to help me, and I repay you by making you feel like prey. Would you like us to go our separate ways?"

"Absolutely not. Like I said, I apologise for my uncharacteristically harsh tone. I... need a while to calm down. Everything will be fine when we get to Nightport. The city is big enough for us to get lost in the crowds very quickly." She reached out to rub Elisandrine's arm reassuringly.

Elise sat up straighter at the touch. "I am sure you are right. Once again, I hasten to add that if they do hunt me, they will not do so for long. That would be a waste of their resources and their time. I can easily be replaced, remember?"

"Maybe the Royals and your mother find you expendable. Just don't judge the rest of the world by their stupid behaviour. Now, let's go look for those boots."

Elisandrine beamed at her and Nessa made an effort to smile back. As she walked into the forest, Elise suddenly pointed a finger at her. "And my socks!"

Nessa laughed. "Yes, I will find the socks, too. While I do that, you should hide the satchel with your family crest on it.

Too recognisable. You can place your things in my satchel. It's bigger than yours anyway."

"Good idea," Elisandrine agreed as she began emptying out the few things she had brought. Nessa glanced over to make sure that she was putting them into the larger satchel, then she focused on her hunt. It didn't take long to locate the mass of socks and boots next to a tree. As she was gathering them up in her arms, Elisandrine appeared next to her.

"I suppose this will do as a hiding place," Elise said, hiding the satchel under some rocks and leaves behind the tree.

"Yes. Job well done. Now, let's get your feet bandaged, and then we can keep travelling. We should see the walls of Nightport soon."

Elisandrine patted the hiding place and stood up to stretch. "I look forward to it. There are only so many leafless trees and endless gravel roads I can see before I ache for the smells and noise of civilisation."

"Spoiled city girl," Nessa said and rolled her eyes to drive the point home. She was rewarded with a slap on the arm, followed by a flirty smirk to ease any ill feelings out of the slap.

A while later, Elise's feet were bandaged, they had both drunk some water, and had a quick rest. Now they were walking again. Or in Elisandrine's case, hobbling.

They must be close to the city now. There was noise in the distance, and Nessa swore she could make out smoke from chimneys when she squinted. There appeared to be more roads and paths converging onto theirs. With that, came more people.

Two women and a small child came hurrying down from a path on a hill. Nessa guessed they had made running down the slope a competition to entertain the little boy they had with them. Their son, she assumed. One of the women, a tall blonde, was clearly winning. She came down first, and because she was busy looking down at the child behind her, she ran straight into Elisandrine.

Nessa saw her companion wince when she had to alter her footing and come down hard on her painful feet. She also saw Elisandrine's pretty features twist into a mask of rage. It was like the difference between light and dark.

"Ah! What in the name of all the gods do you think you are doing, you imbecile?" Elisandrine bellowed.

The blonde stared at Elisandrine for a while. "I reckon I ran a little too fast and crashed into you. I was just about to apologise, but I shan't if you shout at me. There was no need for all that."

Elisandrine snarled. "Really? I think there is a world of need to shout at you. Reckless, thoughtless, and clumsy – that is what you are! I hope you do not represent the sort of people I will encounter in Nightport!"

The other woman looked like she had been slapped. "Me, my wife, and my son are currently on our way to move there. So no, I represent people who are travelling in peace, having fun, and happened to make a mistake."

Elisandrine took a few limping steps closer to the woman, pushing into her personal space. "You represent people who need to watch where they are going and have some common sense. Not to mention some grace. Instead of bumbling about like a drunk marrow-oxen!"

Suddenly the boy gave a sniffle and ran over to hug his mother's leg.

The blonde patted his head gently and then looked at Elisandrine with eyes blazing. "Now see what you've gone and done. I would appreciate it if you don't shout abuse at me while my son is listening."

They all became very quiet. Only the boy's sniffle could be

heard. Nessa saw Elisandrine take a deep but shaky breath. Then she covered her eyes with her right hand. When she removed her hand, that odd transformation happened again. Elisandrine's face went from a look of searing rage back to those sweet features which seemed to hold nothing but joy and openness.

Elisandrine held her hands out. "I sincerely apologise. I seem to, quite foolishly, have injured myself today. That pain, the fatigue, and my quick temper led me to overreact." She crouched down so she was face to face with the boy. "I am sorry I shouted. And that I called your mother bad things. I should not have done that."

The other woman, who had kept in the background, stepped up. "Nor should we have been running without seeing where we were going. We can all learn some lessons from this and put this ugly incident down to being weary with travel. Let's all carry on to the city in peace."

Her blonde partner cleared her throat, eyes fixed on Elisandrine. "I suppose my wife is right. I apologise for running into you. I hope you'll enjoy Nightport and that your injury heals."

Elisandrine stood up. "Thank you. I hope you enjoy your time in the city, too. Especially you, young man."

The boy still looked up at Elisandrine with fear and distrust. There was no mistaking the regret and sadness that was painted on Elise's face.

Nessa wondered if she couldn't be of help here. She crouched down.

"Hello there, young master traveller. I came to Nightport when I was your age. Do you know what I remember the most?"

Hesitantly, he shook his head.

Nessa gave him her biggest smile. "I remember that there was a big toy shop on Core Street. Near the port. It was so very big and had so many different toys. You could almost get lost in there! I've heard that it's still there, and I bet that if you are a good boy, your mummies will take you there one day. At least for a look."

She cast a wary glance up at the two women, and they both looked approving enough. The boy's eyes lit up. Nessa hoped that Elisandrine had noticed and that it had made her feel better.

Elise was ruffling around in her bag. Then she crouched down next to Nessa and tried to catch the boy's eye.

"And if they do take you to that shop. I would like you to buy yourself something small with this." She handed him a bronze coin. "It is my way of apologising for scaring you with my silly shouting."

Slowly, he reached out his hand and took the coin from hers. With a child's quick change of emotion, he beamed at her.

His fair-haired mother tapped him on the shoulder. "What do you say, Bhenjamin?"

"Thank you, shouty lady."

Everyone sniggered at that, except Elisandrine, who merely looked sheepish.

The two women and little Bhenjamin said their farewells and continued towards Nightport, this time at a calmer pace.

Elisandrine stood frozen to the spot, staring after them. "Did I... Did I just pay myself out of my guilt? How disgustingly... *Noble* of me."

Nessa shrugged. "I guess you can think of it that way, if you want to beat yourself up. If you wanted to be kinder to yourself, you could say that you heard me talking about the toy shop and knew you could make his trip a great one simply by parting with a coin. There wasn't much else you could do to make up for scaring him."

Elisandrine gave her a surveying look, head tilted and a

small wrinkle between her dark eyebrows. Nessa looked right back, slightly uncomfortable at the scrutiny.

"What?"

A small smile tugged at Elisandrine's lips. "Nothing. I was merely musing on how lucky I got with fate's choice for a travelling companion."

Nessa felt her cheeks heat up. She looked away. "Let's keep going. Those feet of yours aren't going to hold up much longer, and I don't want you to start calling me names, too."

CHAPTER 11
NIGHTPORT

Elisandrine took slow, limping steps. Her feet were worsening by the minute, pain shooting up her lower legs and distracting her from all else. Until she saw tall stone walls, and the pain became inconsequential. The walls framed large metal gates which, despite their rust, gleamed in the sun. Above the gates were wrought iron letters reading *Nightport.*

They were finally here. She spotted a great, barrel-chested guard slouching against the gates. Behind him Elise could make out towers and the roofs of tall buildings. When she looked closer, she could see the smoke that rose from them to dissipate into the cloudless sky.

She turned to see if Nessa was as excited as she felt. Elise was relieved to see that Nessa seemed possibly even more over-whelmed and infatuated by the city than she was.

Elation surged in Elise's stomach and spread through her like heat. This was their adventure. This was their city, and they were going to claim it. No matter what came next, Elise knew that she had made the right decision.

Freedom. I think I can be free here. Hopefully, I can even be safe.

Part of her wanted to run towards the gates and demand to be let in immediately. But obviously, that was not how things were done. In fact, she realised that she didn't know what she should do to enter the city. What would the guard want from her?

"Nessa, what do we do when we get there?" she asked, pointing at the gates.

"Um, let's see. We tell the guard that we are here to seek work. He'll ask our names and if we're looking for a particular sort of work. He writes our answers down in a ledger and lets us in. At least that's what Layden told me."

Elise stopped and slapped her forehead. "Ah! I cannot very well tell them my name, now can I?"

Nessa paused. "No, I suppose you can't. I didn't think of that. Right, I think you will have to come up with a new name. A new start, a new name. That's not too bad, is it?"

Nessa was watching her, waiting for an answer. Elise hated feeling insecure. What was the point of that emotion? It annoyed her. "I guess not. It is just that this highlights how unprepared I am for all of this. Never mind that now. A new name. Yes. It could be fun. I conjured up quite a few names for myself when I was a child."

"Great! Then maybe you can use one of them?"

Elise scoffed. "Not really. Something tells me that names like Illegoria Stormcatcher or Henrietta Firetamer will not sound very real."

"No, you've got a point there," Nessa said with a laugh.

Elise hummed. "I like that."

Nessa glanced at her. "What?"

"How quick you are to laugh."

"And I like how you make me laugh. However, now is not the time to talk about that. We are not far from the gate and the guard, or gatekeeper or whatever he is called, might think it odd that we're loitering in the middle of the road. Focus on thinking about names."

She dropped her satchel and stretched out her back and shoulders.

Elise took the opportunity to root out the jar of sugar pumpkin and dammon nut oil from the satchel. She applied it to her dry lips and hands while she pondered names.

"Come on. Let's think while we walk," Nessa said and slung the satchel back over her shoulder. They carried on walking, or hobbling in Elise's case.

"All right. I have decided I would like to keep my nickname, Elise. Now I require a surname."

Nessa's face lit up. "Would you like to borrow mine? We can say you're my cousin."

"With my skin darker than yours?"

Nessa shrugged. "It could happen. Besides, you do have light eyes like me."

Elise gave her a pointed look. "Yes, but the wrong colour."

She wouldn't tell Nessa that it wasn't just the fact that they didn't look alike that made her dislike the idea of saying they were family. She had heard that commoners weren't as worried about the taint of incest as Nobles were. Nevertheless, she didn't want to take the risk of them saying they were related. Just in case she couldn't stop herself from asking her new friend for a kiss one night. Or maybe more than a kiss.

"Fine, so you won't be a Clay. What would you like to be called then?"

Elise looked around for inspiration. She saw a pine tree next to them. Unhelpful. Neither Elise Pine nor Elise Tree sounded right. She bit her lower lip and muttered the choices out loud to see if they sounded any better.

"Elise Gate? Or Elise Walls?" She looked past the guard to

the city behind him. "Perhaps Stone?" Her eyes fell on a church in the distance as its bell began to toll. "Church? Bell?"

Nessa broke into the stream of possible names that Elise spouted.

"What about Elise Aelin?"

Elise peered at her. "Where did you get that from?"

"A book. My favourite book as a child, actually," Nessa said. She was looking down at the ground, hands in pockets, kicking at a pebble.

Elise wracked her brain, trying to think of a book with a character named Aelin. But to no avail. "I do not think I know it. We will have to find me a copy to read one day."

"It's a good name. A hero's name. I think it suits you," Nessa said quietly, her eyes still fixed on the ground.

If Elise had wanted to pick another name, the uncertain look on Nessa's face and the pink tint on her cheeks made that impossible. Nessa had chosen a name for her, and Elise was going to keep it.

"Elise Aelin, it is. Remember to call me Elise. No more Elisandrine and certainly no 'milady'. Let us get to the gate and venture into our new home."

Nessa nodded and set off briskly towards the gate. Elise followed her, keeping her gaze on Nessa's long braid to keep from squealing with giddiness at the city behind the gates.

The barrel-chested man looked them up and down with an indifferent expression. He wore shabby clothes, the only clean thing being an armband that said "Nightport City Guard."

"Names an' reason for comin' to Nightport?" he muttered.

Elise scrutinised him. *Ah so that is the Nightport accent that Nessa mentioned. Interesting.*

Nessa took command. "Hello. We'd like to work and live here. My name is Nessa Clay, and this is Elise Aelin."

He made a note in a large brown ledger. "All right. Where are ye from an' what line of work will ye be wantin'?"

Nessa replied, "Ground Hollow. I don't know what work we'll be seeking. Whatever is available. I'm strong, and my companion is very well-schooled. We both know how to read and write and work hard —"

"I'll stop ye there, miss. Don't need yer life story. Just know that if ye can't find work or if ye break the laws of our town, ye'll be out on yer ear an' not allowed in again."

Elise wondered how they could stop offenders from simply coming back in with a new name and new information when the guards had changed. But that was none of her concern. All she wanted was to be let in and see what the city had to offer.

"We understand. May we come in? We have walked far, and we are hungry and tired," Elise said. She added a little extra eyelash batting, because flirting never hurt and she needed to keep her skillset sharp. This city was bound to be filled with interesting women.

He gave a curt nod and opened the gate while muttering, "Be careful. Thieves an' villains always find their way in. No matter 'ow much we of the City Watch try to clear 'em out."

"We will," Nessa promised.

He stood aside, and Elise and Nessa walked in. As she looked around, Elise's heart skipped a beat. A new city spread out in front of her. She wondered if her father had seen this architecture in his lifetime. If he had, it must have been many years ago and this place must have looked quite different. There was no real design style to speak of other than a sense of a sudden, urgent need for housing and buildings for commerce and industry.

She saw what appeared to be a forest of chimneys, all puffing out large plumes of near-black smoke. Most of the buildings were stone, many with towers. Others were tall due to floor after floor having been stacked on top of each other with little regard for safety or aesthetics. Occasionally there were some smaller, unassuming wooden buildings squeezed in.

Elise shifted from foot to foot, trying to get comfortable enough on her painful feet to take in the sights.

The sunlight stood a strange contrast to the dark, grey city. It seemed like a place made for the night. Adding to that sense was the vast amount of wrought iron streetlights lining the crowded, cobbled streets. All gaslight, no candles like Elise had noticed Ground Hollow still had.

The air smelled heavily of smoke, horses, and, under it all, something very sweet. Perhaps it came from the food wafting out of bakeries and various shops. Or the flowers that dirty children were selling on street corners. Highmere had its own scents but they weren't as overpowering as the ones were here.

Elise found herself walking closer to Nessa, partly for safety in the bustling crowd and partly because of the more pleasant smell of sugar pumpkins wafting off both their skins.

A four-horse carriage drove past them. It was black with elegant golden symbols. People hurried along in its wake, shouting to each other in what sounded like playful tones. A man sat outside a barbershop near them and played something cheerful on a raggedy violin.

She heard Nessa suck in a breath. "Isn't it beautiful? I mean, I know it's not traditionally beautiful, like a pretty castle or a sunset. But it's so…"

"Alive," Elise filled in.

"Exactly." Nessa's eyes were bright. "Everything and everyone moves with purpose and speed. Like cogs in a machine. But it feels like they enjoy it, like it drives them to achieve more. There's so much energy and colour. You get the feeling that anything can happen here."

"And that it probably does, on a daily or perhaps nightly basis," Elise agreed.

Nessa stood with her mouth slightly open, taking it all in. Her whole body looked like it was ready to spring into action.

Elise took Nessa's hand. "Just so we do not lose each other in the crowd. Let us keep moving."

They gave a shouting man in white garb a wide berth. He was a preacher, clear from his white clothes and the fact that he was standing outside the church they had seen through the gate. He caught sight of them and bellowed his message, spit flying from his mouth as he did so.

"Do not let alcohol and lust distract you from your true purpose! Our gods want you to work hard, help your neighbours, and fill our town with happy, healthy children. Drink and frivolous bedplay will never fill your heart. Thrale, God of the Sea, wants you healthy. Harmana of the Land wants you reproducing. And Aeonh of the Sky wants you to be kind to your fellow humans."

He held his hands out, indicating his surroundings. "Our factories give us a decent place to work, while the city provides us with nourishment and churches to worship in. Avoiding its sin and time-wasters is the part you must do for yourself. The gods can only stand with you, strengthening your resolve and watching you as you fight against the useless behaviour. Take heed or you will end up a beggar on the street!"

Elise merely nodded at him and picked up her pace. Nessa followed suit, but whispered, "Why do they always only speak of the big three? What about the smaller gods? Are they not important? Ioene was always my favourite."

With a frown, Elise concluded she did not remember that deity. She had never paid much attention in their religious classes, and people at court only really worshipped themselves and the Queen.

"Ioene? What is he or she god or goddess of again?"

Nessa looked at her with pursed lips. As if Elise was merely playing dumb. "You know, the goddess of the moon. The beautiful but lonesome moon goddess. Longing to join with her lover, the sun goddess Sarine, but unable to ever touch her again because she was tricked into swearing her life away to Aeonh, who keeps them apart. Wanting both goddesses for himself."

"Right," Elise agreed. She remembered the tale of the moon goddess now. The lonely and lovesick prayed to her. A romantic deity if there ever was one. It surprised her that this goddess was Nessa's favourite. Perhaps there was more to this practical farmer's daughter than met the eye?

Elise let her gaze roam over the tall, grey buildings around them as they walked. It amazed her how different this city was to Highmere. The capital was made of Centurian marble with elaborate iron gates and balconies, all painted white. Highmere looked like a dessert. White cream with pink lines of winter-berry sauce, gleaming in the frequent sun. Nightport, on the other hand, was made to be used. Perhaps her father would have thought this city ugly and utilitarian? Or maybe he would have relished the down-to-earth feel mixed with grim severity of it, like she did?

Shaking herself out of her reverie, she stopped watching like a visitor and changed her gaze to that of a person preparing to move in. They walked until Elise's eye was caught by a building in front of them, it had a sign that read *Rooms For Hire*. Elise checked the road sign above it. Miller Street. It was opposite a large bakery, giving the whole area a warm scent of bread which almost hid the smell of smoke and horses. A central location on a rather quiet street. Temptingly close for those with aching feet.

Elise tugged on Nessa's hand. "Wait. What do you think of this lodging house? 21 Miller Street. Can you see yourself living in there?"

Nessa scrunched her pale, upturned nose. "What? This one?"

The towering building looked rickety to say the least. The first two floors looked old while the two above them could have been built yesterday, but hardly by a professional builder. The house number was painted on with black paint, barely legible against the grey stone which was stained even darker by years of soot. The whole thing was mismatched and peculiar.

"I know it does not look like much, but one thing you have to learn about cities is that location is key. Here we will be in the centre of town, which will help when we look for work and go to buy supplies. Lots of amenities but still a calm street," Elise explained.

Nessa looked up at the building again. She looked sceptical but then shrugged.

"If you think this is a good choice, then we'll try it. After all, I'm used to living in a place with no windows and a leaky roof. This surely can't be worse."

Elise squeezed her hand. "Come on. I will do the talking, but you should help me negotiate if I seem to be overpaying at any point."

"Oh, count on it," Nessa said, squeezing her hand back.

～

A quarter of an hour later, they were up in their room. *Their room.*

Elise walked in first. Nessa joined her, put her satchel down on the floor, and stood by the door looking around.

Elise smiled at her. "Well, here we are! What do you think?"

"It'll do. I like how light it is. Shame there's no privy or bath. I don't mind using the one down the corridor, it's still luxurious to me to have it so close. But I was hoping for your sake that there would be one in the room. In fact, for your sake, I hoped we'd find lodgings that looked a little less like it might fall down any second. What do you think of it?"

"Well…" She looked around, trying to assess it objectively

and not immediately defend it because it was hers. The first place that was actually *hers*.

"It is rather cramped and might have seen better days." Elise shivered as a draught came from the room's only window, despite it being closed. They might have to see if they could seal that. "But it is so central and affordable. The room looks clean enough and it has everything we need."

Elise realised that was true after she had said it. The room held a dresser, a narrow wardrobe, a slim table with a basin, a mirror, and a worn chair. Two small bedside tables on either side of the bed. The one, single bed. There had been a huge price difference in getting a room with one bed and a room with two beds. So, in a rush of indignation and thriftiness, Nessa had decided that they could keep sharing a bed.

Elise wasn't going to complain about that. She had enjoyed sleeping close to Nessa, despite her embarrassment in finding herself snuggled in on top of her this morning. Elise would gladly continue acting as a cuddly toy for the practical, shy, sweet woman who was currently unpacking her few changes of clothes and putting them into the shabby dresser and tiny wardrobe.

With a happy sigh, Elise whispered, "Welcome home." She wasn't sure if it was meant for Nessa or herself. Perhaps both.

CHAPTER 12

A NEW DAY, A NEW START

The next morning Nessa woke to the view of a large crack in the ceiling. A white-washed concrete ceiling, she noted. So different from the one she had grown up with in Ground Hollow.

She peered bleary-eyed at it, trying to remember where she was. The question was quickly overshadowed by why she was alone. She might not immediately know where she was, but she somehow had a sense that Elise was meant to be there with her. It was startling how after merely two nights she had adapted to sleeping next to Elise. Or on top of or underneath her, depending on how much fidgeting and moving around her bedfellow did.

Nessa realised that what must have woken her was Elise unlocking the door. She now walked in, carrying a paper bag in one hand and a large tin mug in the other.

"Good morning, beautiful. I am sorry that I was not here when you woke up. I went out for fresh bread and some leaf tea."

Nessa looked down at the pillow, letting her hair cover her

face. It was far too early in the day to be blushing, just because her flirt of a roommate had called her beautiful.

"Good morning to you, too. That smells delicious."

"I hope it tastes good, too. Here you go." Elise handed her a roll and the big metal mug filled with what looked like weak tea.

It wouldn't surprise Nessa if the tea was as weak as it looked. It might only have seen leaves from a distance. She was fully aware that most of what Elise had paid had probably gone to paying for the tin mug. She'd have to speak to Elise about being careful with coin. And how to be clever when dealing with overcharging traders.

They ate in silence and handed the mug of tea back and forth.

Nessa cast glances at the woman who now sat on the edge of the bed. Elise was still wearing the clothes she had lent her. Somehow, they looked so much better on Elise, even though they didn't fit her as well as they did Nessa.

She must have missed when Elise washed up and got dressed this morning. Her hair, however, still lay in tangled waves down her back.

Adorable, but messy. Did she go outside looking like that? Odd. Maybe a rebellion against the impeccably styled life of Noble circles? Or perhaps she isn't used to styling her hair without a servant to assist? Well, she'll have to get used to doing it herself. Unless she cuts it short. Would Lady Elisandrine Falk ever cut her hair? Probably not. But perhaps Elise Aelin would?

Elise was focused on ripping up a second roll into little pieces and eating the small morsels. Nessa took the chance to examine Elise's face. Unlike when they first met, Elise wasn't wearing the kohl around her eyes or the red lip tint. Even without it, she had the most captivating appearance Nessa had ever seen, especially those mesmerising eyes. She couldn't look away from them. She remembered when they had been face to face yesterday morning in Ground Hollow. Those sleepy eyes blinking their beauty at Nessa. So intimate, so vulnerable, so near.

We were so close. I could have kissed her then. Or even better, she could have kissed me.

Suddenly Elise looked up, making eye contact with a warm smile. Nessa forced herself to look down at the mug in her hands.

A tingle was starting in her chest and spreading throughout her body. She willed herself to breath normally and not blush. The tingle died down, doused by a realisation. It wouldn't do to be attracted to this woman. She was out of Nessa's league. Besides, there was the description that Elise had given of herself "A sexual woman who likes bedplay for fun, not for relationships or for love." That was the opposite of Nessa, who had little need for bedding someone she didn't want to spend her days with. They were not romantically compatible. Elise was not meant for her. She had to remember that.

Nessa took a big gulp of the watery tea. "Thank you so much for going out to buy breakfast."

"You are most welcome. It was not an inconvenience. Well, in a way it was, since I was hobbling like a three-legged dog. I will have to buy new boots today. It is an unwelcome expense considering we do not have any capital coming in, but I have to be able to move."

Nessa put the mug on the bedside table and picked up what was left of her roll. "Of course. After I have washed and dressed, we'll go to the nearest cobbler and get you some good boots. I assume you'll want a job that is not pure grunt work. That means you'll also need clothes that are practical but some-what stylish."

Elise wiped breadcrumbs off her hands. "I had not thought of that. Yes, new boots and practical but elegant dresses for me. I suppose you would prefer some shirts and trousers which allow for physical labour?"

Nessa considered what jobs she might want, finding none needing a dress. "I think so."

"All right. I will put my hair up and get the coin purse out."

Nessa swallowed the last bit of her bread roll. "Great. I will get ready. Feel free to have the last of the tea."

After going downstairs to ask the landlady about cobblers, they had been directed to the biggest street in Nightport, Core Street. Miller Street was an offshoot of Core Street so it would be easy to find. They headed there now, looking for what the landlady said was a "cheap but good" shoemaker.

Elise was passing the time by badgering Nessa about what she looked for in a job. "Oh, come now. Surely you had something in mind when you thought about moving to Nightport all those years?"

Nessa shrugged, once again noticing the itch on her shoulder which had appeared after last night. She tried not to entertain the possibility that their cheap lodging house had fleas, lice, or something worse. "Perhaps. But what you dream of doesn't necessarily relate to what life looks like. Not when you're trying to make ends meet. I will take whatever job I can get."

Elise waved the statement away. "Yes, yes. I know that. But why not aim for what you truly want to do? Come on. You can tell me. What did you see yourself doing when you dreamed about coming here? Working in that big toy shop? Candle maker? Barmaid? Getting a job in one of the new factories?"

Nessa wasn't sure if she should be honest. Talking about

dreams and plans wasn't done in her home. If she said this out loud, it felt like it might somehow disappear into thin air. Be tainted by reality. Or that Elise would laugh at her high-flying plan.

No, Elise wasn't like that, so she squared her shoulders and forced the words out.

"I've n-never told anyone this. Nor really dared to truly consider it, I guess. But, th-there was one trade I did want to learn. I'm not sure I'd be any good at it, though. I know how to read books and farm land. That's it. Besides, it would take a master for me to apprentice with and they are few and far between. Most of them take a family member as an apprentice anyway, so what chance do I have?"

Elise walked closer to her. "Who can say? Let us find out together. What is the profession?"

Nessa chewed her lower lip, keeping her gaze on the road ahead. "Glassblowing."

When Elise didn't react, she forced herself to speak again. "When I visited Nightport as a child, I saw a man blowing glass and was mesmerised by it. He shaped this blob of unassuming stuff over fire, making the most beautiful but useful objects out of it. Since then, I've never been able to shake how fascinating and versatile glass can be. It's almost become a bit of an obsession. Layden would laugh at me for admiring his array of tincture bottles and glass jars. If there was a skill I could pick to dedicate myself to, glassblowing would be the one."

Out of the corner of her eye, she saw Elise give a quick nod. "Splendid. After we get my boots and the clothes, we will ask around regarding the city's glassblowers. Then we will seek them out and ask if any of them would take an apprentice. If they have any sense, they will see how capable and hard-working you are as soon as they speak with you."

Nessa scoffed. "I doubt it. I will probably be shy and make an idiot of myself."

"Not while I am around. I will not allow it. First things first, however, let us make my feet hate me less."

They arrived at the suggested address on Core Street and walked into the cobbler and shoemaker's shop. Elise marched right over to a man with a giant, bushy moustache. Smiling prettily, she greeted him. He looked up and instantly smiled back, smoothing his moustache and sucking in his beer gut. Nessa tried not to roll her eyes as she sat down to wait.

"I am looking for a sturdy but elegant pair of heeled, black boots. It is a bonus if they do not pinch too much. I should also like… and this is an unusual request, I know. I should also like some addresses for glassblowers in Nightport. If you know of any, that is. I am certain you do. You look to me like a real man about town."

The moustachioed man stood to attention. "Most certainly, Miss. I'll find ye the best black boots I 'ave. Elegant they are, too. An' won't be costin' ye an arm and a leg. Then I'll write down the names of some glassblowers. I know quite a few. Nightport born an' raised, I am."

"Thank you ever so much. I am so lucky to have stumbled upon you and your lovely shop," Elise said, blinding the man with another smile.

The man bowed low and then scurried off to a shelf of black boots.

Nessa leaned back and marvelled at Elise. She had a feeling that the confident and vibrant lady currently looking at shoes would keep her entertained and captivated for the rest of their friendship. She shook her head, smiling.

I never knew people like her existed. Please don't let her get bored of me.

Two hours later they had three new sets of clothes each and Elise had a pair of gorgeous new boots.

They had also traipsed throughout Nightport, visiting nearly all the glassblowers on the list that the cobbler had written down for them. None of them had been willing to take an apprentice.

Nessa's dream seemed to have been left on the narrow, dirty streets behind her. She rubbed her face with her hand. "Was that the last one?"

Elise consulted the list. "No. He wrote down one more. A Josiah Brownlee. It says he works on 32 Orgreave Street. That is next to Miller Street, I think. So close to home – that must be a sign." She gripped Nessa's hand and gave it a squeeze. "Stay positive."

Nessa sighed but followed Elise towards Orgreave Street. When they got there, they counted the numbers out until they reached a building with the number 32 on it. It was a normal house connected to a long workshop with a giant chimney above it. Nessa wasn't even nervous this time. What was the point? There would be no job here either.

Elise knocked on the door, and after a while it opened with a slow creak. A man who must've been in his fifties, with a scraggly beard and a haggard face, peered at them.

Elise took a step forward, back ramrod-straight and a winning smile on her face. "Hello. Are you Josiah Brownlee? The glassblower?"

"I am. Who's askin'?" he barked.

"My name is Elise, and this is Nessa Clay. We are new to the city and looking for work. Nessa here has always wanted to learn the craft of glassblowing and was told you were the person she should learn from. Would you be willing to take an apprentice? She is hardworking, diligent, trustworthy, and a fast learner."

Josiah looked Nessa up and down with a sceptical air.

Nessa felt the need to say something. "I'd work long hours for small pay."

He crossed his arms over his broad chest. "I'd say ye would. My last apprentice lived 'ere. Slept on a mattress in the hot shop; that's a glassblower's workshop, in case ye didn't know. He sometimes helped me an' Mrs Brownlee in our house next door. Cleaned an' did errands, the lad did. All for the privilege of bein' taught a proper profession. His wages used to be a roof over his 'ead an' food in his belly."

Nessa's heart sank even further. She'd heard similar tales from the other glassblowers. Any apprentice had to be young and willing to live with the glassblower, in all but name being a slave. To make matters worse, their querying had confirmed the assumption that glassblowers chose the younglings from their extended family. She was about to thank him for his time when she saw Elise hold up a hand.

"Mr Brownlee. You said 'used to be.' May I ask where your apprentice, this *lad*, is now?"

The old man rubbed his bearded chin and squinted at Elise. "Skipped out on us, didn't he? After pilferin' the month's earnings an' my wife's best porcelain. Why do ye ask?"

Elise hummed. She clasped her hands and shook her head. "From what I hear there is a lot of that in Nightport. Plenty of untrustworthy youngsters growing up on the tough streets."

He was about to say something, but Elise carried on. "Well, my friend here is a hardworking young woman from Ground Hollow. A farmer's daughter who has helped the farm to thrive. She is used to putting in a good day's work without grumbling. Helping those around her without asking for anything in return. Constantly following a strict code of moral conduct."

Josiah looked Nessa over again, this time with a greater interest, but he still didn't look convinced. Nessa saw Elise smile at the old man, grabbing his attention to speak again.

"She would live in lodgings with me just a short walk away, over on Miller Street. I need the companionship, you see. Nessa offered to help, being the good person she is. It seems to me that the few coins you would pay her would be less than you paid your last apprentice, if you factor in what he stole. Nessa only needs enough for rent and some basic food. Pittance, really. She would almost be working for free."

All of a sudden, a woman stepped out from inside the workshop. She opened the front door wider, and a wall of heat hit Nessa.

"Josiah, I've been listenin', and there is sense in what the girl is sayin'. Ye're not a young buck anymore, an' my back is bent like a rusty pipe. We need help with the grunt work. But I'll be drawn behind a cart if I let another skivin', thievin' young scoundrel under my roof. Havin' someone livin' a street away sounds better to me." She squinted at Nessa. "Let me 'ave a look at this farm girl an' see if she's all what her friend reckons she is."

Josiah grunted and muttered, "This is Secilia, my wife. She's a glassblower, too. Does most of the tricky, fiddly work. Ye'd be workin' for us both if we took ye on."

Secilia walked up to them and looked Nessa up and down, much as her husband had a moment ago. After a tense moment, she gave a quick nod.

"Looks trustworthy enough. Honest eyes and doesn't stand there smilin' like some fool. However, looks can lie. Are ye willin' to work your fingers to the bone, girl?"

Nessa knew this was the time for her to do her part. Elise couldn't help her now.

"Yes, Mrs Brownlee. It's been a dream for me to become a glassblower, and I'll work myself into the ground if it means I can make that dream a reality. I'll clean, run errands, do heavy lifting. Anything you need in return for teaching me the trade. Oh, and earning enough coins to keep me in bread."

"Speaks nice and proper, too. Good posture and seems to 'ave some muscle on her bones. We'll give her a chance, Josiah. Take her on for a month, and we'll see how hardworkin' and trustworthy she is."

With that Secilia returned to the workshop, leaving Josiah, Nessa, and Elise on the doorstep.

Josiah drew in a long breath and echoed his wife. "I'll hire ye for a month. I can only pay ye one silver a week. That should be keepin' ye in bread and rent if you're on Miller Street. After that first month, we'll see if ye want to stay on. And if me and Secilia want ye to. Sound fair?"

Nessa felt like she had just been given the best present of her life. "Absolutely. You won't regret it."

Elise broke in. "Excuse me. Will the wages go up if you both decide that Nessa can stay on as apprentice?"

"Of course!" Josiah barked. "I'm not some bloodsucker who keeps good workers on for small coin. If she works hard, does as we say, an' has a knack for glassblowin', we'll be payin' her three silvers a week. Ye can't say fairer than that."

Nessa looked over at Elise, who smiled and said, "Indeed, Mr Brownlee. I certainly cannot. Thank you."

Unable to keep excitement buried any longer, Nessa asked, "When would you like me to start?"

Josiah Brownlee stared at her like she had asked where the sky was. "Right bleedin' now, of course. Ye heard the missus, we need help with the grunt work."

The ground got a little unsteady under Nessa's feet.

Starting right now? No time to prepare or to get used to the idea?

Perhaps that was best, Nessa thought. Perhaps she should simply be thrown into it, much like the trip to Nightport.

She steadied herself. "All right. Will I need anything? Like clothing or tools?"

"No. I have it all right 'ere. Although the apron is made for a man and might be a little big. No matter, I'm sure it won't be too heavy for a lass used to farm work."

Nessa tried to look confident. "I think you're right there, Mr Brownlee. Let me have a minute to say goodbye to my companion, and then I'll be in and ready to start work."

"All right. But don't be dawdlin'. We don't have all day." With that, Josiah walked back in, slamming the door behind him.

Nessa turned to Elise. She was no longer hiding her excitement and probably looked like a child on its birthday. "We did it! I'm going to be glassblower. I'm so sorry that's not much coin to start with, but we have the capital you've brought and soon I'll be earning more. I'm sure of it."

Elise grabbed her by the shoulders. "Of course. Besides, I will find a job, too. We will make ends meet. Please do not fret about that. You simply focus on becoming the best glassblower in Nightport."

Nessa was trying to catch her breath, trying to wrap her head around this. "Well, I suppose I will eat something here for lunch and then see you tonight. Will you be all right on your own?"

Elise let go of her shoulders, smiling reassuringly. "Most certainly. I am going hunting for a job. In the bakery where I bought the bread rolls this morning, I spotted little notices about jobs in the window. I am going to have a look at them and see what is available."

"Good thinking and well spotted. Good luck. And if you don't see something you would be happy doing, don't just take any old job. We will find something that you enjoy tomorrow or the next day."

Elise quirked an eyebrow. "We? You will be busy learning a new craft. I have a feeling Secilia and Josiah are going to work you like a horse. You will be lucky to be home to dinner tonight."

Nessa sighed but couldn't hide her grin. She didn't mind working hard if it was to learn something she would enjoy. Hard work was all she had ever known, but it had always been to help someone else. Today was the day her work would be for her own benefit. Her food. Her rent. Well, not only hers. *Theirs.*

She took Elise's hand for a moment and pressed it. "Thank you for all your help. I couldn't have achieved this without you pushing me and being bold for me."

"I was glad to help. I like helping you, returning the favour so to speak. Congratulations on the new job. Oh and, please be careful around the fire. I will see you later," Elise said before turning back towards Core Street.

Nessa watched her walk away. There was a strange, warm, buzzing feeling in her stomach. She would have to learn to ignore it. Elise wasn't for her. She had to remember that.

CHAPTER 13

WHEREIN ELISE SEARCHES FOR A JOB, BUT FINDS AN ACQUAINTANCE INSTEAD

Elise was happy that Nessa finally found a place she belonged. More than that, she was relieved. She felt responsible for the other woman.

The problem right now was her own belonging. After she left Nessa, she walked over to that bakery and examined the notices in their window. Three of them asked for strong workers with experience carrying and lifting; the other two were for skilled labour.

Dead-end for a Noble woman on the run.

She rolled her eyes at her own melodrama but couldn't stop the feeling taking root.

Since then, she had wandered the streets looking for more notices, occasionally stopping in shops and businesses that might want a highly schooled employee with no real experience. That had been just as much of a dead-end. In the end, she walked into a shop and bought some kohl and lip tint, borrowing a mirror and applying it in the shop. Anything to make herself feel a little more confident. It hadn't worked.

She was tired, dejected, and her feet hurt. She rubbed her temples.

I have enough coin for at least a couple of weeks. I shall simply have to start my search over again tomorrow.

With heavy steps, Elise walked back to their rickety boarding house. It was a dry, windy day, and dust blew up from the cobblestones as carriages passed her. The entire walk, she thought about the shared bathtub at the end of their corridor. It was stained and small, but it would do to get her clean and relax her aching legs and feet. Hopefully she could get enough hot water for a long soak. She could only hope there wasn't a queue.

If only we had the time and coin to find a better lodging house. Oh well. We needed a place to stay and I found us one. We shall make due. I must learn to make due with things.

It was while she was heading for the stairs that she looked down at her new boots, which chafed as they had yet to shape to her feet, causing her to nearly crash into a man.

He was slim, well-dressed, and his square jaw was perfectly shaven. He puffed, out of breath from running down the stairs, as he stopped and stared at her.

"Oh. I am terribly sorry about that. I am late for work." Despite his apparent rush, he raked his eyes over her. "Say, are you new here? I am sure I would have remembered seeing someone so… striking here before."

She looked back at him, aiming to appear neutral. She appreciated a good flirtation, but now was not the time. Besides, speaking to a strange man in a city known to be unsafe seemed imprudent even to her. She should tread carefully.

"Yes, we arrived in Nightport yesterday and rented a room here last night."

If the stranger picked up on that she was hinting that she was spoken for by saying 'we,' he gave no sign of it. He smoothed down his already perfect hair, which was blonde as wheat with a streak of black at the front. It was sleekly arranged in a long ponytail which his hands now clasped. He gave it a theatrical twirl and let it drop back against his red velvet frock coat.

He bowed with a flourish. "Welcome to Nightport and to 21 Miller Street. I hope your stay will be most enjoyable."

Then he gifted her a rehearsed smile. One which he probably thought was roguishly charming, but which reminded Elise of a conman who had weaselled his way into court last year.

She noticed that this man's teeth were unnaturally white and perfect. They looked as if they had been made in a factory. In fact, all of him gave that impression. Unnaturally flawless. It wasn't purely his looks. The accent was unnatural, too. The words sounded like a midlands accent, almost Noble, but the cadence was all Nightport.

Normally she would have been intrigued, but now, she wanted to rest and have a bath. Or even better, a job so she wouldn't have to let Nessa down.

He gave a polite cough and she realised that she hadn't answered him.

"Thank you for your concern. I am certain my stay will be most enjoyable… if I can ever find some employment," she muttered.

He straightened, seeming to have forgotten his haste. "Oh? You are in search of a job? I can help you there. I work for one of the biggest law firms in Nightport. I bring important messages to just about every business, factory, company, and politician in town. Even to the Nightport docks."

She crossed her arms over her chest. "So, you are an errand boy?"

The peacock of a man looked appalled. "Certainly not! I

am an assistant to Mr Rudyard Hampton, the most important solicitor in Nightport."

Elise realised that she had wounded his pride, something she guessed he had a lot of. Out of guilt, she decided to try to mend some of the injury. "Ah, I see. As I say, I am new to the city. I meant no offence."

The man squared his shoulders, puffed his chest out, and once more gave her that white-toothed, roguish smile. "No offence taken. Besides, it is only my day job. At night I have a more exotic position. But you are too new in town to hear about that, Miss…?"

Now that did pique her curiosity. A little.

"Elise Aelin. And you are?"

"Hunter Smith, at your service. Now, I must be hurrying to work, but I will return before nightfall. Perhaps then I can buy you a glass of ale here? The landlady serves bad ale and worse pies. All so she can claim to have food services at her lodging house. We can discuss what employment would fit you then?"

The smile on his face hinted that he wanted to do more than merely buy her a drink, but this was not mirrored in his body language. His feet were pointing away from her, his posture was stiff, and he was crossing his arms over his chest. Nearly hugging himself.

There was something going on with this man, but she was too tired and dejected to care. Maybe after she had managed to get some sleep. Preferably next to Nessa's warm, soft body.

"Perhaps. I am very tired and not sure I shall be here when you return. I might be out with my companion. She does so like to treat me." Elise added a meaning wink to her last words, hoping that this Hunter Smith would take the hint this time.

Although, there was a distinct possibility that even if he did, he would still press his luck. He behaved like the sort of person who thought that they could have any lover they wanted. In short, he behaved as a Noble. In everything but his body language, which was still strangely standoffish.

He looked at her for a few heartbeats. "I see. Even better! Perhaps we can all have a glass of ale around eight tonight? But now I really must hurry. I am monstrously late."

He rushed past her and out the door.

Elise heard chuckling and looked over the desk by the wall. The landlady was there. She was the one who had upset Nessa by informing her of how much it would cost to get a room with two beds. Now, she was looking in the direction of the door, shaking her head. Elise wondered if she had overheard what Hunter said about her ale and pies.

She caught Elise looking. "Beg ye pardon, Miss. He's just such a silly lad. Pretendin' like that."

Elise blinked a few times. "Do you mean the accent?"

"Well, no. Although that is all pretendin', too. Likes to think he sound like a Noble, he does. Sounds plain silly, right? No, I was thinkin' that it's so funny to see 'im strut and prance around young beauties. Like he wasn't all smoke an' no fire."

"What do you mean?"

The landlady made an unpleasant snorting noise. "I mean that Mr Smith takes on the role of famous man 'bout town an' reckons that this means he's to flirt with everyone he sees. Especially if they happen to be attractive or important. Except, most people in Nightport whisper that he prefers a lonely bed."

"A lonely bed?"

The landlady gave her a lopsided grin. "Aye. The pretty specimen of a man doesn't like the... well, ye know... the pleasures of the flesh." The last couple of words were whispered. She continued with eyes twinkling. "But he pretends real hard an' thinks that no one sees through it. All the while, most of Nightport knows that he won't actually bed his conquests. He tends to find a way out before things get… juicy. Broke quite a few hearts in the first few months, he did. That's why I'm tellin' ye this, to keep yer heart safe, Miss Aelin."

Elise shook her head. "No need to worry about me. My interests do not include men."

The landlady looked taken aback but then smirked. "Ah, I see. Keep to grey-eyed girls, do ye?"

Elise gave her a filthy look. "I am not certain that is any of your business. Neither are Mr Smith's sexual habits, surely. Nevertheless, I thank you for informing me, as I am now more likely to take him up on his offer to help me find employment."

The landlady put her hands at the small of her back and stretched. "Aye, I suggest ye do exactly that. He might be a sad case of all smoke an' no fire, but he does know his way around town, an' all the people in it. Get him to set ye up with a job so ye can keep payin' me the rent."

Elise muttered that she'd try and began walking up the stairs. That bath would have to wait. The bed in their room was calling her name, and even though it was only late afternoon, she was going to answer it.

Some hours later, Nessa opened the door. Her noisy fumbling with her keys woke Elise from her slumber. Keys and locks hadn't caught on much in Ground Hollow. Elise really wished they had.

"Oh. I'm sorry! I didn't know you were asleep."

Elise yawned and smiled up at her. "That is quite all right, I was just catching up on some rest."

Nessa closed the door behind her. "Does that mean your job search didn't bear fruit?"

"I am afraid that is exactly what it means," Elise said, rubbing her eyes before remembering that she had applied kohl.

Splendid. Now you look like a black-eyed racoon.

Nessa sat down on the bed. "Don't worry. Tomorrow is a new day. I'm confident you will find the perfect thing for you then. Maybe I can ask Josiah if he knows of someone employing well-schooled women?"

Elise hummed. "Perhaps that would be a good idea. It certainly cannot hurt. That reminds me, I promised a flirtatious young man whom I ran into downstairs that we would have a couple of ales with him tonight. He claimed to know of employers here in town, and the landlady confirmed that he has an extensive catalogue of contacts."

Nessa edged closer, looking sceptical and stern as she did so. "I see. Are you sure that he won't want something in return for this information?"

Elise leaned closer, wanting to flirt and greedy for more of the warmth coming off Nessa's body. She arched an eyebrow and smirked. "Is that concern or... jealousy I hear in your voice?"

That voice. Nessa's incredibly clear, beautiful voice. Why do I never tire of listening to that gods-forsakenly enchanting voice?

Nessa snorted. "Don't be silly. I just worry about sitting down with some stranger you ran into in a notoriously dangerous city. Especially one who was flirty and promised you something that you desperately needed. Bound to be shady."

With that, all flirtation was cut off. Elise sat back, dropping her eyebrow and ending the smirk. She was trying very hard to not feel hurt by Nessa's reaction to the notion of being jealous. Or the overbearing tone in her voice. "I know. I was joking. No need to worry, I can read people and am very well aware that such a person might be 'shady.' However, the young man in question will not pose a danger to us. At least not in a sexually predatory way."

Nessa stretched. "Really? May I ask how you know that?"

Elise tilted her head. "You know what? I believe it would be more entertaining to let you guess when you meet him."

Nessa's eyes narrowed, suddenly paying more attention. "You want me to just trust your judgement about this man? Without any explanations?"

Elise ran her fingers under her eyelids and looked at them to see how much of the black paint she had smudged over her eyes. "Yes. That is the point of our friendship, is it not? We both contribute something that the other one does not have and can advise each other because we come from different circumstances."

She got up to check her eyes in the mirror, wiping away the worst of the kohl as she continued. "I know about people, you know. Especially men who try to take advantage. Highmere was filled with them. When I spoke to this man, he seemed to be trying too hard to be something he could not quite pull off. Our landlady confirmed as much right after he left. Humour me, try to spot the secret he is hiding when we see him tonight."

Nessa chewed her lower lip. "And if I can't? Will you mock me?"

Elise looked past her own reflection, catching Nessa's eye in the mirror. "Of course not."

Nessa was still chewing her lip and now averting her eyes. Elise walked over to her and brushed a few strands of soot-stained hair away from her pale face. "I would never do that. If you cannot guess right away I will tell you. I simply believe it will be a good challenge to see if you can see through him, and if you cannot, it will be a starter lesson in reading people. You will need that skill in the city. There will be no wrong answers, and I will never mock you. Tease you about things you do not mind being teased about? Yes. Mock you? Never."

Nessa gave a brief smile. "All right, I will give your game a go. I bet I can guess, right away. Is he like you? Bedding solely his own gender?"

"No, no. None of that. No clues. You are going to have to read him yourself."

Nessa began to undo her braid. "As you wish. For now, I plan to wash up, change clothes, and try to find a big meal. I need it."

"Oh, of course! Tell me everything about your first day. Did you get to make any glass?"

"No. But I got to sweep floors, clean tools, and handle any customers who came in. At least until they had tricky questions. In between all that, I was given instructions on how to behave in the hot shop to prevent injury to people or any of the materials. Secilia says I will be ready to handle the glass and the furnace in a few days. Josiah thinks it might be longer."

Elise could see the impatience and disappointment on Nessa's face. "I am sorry to hear that."

Nessa combed her fingers through her loose hair. "It's all right. It seems to be common practice when you take an apprentice. I'm glad to know that they are concerned about my welfare and about me learning how to behave in the workshop before I take on any dangerous tasks."

Nessa walked over to the basin. She began to undo the buttons on her dirty shirt, taking it off while talking about the customers who were coming to have glasswork made.

Elise was struggling to pay attention. Her focus kept drifting to the revealing of all that creamy skin, stained with soot anywhere the shirt hadn't covered it. Her own skin seemed to burn with heat, and she found herself clenching her hands to keep them from reaching out to touch Nessa. In the end, she turned her back to be able to pay full attention to Nessa's words.

~

It was nearing eight, and they were walking down the stairs. Elise was rubbing sugar pumpkin oil into her hands and dabbing some on her neck. Exactly as she had on Nessa's neck before they left the room. That touch had been a little too pleasant, a little too tantalising. So painfully tempting to rub that sweet oil further down that neck and coat that soft, fair skin. Reaching in under the clean change of clothes Nessa had just put on.

Elise had quickly suggested that they needed to go. Nessa had, as always, followed her without question.

Opposite the reception desk downstairs were a few tables around a fireplace. This was where the ales and what the land-lady had called "some of the finest pies in Nightport" were served to those who stayed in 21 Miller Street.

Elise chose the table closest to the fire and sat down, Nessa picking the seat opposite. Elise glanced over at her, appreci-ating the pink cheeks and silky hair that had been unearthed when Nessa had washed off all the soot. She bit her tongue to keep from telling Nessa how utterly beautiful she found her and moved her gaze to the fire instead.

The landlady came over with the heavy steps of someone who didn't move a lot but did eat a lot of pie. Elise had to admit that she carried her weight well, though.

"Hello again, Miss Aelin." She spotted Nessa. "And Miss Clay. Are ye both waitin' on Mr Smith and those ales he was going to buy ye?"

"Exactly so. Although, as it is not quite eight yet and we are hungry I think we will buy some ales and a pie each now. He can buy the next round when he arrives," Elise said.

There was a gleam of amusement in the landlady's eye. "All right. Just the two of ye, eh? By the lovely fire. With some intoxicatin' ale and steamin' hot, filling pies then. Good choice, Miss Aelin. Mr Smith can be left waitin' for a good, long while."

Elise ignored her. Not just because of the hints of something romantic between her and Nessa, but because she was not much for gossips. Hunter Smith's fight to hide his disinterest in bedplay was a subject that deserved more sensitivity and less sniggering. Even if she had made it a bit of a game for Nessa to puzzle out. After all, that was about Nessa learning to read which were the real dangers and which were simply grass snakes pretending to be vipers. Although, in Elise's experience, it was more common that vipers pretended to be grass snakes.

"What sort of pies do you serve?" Nessa asked, unaware of what was going on.

"Pig's feet an' dammon nuts or ale an' oxen liver. There's also one with milk cabbage an' shrooms. Y'know, for those poor buggers what don't eat meat."

Nessa didn't look at all worried about those choices, in distinct contrast to how Elise's stomach was turning. She found herself missing Noble meals. Five dishes where you could pick out a bite here and there from a plate so fresh, clean, and... well, yes... piled with only the best cuts of meat. She would have to shake being so spoiled.

"I'll have the ale and liver one, please," Nessa was saying. "And a tall glass of your best ale with it. What do you want, Elise?"

Elise swallowed down her burgeoning nausea. Feet and innards weren't going to sit well in her stomach. "I would like the milk cabbage and shroom pie. Oh, and the same drink as Nessa, please."

The landlady adjusted the skirt that was sliding down her belly and muttered, "Seein' as we only have one ale, pickin' the best one won't be hard. It's sure not to poison ye at least. That'll all be comin' right up."

Elise looked at Nessa with trepidation, but she was busy leaning back and closing her eyes. Her face was so beautiful in repose. Elise also sat back, enjoying the fire and occasionally stealing glances at Nessa.

After a few moments, the door to 21 Miller Street opened and Hunter Smith strode in. He was a little more dishevelled than when Elise had seen him last. Despite this, he was still handsome in his fine clothing, with features so beautiful they could have been sculpted by an artist. Elise smiled at how wasted his good looks were on her.

She felt her smile grow as she realised that if her instincts and the landlady's gossip were right, her own attractive looks were equally wasted on him. Unless, of course, he appreciated beauty without wanting to physically pleasure it.

She looked over at Nessa to see what impact Hunter Smith had on her. Nessa was no longer closing her eyes. She was sitting bolt upright, fidgeting with her shirtsleeves, eyes trained on Hunter. Jealousy soured Elise's stomach.

Do not jump to conclusions. She is shy around everyone. This does not mean she wants to bed him.

She looked from Nessa to Hunter and then back to Nessa again. She couldn't help it. And she didn't like what she saw. Nessa was looking him up and down and swallowing nervously. It was impossible to keep her mind from churning lightning fast.

But she is not nervous around me. Is that a good sign or a bad one when it comes to my chances as a romantic partner? Would she be fidgeting with her clothes and swallowing like that if she was attracted to me?

Hunter Smith caught Elise's eye and smiled, showing those abnormally white teeth. "Miss Aelin. You decided to accept my offer, then?"

"Clearly. I am here, am I not?" Elise snapped. She could feel her temper getting out of her control. That was fast, even for her.

Hunter Smith gave a bow, ending with a little flourish of the hand. When he looked up and locked eyes with her again, his glittered.

Clearly not discouraged by my lack of interest. As I figured.

Elise indicated Nessa. "This is Nessa Clay. My... companion."

He turned towards Nessa, thrusting his chest out. "Good evening, Miss Clay. A true pleasure to meet you. Our dark city needs more pure, radiating beauty like yours." He took Nessa's hand and in a slow, savouring manner, kissed it. Nessa smiled briefly at the gesture and blushed. Elise felt her teeth grind.

"Th-thank you."

He enthroned himself in the chair next to Nessa, legs spread widely.

"No need to thank me, Miss Clay. It is the truth. This city is clogged up with people who need expensive paint and fancy clothes to make themselves attractive. Your looks, however, light up the room without any assistance. The men and women of Nightport will be worshipping at your feet. I know, because I am sure to be down there with them."

Elise's teeth-grinding began to hurt her jaw so she forced herself to relax.

The landlady brought their ales, placing them on the small tables next to each chair. In bored tones, she informed them that their pies would be coming out of the oven soon. She took Hunter's order for another glass of ale and a pie of any kind, and then left them.

Suddenly, it felt important to get to the matter at hand fast and then get rid of Hunter. Elise was no longer invested in letting Nessa practice reading people. She could read other people. Less attractive and less flirtatious people.

"So, Mr Smith. You said you could help me with finding employment?"

Hunter leaned back, switching his gaze to Elise now. "Indeed. First, I must enquire what sort of job you would like and what you are fitted for. Let us begin with if you want manual labour or something more cerebral?"

Elise sipped her ale. "Categorically something more cerebral."

He peered at her. "Yes, I would say so. Judging by your way of speaking and how you treat people, you seem almost like a Noble. A little like me, but I confess to having spent years practising and still falling a little short. A problem you do not seem to have. Anyway, my point is your voice and behaviour speak more of schooling than of strength or skilled labour."

A chill shot up Elise's spine. She thought she had been so careful in not sounding Noble. Was it her pronunciation or her word choice that gave her away? Her instinct was to attack. To act cruel and make him leave. She took a moment to suppress the urge. She imagined her face calm, neutral, and pleasant and hoped it was translating into reality.

"I grew up in a large manor house where my parents where servants to a Noble family," she lied. "I assume I picked up my way of speaking and my thirst for knowledge there." Then, to change the subject: "So, do you know of any job for someone like me? Perhaps some merchant family requires a governess? Or does the law firm you work for need a writer?"

Hunter steepled his fingers. "Not that has reached my ears. And as I am on the streets of Nightport most of the day and a good portion of the night, my ears take in most news. However, the printer who has his press opposite Mr Hampton's law bureau, Archibald Richards..." He paused, looking at them both as if the name should mean something to them. When it didn't, he continued. "He is in need of an extra pair of hands for a sizable project. He does not want to take on an apprentice as this would only be work for a few weeks. However, if you impress him enough, perhaps he will change his mind."

He winked at her. He probably thought it looked suave, but it only looked like he was trying too hard. Particularly as he couldn't keep his other eye open as he did it. She knew that pain. Why was such a perfect flirtation so difficult to pull off?

He ran his hand over his scalp and ponytail, smoothing down tresses which were only slightly less sleek than earlier in the day. "When I spoke to him, he said he was looking for someone who was diligent, intelligent, and who had refinement. The latter I believe was more for his own benefit than a requirement for the job. He is a terrible snob, so I wager he would appreciate someone so like a Noble lady as yourself."

He sat forward. She didn't like the way he was looking at her now. Like he was looking beyond her eyes and all the way into her mind, trying to read her secrets. Well, if he could do that, it would do him no good. If he disclosed her secret, she would disclose his. Although it appeared most of the city already knew his, if their landlady was to be trusted.

She inclined her head. "All right. If you would not mind making the introductions tomorrow, I shall be sure to impress this printer and put you in a good light for recommending me."

"I cannot ask for more than that, Miss Aelin."

He leaned back once more, spreading his legs even wider this time, and then grinned his well-rehearsed roguish smile at her. Elise was in no mood for his strange games. Especially not as he soon turned that smile to Nessa, looking at her as if he was inviting her into his open lap.

Elise reached over, putting her hand lightly on his knee. "Oh, I think you can ask for more than that, handsome. And I plan to give you what you want," she said in her most seductive tone. Just as she had hoped, that wiped the smile from his face.

Yes. I happen to be the real deal. Stop pretending with me, boy. More importantly, stop pretending with Nessa. She is too innocent for your games.

She kept her smirk in place and slowly blinked at him. He immediately snapped his legs together.

"Huh?" Nessa queried.

Elise turned to her. "I am of course referring to buying Mr Smith another ale when he has finished this one. I certainly did not mean to flirt with him, as I have no intention of making him a proposition of any kind. Nor am I looking for him to proposition me." She paused for effect. "No, I merely wanted to extend a grateful and *friendly* hand by buying Mr Smith a beverage. Is that not a splendid idea, beautiful?"

Poor Nessa seemed confused, looking between Hunter and Elise. Nevertheless, she played along with what Elise was saying, as always.

"Oh. Um. Yes, naturally. An ale is a small price to pay for a possible job. We thank you, Mr Smith, and I propose a toast to making new friends."

Nessa lifted her glass so that Elise could clink hers against it. Then both thrust their ales towards Hunter. He picked up his glass and clinked it against theirs with an expression that showed something which looked a lot like relief.

"Friends. Aye. I'm likin' the sound of that. Call me Hunter."

Aha. There's the Nightport buried under the practised accent.

A stab of regret hit her. She should probably pity him instead of besting him at his game, but she wanted him to drop the pretence. Both for his own sake, as she could not understand why he fought so hard and behaved so obnoxiously purely to hide that he did not want to bed them. But, also, because he was annoying her and confusing Nessa. For whatever reason, Hunter Smith needed to be taken down a peg or two.

He was looking over at Nessa while preening, brushing down the front of his shirt and playing with his ponytail. Elise's stomach soured.

Let's face it. You won't be able to keep from reacting if he flirts with her, will you?

She tried to swallow that thought down. Then she gathered her wits, focused on her meal, and on trying exceptionally hard to be polite to their new acquaintance.

CHAPTER 14
NESSA AND ELISE

The too-bright, whitish light piercing through the dirty window woke Nessa that morning. Maybe they should get a curtain of some sort? The bell tower of the nearby church, which she now knew as the Church of Saint Alsager, hadn't rung out yet. The church bells were quiet all night but rang at six in the morning to wake the city. She still had time before she needed to go to work.

She was laying on her side. Draped behind her like a clinging cloak was Elise. A thin arm was gently holding Nessa's waist while every other part of Elise seemed to be pressed close against her. She could feel every curve, every dip, every bone, every muscle, and every deep breath that Elise took.

Nessa tried to steady her own breaths. She didn't want to seem like she was panting or have Elise wake to the feel of her increasing heartbeat. Nothing could disturb this moment. Elise could never know what she was feeling.

The room was so damned quiet. Not a hooting owl, a scurrying mouse, or even the noises of the city from outside. It was too quiet. The gentle breathing of the woman behind her was all Nessa could hear. That and her own thundering heart. She

126

swallowed hard, wondering if she could go back to sleep and escape this confusing mess of feelings and sensory overload.

Elise sighed intensely in her sleep, making her petite breasts push even tighter against Nessa's back.

This was dangerous. It would be easy to overstep. To cross the thin line between friendship and romance. That line was so hard to make out right now.

She tensed as Elise's arm moved, her hand sliding down Nessa's belly to rest just below the navel. Suddenly her nightdress felt too thin. Elise's hand was so warm, the heat from her palm penetrated the fabric easily.

As Nessa lay there, trying to breathe normally, it struck her that Elise might ask her to be her lover soon. If she did, would Nessa have to explain that she didn't want that unless Elise could *love* her? But then, perhaps all of this was simply Elise being best friends? Perhaps this was the way Noble ladies were with each other? After all, Elise was a natural flirt and seemed very relaxed with showing her appreciation physically.

Still…

Last night she had caught Elise reacting badly whenever she agreed with Hunter Smith or laughed at his jokes. Not that she had done much of that. Partly because of her shyness and partly because Hunter seemed untrustworthy. Fake somehow. But when she had done those things, Elise's demeanour had become hostile towards Hunter. Was that jealousy? Or was she merely trying to protect her from Hunter?

Nessa pushed all thoughts of Elise out of her mind for the moment. Too complicated.

Breathe evenly. In and out. In and out.

She focused on Hunter. She hadn't been up to Elise's challenge of trying to read the suave, strange man. She could tell that he was hiding something, maybe trying to compensate for something. But she wasn't sure if she had made that assumption from his behaviour or from what Elise had told her about him. People were a mystery. Why did social interaction have to be so difficult?

The bells of Saint Alsager rang out, and Nessa was relieved at the tension breaking. On the sixth chime, she smiled at the fact that Elise could sleep through all that noise. She put a hand on the arm draped over her waist and gently tapped on the soft skin.

"Elise? It's time to wake up."

"Hmm? Why?"

Nessa's smile grew, hurting her cheeks.

"Because it's morning and I have a job to go to. You, meanwhile, have to go speak to a printer about getting a job."

Elise whined. "But it is so nice here."

Nessa was about to reply when Elise burrowed her face into her hair. Nessa could feel Elise's nose rubbing against the nape of her neck. Nessa noticed goosebumps forming on her forearms. Her entire body relaxed into Elise's grip, yielding to her. It would be so easy to stay here. To sleep a little longer. To relish in the warm softness of Elise. To keep that possessive arm around her. To enjoy the way Elise hummed happily into her hair right now.

Nessa clenched her teeth, summoning up her determination. If she stayed here, she'd lose all self-control. She gently extricated herself and stood up.

"I'll get ready first and then I'll go buy some bread rolls while you wash up and get dressed."

"Sure," Elise mumbled. Then she burrowed her face into the pillow and seemingly went back to sleep. Her thick, black waves of hair splayed out over the pillow and her face, shielding her from the world and from the one, single affectionate glance Nessa allowed herself.

Nessa would happily let her sleep. She just had to get some fresh air. Right away. She had to cool down and take her mind off what her heart seemed to be doing.

It wasn't allowed to do that. She would only be disappointed and hurt. And she would ruin her friendship with Elise. She'd be the clingy, sappy romantic from the countryside who didn't understand how things worked in the world. No. Never.

She tightened her jaw and got ready to go out and buy breakfast.

A while later she had bought the bread and decided to forgo wasting coin on juice or leaf tea today. Water would do. She was returning to 21 Miller Street while thinking about Elise. About long waves of soft, black hair, sandy brown skin that smelled so sweet, and eyes that could light up even the darkest corners of the world. Nessa's heart was aching and confusion twisted her gut.

When she walked into their lodging house, she saw the landlady scrubbing the reception counter with a cloth that smelled of lemon juice and vinegar. Nessa greeted her and got a muttered hello back before she walked on towards the stairs. She had only taken a handful of steps before the landlady spoke again. "Oh, hang on, Miss Clay. A package came for ye an' Miss Aelin just a moment ago. I'm not a postman, y'know?"

Nessa stared at the grumpy woman in confusion. "A package? Delivered here? It must be from Hunter, then. No one else knows where we live."

"T'was most certainly not from Mr Smith. I'd have 'im go deliver it 'imself. This was dropped off by a young lad. He said he'd been paid by a lady wearin' a veil to go drop this off to two ladies stayin' here. She didn't know yer names or room number, but she described ye both down to itty bitty detail. An' when the lad repeated the description to me, I knew she meant ye two. Even mentioned Miss Aelin's yellow eyes, he did."

"Golden eyes," Nessa corrected automatically. "Perhaps light amber."

The landlady looked at her. "Right. Sure. If ye say so." She handed Nessa the package.

Nessa weighed it in her hands. It was light as well as small. It was wrapped in paper dyed midnight blue and had a white ribbon tied around it, finished in a neat bow. An expensive way of wrapping a package, to be sure. There was no writing on it or card attached.

The landlady returned to cleaning the counter, so Nessa took her leave. She put the package into the satchel with the bread. Then she headed upstairs, shaking her head at how eager she was to be back in Elise's company soon.

Gods, woman. You have only been away from her for a short while. No one wants a friend this clingy. Control yourself.

Elise had washed, dressed, and arranged her hair in a perfect knot by the time Nessa came back. Despite this, she seemed barely awake as she dutifully ate her bread in between long yawns. She caught Nessa watching her, and their eyes locked.

Cheeks burning, Nessa looked away. She busied herself by checking the bag for more bread. That's when she saw the mystery package.

"Oh, I forgot about this," she said.

She produced the small, round package in midnight blue paper and handed it to Elise. "It was delivered to our landlady by a boy, who in turn got it from some veiled mystery woman. Apparently, she described you and me and said the package was intended for us. However, she didn't know what room we were staying in. Or our names."

Elise swallowed her mouthful of bread. "But she knew where we lived? Odd. Does that mean she just did not know what names we were staying under? Could it... could it have been my mother?"

Nessa took a moment, chewing the inside of her cheek. "I doubt it. If it was your mother, she'd come in and look for you, right? Not send you a strange, little package. That's probably your paranoia speaking. I bet this is simply a case of mistaken identity. Although... she did apparently describe your golden eyes perfectly," she said with a shrug.

Elise put her roll down and began unwrapping the package. Under the many layers of expensive wrapping paper, she unravelled what first looked like a stone. When she turned it over in her hands she said, "It is a piece of flint. Why would someone send us that?"

Nessa moved closer to investigate it. "Well, that settles it. It must be for someone else. Or someone has seen us on the street and mistaken us for someone they know who wants a piece of flint. Maybe it is a joke that the real recipient would understand? Or a symbol or something? Either way, it can't be for us."

Elise began pacing while letting the flint slide between her fingers. "Hmm. No one knows we are here, and even if they did, why would they send this? Mother or the Royal guards would simply take me back to Highmere or Silver Hollow Castle. They would not give me a present and most certainly not give me *flint*. A Noble person would not even know where to buy flint. Could it be for you?"

Nessa felt her eyebrows shoot up her forehead. "For me? Sent by whom? My parents? Layden? None of them know where in Nightport we are staying. Besides, they wouldn't send me anything without a note. They'd send me a letter or some food if they sent me anything at all."

Elise stopped pacing. "Of course. It cannot be for us. Still, what a peculiar thing to send to someone."

Nessa made a ball of the blue wrapping paper and threw it into the waste basket by the door. Elise placed the piece of flint on top of the dresser. She was standing there looking at it, narrowing her eyes and pursing those full lips of hers. Her posture was erect but graceful, her hands resting on her slender hips. Nessa knew she was staring but couldn't stop. Every part of her was drawn to the elegant woman peering at the plain object. Not for the first time, she simply couldn't take her eyes off Elise.

Seconds ticked by. Elise tilted her head as she kept peering at the flint, as if she could unlock its secret by staring at it. Nessa gazed longingly at the soft skin of her exposed neck, wondering how a shy and plain farmer's daughter like herself got to sleep nestled against that skin every night. Wondering what that skin tasted like.

Then Elise turned, meeting her gaze. Those deep-set, golden eyes penetrated her every defence. Nessa felt her cheeks burn.

Just friends, remember? You're just friends, Nessa. Friends don't look at each other like that. Shame on you.

She looked away, scrambling for something to say. "S-so, I'm afraid I failed the task you set me last night. I can see that Hunter Smith is hiding something. But I don't know what it is. Or why it means that he's not a threat to us."

Elise came back to the bed and sat down. She picked up her abandoned bread roll and took a bite. A crumb landed on her lower lip. "Well. He could still be a threat in as much as that he might steal from us or get us involved in some criminal activities. However, we should not have to worry about him wanting to... bed us."

"Why is that?" Nessa said and took a pull from her water

canteen, avoiding looking at that breadcrumb on Elise's lip and wondering how it would feel to kiss it away.

"As you might have noticed, he tries very hard to seem like the stud ready to mount any willing mare. Or willing stud, for that matter. However, as soon as you scrape the surface or get closer to him, he backs off like a frightened foal."

Nessa yawned as she handed the canteen of water over. "That's a lot of horse metaphors, especially for this early in the morning. Can you cut to what you are actually trying to tell me?"

"From my own observations and those of our landlady, Hunter Smith does not actually like to bed anyone. He simply pretends to. Pretends very strongly, to the point of pushing others away."

"Really? That's sad. Why does he do that?"

"I am not certain. Perhaps it is to prove his worth as a man about town? The landlady hinted at that," Elise said before drinking from the canteen. It washed away the breadcrumb, giving Nessa some reprieve.

"Prove his worth? What does a person's sexual needs and prowess have to do with anything other than where and how they spend the night?"

Elise shrugged. "I would guess that surviving in this harsh city, especially without the amount of coin we brought, means you have to fit in and seem able and willing in all aspects. I am ready to wager that in both the legal and illegal higher eche- lons of this society, you must seem attractive and impressively virile to get anywhere."

"Well," Nessa said, "whatever the reason for his behaviour is, I pity him. Still, I'm glad that that he was able to flag up a possible job for you. And he was good company last night, wasn't he? Gods know that we need a friend in the city. Espe- cially one who knows the ins and outs of it."

Elise yawned and stretched. "Yes, I suppose you are

correct. I simply wish he would stop flirting so blatantly with you."

"Does he flirt with me? Maybe he does. Although I think that's just his way. He flirts with you, too."

Elise rolled her eyes. "Not as much, since I have made it clear that his advances are unwelcome. I called his bluff, so to speak, and then showed my disinterest."

Nessa took another sip of water as she considered that. "It's not like I have encouraged him."

"I know that, sweetest Nessa. But he does not need encouragement to carry on. He needs to hear the word 'no,' I think. You have to let him know where you stand."

With that, Elise stood up, no longer meeting Nessa's eye. "Anyway, I should get going. I do not want to be late for my chat with the printer."

Nessa started at the sudden rush. "Of course. If you get the chance, come by the workshop and let me know how the meeting went. Otherwise I will see you tonight?"

Elise was putting on her coat. "Yes, I will try to swing by. And if unable, I will tell you everything over ale and bad pies tonight."

She crossed the room to where Nessa was sitting on the bed. She stopped for a moment, then she bent down and quickly kissed Nessa's cheek. Her generous mouth was warm and the lips a little wet from the water. Nessa held her breath.

Elise stood up, her gaze flickering away. "Be careful. I will cross my fingers that you are allowed to handle the glass today."

Then she turned and walked out, leaving Nessa on the bed, still feeling the echoing sensation of those warm, soft lips on her cheek. Aching to feel them again.

～

When midday came, Nessa had cleaned tools, fetched coal, gone out to buy supplies, and been told to sweep out the floors. Despite that they didn't seem to need sweeping. She was hoping that the afternoon would bring some actual work around the glass. Or at least some more instruction to further her apprenticeship.

She heard her name being called and looked up from her broom. Elise was standing outside, beckoning to Nessa through the open door. She was beaming and didn't seem to pay attention to the two-horse carriage that nearly scraped her back. Elise had to be more careful; didn't she know how precious she was? The city's carriages were driven far too fast and carelessly, anyway. To think that people were talking about using steam power to make things that went even faster. Just the thought frayed Nessa's nerves.

Elise beckoned again. Nessa looked around and saw that Secilia was busy. She snuck to the door.

"Hello. You look happy," she whispered.

Elise took her hand. "I am. Because I am now hired as a temporary printer's assistant."

"What? Really? Congratulations!"

"Yes! Thank you. I am not allowed to do any real printing work, not officially at least, as you need to be an apprentice for that. But I will be assisting with lesser chores. And probably more, when Mr Richards knows I can be trusted not to tell anyone. Anyway, it is lunch time. Do you think you can get away?"

Nessa looked over at Secilia and saw that she had stopped work to be kissed by her husband. "Probably. They're in a good mood today."

Elise let go of her hand, and Nessa made a concerted effort to not look disappointed. Elise held up the paper bag which had been squeezed between her feet. "Good! I thought we would celebrate with some cheese and shroom sandwiches, which are apparently a Nightport speciality. I also have a dozen miniature figs, some dammon nuts, and a large bottle of sunberry juice. There are so many places to buy food and treats in this city. I nearly bought enough food for five people. If the Brownlees let you go for lunch, perhaps we can sit on the bench at the end of Orgreave Street and enjoy our little feast?"

Nessa's stomach growled. "Only if you promise to tell me everything. You know, about the printer, the job. And how you got it, of course."

Elise's smile was so big it threatened to overtake her face. "Absolutely. I must tell someone presently, or I will simply burst."

Nessa laughed. "All right. Wait here, and I'll ask if I can break for lunch."

Elise nodded, and Nessa went off in search for either Secilia or Josiah, who were both out of sight now. She finally found Secilia stoking the fire.

Nessa cleared her throat. "Master Brownlee. May I be excused for lunch?"

Secilia peered up at her. "I s'pose so. But if ye're gone for more than 'alf an hour, I'll be dockin' yer pay for this morning. Don't come back too full to work; we'll be havin' some lessons regarding raw materials this afternoon."

A thrill buzzed in Nessa's stomach. "Of course, I look forward to it."

"Right. Why ye standin' about, then? Hurry up an' leave so ye can come back faster."

"Yes, Mrs Brownlee."

Nessa hung up her apron and hurried out to find Elise. She was waiting a few steps down the street, her arms full of food. She seemed to pulse with excitement; it was impossible not to be infected by it. Nessa realised that she was probably smiling as much as Elise was. "You've carried that bag for quite a while. Want me to take it for the rest of the way?"

"Why not? Thank you. Thoughtful as always, Nessa."

Carefully, Nessa took the bag from Elise's arms. The transfer was uncomfortable in that it came with too much touching. Why did the mere brushing of fingers with this woman feel as intimate as kissing did with anyone else? Nessa berated her trembling fingers as they grasped the bag.

They walked to the end of Orgreave Street, where there were a few leafless trees surrounding a bench. It was the most nature Nessa had seen in the city, and she found herself appreciating these trees more than she had the ones back in Ground Hollow.

Elise began to unpack their celebration lunch. Nessa couldn't wait to start asking questions until the food was served.

"So, tell me everything. Start with when you arrived at the printers. What was his name again?"

"Archibald Richards. He is a short intellectual in spectacles and a flawlessly pressed suit. Born in a midlands village, so we share an accent. I am not certain how he feels about me. He looked at me as if I were oxen droppings at first. Then he became impressed with my fake tale of growing up in a servant family in a Noble house, as well as how I could keep up with him in literary discussions." Elise paused to hand her the bottle of juice. "And after I passed the test of being able to use the big ink pads, he admitted that I was stronger than I appeared. So, he gave me the job and asked me to start right away. He still seems to be averse to me in some way, though. He shied away whenever I tried to be friendly."

Nessa placed the bottle between them on the bench, trying to hide the smile that she felt coming. "Perhaps that's not a sign that he's adverse to you. Sadly, not everyone is as enthusiastic and social as you are. Or as quick to emotion of all kinds. You might not know it, but your vibrancy can be a little daunting at first. You come on a little too strong for some."

Elise put down the cheese and shroom sandwich she was unpacking and gave Nessa a sour look. "I am cognizant of the effect I can have. I have been informed before. My mother likes to berate me for my impulsiveness and my tendency toward overexuberance. Gods, the Queen even called me 'fire-starter'. So yes, I am *quite* aware."

Nessa reached out to take Elise's hand. The touch reverberated through her, but she ignored it. This was not about her, it was about encouraging Elise. "Please don't think I meant that as a negative thing. You're incredible. It's just that not everyone can handle that you're in hundreds of colours while the rest of us are simply black, grey, and white."

Elise gazed at her for a long time. Or perhaps it was a short moment that appeared to last for hours. Either way, the look in those deep-set eyes made Nessa's pulse pick up. She wished she could read that look.

Finally, Elise spoke. "You could never be just black, grey, and white. You could never be like everyone else, Nessa Clay."

Their eyes stayed locked until Nessa couldn't stand the intense gaze any longer. Her heart was beating too hard. Her mind was too muddled. And her hands were prickling with the wish to touch Elise.

"I'll have to buy you a present to celebrate," Nessa said, trying to pretend that her voice hadn't cracked a little.

Elise blinked a few times and let go of Nessa's hand. "Why? I did not buy you anything when you got your job."

"It's to thank you for making sure we both got jobs. Good, steady jobs to boot. They might not be perfect or pay much, but we could do much worse. We could be cleaning horse manure off the cobbles or selling daisies on Core Street's cold, busy street corners. So yes, I want to buy you a present as a thank-you. If you'll let me?"

Elise looked down while she brushed the knot of thick hair on the top of her head. "Well… I am not the type to say no to a present. I will look forward to getting whatever it is. Now, let us eat before I starve to death."

Nessa couldn't argue with that.

~

It was growing dark when Nessa exited the bookshop on Core Street. She stopped to roll her aching shoulders. She was weary after a day of physically gruelling work and a lot of new knowledge. That didn't matter now. What mattered was how excited she was to give Elise her present. It hadn't been hard to choose what to get her. It had to be the book that she was currently named after.

After searching out and being disappointed by two book-shops, Nessa had finally found a third which had a copy of *The Tales of Princess Aelin*. She bought it and tried not to wince at the hefty coin it cost her.

The Tales of Princess Aelin had mesmerised little Nessa. There was a copy in her school room which Nessa had read from cover to cover. So many times that she had nearly worn the book out, cracking the spine and getting water stains on the front.

She wasn't sure why she had loved the story so. Perhaps it was because it was one of the few stories about princesses, or other Noble ladies, in which the princess was not merely a beautiful maiden waiting for a prince.

Sure, Princess Aelin was described as beautiful and elegant, but her looks were the least important thing about her. Princess Aelin spent a lot of the book proving that she was more than a delicate ornament.

It wasn't something Nessa could relate to. In her world, women were not seen as more fragile than men. After all, it was women who had the agonising bleeding every month and who bore the children, facing the pain and frequent death that came with it. But the Noble world was clearly different. It was interesting to watch Princess Aelin fight against how others saw her. Nessa could relate to that bit. Feeling like there was more in her than others saw. Wanting to break free.

By the end of the book, the princess had saved her kingdom, broken the spell which had cursed her parents into a state of frozen slumber, and explained to the prince that she could not marry him until she had seen the world and decided what her future would look like. It was a tale of a heroine who was overlooked and underestimated until she proved she was the strongest and bravest of them all.

Princess Aelin was meant to have long, red, twirling curls. Completely unlike Elise's pitch-black, soft waves. And Nessa doubted that the princess could have had those unique golden eyes. Other than that, it was hard for Nessa to see the differences between the headstrong princess and the woman she shared a home with.

She now stood outside the shop looking at the book's cover. This one was red, not blue like the book she had read as a child. However, the slanted white letters of the title looked the same. Nessa was taken back to moments of complete joy and escape while reading those pages.

A hint of fear seeped into her nostalgia. What if Elise didn't like the book? Perhaps she should tell her about the chapter where Princess Aelin makes the impossible choice between waking her parents from the curse or saving the kingdom from the attacking gargoyles first. That was the chapter which made her choose the name for Elise since the princess and Elise had that in common, the ability to make tough decisions quickly.

When Elise dithered about her name, it was the first time she had seen her hesitate. She knew that if it had been a bigger decision, Elise would have made it in a heartbeat. Nessa envied her for that. Imagine being able to face decisions without months of going back and forth.

She chewed the inside of her cheek as she ran her fingers over the cover. Perhaps this was a mistake? Perhaps Elise would think her silly? Or maybe she was expecting a more luxurious and grown-up present?

Nessa closed her eyes, trying to find the resolve to go home and put the book in Elise's hands. That was a mistake as she didn't see the young lad selling newspapers rush past. His elbow hit her waist as he hurried down the street to find richer looking people to buy his papers.

Gods curse these city crowds.

She sighed. Then she willed her feet forward. This was the present she had chosen, and she would just have to explain why to Elise. To trust that she would understand the sentiment behind it and not be disappointed. If she seemed disappointed, Nessa would go out and buy her some fancy honey tartlets or a bottle of winterberry brandy.

The walk home seemed to take an age. She had changed her mind, and then changed it back again, twice before she could finally put the key in the door and enter their room.

Elise was sitting at the table, undoing her top knot. The thick hair spilled down her shoulders, and she began combing it out.

"Ah, there you are, I was worried about you. What took you so long? You must have left the workshop more than an hour ago."

Nessa shifted her weight from foot to foot. "I stopped to pick up your present, remember?"

"Oh yes." Elise shot to her feet and put the brush down. "Well, where is it? More importantly – what is it?"

Nessa smiled. Elise's excitement was, as always, infectious.

Without any explanation, she held out the book. In two steps, Elise was standing in front of her and taking it from her hands. She read the title of the book out loud and added, "Oh, so this is the book you got the name Aelin from?"

"Yes," Nessa croaked. Her nervousness was ridiculous, but, somehow, she felt as if she was baring an important part of herself in front of Elise. Worse than that, it was like she was showing Elise exactly how much she had come to mean to her.

Completely unaware of how rude it was, Elise sat down on the bed and began to read.

Nessa knew that she should let Elise read it and come to her own conclusions. Nevertheless, what if those conclusions were wrong? What if she misinterpreted the reason behind the gift?

So, she cleared her throat. "The princess, she, um, reminds me of you. She doesn't necessarily look like a hero at first. But soon you realise that she is the only one willing and able to make the hard decisions and take all the risks. By the end of the book, you end up admiring her, just like the other charac-ters in the book do," Nessa said. She stopped herself there; she was about to start rambling.

Elise looked up at her in silence. A smile slowly formed on her red-tinted lips. Soon, those unique eyes glittered, echoing the smile. Nessa wondered if she was blushing at the sight of it.

"I think that might be one of the sweetest things anyone has ever said to me. Thank you. Both for the gift, which I look forward to reading, and for the compliment. I do not believe I deserve it, but I would like to try to be more like this princess of yours."

Nessa tried to answer, but her mouth was as dry as sand. She licked her lips, looking for moisture to form a reply with.

"I hope you'll like the book. And th-that I didn't step out of line in any way," Nessa said.

Elise placed the book carefully on the bed. She walked towards Nessa, eyes fixed on hers. Nessa heard her heartbeat rush in her ears. When Elise reached her, she kissed Nessa on the cheek. "You most certainly did not step out of line. I truly appreciate your candour."

Unable to answer, Nessa merely nodded.

Elise found a lock of hair that had escaped Nessa's braid and tucked it behind her ear. "I shall start reading the book while you wash off the soot and get changed. Then we should go out, and I will find us some nice supper. I refuse to have those horrible pies again tonight. There is a city out there full of food and drink, and I intend to explore it." She took Nessa's hand. "Get ready, Nessa Clay. I am going to find you some food that Ground Hollow has never even heard of!"

How could Nessa do anything but obey? She would get ready and then follow her dashing Lady Falk out into Nightport, laughing and looking forward to whatever adventure Elise was about to pull her into.

She pushed her trepidation and worry down deep and permitted herself to be happy tonight. After all, she had earned it.

CHAPTER 15

NIGHTPORT AFTER NIGHTFALL

Elise had finally gotten Nessa out of their room and out into the Nightport evening. They were both washed, in clean clothes, and smelling of sugar pumpkin oil. Ready for adventure, and, judging by the growling of Nessa's stomach, ready for dinner. They hadn't properly enjoyed their new city at night yet, and after that lovely present, Elise wanted to gift Nessa with a wonderful evening full of new impressions and memories.

Nightport was so different after nightfall. The faint, romantic light from street lamps gave the dusky buildings and dirty cobbles an almost magical, mystical feel. The noises were different, suddenly all pleasure and little business. The smells were headier and harder to trace. There was a sense of the city's dangers turning from tragic to tempting.

Heat rushed through Elise's blood. She looked at Nessa and saw that she was evaluating the evening version of Nightport, too. She had her hands in her pockets, keen eyes, and an enigmatic smile on her face.

"This place comes alive at night, does it not?" Elise ventured.

"Yes. There's a... sort of beat to it. Well, there always is. This place is like one big heart. Lots of little parts that I don't understand, all needed to keep it beating, all working in a frenzy to... I don't know... repair and produce, I guess? But at night, that heartbeat goes from slow and steady to incredibly quick. I mean, look around."

Elise did. Everywhere people were running to and fro. Or even walking slowly but talking fast, as if they all had so much to do before the day gave its last breath.

They had reached Core Street now. In one direction, it led to the city's life-giving port and in the other, it led to the gate they had entered through that first day. Cutting a long line across Nightport, feeding all the other parts of the city. Core Street was clearly the place to be after nightfall. It was lined with street vendors, selling everything from food to clothing.

They stopped and ate pieces of spiced yellowfish and sticks of toasted bread wrapped in yesterday's newspaper. Washing it all down with gulps of sunberry juice, which tasted watered down. But who cared about petty details as that on such an interesting night?

They moved on, walking close together and marvelling at the hubbub. Every time Nessa stopped and with glittering eyes pointed at something, Elise's heart soared.

Her heart stopped soaring and began to race instead when they passed through a throng of people and came out with an overpowering scent clinging to the air. It smelled like purified alcohol mixed with a heavy amount of lavender.

Her signature perfume. Odd. She cannot be here.

That scent took Elise back to good memories as well as bad. Respect, dependency, and involuntary arousal were all brought to the surface. Elise hadn't expected to ever smell that perfume again after her escape. It belonged buried in her past.

Still, she shook the discomfort off, trying to calm her thudding heart. Lavender was a common scent for women to wear, and gods knew most of Nightport smelled faintly of alcohol. It was far too lovely a night to be haunted by people from her past.

In between the selling stalls were ones where you could play games and place bets. There were tricksters hiding a ball under one of three cups, moving them about and making you guess under which cup the ball was. The ball was never where you'd think. Elise wondered if it wasn't in the trickster's sleeve most of the time. They saw people doing card tricks and even a few doing vanishing illusions with coins and handkerchiefs. Elise couldn't help but notice that many of these stall-dwellers seemed to be helping themselves to the customer's purses when they were distracted by the tricks and bets. The City Guard, who were out in force, seemed to try to stop it to no great avail.

Elise also noticed several pay-to-kiss couples. They passed one such couple, a man and a woman, who seemed to be almost all over each other without any payment.

Nessa scratched her cheek as she looked at them and then whispered, "What are they selling?"

"They are selling their... erm... *affection* for one another. People give them a few coins to watch them kiss and fondle each other."

Nessa blinked rapidly and then frowned. "So, they're pleasure sellers?"

"No, pleasure sellers allow their customers to buy their body and bedding talents. These couples will do nothing more than kiss and touch each other a little. *Only* each other. If you try to touch them or make them do more than that, the City Guard will throw you out. At least that is how it worked in the small, hidden underbelly of Highmere. I am sure it is the same here."

Nessa glanced back at the kissing couple and the crowd

which was gathering in front of them. "Why do people pay to watch that?"

"Well, I would liken it to having a drink before dinner. It gets your appetite going and gives you a treat before the main meal, making you appreciate your food all the more when you get it. Most who pay to watch end up going home to get the… 'main meal'. Either with a lover or with their own hands. If you know what I mean."

"Sure," Nessa said casually. She put her hands in her pockets and looked ahead.

Elise contemplated her. For all Nessa's naivety, she didn't seem to be shy about pleasures of the flesh. Perhaps all commoners were like that? Nessa's eyebrows were still pressed together, though, and she seemed lost in thought.

It does not quite make sense to you, does it? You are not a 'drink before dinner' kind of woman. I wager Nessa Clay would not settle for anything less than a whole meal right away. She would want it all.

Elise felt an unexpected tingle at that thought, making its way down her spine until she shook it off.

They walked along, past more food stalls, people selling trinkets, and even a booth where small wooden statues of the gods were sold.

After a few minutes, Nessa stopped by a booth with two men. They were being paid a handful of bronze coins by a short, blonde woman. Elise was amused to see Nessa's eyes go wide when one of the men winked at the paying woman and then devoured his lovers mouth while grabbing his crotch. Nessa whispered, "he didn't ask first" under her breath. Elise fought hard not to smile at her sweet companion.

Instead, she focused back on the street. Elise breathed in deep. Nightport still had its smoky, dirty scent but that hint of sweetness in daytime was gone, replaced with a more complicated mix of scents of food and drink. In the back of her mind, Elise was relieved that alcohol-spiked lavender wasn't one of them.

Helping the gas lit streetlights illuminate Core Street were metal barrels with roaring fires in them. The fires made Core Street feel warmer than the other streets, and Elise unbuttoned her wool coat. It was the one Nessa had lent her back in Ground Hollow and still smelled faintly of her if Elise burrowed her nose into the fabric by the collar. A crisp, leafy smell under the sweetness of the sugar pumpkin oil. Elise found herself loath to replace it with a new, better-fitting coat.

Her reverie was broken when someone shouted and a fistfight broke out to their right. The sounds of cracking knuckles, spitting, and cursing filled the air.

Nessa cringed. "I hate to say it, but my mother was right. There is a lot of crime and fucking, pardon my language, *coupling* in this city," she muttered. Her upturned nose was scrunched as far as it could go into a stern frown.

Elise resisted the sudden compulsion to kiss the tip of that cute nose. Instead, she walked them away from the row. "Yes, indeed. Does it make you regret coming here?"

Nessa turned to her, hands held up. "Gods no!"

"Glad to hear it. You do not mind crime and coupling, then?" Elise asked teasingly.

Nessa shrugged, putting her hands back in the pockets of her coat. "I don't like crime or anything that has some kind of victim. Coupling, well, I may not be a huge fan of it outside of long-term relationships myself, but I believe that people generally make too big a deal of it. Coupling, lovemaking, bedplay, whatever you want to call it, is natural and fun for most people. So, we should all relax about it."

"That is a refreshing way of seeing it. Especially from someone who I believe means it and is not solely trying to get what they want."

"What do you mean by 'get what they want'?" Nessa asked with a furrowed brow.

Elise sighed. "People tend to say that sort of thing to me, especially after some alcohol. It usually means they wish to bed me. However, in the sober light of day, they will swear to anyone who listens that carnal acts are for procreation and not to be taken lightly."

Nessa nodded her understanding. "Branding you…"

"A harlot? Yes, pretty much. One of the other ladies at court always said that I would have found it easy to be a pleasure seller if I had not been born a Noble."

"Did she mean that as an insult?" Nessa asked, her features grave.

"Yes. Showing what an imbecile she is. There is obviously nothing wrong with being a pleasure seller. They are experts in something most people wish they could master. Anyway, people are constantly judging and making light of my enjoyment of bedplay and flirting. I have ceased caring."

"I'm sorry that you've experienced that."

Now it was Elise's turn to shrug. "That is not the worst part, really. The worst part is that they think that is all that I am."

"How do you mean?"

Elise walked slower, choosing her next words carefully. After their earlier conversation when Nessa gave her the book, being open and honest now seemed important. Even if it wasn't easy. Elise preferred to act rather than to speak. Dwelling on things had never helped her.

She cleared her throat. "Well, what has been your impression of me?"

Nessa hummed thoughtfully, watching a man juggle empty wine bottles for thrown coins before answering. "I suppose I'd say that you are independent, charming, decisive, and brave."

Elise stopped dead in her tracks and surveyed

Nessa. "Huh."

Nessa returned the glance. "What?"

"That was not what I expected you to say. That is not the way people usually describe me. I thought you were going to mention attributes like: wild, fire-starter, impulsive, emotional, or overly carnal. Something along those lines."

Nessa tilted her head, appearing to consider the words. "Well, I can see that you have those traits. But I don't think they define you as much as the things I said. I'd say that anyone who thought they did had never bothered to look very closely at you. Or listen to you. I told you before, you're like Princess Aelin. Your glinting exterior makes people miss the depths below."

Elise stumbled. She felt like everything around them was moving a little quicker all of a sudden. Just a moment ago, she had been the worldly teacher with the innocent farmer's daughter as her student. Now she felt like a blushing girl whose diary has been read out loud.

Her whole body was numb, as if it had been struck by something. In a daze, she carried on walking.

"Thank you," she said after a while, her voice hoarse.

"Just being honest," Nessa said. She seemed utterly clueless of the effect her words had on Elise. She walked along, hands in pockets, eyes on the stalls and performers. The light from the fires illuminated her fair skin and rosy cheeks, making her clear, grey eyes shine like jewels.

Elise was suddenly very aware of how uneven her heartbeat had become. She walked by Nessa's side, unable to take her eyes off her.

Then Nessa broke the silence. "Hey, if they're not too expensive, can we buy some roasted dammon nuts? There must be some around here, I can smell them."

Elise cleared her pinched throat. "Yes, I can, too. We should go find them and buy you a bag."

CHAPTER 16
NESSA ON CORE STREET

Dammon nuts procured, Nessa wondered what new wonders awaited them. Elise seemed excited by everything they saw here on Core Street, but Nessa knew that was nothing compared to her own thrill. Adrenaline spiked in her veins, racing the blood along. It made her feel so hot she might as well have a fever. She hadn't seen any of this when visiting as a child. They had gone back to Ground Hollow long before nightfall.

Experiencing this. Daring to be here in all of this. It reminded her why she had left the safety and comfort of Ground Hollow. There was so much *life* here and new experiences every moment. The living beat of it, the pure, heart-thundering essence of it. It fed into her feeling of being feverish, making her dizzy.

So did the bright colours in a stall where people seemed to be shouting out bets on something. Nessa put her hand on Elise's shoulder, half to get her attention and half to steady herself. "What's happening there?"

Elise looked over to the stall. "Not the faintest idea. Let us find out."

They walked over and saw that the people around the stall were betting on skitter-beetles. Nessa counted seven of them, all waiting in tiny holding pens on a miniature race track, which lay on a rickety table.

Elise clapped her hands. "Oh! I have not bet on anything since the last horse races at Highmere. I know we are being careful with our coin, but can we bet a little? The one with a white dot on its back looks spry."

"Up to you what you do with your coin," Nessa said. "I'm sticking to eating my nuts and watching. I only bet when I know I have a high chance of winning. These insects are impossible to judge."

Elise was bent over the miniature race track, staring at the little critters. "No, they are not. The one with the white dot is moving more than the others. It wants to get out on the track and run. Look!"

With a sigh, Nessa got closer and leaned in to look at the beetle. When Elise turned her head to say something, the tips of their noses brushed. She could smell dammon nuts on Elise's breath. Neither of them moved, and Nessa noticed that Elise was staring at her mouth.

Perhaps she can smell the nuts on my breath, too. That must be why she's looking at my mouth? No. That look is... erotic.

The little hairs on Nessa's arms pricked up, and she felt her mouth water, as if the beauty in front of her was a treat she could devour. One she was starving for.

She chided herself for the umpteenth time that there was no use in all that. They wanted different things.

Nessa stood up straight. She had to take Elise's mind off bedplay and back to what they were here for. "Fine. You bet on that critter, and I'll try to not say 'I told you so' when it loses. Or they all stay still and won't run when they are let out of their pens."

The tension broke. Smiling, Elise rolled her eyes at her and went over to bet. When she came back, they ate some more nuts in congenial silence.

Nessa was just about to say that she wanted a drink when the stall owner announced that the race was starting. Elise grabbed her hand as the stall owner pushed a button which made the little pens open and allow the beetles to get out on the track.

Nessa had been right: they didn't move. One of them actually looked dead now that she looked closer. Another was climbing along the back of its holding cell, trying to get off the table. Nessa couldn't help but pity the small animals.

People booed, but Elise went one step further and began shouting. "What sort of scam is this, Sir? Are these animals drugged? Are they even alive? What have you done to them? I want my two coppers back."

The stall owner shouted back, and soon there was a lengthy argument which ended with Elise and the other betters getting their coins back. Nessa was sure that their coin would have been lost if it hadn't been for the posh, belligerent woman who would not give up.

Even with her coin back, Elise wanted to carry on the argument. Nessa saw veins protruding in her elegant neck as she shouted at the man. He was starting to snarl menacingly at her. In the distance, Nessa saw what she assumed was a group of city guards rushing towards them.

Nessa took her arm and led her away. "Never mind. He's not worth you making your blood boil like this. Besides, he might pull a knife or the city guards might kick you off Core Street. Come away. Please."

Elise seemed like she would argue, but a heartbeat or two of staring into Nessa's eyes seemed to calm her. Her posture was still rigid and tense, but her breathing slowed as she followed Nessa over to a booth opposite. This one was blessedly without any betting, but Nessa couldn't quite understand what it had instead.

"What am I looking at?" she asked Elise.

Elise gently took her by the shoulders and moved her aside to clear her view. "It is a fortune machine."

"It's a what now?" Nessa asked, acutely aware that Elise's hands had stayed on her shoulders.

"It is exactly what the name says it is, a machine that will tell your fortune. Actually, I believe it has a certain number of vague fortunes and will spit one of them out for you at random. So it won't so much tell your fortune as give you a pre-printed piece of paper in exchange for some coins. At least that is what the ones at Highmere were like."

Elise let go of her shoulders and crouched down in front of the contraption. "Yes, this looks very similar to the ones I have seen. They all have a theme of some form of telling the future. The figurines might be witches reading the entrails of animals or prophets finding your future in one of their books. Or like this one, a fortune teller finding your future in her cards."

Nessa stared at the strange object. Elise was right; the automaton was meant to look like a fortune teller. She remembered her father's drawing of his grandmother, who had been a fortune teller. She had been dressed like this machine. The thing in front of Nessa was only the likeness of a woman's torso, arms, and head. There were six ornately decorated cards face down on a tray in front of her. The thing was perfectly made. Although horribly eerie, too still, too realistic.

"Is it run on steam power?"

Elise shook her head. "No. Good old-fashioned clockwork. Even though I know it is a scam and that the fortunes you get will be vague enough to apply to anyone at any time, I still think there is a magical feel to it. If nothing else then because of the intricate clockwork. A lot of artistry and skill has gone into this machine."

Nessa crouched down next to Elise. The fact that this was a machine mainly for children meant that all adults either had to bend over or crouch down.

Annoying. There are barely any children here tonight. Stick it on a table so I don't have to sit down here so close to... her. Gods, she smells so nice. Please don't let our knees touch. If they do, I might lose control and fall back on my arse. Or worse, on her.

Nessa refocused her attention to inspect the clockwork figurine face on. She wanted to see this machine from all angles. To figure out its workings. She had never seen anything operated by clockwork.

"Here, allow me," Elise said and put a copper coin into the slot connected to the figurine.

It made a sound like gears grinding against each other and then came to life. The fortune teller, with movements that were clunky and slow, turned each and every card on her tray. Showing pictures of everything from fools, to strange imaginary animals, to Sauq; the god of death. When she had turned them all, the clockwork woman looked up. Its lifelike, unseeing eyes were now drilling into Nessa's. An icy shiver trickled down her spine.

Just above the slot where Elise had put in a coin, a piece of paper was spat out. It fell to the ground, and Nessa picked it up.

When she held it in her hand, Elise leaned over closer than she needed to and read it:

"You will have a confrontation with someone who has a black heart. Then you will embark on an adventure which will take you far away. Unlucky colour: purple," Elise intoned.

Then she laughed. The warm sound of it hit Nessa like a wave, cresting over her and making her all tingly. She was reminded of their first night together, when they were leaving the castle and Elise laughed as the lux beetles flew too close to her. That sound had captivated her then, and it was even worse tonight. Nessa balled her hands into fists, begging her heart to stop falling for this woman.

"Well, to avoid meeting anyone with a black heart or running into anything purple, I suggest we go home and get some sleep," she said, wanting to break the strange magic of Elise's laugh.

Elise folded the piece of paper with the fortune and stuck it in Nessa's coat pocket. Then she linked their arms. "Agreed. Let's go home."

CHAPTER 17

A MOMENT OF MAGIC ON A RAINY MORNING

It was raining. Heavily. Elise watched the drops hit their dirty window. It looked cold out there, with those dark grey skies brooding over Nightport. The wind that crept in through the uninsulated window was close to icy. Causing a sharp contrast to how warm it was under the covers in their bed.

Elise was laying on her side, face towards the window. Behind her Nessa was on her side, too, facing away. She savoured the warm, solid comfort of Nessa's back against her own. She never knew it could be so wonderful to merely sleep next to someone.

Sadly, she wasn't sleeping now. She was blinking out at the grey skies and dreading Saint Alsager's church bells chiming six. Judging by the light it must be almost time. The last thing she wanted to do was get out of this warm bed and into that cold greyness, only to face a day in the company of the dull and overly precise Mr Richards. Her job provided them with the safety of coin coming in, and she knew she should be grateful for that. But going from a leisurely life at court into working all day would have been easier if the job was more challenging. Or if she could at least work with someone whose company she enjoyed.

She rolled onto her back, staring up at the crack in the ceiling.

Perhaps I should get up and start washing. Why just lie here and wait?

Suddenly, life provided a gift. Or perhaps it came from those gods she had such a hard time believing in. Before the church bells had time to ring out, Nessa turned and embraced her. One leg landed heavily over Elise's and an arm was carelessly tossed over her torso.

Nessa was fast and brusque in her movements when she slept. Elise was getting used to it, though. Besides, how could she mind when the end result felt this good? The warm weight of Nessa's limbs, the deep breaths against her ear, and the forbidden pleasure of Nessa's crotch pushing against her hip. Only two thin, short nightdresses separating their skin.

Nessa stirred, sighing in her sleep. She made tiny movements, adjusting to her new sleeping position, something which accentuated every place where her body touched Elise's. They were so closely entwined now. It would be so easy for this to move from something platonic into something erotic. A rush made its way from Elise's stomach and poured out into every part of her body, warming her and tingling her every nerve ending.

This is wrong. Nessa is your friend, nothing more. Besides, she is asleep. Stop being so wanton all the time!

Her rampant heartbeat wasn't listening. Elise breathed in deeply to calm herself and picked up the smell of rain from the draughty window, the sugar pumpkin oil on both their skin and on the bedding. And under all that, the comforting, crisp, and intolerably intoxicating smell of Nessa's skin.

Elise didn't dare to move. What if she woke her and she moved away?

Nessa gave a soft, little grunt and nuzzled her face down against Elise's shoulder. It felt like she was itching her nose, right next to the strap of Elise's nightdress. The gesture was more sweet and childlike than erotic.

Nevertheless, it gave Elise goosebumps of pleasure.

If she had magic, she would make time stop in that moment. She would make it so that she could always stay in that fragile, fleeting moment of pure, almost painful beauty. Nervous excitement, blissed-out comfort, and the tingling of infatuation all crowded in her mind and heart. Not only was she extremely aware of every spot where her body touched Nessa's, she was also aware of exactly how drawn she was to her. Drunk on infatuation. Terrified of rejection.

Nessa moved her face against her shoulder again, and Elise felt something warm and damp. It could only be Nessa's lips.

Her mouth is on my skin. Oh gods! What do I do?

To her shame, Elise felt a pull in her lower stomach emanating into liquid warmth between her thighs. Dizzy. She was suddenly so dizzy. Was she breathing too fast? Was she breathing at all?

Nessa made a snuffling noise. Her arm, earlier just flopped over the Elise, now tightened around her waist. Was that a sign of some sort?

Elise stifled a groan. She had never felt anything like this. This went beyond any love, and certainly any lust, she had ever felt. How could something this lovely be so bewildering and frightening?

Saint Alsager's bell began to toll six. Morning was here. The magic was broken.

Nessa rolled over, stretched, and with a mumbled 'good morning,' she slowly got up to wash and dress. Elise was left alone in the bed. She had a strange feeling that she was being punished for her wanton reaction to Nessa's body by that fragile, magic moment ending.

The rain grew heavier — mirroring her mood.

ONE WEEK IN NIGHTPORT

They had lived in Nightport a week now, so Nessa's walk to Orgreave Street and the Brownlees' hot shop was familiar. Her feet knew the way, freeing her mind to think about Elise.

She was thinking about Elise far too often, and telling herself to stop wasn't working. Last time she found someone on her mind this often, it had been Henrico. They had been together for two years after he came to help with her parents' overgrown barley fields. He had stayed to be with Nessa, and they had been inseparable until he wanted to move on and get their own farm somewhere else. She couldn't do that, she had to stay and help her parents. It had been the right thing to do, letting him go. She knew that now.

Hurt like being rammed by a marrow-oxen, though.

She ran her hands though her hair, brushing away the unwanted memories. Why was she thinking about this? Oh yes, Elise. Fascinating, beautiful Elise. It was a shame that her roommate only wanted to be friends. And possibly lovers? Nessa's inkling that Elise wanted that, to make them lovers, was increasing. But then they both knew that Elise enjoyed bedplay and she hadn't had any lovers in Nightport yet. So that was probably why she clung to Nessa so tightly. Perhaps she should encourage it. Maybe she could enjoy pleasures of the flesh without a relationship? At least if it was with Elise.

No, you idiot, that way lies heartbreak and the ruination of your important friendship.

She moved aside for a woman who nearly ran into her. The woman quickly apologised and moved on. It was lovely, the city life. No stopping and chatting, no recognising Nessa. Not making her heart race by talking to her. Not forcing her to try to figure out what to say or how to say it. The citizens of Nightport didn't know all of Nessa's business and didn't judge it. They didn't care one whit that she hadn't settled down. Or that she hadn't had children. Wasn't four years into a job and thriving. They didn't know, and they didn't care. Just strangers minding their own business. There was such freedom in that. Her nerves seemed to be relaxing more every minute she spent in the city.

She knew that Ground Hollow was perfect for her parents and for Layden. They, and most other citizens of the village, thought it was the most wonderful place in the world; it fed and healed them. Her, on the other hand, it strangled. Ground Hollow was safe, and she had loved that as a child. But now, its safety wasn't enough to put up with all the negative aspects. And that was coming from someone who valued safety very highly indeed.

She looked around. Everything was so different here. So new. So big. It was what she had loved as a visiting child. The sense that everything seemed to be changing and evolving. The fear of the unknown was overshadowed by the thrill of a place that didn't settle down. Didn't become stale. Didn't stop. The people here had open minds, willing to learn and change. She wanted to be like them. She *would* be like them. She would make this city hers. Make it feel safe. Somehow.

Gods, help me be brave and open-minded. Help me fit in here. Help me be more like Elise.

Elise. She was back to thinking about Elise. How had that happened?

Oxen-shit. Stop it, woman. You're friends. Just stop!

Disrupting her furious thoughts was the sight of the door to the Brownlees' workshop. She put her hands in her pockets and picked up her pace. She wasn't the type to be late or to shun work. That wasn't how she had been raised.

It was nearing midday. They were making drinking glasses today, and for once, Nessa was invited to do more than watch. Secilia was standing next to Nessa with the blowpipe in her hands. She was showing her how to blow quick puffs of air into the blob of molten glass attached to the end of the blowpipe.

"There. See, nothin' to it. Have a try, lass."

Nessa bit her lip. "Thank you, but I'm not sure I'm ready for this. What if I make a mess of it?"

"Ye've got to stop worryin' so much, lass. If somethin' gets broken, it can usually be mended. Ye can never work with glass unless ye are prepared to try somethin' an' fail. If ye hesitate, the time when the glass is the perfect temperature an' shape will be missed. Then it'll be near impossible to work with."

"I just don't want to r-ruin the glass. Or let you down, Mrs Brownlee."

Secilia frowned. "Ye'll only be lettin' me down if ye don't dare try. It's all about the glass, an' it's waitin' on ye to help it be the best an' prettiest it can be."

She handed Nessa the blowpipe. Nessa's hands sweated profusely as she took it. Not just because of the furnace or the hot workshop.

You can do this. You're not even shaping it, only blowing it and starting the process. You won't ruin it. Not yet anyway. Take the chance.

She began puffing the short breaths into the blowpipe and saw the mass of molten glass react. It was working.

Outside, the bell tolled twelve. Nessa puffed into the pipe as it rang out.

"Stop, stop. That's enough, lass. Good. Now hand 'er over. I'll do the rest. Ye go talk to that lady of yers and be back after lunch."

Nessa gave her the blowpipe and glanced in the direction that Secilia had been looking. Standing right outside the open door of the workshop was Elise. She held a paper bag in her hand.

Lunch, Nessa assumed. She felt a rush and put it down to having used the blowpipe for the first pipe and the fact that she really wanted lunch. Purely that. Certainly nothing else.

She hurried towards Elise, whose smile didn't look as confident and merry as usual. Her gaze flitted between Nessa and the ground.

Nessa was in the doorway, right in front of her now. "Hello there. What's in the bag?"

"I am doing very well today. How are you?" Elise asked pointedly.

Nessa chuckled. "Fine, fine. I'm sorry. *How are you?*"

"Very well, as I said. Thank you for finally asking."

"Can I know what's in there now?" Nessa said while grabbing for the bag. She accidentally brushed Elise's hand and saw her gasp at the touch.

Nessa pulled her hand back. "Are you all right? Did I hurt you?"

Elise was frowning. She cleared her throat. "No, no, of course not. Sorry. I had a bit of a strange morning, and it seems to still have me in its grip."

"Oh? Something happened at work?"

Elise peered at her, like she was trying to read her. Or decide something perhaps? Nessa looked back, unable to help herself from enjoying the view.

Gods, those amber eyes are so bright and pretty.

Elise licked her lips. "No. Not really. It was… you know what, never mind. Let's just go to our bench by the trees and eat. I have sandwiches filled with yellowfish covered in soured cream today. Who knew that they actually do make sandwiches with something other than than cheese and shrooms in this city?"

"Ha! I certainly didn't. But I'll be glad for the change. Let's go."

They sauntered over to their usual spot. Elise walked some distance from Nessa, looking like she worried what would happen if they touched. She didn't seem angry or frightened, though, so Nessa didn't think she had done something to upset her. When they sat down, Elise sat further away than usual, though she kept glancing over at Nessa, often licking her lips as she did so.

After a moment's chatting and eating, the awkwardness seemed to pass. Elise began admiring the clothes of the passers-by and telling funny stories of what happened at the printer's that morning.

Nessa shoved the awkwardness out of her mind. Elise had probably just slept badly. Come to think of it, she had seemed a bit strange when they woke up together. Maybe an early night to catch up on some sleep would be a good idea.

CHAPTER 19

NORTHMEN, A HAIRCUT, AND A PEDAL CYCLE

Elise woke up with a start. The nightmare was still alive in her mind, haunting her, making her heart race. The room was dark. She leaned on her elbows, peering into the darkness to ensure that none of the monsters had followed her from her horrible dreams.

An arm draped across her chest, pulling her into lying down again. Nessa hummed softly in her sleep and cuddled nearer. Elise's heartbeat began to slow. Everything was fine. Nessa was here. She was so close, so warm, and the arm that held her was strong but gentle. Elise couldn't remember being comforted so fast and so completely since she was a child. The breaths that tickled her ear were steady and deep. Elise allowed them to lull her back to sleep.

The next time she woke, it was to the sound of the church bells chiming six and to Nessa, who was yawning loudly while stretching. Elise blinked to try to get the world into focus. She felt like she was still asleep and knew that if she stayed in bed, she'd fall back into bottomless slumber.

She quickly sat up and without thinking, bent her head down and kissed Nessa's temple. The warm skin felt so good under her lips. Nessa smelled so lovely. She placed another soft kiss on that temple, a longer one this time. She sat up, looking at Nessa, wondering if she was going to give an indication on if the romantic advance was welcome or not. Suddenly, Nessa's reaction seemed intensely important. She waited, shallow breaths moving over her slightly parted lips.

Nessa yawned again and then muttered, "Good morning." Her eyes were still closed, and she was still stretching. Then she added, "Would you mind going out for breakfast today? All the sweeping I've done lately is catching up with my muscles, so I want to stay in bed and rest my body a little more."

Elise's lips closed with a pop. She covered her body with the sheet, even though she was in her nightwear. "Of course. You stay in bed. I will hurry back."

Elise got up and started to get ready. As she washed, dressed, and braided her hair, she tried hard to focus on the day ahead and not on those stolen kisses. She was still trying to charm Richards and make him feel like she was the right woman for the job; she couldn't afford to be distracted.

It was late afternoon, almost time to close up. Throughout her first few days as a temporary printer's assistant, Elise had been given all the instructions that Archibald Richards felt she needed to help him operate his expensive printing press. Plenty of practice, too, when he noticed what a quick study she was. While he was dull, the process of printing was exhilarating. She had always loved newspapers and books, and now she would be the midwife who brought them into the world.

At that moment, when they printed the last copies for the day, it wasn't solely excitement that got Elise's blood pumping. It was also the fear that hit her as she bent over to close the heavy lid of the printing press to squeeze the paper.

Archibald usually did this part, but he had just stepped out to discuss something with a client. Elise was alone and had to bend over to really get her full power into closing the lid. Meaning that she almost put her braid of ebony hair into the printing press.

Luckily, Archibald was still out and didn't see the near accident. She felt certain that he would have thought her a bad candidate for the job if she had caused a scene by hurting herself in her first week. Or even worse, by hurting the printing press.

She promised herself that she would stop by a barber and get one of the short haircuts she had seen women in the city wearing. It would reduce the time of her morning ablutions as well. Combing out her thick mass of hair each morning took an age.

Archibald came back in, and she pretended like nothing had happened, still feeling panic quickening her heartbeat.

"Right, Miss Aelin. It is time to call it a day. You performed in an adequate way, as you have these past five days. The day after tomorrow will be a full week in my employ. Please continue to not disappoint me."

As usual, he took her daily wage out of his coin purse, and Elise took the coins without counting them.

She curtsied ever so slightly. "I know I said this on my first day here, but thank you again for giving me the chance to help you with this project."

"No need to keep thanking me. I am glad to employ a fellow midlands-native. Besides, Hunter Smith would not have recommended you unless he believed I would be happy with your performance. He knows I have far too much sway in this city to risk angering me. I still recommend that you strengthen your arms and back. I see you struggle when you help me turn the handle for the press."

"Of course, Mr Richards. I will work on my strength so that I am of better use to you during these coming weeks. I know this is an important project. These urgent report leaflets need to reach the public, and they need to do so before the information is old news, so to speak."

He looked grave. "Precisely. All of Arclid needs to be told what those Northmen are doing. They need to know that what started as experiments with a steam engine and new ways of transport has now changed the very fabric of their society. Everything in Storsund is trains and tracks now. They are racing to the future with steam and leaving us behind."

Elise had heard some of this at court but never cared enough about what happened on the other three continents to bother finding out more about the railroads being built in Storsund. She was more intrigued now that she had seen the pamphlets they were printing. Besides, getting away from court had made her see that there was a whole world out there. One which was so much more interesting than court intrigue and the latest dance styles.

So, she prompted him on, despite being hungry, tired, and wanting to go out and get her hair cut. "Is that so?"

He clasped his hands behind his back and peered at her over his spectacles. "Yes. Unlike us, the Northmen do not transport their goods via manmade canals and over seas. In fact, they only use ships for transporting to the Western Isles, Obeha, and us these days. Storsund sees us as all as backwards colonies to grow things for them as they evolve. Ever since they laid those tracks and made their steam-powered monstrous creations travel on them. The *locomotive* and her beastly carriages." He shook his head. "Terrifying things. Nevertheless, incredibly useful for their economy. The Storsund factories grow huge because they can transport goods in and out without waterways. While we may not want to emulate them, we should not be left behind or be ignorant."

"I think you are exceedingly correct. I better be going. Have a pleasant evening, Mr Richards. I shall see you tomorrow morning."

He gave a curt nod. Elise hurried out towards the barber-shop, which she had seen on the corner where Miller Street crossed Core Street.

Half an hour later, Elise walked out of the barbershop with her hair now only reaching as far as her jawline. It was so strange to feel the air against her neck without the weight of a braid or the fullness of a bun. Every time she reached up to touch her hair, she felt a tingle of excitement but also of fear. What if she would regret it? Noble ladies saw their hair as a prime source of beauty and now that source was all but unusable to her.

It does not matter. I am not in Noble circles. I am free to live my life as I wish here in Nightport. All that matters is practicality and my own satisfaction with my looks.

The woman who had looked back at her in the barber's mirror had been a revelation to Elise. In her new hairstyle she looked more capable, tougher and more confident – or perhaps that was all in her head.

Eager, but still with that worry of regretting the cut gnawing away at her, Elise hurried the short distance back to Miller Street. She passed a large, four-horse carriage. Its driver leaned over and wolf-whistled after her. Elise tried to let her glare show that she did not appreciate being reduced to something which strangers could give their opinion on in regards to attractiveness. That familiar feeling of anger was beginning to thud in her veins.

"Aw, don't be grumpy. C'mon, pretty. Why so glum?" the driver shouted.

"Perhaps because you are whistling and shouting after me as if you had spotted a carriage you would like to test drive," Elise snapped. "I am a human being and would like more respect."

He looked as if she had stepped on his foot. "Blimey! 'Scuse me. Most of the lasses I know would love to be whistled at when leavin' the barber's."

"Then I suggest you stick to whistling after them. Leave strangers, who have not invited your judgement on their attractiveness, alone."

Sure, she wanted confirmation that her new hairstyle looked good, but she wanted it in circumstances where she felt comfortable. She had endured being treated like an ornament, or a prize mare, in Noble circles. She would not abide being treated that way here.

However, glaring at the carriage driver who was sheepishly driving off meant that she wasn't looking ahead and therefore did not spot the danger hurtling towards her. In a flurry of limbs, metal, and shouts, Elise and the offending party fell to the ground.

"Ugh. Blimey… Elise?"

She looked up at the sound of her name to see that the idiot who was getting up and casually brushing himself down was none other than Hunter Smith.

Elise pursed her lips as she rose. "You. Why is it always you?" she snarled.

"I'm sorry. I was distracted by the pedals stickin' a bit. Have ye seen my new pedal cycle? Ain't she smashin'?" he asked, slipping into his Nightport accent.

Elise looked at the machine — thick metal rods connecting two wheels, a seat, a couple of pedals, and a bar to hold onto. Hunter was currently picking it off the ground with the care of a loving parent.

"A little too closely, you ox-brained cretin! That front wheel nearly smashed my shin. What were you doing driving that contraption so recklessly? I will have huge bruises in the morning thanks to you."

As with the steam engine in Storsund, Elise had heard of these new transport vehicles at court. Unlike the steam engine, this was an Arclid invention. However, when the subject of these pedal cycles arose, it had always been stated that Nobles travelled by horse. Walking, or in this case pedalling, made you perspire and get out of breath, physical reactions only acceptable in Nobles when engaged in duelling or bedplay.

Hunter winced. "I apologise once more, Miss Aelin." He gave a stiff bow, eyes fixed on the ground.

Elise quirked an eyebrow. Why was he being so deferential and formal? Not to mention, back to his faked midlands accent.

"I hope you are not seriously injured," he added.

She noted that he did look truly sorry. And more than a little embarrassed. This wasn't like the showy, arrogant man she had met before.

She forced herself to calm down and softened her tone. "Nothing but the bruises and some scratches. All things that the printing press could have caused as well. Speaking of which, you neglected to tell me how physical this work would be. I should not complain, of course. It is a good job, and Archibald does the most demanding tasks. Nevertheless, I would have been able to prepare better if I had known."

He was still not meeting her eyes. "Then I apologise for that too. I did not take that into consideration. I only knew that you needed a job and that old Archibald would adore you."

She shifted uncomfortably. "We seem to get on well, yes."

She paused, gathering the will to say the next words. "Thank you so much for suggesting me for the job."

That made Hunter face her again. Elise saw his worry melt away to be replaced with a small smile. "Well now, that 'thank you' took some effort."

Another carriage was on its way, so she and Hunter got off the road and up to the pavement.

Elise rolled her eyes, but couldn't help but smiling. "Yes, I suppose it did."

She was smoothing out her dress and brushing the remaining dust off her shoulders and the back of her freshly cut hair. When she looked up again, she caught Hunter staring at her.

"What are you looking at?" she asked.

"You. Trying to figure out why you dislike me so much."

The honesty caught Elise off-guard, as did the question itself. She simply wasn't sure. She was, however, sure that she wanted to return the honesty. It had been a luxury she couldn't always afford at court.

"I will be utterly frank with you. I am not completely certain why."

Hunter scratched the back of his neck, nearly dropping the heavy pedal cycle which seemed to require both hands. "Well, then. Let us try to figure it out together. You were a little cold at the start of our acquaintance. Nothing strange in that, some people react like that to me at first. However, most of them thaw to me, while you merely grew colder. That night when the three of us ate together, your annoyance only seemed to increase, no matter how I tried to charm you."

Elise stalled for time, stomping road dust off her boots. How much did she want to say? She knew that she was not ready to talk about jealousy and Nessa.

"I believe one of the reasons is that I feel that I cannot trust you. You put up a front, and I suppose that is something

I struggle with. My parents had a polished, forced façade, which is common in Highmere. I grew up trying to get behind it. To get to the people I loved, hidden under all that pretence. The life I led before coming to Nightport — it was generally rife with insincerity and people playing games." It was hard to talk about this and avoid the words 'Noble' or 'court'. She bit her tongue.

Hunter was quiet for a moment. "Yes, I do have a front. My fathers raised me to have it when they realised I was different. What way I am different does not matter now. What matters is that growing up in Nightport is hard. Especially when you grow up poor. These streets can swallow you whole and spit you out into a life of crime and poverty."

He stopped speaking and looked down at the pedal cycle in his hands. Elise could see him grip the handle bar tighter. When he carried on, his voice sounded almost confrontational.

"That was what happened to my birthmother. That and the fact that she was not parent material, made her adopt me away to my fathers. Something I do not regret. They may have suggested I cultivate a facade to hide how different I was, but they did it out of love and care. They did everything for me out of love and care."

"They sound like good parents," Elise said, trying to calm the waves.

"They were. We never had much coin, but they lived an honest and hardworking life and made sure I always had food and shelter. Which was much more than most kids in Nightport had before the factories opened and the city grew."

"It sounds tough. Tougher than I, with my sheltered childhood, can imagine," Elise admitted.

Hunter shrugged and tried for his charming smile. He couldn't quite manage it, and it died on his lips, leaving him looking vulnerable.

His chin trembled. "My front... do you know what it

hides? Has someone told you? You seemed to have guessed when we spoke the other night, and you are not asking any questions about it now."

Elise opened her mouth to play coy and pretend not to know what he meant.

Honesty, Elisandrine. Remember?

She lowered her voice so no one on the street could hear her. "When we met, I assumed you were hiding something. You appeared to be compensating for something with that over-the-top flirting. Then our landlady confirmed that you… do not have the voracious sexual appetite you pretend to have."

He blew out a shaky breath. "You could put it like that. The truth is that anything more physical than a friendly embrace makes me break out into a cold sweat. I cannot see what is so enjoyable about physicality."

Elise wasn't sure what to say. She had always been very fond of being physical with people, be it stroking a friend's hair or a lover's breast, but she'd never analysed why. It had simply seemed natural.

Hunter continued. "I am glad that you know my secret. My employers — both Mr Hampton and the employers I work for in the evenings — are asking questions and throwing jibes at me. I need to produce a sexual partner to show them soon or they will start asking more serious questions. I think you would be a wonderful choice to act the part. Purely act, mind you. No actual bedplay involved. You know my secret, you are a good person, and you are attractive. Anyone who would see you on my arm would think I have struck gold!"

Elise felt her forehead furrow. "I… I do not believe that is a good idea. These deceptions never work for long. And it pains me to see you working so hard to cover who you really are. You should be proud of yourself. What does it matter to them if you take a lover or not? Just tell them the truth. They might react at first, but if you weather that shock, I am certain they will come to regard it as normal soon enough."

Hunter scoffed. "Not in this town. Especially not in the night-time enclaves. You fight and fuck or you are a nobody, an outsider without power or stature."

Elise shrunk back at the profanity.

Hunter held out a hand. "I am so sorry for my language! I am growing desperate as I receive more and more questions regarding my personal life. My deepest apologies. I have offended you and will not press the issue further."

She nodded, unsure. She couldn't hide being flattered that he had chosen her to be his acted partner, but the whole situation had made her uncomfortable. Her attraction to Nightport had taken a serious blow at hearing Hunter's story.

He peered at her from under long lashes, like a dog fearing a beating. The silence marched on; Elise was growing impatient and hungry.

Hunter looked down at his dapper clothes. He must have spotted that his initial brush-off had only gotten about half of the road dust because he attempted to brush down his yellow waistcoat and cream shirt with one hand. When he spotted that his tweed trousers were in even worse condition, he began to look around.

"Where can I lean this?"

"Anywhere but the wall next to us," Elise replied.

She was in no doubt that he could smell the stink of the paint that was freshly applied to the wall. He grunted in agreement. His eyes kept darting around for a place to put the cycle. She could see his knuckles turning white with the panicked grip on the cycle and his nose scrunching up when he looked down at the dirt on his expensive clothes.

Elise sighed. "Here, let me help you. Take your time. Your pedal cycle and I are not going anywhere."

With gentle hands, she took the cycle out of Hunter's grip.

He immediately began to slap the dust off his trousers and wipe at his waistcoat and shirt. When he was as stainless as he could be without water, he smiled up at her, carefully at first, but the smile grew much bigger than the gesture should warrant.

"Thank you. Does this mean you are warming to me?"

Elise quirked an eyebrow and tersely replied, "I make no promises, Mr Smith."

"Ha! You really do blow hot and cold, don't you?"

"So I have been told," she answered.

Too temperamental. Too impulsive. Those moods swings of yours will get us all in trouble one day, my girl. You start fires wherever you go, simply by letting your heart dictate your mouth and your actions.

Elise could hear her father's words as if he had spoken them into her mind just now. The pang of missing him returned in full force. She shrugged it off best she could, raising an eyebrow at Hunter and asking, "Speaking of hot and cold, are you not freezing without a coat?"

He puffed out his chest. "No. Being on the move has kept me warm. Besides, this waistcoat is very thick as well as being new. Is it not to die for?"

Elise looked at the garishly yellow waistcoat. "It is certainly… unique. Catches the eye."

Hunter beamed as he took the pedal cycle back. "You know, you seem to like me better when I am not flirting. Especially when I am not flirting with Nessa. I cannot figure you two out. One moment you seem like new friends and the other like lifelong lovers. May I ask what you are to each other?"

Elise crossed her arms over her chest. "No, you may not."

He whistled low. "There is a lot of passion and fire in those golden eyes all of a sudden. Definitely not just friends then. Lovers?"

She scoffed, feeling herself grimace and fidget. Maybe she should leave before this got even more private?

"Aha! That body language puts you in either the lover-with-issues bracket or perchance the unrequited love bracket. Does the lovely country lass not share your passion? Could someone resist the impressive Elise Aelin?"

He stopped smirking at her since he was busy checking the pedal cycle for damage. She took the chance to mull over how much she was willing to divulge. Nothing about where she was from, of course. There was a tiny chance that she was still hunted. But what could it hurt to tell him about Nessa? Gods knew she needed to air her thoughts.

"I am unsure what she wants. For someone so transparent and honest, she is strangely hard to read at the present." Elise's voice sounded petulant to her own ears, but she didn't care. It wasn't fair that she didn't know where they stood.

"But *you* want her in your bed?"

"Actually, she already is. We share a bed to save some coin."

Hunter rolled his eyes. "You know what I meant. In your arms."

Elise sighed and looked up at the sky. "She is quite often that, too. We sleep in each other's embrace most nights. It is a small bed, and the draught from the window means body heat is necessary. Nevertheless, I understood your meaning. And yes, I want to be in her heart."

Hunter waggled his perfectly shaped eyebrows. "What about between her legs?"

She slapped his arm. "Show some respect, you knave." She gave a reluctant shrug. "But yes, that, too."

Reading the tone in Elise's voice or perhaps the look on her face, Hunter dropped the subject.

"Oh, by the way, I like your hair like that. It suits your personality. Forceful and attractive."

Elise searched his face. For a moment she thought he was back to hiding behind the façade of the master seducer. Looking closer, she decided he was in earnest.

Elise adjusted her hair, curling it inwards towards her face. "Thank you. Do you…" She hesitated. Should she really give him something to mock her for? She'd have to risk it, she needed a friend in this harsh city. "Do you think Nessa will like it?"

He smiled, not unkindly. "Yes. I think she will love it."

Elise fidgeted with the sleeve of her coat. "Would you come with me and find out? We can go pick Nessa up, and later you can buy me one of those terrible pies as an apology for driving that contraption right into me."

Hunter beamed. "It would be my honour to do so. I was heading back to Miller Street, anyway."

They walked the short distance to the lodging house with the pedal cycle between them. It seemed to have taken the place of the animosity that lingered before.

Elise found herself knocking on her own door. She didn't want to let herself in with Hunter in tow. What if Nessa was changing her clothes? Or lying down for a nap before supper?

After a moment, Nessa opened the door. As soon as she saw who it was, she asked, "Where have you been? You must have left work quite a while ago."

Then she stopped and looked at Elise in puzzlement. Soon the facial expression morphed into joy.

"Your hair. It's so short! Don't tell me your master cuts your hair? The Brownlees won't even share a water glass with me," Nessa joked.

Elise shook her head. "You know very well that I am not allowed a master, only an employer. You are an apprentice learning a craft; I am a mere assistant doing the dullest of the chores, acting as a conversation partner for a bored printer. Who, I hasten to add, would not be allowed to come anywhere near my hair."

Nessa sniggered. "Well, whoever cut it, I like it. It's going to be so much more practical for you. No long hair to spend an eternity washing in the bath. Or to comb and braid every morning."

Elise hummed her agreement. "In addition, it will not get stuck in a printing press or dipped in ink either."

"It will also keep your neck cool in the summer. Although you can't do this," Hunter added while twirling his long pony-tail in a coquettish manner, making them all laugh.

"Good evening, Hunter. Sorry for not seeing you at first," Nessa said.

"Not a problem. You seemed busy admiring Elise."

Elise elbowed him in the ribs.

"Oof. I mean to say, Elise's new hairstyle," he amended.

The usual pink blush painted Nessa's cheeks. "I guess I must h-have been. Um, what is that?" She pointed at the pedal cycle in an obvious attempt to change the subject. Both Elise and Hunter played along.

Elise scoffed. "*That* is what he used to run me over in the middle of the street. This is apparently how Mr Smith makes friends."

"Oh, we are friends now?" he asked with big eyes and a playful smirk.

When Elise didn't answer but simply rolled her eyes, Hunter looked back at Nessa. "It is my pedal cycle. Now, I have promised to buy Elise a pie as an apology for our run-in. However, after we have all braved stomach ailments by eating the pies downstairs, I can show you how to ride the cycle if you like?"

Nessa looked like a child seeing the sun after a long winter. "Yes, please!"

~

Elise sniggered at Nessa's attempts to open the door to their room. Drunk on too many ales and exhilarated by her ridiculous attempt to ride the pedal cycle, Nessa tried to get the key into the lock and had to give up.

Elise snatched the key from her. "I will do it as I am less inebra... inabr... inibriated."

"Thank you. The door hates me," Nessa slurred.

Hunter misjudged the distance between himself and the corridor wall, causing him to crash into it more than the suave leaning he had probably been aiming for. "So tired. I am going to go in search of my room. What floor am I on?"

"Um. Third, I think," Nessa replied.

"Third?" He seemed to ponder it while he adjusted his waistcoat. "Yes, third."

Elise managed to unlock the door and nearly fell through as it opened.

"Thank you for a lovely evening," Hunter mumbled.

Elise looked at him with scepticism. "Not much to thank us for. It was merely some bad pies, far too much ale, and then you two falling about on that cycle and nearly hitting a man rolling his vegetable cart home."

Hunter shook his head violently. "It was something to thank you for because it was an evening where I could unwind and be honest. That is the base of our alliance now, is it not? We are honest with each other. All the time." He looked directly at Elise when he spoke those last words.

She swallowed, wishing she dared to be completely honest with him. "Right, yes. Of course. Anyway, we should go in before Nessa falls over. Goodnight, Hunter, and thank you for the pie."

He inclined his head. "Thank you for buying most of the ale. Have sweet dreams." Then he poked Nessa's shoulder. "Make sure no nightmares haunt my new friend's sleep. I am making that your official duty."

Nessa gave the traditional raised fist of the Arclid Navy. "Aye, aye, captain!"

Hunter guffawed and then trotted off while humming the Navy's official song.

Nessa followed Elise into their room and stood there, smiling at her.

"What?" Elise asked while closing the door.

"You're so pretty. I love your hair like this. It was beautiful before but this… this looks more like the real Elise."

Nessa ran her fingers through her hair, getting her fingers stuck on a snag on one side. She abandoned the snag and began drunkenly patting Elise's hair instead. "It's so thick and nice to touch. Whoever ends up as your lover in the city, they will be lucky to get to play with this soft, short hair. Lucky, lucky them."

Nessa let go of her hair and began clumsily taking her coat off and hanging it up. Elise was left standing there, dismayed to find that her heart ached at the thought of Nessa not even considering herself an option. Or perhaps she didn't want to be her lover?

Perhaps I should simply ask her.

No, their friendship and status as roommates were essential to Elise. Nessa had quickly become her safety. Her home. Nessa wasn't as much of a social creature as she was; if she made Nessa uncomfortable, it was possible that she would cut ties and go it alone.

I must avoid that. I need Nessa. Curse it all. What if I need her as more than a friend or roommate? What if I need her as more than even a lover?

She shook her head to clear it and too keep herself from starting to question why she wasn't attracting Nessa to her. Best to get ready for bed and sleep the ale off. She had work in the morning.

Although it was no use. Her mind churned on, trying to figure out why Nessa didn't want her as more than a friend, travel companion, roommate, and cuddly toy.

Because is that going to be enough for me and my dumb heart? If so, for how long? Perhaps fate did not choose so perfectly for me after all.

CHAPTER 20
SWEET CREAM AND LEMON
WATER

Nessa woke up feeling uneasy. The memory of Elise shying away from her all night haunted her into the waking world. Elise had seemed to refuse to sleep near her, meaning that she was so on the edge of the bed that she was nearly falling off it. Elise avoiding her touch made Nessa's stomach roil and ache. She had to snap out of it.

She opened her bleary eyes. All she could see was smooth, sand-coloured skin. Nessa blinked the worst of the sleep grit away. Into focus came a jugular, the start of shoulders with white straps of a nightdress, and a pair of exquisitely sculpted clavicles below. Nessa blinked again. Elise was so close to her that she could see every pore of the skin on her throat and every deep breath making the shoulders and clavicles lift and sink.

It was hypnotizing. She had never seen waves move in and out against a shore, but she imagined it would look like this. Elise was always beautiful, but sleeping so innocently, she was exquisite. Nessa lay still as a statue, feeling her cheeks heat up. It was like she was watching something she shouldn't. Something too intimate for people who weren't lovers. Something too intimate for people who had slept in the same narrow bed without making contact all night.

Their bodies were so close to each other right now that she could feel the warmth coming off Elise's skin, but no part of them was touching. There appeared to be a thin wall of air placed there to keep them apart. Nessa watched the slender neck in front of her as Elise swallowed, the movements so delicate and slow.

She wasn't quite sure why she inched forward so that her nose nearly rubbed against the column of Elise's throat, but she did, as if pulled in by magnetic force. She wasn't quite sure why she breathed in so deeply either. Elise didn't smell of the sugar pumpkin oil or the shared bathroom's rose-scented soap. Nor of the printer's ink that sometimes clung to her clothes and hair after work. She smelled only of herself. It was that secret scent which Nessa had found herself appreciating every morning. She wasn't very good at describing smells, but since she got to know Elise, and her overly keen sense of smell, she had been inspired to try it out.

What exactly does Elise smell of?

Nessa tried to pinpoint it, wanting to distract herself from thoughts of what had made Elise so distant last night. She filled her nose and lungs with the scent. It was warm, sweet, but with a vaguely tart, fresh edge. Sweet cream and lemon water? Close, but not exactly right. It could only be described as the smell of Elise. Her Elise. No, she wasn't hers. Elise could never belong to anyone, but particularly not to a dull, farm mouse like Nessa.

Elise sighed in her sleep. It sounded sad. Nessa winced at the sound of it.

Did I make her sad? Did I say or do something inappropriate last night in my drunken folly? Why did I have all those gods-forsaken ales?

This was what she got for drinking mindlessly while

listening to Hunter talk about his pedal cycle and tell tales of famous Nightport people. Everything from noted singers to Eil Cowalski — Nightport's most famous serial killer, who committed more than a dozen brutal murders before being caught.

Thoughts of the darker side of Nightport made her recall Elise saying that Hunter had some less respectable part-time job outside of his work for the solicitor. She would have to ask her about that. If Elise was still speaking to her.

Her stomach ached even more now, and she knew it wasn't because of hunger or her hangover. She had to get up and get some breakfast. Focus on the real world and not brooding about Elise.

Nessa pulled the collar on her leather coat up, but it wasn't keeping her cheeks safe from the foggy, chilly morning. She was walking back to 21 Miller Street from the bakery, breakfast procured. She dodged a tatty child who appeared to be running right for her. A few days ago, she'd been warned by Secilia about beggar children who smashed into you and emptied your pockets as you were both getting up. Nessa was slowly but surely learning the ways of the city.

Thinking about the child reminded her of that strange package that was dropped off with their landlady by a little street urchin. Strange that they never heard any more about that. Still, that must prove it was a mistake. The odd package in the expensive midnight blue wrapping paper and white string was clearly meant for someone else. What other solution could there be?

Her stomach growled, taking her mind off both children and strange packages. Since they were both were in employment, Nessa had sprung for some more expensive, sweeter rolls today. These ones might not have dust or ash added to the flour to fill them out. She had even picked up a bottle of honeyed winterberry juice.

The warm, sweet scents in the bakery had made the badly hungover Nessa, feel famished. She had begun nibbling on one of the freshly baked rolls the second she had paid for them. She was still eating one now and was therefore reduced to a simple nod when their landlady looked up from surveying her nails to greet her.

As she walked upstairs, her thoughts were on Elise. Was there something wrong between them? If there was, would they be able to talk about it? How she wished she were better at these things.

Let's face it, my awfulness at serious conversations could be overcome if she was less impressive. How can I talk about my feelings and shortcomings with someone so superior? How can I make her understand how my mind works?

Steeling herself with a deep breath, Nessa opened the door to their room and snuck in to wake Elise.

CHAPTER 21
A VISITOR FROM GROUND HOLLOW

Elise woke up to the smell of baked goods and the sensation of someone brushing hair out of her face.

She heard Nessa softly say, "Good morning. I bought some sweet rolls and winterberry juice. It does wonders for an ale-drenched head. According to the man at the bakery, Saint Alsager's bells are going to chime six soon. So, you'll have to wake up now if you don't want to hurry while hungover."

Elise left her eyes closed for a moment longer, determining how she would behave towards Nessa. Last night's thoughts of Nessa not returning her burgeoning affections had weighed heavy on her during the night, making her avoid touching Nessa. Considering how drunk Nessa had been, she probably hadn't even noticed.

But she would notice today, so how should she behave? The decision only took a moment. It wasn't Nessa's fault that she didn't feel the way Elise did. It would be unfair to punish her for it.

Elise forced a smile and opened her eyes. "Good morning. That smells lovely. Give me one of those rolls, please?"

She saw Nessa smile back at her and tried to read that smile. Was that relief?

"Of course. Hang on," Nessa said. She began rummaging in her satchel and produced two and a half sweet rolls. The half one had clear bite marks.

Elise laughed. "How many rolls were there before you starred chomping?"

"Um. Four," Nessa admitted with a sheepish grin.

"Well, it would seem I will have to try to catch up then. Could you pour the juice? We will need to drink a lot to flush the ale out of our bodies. I learned that at court."

Nessa raised her eyebrows. "Hmm. I guess that makes sense."

Elise took a bite of one of the rolls while watching Nessa reach into the bag to get the winterberry juice. She thought about asking where their tin mug was but realised that her new life was one where you drank straight from the bottle. Mainly to save yourself having to wash your mug fifteen times a day.

She watched Nessa's hands as they held the large bottle and uncorked it deftly. They were practical, slightly calloused hands, used to work and heavy lifting. And yet they were so nimble. So elegant and feminine in their quick, lithe movements. Realising that her gaze on those slender fingers was turning distinctly erotic, Elise returned to eating her breakfast with shame burning in her belly. She had to respect Nessa's wish to be platonic. From the corner of her eye, she saw Nessa sit down on the bed and rub her temples.

"Headache?"

Nessa gave a curt nod. "Like a dozen little carpenters are working with hammers and nails inside my head."

"Reaping the reward of all that ale. Now, drink as much of that juice as you can. You have to go be a good little apprentice soon and that hair of yours is not even braided properly, more strands than normal are falling out."

Nessa groaned and downed gulps of juice.

Elise hesitated. This was unquestionably a bad idea, but so irresistible. "Would you... I mean, I could... would you like me to braid it for you?" she asked, heart pounding.

Nessa swallowed her juice with a loud gulp. She looked wide-eyed at Elise for a moment. Elise's palms were growing damp. She wished Nessa would hurry up and answer.

"Um. Well, I s-suppose you don't have to braid your own this morning, so sure. If you don't m-mind?"

Elise gave a minute shake of the head, fetched the brush, and stood behind the bed Nessa was still sat on. She undid the messy braid Nessa had made before going out and watched the long strands of straight, almond-brown hair drape over Nessa's shoulders and down her back. She picked up the brush and began running it through the tresses, an intimate and familiar gesture. Like their mothers had brushed their hair. Like animals groomed each other. Like lovers caressed each other.

Her heart pounded so fast that it ached. Or maybe the pain was more connected to emotion. She kept combing, turning adorable tangles into a beautiful, smooth mane which glistened in the morning light. She wished she could do the same with her feelings. And Nessa's apparent lack of them.

Nessa winced loudly as Elise hit a tangle.

"Oh, I am so frightfully sorry."

Nessa laughed. "Don't sound so anxious. It hurts when someone brushes out the snags. You know that. Relax, I can take it."

Elise swallowed thickly. "Yes. Right. Of course."

She continued brushing, more carefully now. She tried to sing as she did it, to prove her comfort with the situation. But as her voice trembled unpleasantly, she soon stopped. When she was done combing, Elise put the brush down and hesitated with her hands hovering over Nessa's head. It felt strange to plunge her fingers into the curtains of hair. Into something so intimate and deeply connected with Nessa. She always had her hair in that braid, seeing it down was a rare treat. Touching it while it was down, now that was a gift. Elise bit her lip hard.

Get yourself together. Nessa is a practical woman. She does not see a gift here, she sees a person helping another person of the same household get to work faster.

She slid her fingers into the mane of hair and began dividing it into three parts to braid it. The hair felt warm and even softer now that it was brushed. The sensation of its texture against her fingers was wonderful, and so she took her time.

She wondered if Nessa had her eyes closed. She wondered if Nessa enjoyed it when her fingers accidentally brushed her neck occasionally. She wondered what she could do to make Nessa want her in the way she wanted Nessa; every way.

Elise had been kept late by Archibald, who wanted to discuss the riots in Nightport's clothing factories. He was appalled that the workers demanded better pay and shorter hours. It was all Elise could do to not tell him that he was severely lacking in empathy.

She was finally walking home now and felt her shoulders relax as she thought about a quiet evening with Nessa. And preferably food that wasn't those awful pies.

She looked up as she neared 21 Miller Street and saw Nessa standing outside, speaking to someone. It was a tall, dark-skinned, broad-shouldered man. They were close to the wall and speaking in hushed voices, faces close to each other to hear over the commotion of the street. When Elise could see the man's profile and the spectacles on his nose, she recognised him as someone she had met once – Nessa's friend Layden.

Nessa was biting her lip and frowning. Elise hurried her steps over to them.

"Good afternoon, or evening, if you prefer. Is everything in order here?" she asked.

Nessa jumped ever so slightly. "Oh, it's you. Sorry. Layden just found me. He, um, came all the way from Ground Hollow to tell me something."

Layden bowed to Elise. "Hello, milady... I mean, miss. I should have come earlier as the events I was reporting on took place three days ago. But Isobel has been poorly so I've been caring for her and our daughter."

Elise looked from Nessa to Layden, before saying, "I am sure that is fine. What was it you came to tell us? Or was it solely news for Nessa? Are her parents safe and in good health?"

"Oh yes, Carryanne and Jon are fine," he hurried to reassure her. "They send some supplies and their regards. In fact, what happened to me happened to them as well."

"And what was that?" Elise asked while stretching her stiff neck. She was trying to ignore her empty stomach and aching muscles. This was bound to be something important.

Layden swallowed. "A gang of men on horseback came to ask me questions. Questions about Nessa and about you."

Elise looked to Nessa for confirmation. "About us? Not just me?"

Nessa frowned. "No, and Layden told me that they didn't look like Royal guards."

"No, they wore some sort of dark green uniform, like they were trying to blend into the forest. Not the Royal colours. The uniforms certainly didn't have the crest on them either. When I asked how long Macray would search for you, trying to get more information, they laughed and said that Macray wasn't behind this. One of them said that it was common knowledge that he is already happily engaged to another lady in waiting." He dropped his gaze. "And from the rumours around town, he is not waiting and being chaste for the lady in question. Several villagers have been up to the castle to… pay him a visit."

Elise scoffed. "Well, that is one part of all this that does not surprise me."

"Never mind what the prince does. I'm more worried about these strange men in forest green," Nessa said.

Elise felt her forehead furrow as she looked back at Layden. "They were definitely not Royal guards?"

He straightened, looking affronted. "I come from a village which neighbours one of the biggest royal castles. Do you honestly think I can't spot Royal guards? I grew up with their big horses frequently trampling my mother's garden and laughing at her when she had to replant. I know Royal guards when I see them."

"Yes, yes of course. I did not mean to doubt you. It is simply that I cannot think of anyone other than the Royals who might wish to find me. It cannot be my mother since she would, if she against all odds did want to find me, do it quietly and discreetly. My very existence shames her now. She would come herself or send a couple of footmen, not hire 'a gang of men' as you put it, Layden. Too much attention."

Nessa put a hand on her arm. "Well, I am fairly certain it's you they're after. I'm of no value or interest to anyone but my parents. Think harder. Can you think of anyone else, friend or foe, who might want to find you? Perhaps just to speak with you?"

Elise sifted through everyone at court and in her old home. "No. The Queen, Macray, and my mother are the only ones who would care if I vanished in a cloud of smoke. To be honest, they all want me to vanish. Probably even the Queen, considering how I disobeyed her marital decree. I would be more use to them forgotten than brought back and punished – that would only make them look bad as they could not keep me in check. No, I cannot think of anyone."

Layden hummed. "Well, I recommend that you keep thinking. They were very insistent on finding you."

"What exactly did you tell them?" Nessa asked.

"The truth seemed best since they already knew that you had left together and that you were heading to Nightport. I don't know if they got that information from your parents or someone else."

"Probably from Macray, if they managed to get an audience with him between copulations," Elise muttered.

Layden spluttered out a cough. "Yes, perhaps. Either way, they knew that much and merely asked if I knew where in Nightport you were heading and if you planned to stay there."

Nessa stopped biting her lip. "And you answered?"

He shrugged. "That I didn't know. That you didn't give details."

"Good lad," Nessa said and squeezed Layden's shoulder.

"Let us hope everyone said the same. At least no one knew where we were going to get rooms. Especially not that loose-lipped Macray," Elise said. Something hit her. "Wait. How did you find us?"

Nessa chuckled. "Hunter. Layden showed up at the gates to Nightport this afternoon and started asking anyone who passed about us. Hunter has ears everywhere and came to the glassblower's to tell me about it, with a description of the man asking for us. I begged my masters for some time off and promised that I'd be back tonight to clean up the workshop. Then I made my way down to the gates and picked Layden up."

Elise squinted at him. "How exactly did you enquire about us?"

"Pardon?" Layden asked with knitted brows.

Nessa gave Elise a warm smile. "Don't worry, heartling. He didn't mention who and what you are. He merely described our looks and when and how we must have arrived."

Elise let out a long breath. "Good. That is all right then." There was a strange tingling going through her body.

Heartling. Did Nessa really call me heartling?

"Yes. Oh, right, that's what you meant. Nessa did tell me that you were hiding your Noble origin," Layden whispered.

Elise smiled to put him at ease. "Hence you stopping your-self from calling me 'milady' earlier. Thank you for that concern. Well, we should not be discussing this out here. We can go to our rooms so you can leave your satchel there and wash the road dust off. Then perhaps we can all have a spot of supper and take a stroll? You can show us where you used to study, Layden."

Nessa crossed her arms over her chest. "Ah, no. I need to get back and clean the workshop, remember?"

Elise took in the sulking beauty in front of her. "There is only one thing for it, then. We shall all go clean the workshop."

Nessa and Layden both stared at her.

"We?" Nessa asked.

"Yes. We will bring a bottle of winterberry brandy and make the chore a light one. Sweeping is so much more fun when you are drunk and singing rude songs," Elise said.

Layden laughed. "Look at that smirk. You have mischief in your blood, don't you? Well, as long as I can have some bread with that brandy and a place to put this satchel." He stopped to point at Nessa. "Which your mother stuffed with glass jars of scented oil and dried fruit, by the way. Then I am willing to help clean and sing rude songs."

Nessa was chewing her lower lip. "Yes, I suppose we can

get it done quicker that way. Then get back to discussing who it is that is asking questions about us."

Elise observed Nessa's stoic expression and rigid posture. She was going to help this woman stop constantly worrying one day. Maybe it was tonight? She hoped it was tonight. She wanted to see Nessa relax and enjoy herself.

And she really wanted Nessa to call her 'heartling' again.

CHAPTER 22
THE GOBLIN'S TAVERN

Doubt crept up Nessa's spine. Was this really a good idea? The brandy was already clouding her judgement even though she had only had a few mouthfuls. What if she missed cleaning something? She forced her mind to clear a bit and went through the list in her head.

One. Sweep the floors. Layden was doing that, and as someone who had apprenticed under a master apothecary, he clearly knew how thorough you had to be. No dust or dirt could be allowed to swirl around the workshop and tarnish the melted glass.

Two. Check on the furnace. She had just finished that job, one she knew Josiah was very particular about. A glassblower's furnace had to keep an even temperature so it was never allowed to go out. That was why most glassblowers lived so close to the furnace. But when Nessa was around, it was her job to keep the fire burning. It roared perfectly now, despite the drunkenness of its current maintainer.

Three. Make sure all tools are cleaned and in their proper places. With some direction, Elise was doing that. It had seemed the least physical job but the fiddliest, so Elise had been the obvious candidate for it.

Nessa squinted over at her, wondering if she should help her hold the heavy blowpipe Elise was currently struggling with. Working with the printing press might be giving the Noble lady more muscles, but they weren't ready for glass-blowing work, that was for sure. Still, she managed it and was clearly making a real effort to be respectful and precise. Blowpipe in place, Elise went back to the bottle filled with reddish-brown liquid and took a swig.

Nessa stood up, wiped her brow, and went to join her. She didn't know why. She should check on Layden. Why was she heading towards Elise? It wasn't for the brandy, although that was what she was going to use as an excuse.

The room smelled of burnt wood, molten glass, and hot metal. It was a heavy but wonderful smell, not stifling like the one that always came from the open windows of Nightport's factories. As Nessa got closer to Elise, the smell mixed with the strong brandy on their breaths and the sugar pumpkin oil that Elise was wearing. She was using the oil frequently now, not solely in the morning and evening. Nessa would catch her sniffing the jar and smiling before applying it liberally. It was a good thing that Layden had brought more little jars from back home. They were close to running out.

Elise had put the brandy down and was wiping something off with a rag, her movements big and exaggerated by the drink. Nessa tapped her on the shoulder. "How are you getting along? Any questions?"

"No, I think I am just about finished. This is that pointy thing which you said lays next to the windpipe —"

"Blowpipe," Nessa corrected.

"Yes, that. I am placing it in its little home right now. There, all done. How are you getting along?"

Nessa took a swig of the winterberry brandy. It was deceptively sweet at first, right up till the point where the alcohol stung her mouth, throat, and all the way down to her stomach.

"Good. The fire has plenty of fuel to keep it going for hours now. However, it looks like the windows need a wipe down. I forgot that yesterday. If Secilia notices, I'll get a bollocking tomorrow. Layden hasn't finished sweeping, anyway."

Elise smiled as she took the bottle. "Sounds like I will have to start the singing on my own, then."

"I can sing and sweep," Layden piped up from behind them.

Nessa cringed. She knew what Layden's singing voice was like.

"*Oooooh, there is a lady in Highmere. Sheeeee'll mount you like a mare,*" he sang off-key.

Nessa shook her head. Someone could overhear them. There might be children outside. Sure, the walls were thick, but there were windows. She looked at the windows, maybe they weren't so dirty after all? Maybe they could leave?

Elise on the other hand merely laughed and joined in. "*And many deserted loooovers say there is no man ooor beast who can compare.*"

Nessa looked at Elise. She had a nice singing voice. Sweet and high-pitched, like little silver bells chiming. She cursed inwardly. Was there anything about Elise that wasn't going to go straight to her heart?

Layden came closer to Elise, leaning on his broom right next to her. She put her head on his shoulder and together they sang, "*So the lesson in the tale in thiiiis, proper mounting sure is rare!*"

They all laughed until Nessa collected herself. "You can't be singing that so loudly."

"Why not? Sweet Nessa, you must stop being so worried

and so proper. We are all adults here and drunk enough not to worry about decorum," Elise said in a drunken drawl.

Nessa crossed her arms. "*You* are giving *me* lessons on behaviour?"

Elise pursed her lips. "Fine. All right. No more singing."

Layden cleared his throat. "Well, as we seem to have left the merriment behind now – has anyone had any ideas about the men in the green uniforms?"

Nessa shook her head once more, this time to clear it. Changing topics so quickly was hard when her mind was fogged with brandy.

"No, not really. I know no one outside of Ground Hollow, and none of the villagers would have reason or silver enough to hire men to find me. I still say they can't have come for me," Nessa said.

Elise sucked her teeth. "And I cannot think of anyone who would want me found."

"So, no closer to an answer, then?" Layden asked while reaching for the bottle.

Nessa sighed. "No. As much as I hate to say it, we will simply have to wait and see if anything comes from it."

"I think we should take some precautions, though. Just in case these people who seek us have nefarious intentions. Perhaps we should ask Hunter to keep an ear out for anyone searching for us? And maybe change residence?" Elise suggested.

Nessa gave it some thought. "Yes to asking Hunter to keep tabs on the situation. No to the idea of moving. I like where we live. Besides, neither these men nor Layden could find us. Not until Hunter got involved, anyway."

"True. We can go find Hunter when we have finished here. Would you like to meet him, Layden?" Elise asked.

Layden handed Nessa the brandy. "I'm sure I would like

to. But it's getting late and I should be getting back. I need to be home to open the apothecary tomorrow morning."

Nessa packed the bottle into her satchel, worry churning in her stomach. "Are you sure you should walk so late at night?"

"I'll be fine. I borrowed the Haydens' donkey and rode here, so the trip should be faster, and I'll be harder to catch than if I was on foot. If, despite this, I am attacked, I'm armed." He opened his coat to show the glimmer of a knife hilt in his inner pocket.

"You came here on a donkey?" Elise slurred. The brandy was truly making itself known in her behaviour now.

Why did she drink so much? I usually get drunker than she does.

"Yes. I left it with the guard at the gate. Apparently, he grew up in a family that bred donkeys so he was only too happy to look after Beeny."

Nessa laughed. "Good old Beeny! I didn't think of him as a mode of transportation when I headed out. He must be a hundred years old by now!"

Layden grinned. "Almost. But he still rides pretty fast."

"Even with a big, strapping man like you on his back?" Elise asked.

Was that flirtation in her voice?

Nessa shrugged off her annoyance. Flirting was second nature to Elise.

Layden nodded at Elise. "Yep. Beeny likes to get places fast so that he can spend more time sleeping in new locations. Anyway, I'm going to finish up the last of the sweeping and then come with you to fetch my satchel."

Nessa frowned. "Are you certain? I feel so bad for making you spend your evening in Nightport doing my chores."

"I'm utterly sure. Sweeping isn't so bad. The good company, and even better brandy, made it child's play," he said.

"Well, when we go back to Miller Street, you can at least point out roughly where you apprenticed. Then we can stop for a quick drink and a sweet tart at one of the pubs on the way to the gates. Journeying on a full stomach is easier," Elise suggested.

"Aye, I won't say no to that, milad... I mean... ah, you know what I mean."

As they all laughed, Nessa ached at how Elise's charming laugh and twinkling eyes made her want to kiss her.

With his satchel over his shoulder, and a belly full of tart and brandy, Layden was leading the way to the gate at the bottom of Core Street. Nessa had enjoyed having him with her tonight. But a part of her, a betraying and confusing part, wanted him to leave so that she could have Elise to herself.

At the gate, Layden put down his satchel. "Ah, this thing only weighs half as much now that I've has dropped off all the scented oil and dried fruit from your mother."

He enveloped Nessa in a close hug. So close that she could smell him as clearly as when they were kids play-wrestling in the fields. He smelled of herbs, sunshine, and the tiniest hint of sweat. Only the herb smell that came with his trade reminded Nessa that he was a grown man, not the boy she used to chase through wheat fields.

Now Nessa regretted that any part of her had been glad to see him go. A stinging ache of homesickness filled her chest as unshed tears blurred her vision.

Damn that brandy.

She pushed him away before she became too maudlin. "Hurry up and go or Isobel will come and fetch you. Something which would probably end up with me getting killed by her sharp tongue."

He scowled at her. "What's with the tone? Has knowing her motives for disliking you changed nothing?"

Nessa shrugged. Out of the corner of her eye, she could see Elise taking a studiously slow sip from the bottle. When had she grabbed the brandy bottle?

Switching her focus back to Layden, Nessa replied, "I simply find it hard to believe that someone could be enamoured enough with me to cause such a strong response. That can't be it."

Layden was still scowling at her. "Yes, it can. You find it hard to think that anyone could be enamoured with you, full stop. The few partners you have had were all but forced to fill out a form stating their intent to romance you. Including a copy to your parents, so they could open your eyes for you."

Nessa crossed her arms over her chest, the brandy in her blood making it a tricky manoeuvre. "You're exaggerating. Now, say goodbye to Elise and be on your way."

His serious look changed into a grin. "Aye, Mother."

The grin vanished as he looked over at Elise. He shuffled his feet. Nessa could guess what he was thinking. He and Elise had spent time making drunken small talk and singing awful songs most of the night. Still, they were new acquaintances and Layden was one of the two people in Nightport who knew of Elise's high social status. So he did not shake her hand. He did not give her a friendly embrace. He didn't even give his customary, diffident bow.

When it was clear that he was just going to stand there, shifting his weight and looking at Elise while swallowing thickly, Elise took charge. She stepped forward and gave him a one-armed hug, her other hand clutching the brandy bottle.

Layden seemed about as comfortable as a mouse in a room full of cats. Clearly noticing that, Elise let go of him quickly. "That is enough of that. Go home before your wife strides in and gives Nessa the spanking of a lifetime."

The brandy allowed Layden to not be shocked at her saying something like that. Or perhaps he had gotten used to her way of speaking her mind, appropriate or not. He merely chortled and turned to leave. He waved over his shoulder as he walked out the gate and turned a corner. Probably looking for Beeny.

Nessa missed him already.

Light, chilly fingers brushed aside a couple of hairs which had fallen out of Nessa's braid to tickle at her cheek. The movement soon became a caress, as soft as Elise's voice when she said, "Time to go, heartling. The night is not yet spent. Let us go have some fun before we fall into bed."

Nessa chewed her lower lip. "We should go home, have a bath, and get some sleep. We have to work tomorrow."

"Yes, I know. Nevertheless, you are sad and I am peckish. I should have had a tart, too, but I dislike when they mix figs and sunberries in them. Anyway, you being sad and me being hungry is no way to go to bed. We can sleep the day after tomorrow instead. That will be Worshipday, our first day off from our new jobs. Remember?"

Nessa put her hands in her coat pockets. "I'm an apprentice. I'm not meant to get a day off."

"I understand that the custom is that tradesmen and their apprentices work full weeks. But the Brownlees wanted the day off, just like most people in Nightport. That means you are free, too."

"Having a free day seems wasteful," Nessa muttered.

On the farm, they had not cared what day it was. You worked every day, right up until sunset. Then it was time for food, drink, and fun with those near to you. However, she had heard of the free day at the end of the week that the cities had brought into use. Layden had told her that it was so that the factory workers would get some time out in the fresh air.

Nessa watched Elise turn and squint down the street. They

were too far down Core Street to see any of the stalls and booths. The gas in the streetlights was burning low, making it hard to pick out any details beyond the occasional late workers going home and one or two people daring to leave through the gate and travel the roads after dark.

Nessa looked in the direction from whence they had come. A small cut-through, made up of a side road which went past the small tavern where they had stopped for a tart with Layden, then another cut-through over to the Brownlees' workshop on Orgreave Street, and from there, a quick walk home to Miller Street.

But Elise had been right, she was sad and didn't want to go home and sleep.

She looked in the other direction, up Core Street. She took a few tentative steps in the direction she knew she'd find noise, people, and fun. Then a few steps more. She could almost hear the music and the revellers now.

Elise linked their arms and whispered in her ear. "Come on. Time to go have some fun, beautiful."

They walked on. Nessa still not sure if she shouldn't simply go home. After all, they might not have to work on Worship-day, but they certainly had to tomorrow. Also, there was something she needed to deliberate on - the people asking about them back in Ground Hollow.

"Maybe we should go find Hunter? We said we'd ask him to keep an eye and ear out for anyone looking of us," Nessa pointed out.

"I am certain he will do that without us asking him. He told you right away when Layden arrived and was enquiring about you, did he not? Furthermore, if you want to find Hunter tonight, he will be somewhere in the city centre, working. Probably in the busiest part of Core Street. We might run into him if we keep walking."

The evening was growing colder. Nessa linked their arms

tighter so they walked closer to each other. "I suppose so. What does he do exactly?"

"Last time I spoke to him outside our lodging house I asked exactly that. He said vaguely that he worked for the taverns, bars, and the gambling houses. Oh, and the brothels, too. You know what he is like. He avoided going into details because he likes to make himself sound more important than he is."

The lights were getting brighter now, and they saw the street's first big tavern. It was painted a dark olive green, standing out in a row of buildings that were all drab grey stone or unassuming wood. It had a large, yellow sign which was framed by two lit torches. Nessa squinted up at it. Painted on the sign were a gruesome green face and two words in bold letters: Goblin's Tavern.

Elise clapped her hands. "Goblin's Tavern! That sounds splendid. It must be a grand and famous tavern if it can afford such a big sign with lit torches. Not to mention painting the whole building. Nessa, we need to try it. There must be all kinds of interesting liquor in there. Probably food, too."

"Which will be awful. Look at this place. It looks rough. Any food served in there'll probably poison us," Nessa muttered.

"It cannot be worse than the pies we get at our lodging house. Come on, beautiful." She took Nessa's hand and began walking towards the entrance to the tavern.

Nessa knew she could just say no. Then they would go home. She could get some sleep, and the hangover wouldn't be too bad tomorrow. She might even get a good day's work done without a brute of a headache. That was the sensible decision.

Then she saw Elise's small frame buzzing with energy and her full, perfect lips smiling in a way which spoke of mischief. If Elise was going into that tavern, that was where there would be an adventure tonight. That was where memories would be made.

Nessa let herself be pulled along. She could work harder next week. She could worry about the people looking for them on her day off. The gods only knew how many days of work and worry she had clocked up, but the nights of risk-taking and adventure could be counted on one hand. Tonight, she was going to add another one.

The wooden doors to the Goblin's Tavern looked like they had been broken and mended too many times to count, the flaking green paint not helping their appearance. Elise pushed them open and strode in. Once inside, Nessa watched her look around, sizing the place up. She had a feeling that Elise was calculating where the optimal point of fun and safety met. Although, that might only be in her head. Perhaps Elise was picking out a lover to go home with tonight. There weren't many women in the tavern, Elise would have slim pickings.

As Nessa's jealous eyes scanned the crowd for someone that Elise might leave with, she caught an interesting sight. At a table in the corner, right under one of the room's scarce gas lamps, sat a group of four, speaking and laughing heartily.

They didn't look all that rough, compared to everyone else. Having cleaner clothes and tidier hair than the people at the tables around them helped. The person who had caught Nessa's interest was the tidiest with ebony hair like Elise's but shorter. The two people to the person's right looked male and the one to their left looked masculine but still clearly female. But this fourth person… Nessa could not make out their gender.

Her curiosity made her move closer. She saw hair so black it was nearly blue, pale skin, and slanted eyes which were as black as the hair. A slight, waifish build melded with rough, handsome facial features. Nessa tried not to stare too obviously as she attempted to guess the person's gender. Or if this was one of those people who was neither gender? Maybe even both genders? She had heard of them, of course, but there had been none in Ground Hollow.

She checked herself. She was acting like the country lass she was. Staring at someone who was different? That was not who she wanted to be. Even if her intent hadn't been negative.

To her embarrassment, the striking fourth person caught her staring. Nessa felt her cheeks grow hot when they smiled in her direction. Suddenly she felt Elise's hand on her lower back.

"Looks like you have made a friend. Let us go over and introduce ourselves," she said against Nessa's ear. She was barely audible over the din of laughter, clinking glasses, and what sounded like a harpsichord being played somewhere in the back.

Nessa followed Elise who was making a beeline for the corner table.

The smell of alcohol and pipe smoke grew stronger as they walked further into the tavern. The walls were a gloomy olive colour with goblin faces contoured in white paint everywhere. Simple, cheap lamps burned low, and a fireplace roared as a brawny, bald man stoked it.

One of the men at the table spotted them when they were almost at his side. "Good evenin', ladies. Lookin' for somewhere to sit? I'm Jac. This is Sanjero, Cai, an' that's Fyhre at the end. Won't ye join us?"

Nessa looked closer at Cai, her mystery person. She decided that a closer look didn't give her any more information, neither did the name as it was used for both genders. She pushed her curiosity down. It didn't matter what gender this person was. It mattered if they were a good person, who would be good company tonight.

"Perhaps we shall. But only if you promise not to be annoying, boring, or spend the entire night trying to get under our metaphorical skirts," Elise said with hands on hips.

The man who had been pointed out as Sanjero gave a belly laugh. "Seein' as we're two monogamous couples, ye needn't worry 'bout any unwanted advances. The 'boring' or 'annoying' part on the other hand, well, that is subjective, innit?"

Nessa looked at him. His russet brown skin was heavily tattooed, the skin art peeked out from under a light grey, worn linen shirt and trousers in the same colour. Cai and Fyhre wore the same outfits. All snugly fitting and with their sleeves rolled up high, showing strong arms. Those were the uniforms the city gave to anyone who came and agreed to work in whatever factory needed workers. It was meant to be an incentive to work in industry. That and a midday meal of bread and honeyed water. Nessa had heard that many people came to Nightport without more than the ragged shirt on their back and would be thrilled for a job and some whole, clean clothes to wear. The tattoos were not usual fare for those workers, though. Those cost heavy coin to have made.

"I see ye're admirin' my ink," Sanjero said to Nessa. He sounded different from other Nightport citizens she had met. The words were the same, the casual, fast-paced slang which the city folk prided themselves on. But the cadence sounded different, more melodic. It reminded her of the accent Layden's grandparents had, meaning somewhere from the Western Isles. Everyone seemed to move between the four continents after a few generations on the same landmass. Leading to a great blend in the populace. Stuck in Ground Hollow, it had been a comfort to see that, at some point, everyone had emigrated and immigrated. It made her feel like moving around was her fate, too, no matter how nervous she was about it. She decided to ask Elise about Sanjero's accent when they were alone.

"Huh? Oh, yes. I was thinking that it's rare to see those on factory workers. It looks like you have an impressive collection. Oh, and call me Nessa. And this is Elise."

"Well, Nessa, I thank ye. And yes, I've my fair share. Six years on the wild seas. A nice, big tattoo for every port."

The man who had spoken to them first, Jac, ran his fingers over the tattoos on Sanjero's neck. His fingernails were black and there were a few cuts and scars on his calloused hand.

"Aye, pretty they are, too. I always wanted me a man with tattoos an' the gods provided," Jac said dreamily.

Sanjero reached over and gave him a peck on the lips.

Nessa wanted to stay. These people seemed nice and had offered that they could join them. But was it wise to sit with strangers in a place like this?

Without warning, Elise took Nessa's hand and sat down on a proffered chair. The hand-holding meant that Nessa had to sit down on the chair between Elise and Jac, but she would have done that anyway. Elise's hand was cool, and her grip was just on the right side of tight. Confident and comforting, not painful. Flanking Elise was the mysterious Cai, who must be in a relationship with the surly-looking Fyhre.

Jac didn't wear the uniform of the factory workers but he must work with his hands considering the state of them. Nessa's curiosity was bursting through her shyness. Her stomach fluttered at the thrill of meeting new people. It was another bonus of city life. Another bonus of Elise making her try things.

Nessa let go of Elise's hand and sat forward to be heard over the noise of the tavern. "So, what do you do for a living, Jac?"

"I'm a blacksmith. An' hope to be one for as long as I can 'fore factories an' their new, fancy steam-powered machines takes the place of my skills an' my forge," he replied with a sigh.

"Aye, and ye can see what we three do," Sanjero said, indicating their clothes. "What about ye? How do ye earn yer coin?"

Some hair had broken loose from Nessa's braid and was tickling her cheek. She was about to brush it away when she felt Elise's gentle fingers caress it into place behind her ear.

That's nice. She wants me to be able to focus on answering the question. So thoughtful.

"I'm a glassblower's apprentice for Master Brownlee and… well, the other Master Brownlee. Elise is working for a printer at the moment. The way things are going, we might end up having to compete with factories one day, too. It seems like they can make machines do just about anything these days."

Jac nodded soberly. "Aye, but it still needs people to put in the blood, sweat, an' tears."

Fyhre cleared her throat and spoke for the first time. "I'm thirsty. Want more ale. I s'pose ye'd like me to ask the barmaid to bring us a pitcher an' two more glasses?"

"Yes, please," Elise piped up immediately.

Nessa evaluated how drunk she was. The brandy was still in her body, dimming her mind and relaxing her tired muscles. But she was sobering up. She should be able to have some ale without becoming legless.

She nodded up at Fyhre who was now standing, showing that she was as tall as she was muscular. "Yes. Ale for me too, please."

Fyhre gave a curt nod before walking off with the empty pitcher from their table.

Sanjero leaned over to be out of Fyhre's earshot. "Excuse 'er behaviour. She might seem rude, but she's just the big, silent type. She's a kitten, really. Ain't that so, Cai?"

"Aye, she certainly is. My big, grumpy kitten. So, since ye two are so steadfast on not bein' flirted with, are ye lovebirds as well?" Cai asked in a low, hoarse voice.

Nessa could have sworn that she physically felt Elise's gaze on her. Intently, intensively fixed on her. *Strange.*

"No. We're friends. Travel companions who have become living companions," Nessa answered.

There was a tense moment as the three peered over at Elise. Nessa looked over, too, and found Elise examining her fingernails very raptly.

Suddenly, Cai laughed. It was a raspy laugh, almost like a cough. Nessa saw that Cai was still looking at Elise who appeared to be rolling her eyes and laughing back.

"Am I missing something amusing?" Nessa asked.

Jac watched her with what looked like pity. "Ye certainly seem to be missin' somethin', sweetest heart."

Nessa was about to ask what when Fyhre came back with two stacked glasses and a large pitcher filled with dark brown ale. It smelled like bread and sweet spices.

"Ah, Goblin's Tavern ale. The quickest way to get a meal, get drunk, clean out yer belly, and wreck half yer mind – all in one badly washed glass," Sanjero said.

"Ordered another pitcher. Barmaid will be bringin' it over soon," Fyhre muttered.

She sat down and began to fill everyone's glasses. The ale ran out before she got to Cai and she mumbled, "Sorry, my cherished."

"No bother. Me an' our two new friends will be gettin' the fresh stuff from the next pitcher," Cai said with a smile and a nod to Elise and Nessa.

Sanjero swallowed a mouthful and said, "Ha! This stuff ain't never been fresh, mate. T'was born gritty an' well-aged."

The barmaid brought over another pitcher. Fyhre thanked her and took it to fill the three empty glasses.

"To new acquaintances," Elise said as she lifted her glass in a toast.

They all echoed the toast, with Fyhre only mumbling the last word. Then they drank deep. Nessa found that the ale didn't taste as much of bread as it smelled. It was earthy, thick, and tasted of spices and honey. She liked it. Out of the corner of her eye she saw Elise make a face which showed that she didn't.

Jac laughed. "It'll taste better after the third glass, Miss Elise. Even yer posh soundin' tongue will get used to it."

Elise held up her glass. "If it gets me inebriated, then yes, I believe I can get used to just about anything."

With chuckles and clinked glasses, they had another toast to that and another large gulp of the cellar-chilled ale.

Nessa heard a gruff, very obviously drunk voice behind her say, "Hey, 'scuse me. Me an' me mates over there have been lookin' at yer scruffy crew. We saw three women an' two men an' then we saw ye." He pointed to Cai. "We have a bet goin' on if ye're a lad or a lass. Settle the bet for us."

They heard laughter and cheering from the table over, clearly the drunken man's friends.

Cai, looking like this happened twice a day, sat back and smiled. "I'm not sure what that matters. Or if it's any of yer business, friend. Say ye all lost the bet and I'm a goblin!"

Both Nessa's table and the drunken man's erupted in laughter. Nessa assumed that would settle it, the drunk would stagger back to what looked like a glass of brandy and they could return to talking. Sadly, the drunk man wasn't smiling. He drew himself up to his full height and his sunburnt, wrinkly face frowned to a mess of reddish creases. His grey factory uniform was just as creased and had stains down the front.

"Don't ye be tellin' me what is or is not my business. Answer the gods-cursed question," he snarled at Cai.

A tense and uncomfortable mood crept in. People at the surrounding tables were casting wary glances, squirming, and scowling. Even the harpsichord seemed to sound less joyous.

Cai blew out a long breath. "Fine, to keep the peace an' to get us all back to our drinks... I'm a little bit of both. There.

I've shared more than I liked, be pleased with that and get back to yer friends."

The drunk laughed and was just about to say something which promised to not be very nice, when Fyhre pushed her chair away and stood up.

"Go back to yer table. Let's all have a good night 'fore we have to go to bed and prepare for another shitty day of work tomorrow," Fyhre said through gritted teeth.

Now the drunk was smiling. "Lookin' for a fight, big girl?"

A little of Nessa's love for humanity drained. This was never about Cai or any bet. This man was miserable and wanted to punch his hate and venom into someone's face. She had seen this far too often in Ground Hollow. Unhappy people loved nothing better than to make others unhappy. And if they were big, brawling men who couldn't talk about their problems, they drunkenly brawled about them instead. She could see no way out of this. No matter what they did or said, this man was going to hit someone. Soon.

Elise leaned in and whispered, "This, well *he*, is gods-cursed unacceptable. Should we tell the people who work here?"

"They won't get here in time, and they might not even care. This is a big, busy place – they can't police every fight. Don't worry, this will sort itself out," Nessa replied.

She was trying to calm Elise's temper so she wouldn't cause more trouble. But this wasn't going to sort itself out. She could feel her fists clenching under the table and she was wrapping her thumb between the second and third knuckle. She remembered how to angle her wrist and was ready to throw a punch if she had to. That was the thing about being from Ground Hollow, you learned early on how to throw a punch.

"Not lookin' for anythin' but a good time and bein' left in peace. Go fight someone else, knucklehead," Fyhre answered slowly.

Her conversation with this man was the most she had spoken tonight. It was impossible to miss that her body was speaking as well. Feet planted firmly, her shoulders squared, her biceps twitching as she tensed her arms and fisted hands.

Elise clearly couldn't stand the silence. She glared daggers at the man. "This is utterly ridiculous. Surely you have better things to do with your time."

Nessa looked over at her and saw that the mask of rage was back on Elise's face. A vein pulsed in her forehead. An explosion wasn't far off. Nessa took a shaky breath and placed a warning hand on Elise's arm.

Sanjero stood up and held his hands out to the drunken man. "C'mon, mate. The two ladies on the other side of this here table are new to Nightport. Let's show 'em that it doesn't live up to its violent reputation. Let's show 'em that we city folk are more civilised than the country-dwellers."

Sanjero was smiling kindly at the would-be brawler and to Nessa's surprise, the wrinkled, soused man smiled back. Then he threw a jab which hit Sanjero square in the jaw. Nessa was surprised it had hit home considering how the man could barely stand up without swaying. He must have some practise at this. Even over the din in the tavern, Nessa heard the blow connect. Sanjero's head flew back and he lost his footing, half from the punch and half from the surprise, by the looks of it.

Fyhre didn't hesitate. She clocked the drunken man straight in the chest with her fist. The man coughed and splattered before he began to scream obscenities. His friends from the table next to them were on their feet in an instant and one of them rounded on Cai and Fyhre.

Wheels were set in motion. It was easy to see how this would play out. They'd all be covered in spilled ale, splattered blood, and bruises soon enough.

Nessa saw it all happen in her mind's eye and once more

went through how to make a fist and throw a punch. But she never had to use her fists.

Lady Elisandrine Falk climbed up on the table... and screamed. She screamed so loud that it would have shattered her ale glass if it hadn't been so thick. It was a good thing that it didn't shatter, because she was clearly gearing up to use it. She threw the glass, contents and all, in the face of the drunken man. The ale went all over him and the heavy bottom of the glass hit him on the bridge of his nose. After doing serious damage to his nose and forehead, the thick glass fell to the ground and cracked in two.

The drunken man screamed. The scream wasn't as high-pitched as Elise's but just as loud. He covered his heavily bleeding nose with his hands and, with a wobble, fell to his knees.

When his scream died out, Elise used the shocked pause to her advantage. She put her hands on her hips and loudly and clearly said, "We do not want a fight. We wanted some drinks and to make some new friends in peace. As that is not likely to happen, we simply want to leave here unharmed. So, I and my friends are going to walk out of this tavern and then you can all fight, or make insulting bets or whatever it is you wish to do."

She stepped off the table with poise, took Nessa's hand and led them out the door. Walking, but doing so briskly. Nessa saw that Fyhre, Cai, Jac, and Sanjero followed suit.

"How in the name of the gods did you know how to do that?" Nessa asked.

"What? Stand on a table, scream, and throw the nearest thing in the face of someone who annoyed me? Normal day at court, heartling," Elise said with a shrug.

They were almost at the door when one of the drunken man's friends, a tall, gangly man with greasy hair, decided that he wouldn't let them leave so easily. He came running after them. They all rushed out into the street with the angry, lanky man right behind them. When he made it out to the street, he was met by a nicely crafted, burgundy leather boot which was extended out to trip him. He fell face first onto the cobbled street with a mighty thud. He rolled onto his back, groaning while wiping blood and splotches of horse manure off his face.

Nessa turned to look at who had tripped up their attacker.

"Why am I not surprised that you two have managed to find yourselves some real Nightport trouble?" Asked a grinning Hunter Smith.

Elise didn't bother replying or greeting Hunter. She was busy using her own boot. The much smaller, heeled black boot was firmly placed on the fallen man's neck.

"If you move, I will stand on your throat. I might not weigh much, but I wager that my bodyweight will be enough to crush your windpipe. The same will happen if any of your buffoon friends in the doorway come out here."

The last words were directed at the drunken brawlers standing in the doorway, staring open-mouthed at what was happening to their friend. Clearly, this fight wasn't turning out the way they expected. Clearly, they had never met Elise.

"I might also mention that I have this," Hunter said and pulled a long, gleaming knife from a hidden sheath inside his coat.

The men looked from Elise to Hunter and then backed up, grudgingly retreating into the tavern.

"I'll stay down. Just get yerself off my neck, lass," the lanky man spluttered.

With some hesitation, Elise stepped off him. He stayed on the ground, wiping away more of the blood pouring from a gash on his chin.

Elise adjusted the complicated flares on the lower part of her dress which created the traditional bell shape. "Good evening, Hunter, thank you for the assistance."

"Looks like you did not require it," Hunter said merrily, tucking the knife back into its hiding place.

As if following unheard orders, they all quickly, but with dignity, walked further down the road. They heard the lanky man scramble up and presumably back into the tavern. Soon they had a safe distance between themselves and the Goblin's Tavern.

Nessa laughed. "Fancy running into you, Hunter! What are you doing here?"

"I go where the action is." He bowed to the group. "Allow me to introduce myself. Hunter Smith, the night-time version, at your service. If you want gambling - I know the best dens. If you want drinks - I know the least toxic taverns. If you want adventure - I know of things that do not quite fall within the law but that will make your night very *memorable*."

"Mm, and I'm sure all these places pay you handsomely for gatherin' up some customers for 'em?" Cai asked.

"A man must eat, gorgeous," Hunter said. He looked Cai up and down with over-exaggerated appreciation.

Nessa caught Elise rolling her eyes at him and bumped her shoulder to keep her from saying anything.

"Well, at least now we know what it is you do at night," Nessa said.

"I did not explain that to you before? Strange. I could have sworn I did," Hunter mumbled, busying himself with wiping imaginary lint off his burgundy tail coat.

"Hang on, I know ye! Ye took me to that there card game by the port last week," Jac said excitedly. "I made a killin' that night. Enough to buy new tools an' a romantic meal for me an' the better 'alf."

"Aye, sadly that 'romantic meal' gave me a bad case of the shi… hrm… food poisonin'. If my memory serves, Jac got the name of the restaurant from ye as well," Sanjero added with a glare at Hunter.

He sounded furious. Probably as much due to the memory of the food poisoning as the pain from the blow he had taken. Nessa looked closer. Sanjero didn't look particularly injured but it was likely that one hell of a bruise was starting to form as they spoke.

"Ah, well I cannot take responsibility for everything that is done in these locales," Hunter said. "This is Nightport, simply walking the streets is a risk. Although, tis a risk worth taking. As you have outstayed your welcome at the Goblin's Tavern, perhaps I can interest you in some drinks and a game of Fool the Angel down at the Scarlet Crow? They have wonderful sugar pumpkin wine."

They all looked at each other.

"Well, I'm in. I can't stand havin' the night end on such an unhappy note. I want wine an' card games," Jac said with a carefree smile.

"I go where this 'ere cheerful sap goes," Sanjero said lovingly.

Cai stepped up next to them. "Aye, I'm with Jac. I need distraction."

Fyhre nodded and wrapped her sculpted arm tightly around Cai.

Elise turned to Nessa. "I am not certain what I wish to do. Part of me wants distraction, too, another part is starting to falter. There has been a lot of cleaning, drinking, and fighting tonight."

Nessa nodded and made the decision for them. "I think you need to rest. When your adrenaline wears off, you'll be exhausted. So will I, come to think of it. I'd like to take you home and make sure you are safely tucked in bed."

The others smiled and broke out in noises that sounded a lot like when you see cute kittens.

Nessa watched them, perplexed at why they all looked at them that way. Just as she was about to ask what she had missed, Cai spoke. "Ye work for the Brownlees? I reckon I know where their workshop is, it's not far from our factory. If ye don't mind the company, me, Fyhre, and Sanjero might come over after work and walk ye home. Maybe pick up Jac and Elise an' take ye all out for some food and drinks? I'd hate to have this be our first and last meetin'. Nightport people are usually lovely, an' I'd like to prove that to ye."

Nessa smiled at Cai. "I'd like that."

"Me too," Elise said before yawning.

They said their goodbyes, and the others headed for the Scarlet Crow, which Nessa assumed was a tavern. Elise and Nessa on the other hand, took tired, heavy steps towards 21 Miller Street.

CHAPTER 23
THE SCARLET CROW

It was three days later, and Elise had woken up refreshed this morning. It was amazing what having yesterday off could do. They had explored Nightport with their four new friends, singing songs and trying out interesting new food. Then she and Nessa had spent the rest of the day reading books borrowed from Cai. Even Nessa had been forced to admit that their day off was as restful as it was invigorating and not a waste of time at all.

This morning Elise had eagerly gone out for breakfast. She was awake anyway. Moreover, waking up snuggled with Nessa every morning was becoming increasingly complicated. There was far too much desire and longing coursing through her in those waking moments when she was surrounded by the feel and smell of Nessa. She had started tenderly kissing Nessa's cheek, hair, and even her shoulder when she got up each morning. Gestures which Nessa ignored.

It was odd. Elise had always believed that bedplay was the most intimate thing you could do with someone. Or several someones when she was exceedingly lucky. However, sleeping next to someone, not for erotic pleasure or even for frugality anymore as they could now easily afford another bed, but for pure affection and comfort — that was far more intimate. Nessa had seen her dream, seen her almost fall out of bed, and probably even snore. Nessa had held her when she was the most vulnerable — when she was not conscious. And vice versa. It was creating a bond. Well, the growing bond between them wasn't *solely* created by sleeping in the same bed, but it was a big culprit, she was sure of it.

This morning she could no longer stand laying snuggled up to Nessa's side. Not without being allowed to let her hands roam over the creamy planes of supple, warm skin under Nessa's nightdress.

The scent of Nessa's skin and the sugar pumpkin oil was all over Elise. She felt like could even smell it in the fragrant bakery. It was marking her as Nessa's. She found she liked that, and the new thought panicked her. This was not just for fun anymore. Had it ever been purely for fun? Nessa had always been different. Always mattered more than anyone before her. Elise's thoughts and feelings scared her and fear made her need Nessa.

She is the cause of your fear AND the remedy to it? What is wrong with you, you complicated mess of a woman?

Elise hurried to make her purchases and get back to 21 Miller Street. She was almost by the door when a young boy stopped her. Wordlessly, he shoved a package into her free hand and then ran off.

"Wait! What is this?" she shouted after his retreating form.

He was soon out of sight, so she looked down to the package he had thrust into her hand instead. It was wrapped in midnight blue paper and tied with white ribbon, just like the last mystery package. She had almost forgotten about that. That package had been smaller, only containing a bit of flint. What was in this one? She stared at it, as if her gaze could penetrate the dyed wrapping paper and see what it hid.

She hurried upstairs and into their room. Nessa was dressing and quickly pulled the laces of her britches closed when Elise rushed in.

"What's wrong? You look like gargoyles are chasing you."

"I... we... got another package. I had to hurry here so we could open it together."

Nessa frowned. "Go on, then. Open it."

Elise put the satchel with breakfast rolls and juice down on the floor. With careful hands, she unwrapped the package. Inside was a smallish bundle of fabric. It was charred and smelled awful.

Nessa came over and gently took the fabric from Elise. "This is char cloth." She looked up at Elise. "Why would anyone send us a bundle of char cloth?"

Elise bit her lip as she stared at the cloth. "Absolutely no idea. We must have been right when we said that someone has mistaken us for someone else. Or that this is some sort of prank. Perhaps sending people strange objects is some form of Nightport humour?"

"Unless this is connected to the people asking about us back in Ground Hollow."

Elise looked up at Nessa. "Why would you say that?'

"Because the questions by the men in green and the packages make two mysterious occurrences in the same short time period. One mysterious occurrence is to be expected in life. Two... now that's unlikely."

"Unlikely, yes, but far from impossible," Elise argued.

"True." Nessa turned the cloth over in her hands. "Maybe it's my lack of experience with the world, but these two things seem a little too mysterious to be coincidences."

Elise shrugged. "Be that as it may, do you have any other explanation?"

"No. Not at this moment."

"Well then." Elise tried to give a carefree smile, but she felt the corners of her mouth drop right back down. Nessa was probably right, and it bothered her that she couldn't find a solution to this mystery.

The sound of Nessa's stomach growling broke the silence.

"Um, you did bring breakfast as well, yes?"

This time Elise's smile managed to grow strong. "Yes, my ravenous little vixen. There is bread and juice in the satchel."

∾

Evening was setting in. Elise was perched on some stacked wooden crates filled with new printing types and paper, counting down the minutes until the workday ended. Archibald was passing the last moments of the day debating politics with the butcher next door. She wished he would close up a few minutes early. But no. The workday ended at seven and that was that.

Elise shook off her annoyance. She steepled her fingers and tapped them against her chin. Concentrating on what she had heard Layden say to Nessa about her being oblivious when someone wanted to be romantically involved with her. Could this be what was happening between them? Could Nessa be so clueless she didn't see her advances — all those terms of endearments, kisses, and flirtations? Or did she just not see the advances as romantic?

What if she has noticed them and simply does not care for me?

Elise shook her head. Nessa was honest and straightfor-ward. If she had noticed the gestures and didn't want a romantic entanglement, she would say so. Not keep cuddling, holding hands, and smiling that wide, loving smile.

Outside, the church bells tolled seven times and Elise jumped off the crates. Archibald came back inside, cutting the butcher off mid-sentence. He got some coins out and handed her the daily wages. She took the coins with her usual curtsy.

"You are free to go, Miss Aelin. I shall see you tomorrow morning. Try to be awake and alert. I need you at your best, not sleepwalking," he said before heading back towards the butcher.

"Of course, sir. Thank you and have a good evening."

With that, she walked out and nearly bumped into Hunter Smith. He was wearing layers of emerald green tonight. Topped with a black, velvet coat and a matching top hat.

"Hunter? What are you doing here? Honestly, are there five of you? You seem to be everywhere in this town."

He gave his roguish grin. "This city is my world, I can travel it quickly and I know how to be at the right time and place. Moreover, I was offered a pretty set of hair ties in return for finding you and fetching you to the Scarlet Crow."

"Fetching me to the Scarlet Crow?"

"Yes. The lovable gang you and Nessa found in the Goblin's Tavern are there. The tattooed Western Islander... Sanjero, is it?... traded me some of his hair ties in return for finding and handing you over. They know where Nessa works so the muscular woman went over to Brownlees' workshop to fetch her.

"Firstly, Fyhre is the name of the woman. Secondly, yes, Sanjero is the man from the Western Isles. Should I go home and wash up and change?" Elise asked, looking down at her practical dress, cardigan, and coat combination.

"My heartling, this is Nightport, not the Noble circles. No one goes to change before drowning their sorrows in greasy meat and ale."

"Oh? Ah. Um. Well. What would I know about the Noble circles?" She tried for a laugh, which sounded as false as a badly tuned fiddle, but Hunter was ignoring her completely.

He was busy smiling at a young man who had walked past him, throwing admiring glances at Hunter. Or perhaps at his clothes. When the man returned his smile, Hunter took a step closer to Elise. "I think they chose to go to the Scarlet Crow tonight as you ran into those ruffians in the Goblin's Tavern."

"Is the Scarlet Crow safer?" Elise asked.

They stepped aside, allowing a group of four city guards to pass in a hurry. Were they following the man who had looked at Hunter? Elise couldn't tell.

"Mildly, yes. The Scarlet Crow is a Nightport staple. Nearly as old as the town. Everyone goes there and management keeps the ruckus to a minimum. As long as you do not go down into the basement."

Elise edged closer to him. "Why? What is down there?"

"Another tavern, of sorts. The shadier twin of the Scarlet Crow - the White Raven," Hunter explained.

"Oh my, the people of Nightport really like their painted birds. Two taverns with colourful bird names in the same building?"

"They used to be just one tavern. The White Raven is named that because it has three of Arclid's rare white ravens. The Scarlet Crow was named such because someone once recommended the White Raven to some dignitaries and got it completely wrong. The owners liked the new name. So when the tavern was split into a secret basement for card players, arranged fights, and powder use, and a respectable old-fashioned tavern above it, they named the upper part the Scarlet Crow."

Elise gave him an appraising look, trying not to look too impressed. "My, you really do know everything about this city."

He pursed his lips. "Well, in this case it is hard not to. I was the one who got the name wrong and called it the Scarlet Crow."

She bit back a laugh. "What?"

"I was only twelve and nervous as a skitter-beetle. It was my first night working the crowds, trying to gather up clientele. No one has ever let me forget the slip-up. These days, I often have to direct punters to either the Scarlet Crow or the White Raven. And far too often... I must tell this story. Like now."

Elise suppressed a smile. "You were not joking when you said this city was your world. It seems utterly entangled with your life."

He looked grave, staring ahead. "It is. I would go as far as to say that it is a part of me. The streets of this town are like the veins in my body."

Elise made no comment, merely quirked an eyebrow.

They walked for a quarter of an hour. Hunter told her about the flock of white ravens that flew over Arclid. Always chased by hunters who knew what fortune those rare birds could bring in. The three kept in that tavern basement were a good example of that. Just one of them had cost more than Archibald would pay her for all her work. He expanded on how they were hunted, refused their freedom because of their rarity. He stopped when his voice quavered ever so slightly.

When their walk across town dragged into half an hour, Elise wondered if they shouldn't have hired a carriage to take them. Her clothes now smelled as much of road dust as printer's ink, and her hair had been blown around by the wind, making her curled bob an unruly mess.

A few more minutes and Hunter stopped. With a flourishing hand gesture, he indicated a worn black door. On the door was the faded outline of a scarlet crow in flight. No name. No sign. Only the crow. She supposed that was all that was needed if this tavern was such a Nightport staple.

"This is where I leave you," Hunter said with a faint smile.

"Not coming in with me?"

He shook his head. "No. No rest for the wicked. There is work to be done."

"Are you sure? You seem a bit drained. You bring

messages for solicitors in the day and customers for the town's nightlife in the evening. Do your legs not get tired? Or your mind?"

"This is how Nightport works," he said dismissively. "If you want power and influence here, you need to bleed and sweat for this town. She expects nothing less of her children. Work and she will favour you."

Elise tilted her head. Was he being serious? This sounded like superstition. A city was just a collection of buildings and people. It had no soul. No expectations.

She patted his upper arm. "As you wish. If you change your mind and want a glass or two, you know where we are."

"I do indeed. Good evening to you, Elise."

He took off his black top hat and bowed to her. When he put the hat back on, he peered at her. "Before I go, may I be bold and suggest something?"

She blinked a few times. "Well... yes, I suppose you may."

"Time is precious. You see that in this town. People can disappear out of your life so fast and so mercilessly. If you have someone you value, tell them so. Keep them close."

"I am not certain what you are implying here, Hunter."

"You know exactly what I mean. You told me when I hit you with my pedal cycle... you are in love with Nessa. It is becoming more and more obvious as the days pass. For everyone else but her, it would seem. Is it because she is a country lass? Or due to her low self-esteem? Either way. I would recommend you tell her how you feel. Do not let time slip away."

She pushed the notion away. "Never mind me saying you seemed drained. 'Downright morose' is a better fit."

"I just see what you have and how you do not claim it. Me – I am not free to live my life the way I wish, and, therefore, I am not likely to find love. I have as little life and freedom as those ravens." He sighed. "Or maybe it is merely the lack of a good meal. I will go get myself some bread and cheese before getting back on the streets."

She looked at his worn face. He had put light powder over the dark circles under his eyes. She could see that as clearly as she saw the frown lines by his mouth.

It is not hunger, and we both know it. It is loneliness and the pain of having to pretend to be something you are not. Poor wretch.

"Perhaps I will take your advice. We shall see how the evening goes. Thank you for caring, and I hope you have a fruitful evening. With any luck you will manage to impress your so-called mother." She pointed to the street, indicating the city in general.

He seemed to take her meaning and nodded before walking off.

Elise walked to the tall black door and opened it. Inside was a typical tavern. Not much different than the Goblin's Tavern. Well no, it was a little better kept, quieter, and painted more conventionally. And, blessedly, it had no ill-tuned harpsichord.

She soon found Fyhre, Cai, Jac, and Sanjero. She walked over to them, happy to see her new friends again. Fyhre pulled up a chair for her, and she sat down.

"Hunter found you! He's an excellent retriever," Cai said.

Sanjero put his glass down with a thud. "Aye, 'course, he did. Those were some splendid hair ties, mate."

"I shall attempt to be good enough company to make up for your loss," Elise said in a honeyed voice. She batted her eyelashes at him theatrically.

Everyone laughed and Fyhre pushed a full glass of something brown towards her. She took it and gave it a sniff. Sweet, warm, and strong. Winterberry brandy. Just like they had drunk with Layden a few nights ago.

"No ale tonight?" she asked the table in general.

"The ale 'ere is oxen-crap," Jac said. "But the food is good. We've ordered platters of smoked ribs, dried yellowfish, an' spiced bread. There's likely to be 'nuff to feed all of Arclid's Navy."

"Oh, that sounds splendid. I will join you in that and give you coin for it later, if that is acceptable."

"Aye, Miss Fancy. That is 'acceptable' indeed," Jac said, imitating her posh accent.

She grimaced at him, sticking her tongue out like a child, and got another laugh.

Jac and Sanjero shared a long kiss, seeming extra affectionate tonight. Everyone else busied themselves with their drinks. It was good brandy, Elise mused, and she drank deeply. The boring day and worry about her relationship with Nessa melted into the brandy as it warmed her stomach.

Nessa. Wait. Why is she not here?

Elise turned to Fyhre. "Where is Nessa? Hunter said you had gone to fetch her?"

Fyhre nodded. Looking at her face, Elise realised that the taller woman had extremely long eyelashes framing heavy-lidded, clear, green eyes. Elise hadn't noticed that last time. She had only gotten an impression of a big build and endless frowns.

"Went to see her at the glassblowers. Secilia Brownlee said they wouldn't be finished until late. They 'ave some big shipment to make before mornin'. I told Nessa where the tavern is. She'll join us later."

Those words had done wonders for the emptiness in Elise's chest. One that she hadn't really registered until now. Nessa was coming soon.

Was it only this morning I saw her? It feels like weeks ago.

Elise briefly placed her hand on Fyhre's forearm. "Splendid. Thank you."

Fyhre only nodded again.

"Missin' yer lady?" Cai asked, all cheeky smirk and glinting eyes.

Elise felt a muscle in her jaw twitch. "Never mind all that. I have a question, have any of you ventured downstairs to the White Raven?"

They all looked at her. She waited to see if they would let her get away with the change of topic.

Finally, Jac smiled and replied, "Aye, I have. It's a much darker place than this one. Darker than most places in Nightport, I'd say. And that is sayin' a lot."

Elise drank more of her sweet, potent brandy. She was thirsty tonight. "Sounds interesting."

Sanjero giggled. "That'll be one word for it, sweet eyes. Dangerous is another one. The customers down there be as dirty as the place is clean."

Elise tilted her head. "Clean?"

Sanjero nodded, his ebony eyes wide. "Aye. But those scrubbed white walls can't make the card games, powder takin', an' bloody fights any less dark. When the fights are bad, the blood splashes onto them there white walls. Some say the staff be needin' to wash the white ravens in their cage to get the blood off 'em at the end of the night."

"People say a lot of things," Cai said calmly.

Fyhre inclined her head. "Most of it likely to be true. Got my first black eye down there. For nothin' more than askin' for another drink."

There was a low whistle behind Elise and the words "Sounds like a lovely place" rang out in Nessa's clear voice.

Elise's heart did a somersault in her chest. Nessa was here. It was like the sun had just come out on a cold, bleak day. Elise had to resist the urge to stand up and hug her close. Maybe even kiss that soft, almond-coloured hair. She groaned quietly. How could a person's mere presence have this effect on her? How pathetic could she get?

"Good evenin', Nessa," said Jac. The others echoed the greeting and Sanjero found her a chair.

Cai grinned at her. "So, the old codgers finally freed ye, huh?"

"Yes. After some work and much marital squabbling, we finally finished the shipment. Well, the Brownlees did. I just packed it all," Nessa replied.

Fyhre, in charge of drinks as usual, handed Nessa a glass, who took it and examined it. Elise leaned in to whisper "It is winterberry brandy" in her ear. She wasn't sure why she had done that. There was no need to whisper, was there?

Admit it. Anything to get close to her, right? To smell the sugar pumpkin and the gods-cursed loveliness of her natural scent on her skin. To show the world that she is here with me.

Nessa thanked her with a nod and a smile.

Out of the corner of her eye, Elise saw Sanjero and Jac kissing and wished that this was how Nessa would have thanked her.

A moment later, a wiry barmaid brought over three large platters of food on a tray which looked like it might slip from her grasp at any moment. The faint smell of alcohol and pipe smoke in the room was overtaken by mouth-watering scents of food. Smoked meat in rich sauce, buttery fish, and the spices in the freshly made bread. As soon as the platters were on the table, everyone began eating.

Everyone but Nessa, who took out her coin purse. "How much for me and the fancy lady to get some of that?"

"Jus' buy the drink for the rest of the night an' we'll call it even," Cai said, mouth full of yellowfish.

Nessa put the coin purse away, reached over Elise, and grabbed some ribs. "Good, I'm starving," she said and tucked in.

Elise took some bread, tearing off a corner and eating it. Slowly. With some dignity.

They all ate in silence for a while. Long hours of work appeared to have made them all starving. It was such a contrast to Elise's time at court. There, food had been a pleasure and come with meticulous, time-consuming rituals. Here it was fuel, which seemed more honest somehow. More real. Everything in Nightport was raw and unmasked. It was strangely relaxing.

When she was full, Elise decided to sate her curiosity as well as she had her appetite.

"Can I ask more questions about the White Raven? I am terribly curious about the darker side of Nightport."

Jac swallowed a mouthful of ribs and dried his mouth with the back of his hand. "Sure. Ask away."

Elise pondered where to start. "Well. Is it truly as bad as it seems or is it all purely talk?"

Fyhre chuckled. "Plenty of empty talk in Nightport. To seem tough, to seem interestin'. But not when it comes to the White Raven."

Jac nodded. "Fyhre's right. Most taverns have brawls an' card games. There's even other places that put on fights an' where forbidden powders are sold over the bar — but nowhere where it's as organised an' commonplace as in the White Raven."

Sanjero put his glass down. "Aye, it has the biggest card games, the strongest imported alcohol, the most anticipated fights, an' the purest powders."

"Do you... take powders?" Nessa asked, looking from person to person.

"No," Jac said. Sanjero echoed the statement. Fyhre shook her head and then glanced over at Cai.

There was a beat of silence.

"Not anymore. Never again," Cai said quietly.

Nessa didn't reply. She merely took a big gulp, looking sheepish. From the sympathetic glances and fidgeting of Cai's three friends, Elise gathered it was time to change the subject. "So, what card games do they play down there? Fool the Angel?"

Sanjero cleared his throat. "Oh, nothin' so wholesome. It's mainly Four of a Kind and Thicket. Heavy bettin' in those games. People lose their life savings nightly."

Elise had to admit to being curious about the place. She also had to admit to being on her way to drunkenness.

She rubbed her forehead. "Is it just me or is this brandy biting unusually hard?"

Fyhre shook her head. "It's cos ye've been drinkin' most nights of the week. No time for yer body to mend."

Cai laughed. "Aye, she's right. It's a thing that most people who are new to Nightport go through. Getting used to poisonin' yer body with strong drinks with gods know what by-products in 'em. Newcomers also tend to drink a little too deep, too often. Look at yer glasses and then look at ours."

Elise looked at her glass and then Nessa's. Theirs were nearly empty while the other four had plenty in their glasses.

"Well, that won't do. Me and Elise will have to slow down. But you four have to catch up, because we're buying the next round," Nessa said with her wide, contagious smile.

Friendly laughter followed, only interrupted by Cai slapping Nessa on the arm. "I 'ave to say. Sharin' yer coin. Sharin' a room. All this and spendin' all yer time together? Ye and Elise sure do sound like ye're more than friends."

With a bewildered frown, Nessa said, "It's only practical. When we set out, we pooled what we had and stuck together. Why should we change something that has worked so well?"

"Why indeed," Jac said with a wink in Elise's direction.

They knew. Of course they all knew. It was obvious to anyone with eyes how she had fallen for Nessa. Elise rubbed her forehead. "So. Yes. Right. Let us go buy our first round of drinks and then you can all explain the rules of Thicket to me.

I have played Four of a Kind at…" Elise stopped herself just before she said the word 'court.' "…at parties and in taverns. But Thicket is new to me. Nessa, come with me to the bar and order the drinks?"

Elise stood up and Nessa followed suit.

"Does everyone want more winterberry brandy or should we try something new?" Nessa asked.

"Brandy's fine by me," Cai said.

Fyhre gave a quick nod.

"I reckon I'll switch to some nice, safe sugar pumpkin wine," Jac said before emptying his glass of brandy. "Ye should, too, my cherished," he said to Sanjero. A look passed between them.

Sanjero grinned wickedly. "Sounds like I'm bein' kept sober for some reason. Wine for me, please."

"We'll get a pitcher of wine and one of brandy," Elise concluded.

She headed for the bar and felt Nessa behind her. She seemed to always feel Nessa's presence, even if she couldn't see her.

They ordered and paid. Elise trying to ignore the desire to turn to Nessa and ask why she wouldn't see her as a romantic option. Or to beg for a kiss. Nessa felt so close now. Right there at her elbow. Smelling of sugar pumpkin oil and smoke from the glassblower's furnace. She was so tempting and so unattainable.

Perhaps I should stop spending so much time with her? No. Not until I dare to ask her why she will not be mine. Perhaps she simply needs me to ask. I will never know unless I…

Nessa interrupted her thoughts by waving a hand in front of her eyes. "Elise? Are you all right? You look like your mind is miles away."

"My apologies. Just thinking."

Elise grabbed the pitcher of pale yellow wine that the

barmaid gave her, leaving Nessa to deal with the brandy that was being poured out from a vat.

When they returned to the table, the topic had changed from card games to something more modern.

"They've apparently laid tracks all over Storsund. An' I read that the Storsund Trading Company wants to lay tracks in Arclid's highlands, too, all the way to the harbours there. Then the goods can be shipped across the water to their port, which'll obviously 'ave tracks. They're sayin' that it'll speed up trade 'tween the two continents," Jac said.

Sanjero's forehead furrowed, making his bald head seem to move forward. "An' those huge contraptions driven with steam go on these tracks?"

"That's what the newspapers are sayin', aye," Cai supplied.

Fyhre scowled. "Wouldn't want to travel by somethin' like that. Unsafe."

Jac and Sanjero poured wine into their glasses. Elise noted that neither of them bothered with rinsing out the brandy first. At court, no one would drink wine out of anything but a wine glass, and a clean one at that. Here there were three kinds of glasses. Tankards, either thick glass or tin, for ale. Some mystery tiny glasses, which Elise mainly saw gather dust on shelves in the taverns. And then the normal glasses which they drank from now, which could be used for any alcohol. She sighed, not certain if she was missing Highmere or if it was brandy and sadness making her see her past with rose-coloured glasses. She had hated Highmere and no nostalgia over pretty glasses and social rituals could change that.

She was happier here. Here with Nessa. She brushed away thoughts of how she could be happier if she truly was *with* Nessa and took a deep drink, trying to drown the sadness taking root in her belly and spreading its cruel tendrils through her body.

They all drank in companionable silence for a while.

Cai looked up. "Somethin' else the newspapers are talkin' about is the strikes. Are we ready to take sides if the conflict comes knockin' at our factory? Ready to down tools and stop makin' the plates?" Cai's eyes were fixed on Sanjero and Fyhre.

Elise was glad that she and Nessa weren't going to be directly involved. She believed in the need for better conditions for the industry workers, but she also knew how many deaths and injuries had come out of the strikes that swept the land. It was one of Archibald Richards' favourite topics.

"Aye," Sanjero said. "I reckon we'll all stand and fight to be treated as humans. But let's not be talkin' about these serious things now. I got wine to drink and a pretty man to kiss." With that, he took a big gulp of wine and blew a kiss in Jac's direction, as if to prove his point.

Jac raised his glass. "A toast to decidin' on paths when we reach that fork in the road. And to just havin' fun tonight."

They all toasted to that and took a drink.

"Is this brandy stronger than the last batch was?" Cai asked with a grimace.

"It does taste like it, yes," Nessa agreed.

Elise took another sip. Yes, it might be stronger. Either in flavour or in alcohol procentage. Either way, it was helping her feel less hollow. Killing that sadness in her belly, or at least muting it. She took another mouthful.

"Slow down there, mate. What did we tell ye about drinkin' so much and so often?" Cai said cheerfully.

Elise raised an eyebrow and then, maintaining eye contact with Cai, drank a huge gulp.

Fyhre chuckled. "That's right. Stand yer ground. After all, it's yer head in the mornin', lass."

Out of the corner of her eye, Elise saw Jac lean in to Sanjero. He whispered something in Sanjero's ear. Whatever it was made Sanjero laugh and turn to kiss Jac's mouth. When the kiss ended, Jac cleared his throat to get attention.

"Well, my heartlings, it looks like me an' my lovely gentleman will be callin' it a night. Enjoy yerselves an' don't get into no trouble."

"I'd say the same to ye, but we all know what ye two are goin' home to get into." The hoarse, gravelly nature of Cai's voice made the innuendo sound all the naughtier.

Sanjero flashed them all a wicked grin. Then he got up, took Jac's hand, and said his goodbye.

The two men walked away from the table, looking a lot less drunk than Elise felt. She was losing focus. She considered stopping, or at least slowing down. Maybe have one of the ribs? She looked at the plate where they were slowing growing cold in congealed sauce and decided against it.

Nessa touched her arm. It was a brief touch, but it almost burned. "Hey. You look strange again. Are you certain you're all right?"

Elise searched for a way to answer that honestly. She found nothing.

"I… want to drink something that will come in those tiny glasses with the slim stems. We have seen them in every tavern, but I cannot recall seeing anyone being served something in them," she mumbled, hoping all the words had been understandable.

Cai looked up at a shelf above the bar, which was filled with the little glasses. "They're only really used for sunberry essence, mate."

Nessa swallowed a gulp of brandy. "Sunberry essence? I've had lots of sunberry juice. But I'm guessing it's not the same?"

Cai gave a wry chuckle. "The juice is just a few smashed up sunberries, lots o' water, an' a dollop of honey. This stuff? It's the priciest drink ye can get yer paws on. In Nightport at least. It's five times stronger than brandy and about as much more expensive."

Nessa wrinkled her nose. "For that price it better taste

238

incredible."

Fyhre nodded. "Stings yer mouth and belly like fire. Over that it's very little ye can taste. Some sweetness, I 'spose."

Cai looked conspiratorially from Fyhre to Nessa and then to Elise.

"Want to buy some? If we all pay a bit, I reckon we can afford a glass. That way we can all 'ave a sip. Me and Fyhre haven't drunk it since one night when we got a reward for returnin' a lost little lad to his mum. We blew all the coin on a glass of sunberry essence each."

Elise worried her lip. She had drunk sunberry essence quite a few times at court. The Queen sometimes liked it as a chaser to her nightly glass of winterberry brandy.

What a spoiled life you have led. How much you took for granted.

Elise sat forward, trying to sound sober. "It occurs to me that I came here with quite a bit of coin and now that I have a weekly income, I do not need to save it as much. I can buy us at least two glasses to share."

Fyhre held up her hands. "We can't ask ye to do that."

Elise gave her a smile. "I do not care what you do or do not ask. I am buying two glasses, and I should hope you will not let me drink them both alone. Anyway, you can see it as payment for the food since the boys barely touched their drinks. Which reminds me, we still have wine and brandy. Do not gobble it all before I am back."

Cai gave a seated bow, and Fyhre actually smiled. Elise went back to the bar, happy to be able to treat her new friends. That warmth and inviting smell was at her side again. Nessa had come with her. Of course she had.

"Are you sure you want to spend your coin on this?" Nessa asked, shouting to be heard over the loud drunks at the bar.

Elise didn't look at her. "Are you certain that you do not want to ask if I want to spend *our* coin on this?"

There was no immediate reply.

Then Nessa shook her head, wide-eyed. "What? No! We pooled our income, but most of the coin we brought was yours. Spend it how you wish. I suppose I'm just being a coinless farmer's daughter. Sensible, careful, dull."

Elise immediately regretted her tone. She faced Nessa. "Don't say that. You were right to ask. It is our coin, I truly believe that, and I should have checked with you. I am a bit testy tonight. Ignore me. Would you mind if we just... blew the cobwebs off by having some sunberry essence?"

Nessa grinned, putting her hand on Elise's shoulder. "I don't mind. No more being sensible. Let's be Nightport newcomers and get drunk pretty much every night of the week."

"And on overpriced alcohol at that," Elise added with a wink.

Nessa laughed and squeezed her shoulder. It filled Elise's heart with sunshine, and for a moment the ache deep inside it was gone.

Soon they were back at the table, armed with two glasses of bright yellow liquid. Fyhre, or possibly Cai, had refilled their brandies.

Elise held up one of the glasses of sunberry essence by its stem. The light caught the thick, concentrated liquid and glinted in it. It looked almost magical. Although that was probably the brandy dimming her brain.

"Here's to extravagance!" Elise shouted.

She drank half the contents of the glass and then handed the rest to Nessa. Cai took the other glass and drank half of it before passing the glass over to Fyhre.

It was a new sort of social ritual. A mix between Elise's past in Highmere and her current life here. She had shared something with these three people, and they all seemed somehow closer to each other now.

CHAPTER 24
FASTENINGS

Hours later, Fyhre suggested they call it a night. Nessa had quickly agreed. She had watched the crowd in the Scarlet Crow change from groups of cheerful workers having a drink or two, into a much more sinister clientele. The people who were here now were in small groups, barely talking. Just scowling at the other groups. Quite a few were looking over at a small door next to the bar. A small, black door with a white raven on it.

They said goodbye to Cai and Fyhre who were heading towards their rented rooms close to the port, hand in hand. Giggling and kissing.

Nessa threw furtive glances at Elise, who was dragging her feet and singing under her breath, as they walked back to 21 Miller Street.

Why did she drink that much tonight?

Nessa had tried to keep up with her, not wanting to seem like the boring country cousin. But it had been hard to keep up as the brandy poured into the petite Noble. It had been even harder to read Elise's mood. Was it the hired men who had been asking questions about them which bothered her?

No, it had seemed localized to her, to Nessa. Again, she wondered if Elise wanted to take their relationship from friendship to bedplay. Or maybe she was bored with Nessa and her need for safety and frugality? Her thoughts muddled; it was tricky to keep one line of thought in place long enough to get answers.

Nessa swayed as she moved to make room for a man on a pedal cycle and all those musings evaporated. Her focus was on the man, who looked neat, tidy, and well-dressed. And irate, of course. Nessa wondered if he worked nights.

"You drunkards ruin this city," the man shouted as he whizzed past.

Normally, Nessa might have been offended. But the brandy, wine, and sunberry essence meant she couldn't be bothered by such things.

"My apologik… aplogi… apologies, sir. Have a lovely night," she called after him.

Elise laughed and Nessa laughed with her, not sure what they were laughing at. She seemed to be walking on clouds in a blissfully warm and dizzying world. The only thing in focus was Elise.

The walk dragged on and Nessa was relieved when they were finally home. Elise struggled with the key to their room and mumbled, "We have to stop drinking so much."

"Sure! Why don't you start?" Nessa said. She was aware that this made no sense but it didn't seem to matter.

The keys finally did their job. Elise walked in and, with clumsy hands, lit the lamp on the dresser, giving the room a small source of light.

Nessa followed her in, shutting the door behind them while Elise took her coat, boots, and socks off. The closing of the door was loud; Nessa had pulled it shut too hard. She shushed the door, making Elise giggle. So, Nessa shushed her, too. The walls weren't thick enough to guarantee that the people in the other rooms could sleep with them thudding doors and giggling. She was aware that the people in the other rooms had probably stopped at a glass of wine if they went to a tavern tonight. And probably gone to bed hours ago.

Nessa took off her coat while humming quietly. Elise pulled her knitted cardigan off and threw it onto the dresser. Then, fumbling, Elise began to undo the many clasps on the side of her high-collared dress. It was an impractical design for a garment; Nessa had said so before. The clasps started at the side of her neck, went down her chest, around her armpit and then down Elise's side, ending at the hip.

Nessa got closer, wanting to help Elise who was struggling with the small metal fastenings. When Nessa was standing right by her side, she saw that there was an ink stain on Elise's ring finger. Without thinking, she wet her own fingers on her tongue and rubbed at the stain.

She looked up at Elise to say that the stain was gone and get a 'thank you.' Instead she found a strange look on Elise's face. She reeled a little. Confusion and alarm were trying to creep into the drunken fog of her mind.

"I wanted to help you with the clasps," Nessa said quietly.

"Then help me," Elise replied. There was a slight slur in her speech, alarming Nessa regarding their drunkeness and lack of control. Sadly, thoughts came and went in her mind like passing clouds, meaning that the alarm was gone as soon as it had arrived. Left was a feeling that everything was rosy and that Elise needed help with these silly clasps. Wonderful Elise. Of course she would help her.

Nessa watched her own hands go to Elise's throat and start undoing the fastenings. Now she understood why Elise had struggled, and she thanked the gods that corsets and bustles had gone out of fashion, more complicated garments would have been the last thing they needed. She bit her tongue, trying to focus. It was like her fingers were reacting a few moments after her mind. When she thought she was on her way to the next clasp, her fingers were still struggling with the old one. The dim light wasn't helping. But she was halfway through now, by Elise's ribs, which were undulating with her quick breaths.

Nessa kept undoing the fastenings, trying to focus her eyes on the small metal things which appeared to be moving. As the clasps opened, the dress fell away. Over Elise's warm, round shoulder, then over her petite chest. Now it looked more like a skirt. As she undid another set of those pesky fastenings, Nessa felt more and more of Elise's warm skin under her hands.

That was when it hit Nessa. *Skin.* She was seeing and feeling skin. Where was Elise's undershirt?

"Why are you naked? I mean, under the dress. On the top of your... body," Nessa said, barely understanding her own meaning.

"I stopped wearing an undershirt to work. I get too warm manoeuvring the printing press in these thick dresses. I can take a cardigan off when I get to work; I cannot do that with an undershirt."

Nessa felt like a cannonball had hit her.

"Are you... are you... too warm for nether coverings, t-too?"

Elise made a noise, somewhere between a hiccup and a laugh. "No, I am wearing those. I bought lots of them when I purchased my new work clothes. Have you not noticed that when I undress every night?"

Nessa shook her head, a mistake as it made everything more out of focus. "Of course not. I never look at you when you change. It'd be rude and improper."

"But welcome."

"What?" Nessa asked.

Elise swayed where she stood and put her hand on the wall

to steady herself. "Nothing. I am wearing nether coverings. However, they are shorter and thinner than yours."

Nessa nodded. She didn't trust herself to find words. She was starting to feel very warm. And the soft, fuzzy feeling in her belly was growing into something more energetic. Something more dangerous.

She carried on with the clasps. Undoing them along the bottom of Elise's thin waist. Trying not to look at Elise's breasts which must be exposed. She focused on the clasps, ignoring her racing heart. More and more skin appeared, and it felt like magic.

When Nessa reached the hip and undid the last three clasps there, she saw the nether coverings underneath. Grey, sewn with black thread as a low-cost form of decoration. She heard herself gasp and with shame understood that she was getting aroused. Not by the nether coverings, but by who was in them.

Silly fool, she is not for you. Wait, why was that? Oh yes. Doesn't want love. You do. Right. Yes. Where was I? Why is she the most beautiful thing I have ever seen? Prettier than a sunset, more tempting than honey tarts. This hurts. I want to kiss her. Gods help me.

She pulled her hands away and took a step back. "The clasps are done now."

Elise wasn't looking at her. Her eyes were closed. She was still swaying where she stood.

"Thank you." Elise let go of the wall and clumsily tugged the dress down until it lay in a large pool around her feet. She stepped out of it and picked it up.

Nessa watched as she smoothed it out and put it on the dresser, on top of her cardigan. Nessa could no longer stop herself, she took in the sight of Elise's bared breasts. The skin of lightest brown and the nipples of rosiest pink. The nipples were rather big for such small breasts, and Nessa found herself drawn to them as if they were trying to get her attention. She cursed her drunk brain and squeezed her eyes closed.

"You can look. In fact, I want you to look. I want you to see me. I want you to do more than just see me."

Nessa opened her eyes. Elise was standing before her, dressed only in those mist-grey nether coverings. Some of her hair was slicked to the underside of her jaw and Nessa tried to focus on that. All to avoid the shapely legs, those tempting breasts, and everything between. Her eyes still betrayed her, slipping down to the slim neck, the pronounced collar bones, and then to those beautiful breasts again.

"Please do not look away, Nessa. See them. See me. I am more than someone to travel with or a cuddly toy to warm your bed. I want to warm *you*, inside and out." Elise still sounded drunk, but more in control now. Utterly earnest.

Nessa swallowed hard. Her heart was thudding in her chest, so hard that she could hear the blood rushing in her ears. She didn't know what to say. What to do.

Elise tilted her head and then sighed deeply. "May I at least kiss you? Please?"

Nessa had no words. Her mouth felt dry and useless, unable to form the simplest of syllables.

She nodded. Once with hesitation. Then again, with conviction.

Elise took her face in her hands. Nessa felt her feet go up on tiptoe to be the same height as Elise. It wasn't done consciously, it was just her body reacting, her mind left somewhere far behind.

Then Elise's lips were on hers. They were eager, demanding, and velvety soft. Nessa groaned into the kiss and parted her lips, granting Elise access to her mouth. The world was slipping away. Or perhaps spinning out of control. It didn't matter. Only Elise's lips against her own, Elise's hands on her cheeks, Elise's breasts pressed against her own... only that mattered. Suddenly her clothes bothered her, they were keeping her and Elise's skin apart. They had to go. She pushed away, making Elise look mortified.

"I need to be undressed," she explained.

Elise's face changed from concern to determination. "Yes. You do. Come here."

She pulled Nessa closer and quickly undid the laces at her neckline. Then she pulled the shirt over Nessa's head, barely waiting for her to raise her arms properly. The undershirt suffered the same fate. They were thrown next to the bed, discarded as punishment for separating the two bodies that were so eager for each other.

Elise began to undo the fastening on Nessa's trousers. Nessa groaned as she felt Elise's breaths hit her bare shoulders and breasts. The whooshes of air were hot and rapid. Part of her wanted to tell Elise to breath properly so she didn't become dizzy. But she knew she couldn't form the words. Not anymore. Between the drink, the desire, and the deeper feelings which prodded at her heart, she couldn't even tell Elise that she was still wearing her boots.

Instead she gently removed Elise's hands and bent over to undo the laces on her boots. Her vision filled with smooth, sand-coloured skin and black hair, as Elise crouched down to help her. She soon had the laces undone and Nessa kicked the boots off, not caring that they went flying across the room. The socks soon followed. Nessa did her part, pulling her trousers down and then off.

Now they were both in only nether coverings. Nessa felt a hot wave of shame to see how much longer and dowdier her own were. But Elise didn't seem to even see them. She was staring a line from Nessa's eyes, all the way down to her breasts, and then back up again. When her gaze dropped once more, her hands followed it to the breasts.

As she cupped them, she whispered, "I knew they would

be too big for my hands. I have imagined this so many times. Gods, how I adore your curves."

It didn't surprise Nessa that Elise had thought about this. Still, Nessa's drunken mind was flattered. She might never get Lady Elisandrine Falk to be her spouse. But she was at least the beautiful woman's wet dream. And soon-to-be actual lover. That would do fine for now.

Elise leaned in to kiss Nessa's neck. Tenderly at first, but as her grip on Nessa's breasts tightened, the kisses turned rougher. Nessa felt teeth raking over the column of her throat. It made her aware of all the sensations in her body, the rush of blood, the increased sensitivity. And that there was now an ache between her thighs that demanded to be acknowledged. She hadn't let that part of herself be touched for a long time, not even by herself. She wasn't sure why. Right now, it seemed like that was all her world revolved around.

Distantly, she felt Elise tug her nether coverings off and when she looked down on them on the floor, Elise's were next to them. A fire lit in Nessa's belly. Elise was naked. And hers to enjoy.

She drew her eyes over the naked woman, feeling almost animal in her hunger. She grabbed Elise's waist and manoeuvred her over to the bed. Elise let herself fall, groaning "yes" as she landed.

Nessa was on top of her, and all over her, faster than she could register. She was tasting it all. Remnants of sugar pumpkin oil on Elise's pulse points, a hint of salt from the heating skin between her breasts, another ink stain on a slender finger. She even dipped her tongue into the tangy slickness between Elise's legs. She felt a strange need to sample all of it before deciding where to start. In the end, that choice was taken from her.

"I need you on top of me. I need your mouth on mine," Elise croaked.

Nessa obliged without question. She kissed her, hurriedly and passionately. As her tongue slid into Elise's mouth, two of her fingers slid into the soaked heat she found between Elise's legs.

Elise opened fully to her in both places. Taking Nessa's breath away with her exquisite silky warmth. As she pushed her fingers in and out, she felt Elise move her pelvis, rubbing her swollen pearl against Nessa's wrist.

As she made love to the woman who had become the most important person in her life, Nessa felt overwhelmed. Bewildered and filled with feverish thoughts. That didn't matter right now. All that mattered was the whimpering woman writhing underneath her. Still, the thoughts haunted her. What was this? It was purely fun for Elise, right? Just bedplay. That's all Elise wanted. All she needed. But then why did Elise kiss her shoulder so tenderly? Why did she whisper her name so reverently almost every time Nessa entered her?

She pushed all thoughts away and focused on leading Elise further into pleasure. Rolling her fingers around, curling them to find every groove, and to push against the most sensitive spot inside her lover. Soon she felt Elise grab hold of her shoulders and shudder against her body. Pushing herself tightly against Nessa's wrist until oily, hot, wetness trickled down it. Elise yelped and then buried her face in Nessa's neck. Her breathing was lightning fast and her heart beat so hard that Nessa felt it as if it was in her own chest.

Soon Elise softened, her whole body seeming to relax. She was silent until a single word slipped past her lips, brushing against Nessa's neck. The word was "again."

Nessa smiled. She could make a joke about spoiled ladies of court. Snigger and call Elise greedy. She could claim her own right to go next. She could do these things. After all, that ache between her legs was still there. But what she most wanted to do was take Elise again. Make Elise give that high-pitched yelp of pleasure again. But this time, she wanted to see her.

"Yes. But only if I get to watch you. Only if you are on top," Nessa whispered back.

She hadn't thought any further than that. No details on the position. She just wanted to watch Elise get her next dose of pleasure.

Elise's nostrils flared, and her golden eyes glinted. For a brief moment, she looked like the hungry animal Nessa had felt like earlier. Then this waif of a woman managed to roll them over and straddle Nessa without any apparent effort.

Nessa felt the air leave her lungs as she was pushed over and into the mattress by the goddess sitting on her, coating the hair on her pubic mound in hot liquid.

The straddling woman began to move. Pushing herself back and forth over the top of Nessa's sex. She closed her eyes, and Nessa watched the pleasured expression change to frustration.

"Not... enough... friction," Elise panted.

Nessa didn't know whether to apologise or to offer her hands and mouth. As usual, she didn't have to worry. Lady Falk would know what she wanted and ask for it. Or in this case, go for it.

Elise moved so that she was a little to the right. Pressing her wetness, especially the hard nub, against Nessa's right hip bone. Nessa had always hated how much her wide hip bones protruded, but now she was grateful for it. It was as if they had been made that way to pleasure Elise.

Elise began to thrust herself against it. Hot, wet liquid coated Nessa in a new place, and it felt natural, dirty, and sacred in a strange blend.

Nessa grabbed Elise's hips and helped her roll them, making the ride faster and smoother. Elise was panting and moaning now, grabbing Nessa's shoulders to steady herself. It felt possessive. As if she was holding Nessa still for her. Claiming her body. Nessa couldn't remember the last time she felt such a rush. Elise looked confident and dominant, moving so fast that a sheen of sweat coated her slender torso. The effect was making Elise look like a gleaming goddess in the process of claiming her worship. And Nessa was so ready to worship her.

Elise's eyes rolled back, and she gave another of those high yelps. She collapsed onto Nessa, nearly knocking their heads together as she fell.

Nessa held her again. Held her tight as she whispered, "You're magnificent, Elise."

"I am exhausted. That is what I am." She looked up into Nessa's eyes, gold meeting grey. "But not too exhausted to claim what I have been wanting since that night you climbed the castle wall for me. I am having your body. And I am going to do bad but delicious things to it," Elise panted hotly against her ear.

Nessa felt her sex respond, twitching and clenching. She must be soaking the sheets below them.

Elise's hand snaked down between their bodies, and her fingers found their target. Nessa gasped as they gently felt around, getting their bearings. All too soon, they stopped.

"Wha... what happened?" Nessa whined.

"I realise that I have to taste you. Everything that comes out of Ground Hollow is delicious, be it grains or fruit. I bet the women are just as flavoursome."

Elise shimmied down her body, kissing Nessa's overheated skin as she went.

"Spread your legs," Elise growled, her voice rougher than usual.

Nessa didn't have to think, her legs parted by themselves. She was rewarded for her obedience immediately. A hot tongue sliding against the neediest part of her. Moving from up across the slit and over the hood and then back again. Over and over in a maddening rhythm.

Nessa felt her breath pick up. Her heart thudded against her ribcage in time with the tongue strokes. Those strokes were like a metronome, steady and measuring out her pleasure in beats. Then the pace picked up as Elise's mouth fastened onto her clitoris. Nessa's heart pounded and her breathing raced towards a peak, making her dizzy and out of control. Climbing, climbing. Her vision filled with colours and her mouth was dry from the hot breaths. The race to the top came to the part where Nessa felt that if she breathed any harder, she'd pass out. She had reached the top of the mountain. It was time to stop that race and calm both heart and breathing down again.

"That's it. Yes. Stop. Thank you, heartling," Nessa said breathlessly. She sounded like she had run here all the way from Ground Hollow. And her body felt as if she had, too. Her lungs ached from the hard use, and her heart was grudgingly agreeing to calm back down.

When she was settled enough to focus on something other than calming down, she craned her neck to look at Elise. She found Elise looking up at her. Propped up on her elbows, chin wet and light amber eyes searching Nessa's face.

"What?" Nessa panted.

"Why did you ask me to stop?"

"I had finished."

Elise looked confused. They searched for answers in each other's eyes for a moment.

"Surely you did not climax? You cannot have."

"Oh. Why the blazes not?" Nessa asked.

"There was no... reaction. No clenching inside your entrance, no extra liquid, no noises, no tension in your body during it, and no release of tension in your muscles now. You seemed more like you exercised than orgasmed."

Elise furrowed her brow before continuing. "I have had

quiet lovers who imploded rather than exploded, but I have never had a lover who did not have at least have the tiniest hint when climaxing. Unless I missed something?"

Nessa shrugged. She tried not to sound annoyed as she said, "My orgasms are different than some people's. It just doesn't seem to affect me much."

"What do you mean?"

"I mean that the tension builds and builds, it gets increasingly hard to breath, and then everything feels sort of overwhelming. That's when I know it's time to stop. I push myself full speed into the pleasant feeling, making myself really think about enjoying it. And then it's, well, as I said – time to stop."

Elise's brow furrowed deeper. "Time to stop?"

"Yes. Because after that it gets to be uncomfortable or hard work. So I stop where it's sort of... almost too much. That's my climax."

Elise bit her lower lip. "Heartling. I... do not mean to lecture you about your body, you know it best, but I do not believe that is a genuine climax."

Now Nessa was seriously annoyed. What right did Elise have to talk about this? Why did it matter? It was fine the way it was. Nothing to be dug into. A feeling of discomfort rushed through her... and there was still that infernal ache between her legs. Still throbbing.

Elise's eyes radiated kindness. "Can I please try again?" She kissed the inside of Nessa's thigh, more tenderly than sexually. "Perhaps this time, when it becomes overwhelming — do not think about it or try to push yourself into something — simply tell me. And we will shift what we are doing and see if that makes... something else happen."

Nessa wanted to protest. But something deep inside her reminded her that her reactions to coupling had always seemed more muted than that of her lovers. She had not wanted to think more about it. She now realised she had – deep down – worried that something was wrong with her.

She gave a curt nod and laid back comfortably. Soon she felt Elise's precise tongue moving through her slickness again. She seemed to be making love to every part of Nessa now, kissing, sucking, and even nibbling. Nessa swore loudly, not sure why. Elise's hands caressed her hips, her sides, and up to rest at the lower parts of her breasts. They soon found her nipples and she began flicking at them as her tongue did the same with Nessa's clit. Incredibly fast. Incredibly pleasurably.

Nessa found herself fighting to stay in control and willed herself to let go. To not analyse what Elise was doing, or what her heart and breathing was up to. Not to hurry herself. She reminded herself that it was all fine. That she was safe. That they were both enjoying this. She tried to concentrate on the flicking sensations. She found her brain diverting from the path, thinking about how she was sweaty and if the tongue on her clit might feel nicer if it was a fraction slower.

Am I taking too long? Is her tongue getting tired? Should I pretend to have climaxed? Scream a little or something?

She curled her hands into fists as she tried to shut her thoughts down.

She thought about the flicking as something that was happening out of her control. As if the body she was in was not truly her own. She observed it and found it steeped in pleasure. In fact, her blood thrummed with it. She simply had to take her mind out of the picture. Without consciously deciding to, she busied it with trying to imagine what they would look like to an outsider. Her pale body lying flat and quivering ever so slightly, legs spread obscenely wide. And between them… the most beautiful woman in the world. Her stunning features against Nessa's wetness and that darkly pink tongue flicking so fast over her erect nub.

Suddenly, seeing that so clearly, the sensation filled Nessa.

She wasn't aware of her heart beat anymore, nor her breathing. Nor did her brain seem to be working on anything besides picturing that erotic dance that the tip of Elise's wet tongue was doing against her equally wet clit. So pretty, so dirty, so perfect.

Then there was a sensation that was new to Nessa. It was like a tug on a thread which threatened to unravel her. It was extreme bliss but also a little frightening. Like staring into an abyss and feeling equal amounts of thrill and fear at the fall.

A moment, or maybe an eternity, passed. Then Nessa's blood rushed with energy as that thread let go and the stitch began to unravel completely, skittering through her belly and darting down her thighs in overtaking spasms of pure pleasure. Her eyes squeezed shut and every muscle in her body seemed to tighten. It was like she couldn't breathe or that she no longer needed to. She wasn't sure. Everything was blinding light and indulgent rapture. Distantly, she noticed her hands grab onto whatever they could reach and her legs kick, but couldn't control them. All she could do was ride the wave of pleasure cresting over her and hope she wouldn't drown. She heard herself moan, guttural, like an animal. Over and over again. Powerless to stop.

Another moment. Another eternity.

Then her mind began to return to the world around her. She felt control over her body seep back in. Her entire being filled with heat, light, and tiny bursts of satisfaction.

Elise looked up at her, lips wet with Nessa's essence and her eyes almost as wet with emotion. "Oh, my treasured one. *That* was a climax. And as I secretly presumed, you are the explosion type, not the implosion type. That is the way you are, private, but when you choose a person, you gift them with every thought and feeling you have. It makes sense that you would be the same in bed. You are exquisite. Are you all right? Did I push you further than you were ready to go?"

"You…" Nessa stopped to take a deep breath. "You pushed me right over the edge. And the fall was glorious."

Elise smiled bashfully, and kissed Nessa's lower stomach. She moved up, trailing kisses until her chin and lips felt dry against Nessa's skin. When their mouths were finally reunited, Nessa could taste herself on Elise's tongue and felt a jolt of belonging. It was such a shame that Elise was solely looking for fun and would soon move on, like a butterfly in summer. Nessa could have gotten used to this every night for the rest of her life.

Exhaustion numbed her mind. She struggled to say something but was shushed by Elise.

"Sleep. We will talk in the morning," Elise mumbled before snuggling up. Her head resting heavily and reassuringly on Nessa's chest.

Nessa didn't have time to agree. She fell into a deep sleep, fuelled by sexual satisfaction and an alcoholic haze.

CHAPTER 25

THE MORNING AFTER

Elise rubbed her forehead, eyes still closed protectively against the morning. She and Nessa had not really been in the right state of mind to make a decision like that last night. Nevertheless, they had been equally tired and drunk; neither had possessed any self-control. And now it was done. They had made love, and it had been wondrous. Elise had fallen far too deep. Last night had been the point of no return, and she had galloped past that point riding a wave of desire, love, and alcohol. *Stupid.* She breathed in through her nose.

Somewhere in her chest, something was buzzing. Like the delicate wings of a thousand minute butterflies. The sensation was starting to take over from the regret. Even if it had been a mistake – because it was too soon and because they had not talked it through – it had been wonderful. It was the the most profound connection that something physical had ever given her.

She braved opening her eyes. Nessa was lying next to her, on her back as well. She was breathing deeply, almost snoring. She wiggled her nose a little, probably because a few strands of almond hair were tickling it. With gentle fingers, Elise caressed the long hairs away from her face. She felt her cheeks hurt from how much she was smiling.

She kissed Nessa's soft cheek a few times and saw her face go from soft repose into awakening. She cuddled close while Nessa woke up properly.

"Good morning," Nessa mumbled.

"Good morning, heartling. Sleep well?"

Nessa grinned as she rubbed her face. "As soundly as you always do after a long night of drinking and fucking."

The coarse, countryside word ground against Elise's nerves. She decided not to comment on it. "I am glad you slept well. I have been thinking, and I believe we should both take the risk of not going into work today. We need to catch up on some sleep. More importantly, we need to discuss how this will affect our relationship."

Nessa turned her head and kissed Elise's temple. Her body language and facial expression radiated languid relaxation.

"Discuss? Nothing to discuss, was there? We got far too drunk and let off some steam. It's good that it was with each other. Saved you the bother of finding your way home from some other woman's rooms. Oh, and I need to hurry to work soon."

Every muscle in Elise's body tensed. "Pardon?"

"Well, I can't risk losing my apprenticeship. I'm going to get up and get ready in a minute. You should, too," Nessa said while stretching.

Elise sat up, quickly enough to give herself a head rush and start the hangover crashing in her skull. "I am not sure I like the way you are speaking. How dare you?"

Nessa blinked a few times as she yawned. "What do you mean? Take it easy. Lay back down, and I'll go get us breakfast."

Elise balked at her tone. As if nothing had happened

between them last night. Like they hadn't shared everything. She stared at Nessa. Could she really be this clueless? Could last night truly have meant nothing to her?

There it was. The pounding of her rage beginning to sound. She grabbed onto the pillow and squeezed. "I mean that you are being equally thoughtless and dumb as the old cliché of a country wench. I thought you were better than that."

That seemed to wake Nessa up. She stared straight into Elise's eyes. "What did you just call me?"

"Thoughtless and dumb."

Nessa sat up. Elise tried her best not to look at her body, which she had fallen in love with last night. Almost as much as she had fallen in love with Nessa's heart and soul this past fortnight.

Nessa looked confused at first. Hurt maybe. Then she scowled, maintaining eye contact. "I see. And what were your reasons for that? Other than becoming belligerent when you're hungover and hungry. Is it that I refuse to be late for work, or even skip work, and risk losing my apprenticeship? Surely whatever conversation you think we should have can wait until we come home. It can't be that important."

Elise's head now felt like it was filled with more pain and rage than brains.

"How can you sit there and say that? After what we shared last night? After what you allowed me to see? To be the first to make you... and... and... to see you so vulnerable," Elise spluttered.

She knew she wasn't making sense, but she was just one ridiculous comment away from being overcome with rage.

Gods help us then, because I will certainly say things we shall both regret.

Nessa pursed her lips. "I don't understand your meaning. What's made you angry this time? Was it something I said last night? I was horribly drunk and may have run my mouth. I'm sure there's quite a bit I have forgotten."

Elise jumped up, not caring about the cold of the room against her naked body. She only cared about shaking some sense into the frowning woman on the bed.

"Nessa. I know you are clueless about how things work in the world, but surely you cannot be so clueless that you have not seen what has been happening here? Everyone sees it! You must see it."

"I 'must' nothing. Don't tell me what I see and don't try to muddle my mind by saying that everyone sees something I don't. Especially not when it's fogged over by drink and sleep. It's not fair," Nessa shouted, her hands balling into fists at her sides.

A little voice of spite and hurt in Elise's head told her that she had hit a nerve and that she should continue. "I am not muddling your mind. But if you cannot handle conversations of this calibre, perhaps you should go back to Ground Hollow where things are simpler?"

"What? Is that what this is about? You don't believe I fit in? Because I won't play whatever game this is, I don't fit in here?" Nessa's increasingly loud voice cracked.

"Perhaps not. Maybe you are not ready to leave the sweet and innocent Ground Hollow. But..." Elise paused for effect, her rage driving her on. "You know what, while you are clue-less as a child about these things, you are not that dumb. So what is it, Nessa? Are you afraid? Is that what this is? You are ignoring what is growing between us because you are frightened?"

Nessa blanched, mouth open. "What? Growing between us? Stop. Do you mean wanting to bed me? You are the one acting strangely all the time. Furthermore, what have I done to deserve this abuse? What in the name of the gods gives you the right to speak to me like that?" Nessa stood up, too, facing

Elise. "I'm not scared, little Miss Noble. I'm realistic. I might not be worldly, but at least I live in the real world."

"Pardon?" Elise managed to get out between clenched jaws.

"I live in the real world and see things for what they are. You live in some sort of courtly fantasy and don't see what is happening here."

Nessa crossed her arms over her chest, seeming to want that to sink in before she continued. "What's happening is that the spoiled lady who likes new conquests and adventures ran into something new – a person who wouldn't simply jump into bed at the first flirty blink of those golden eyes."

Elise tried to break in to protest, but Nessa raised her voice, continuing her tirade. "So you became interested because you found something you couldn't just have in an instant. Well, now you have it. We've lain together. That was what you wanted, right? That's all you ever want. Pretty distractions and meaningless bedplay? That's fine. It's not what I want, though. I am built for serious relationships where connection comes first and bedplay later. But you like shiny new things, and having those things between your legs. Well, you succeeded. So why in the names of the gods are you insulting me now?"

Elise stared at her, feeling her temples begin to throb. For once in her life she was lost for words. All her muscles tensed and she felt her breathing rush through tightly shut lips. If her quick temper had caused her to lash out before, every little stopper now popped out. Everything and anything was fair game now.

"You are wrong, you know. You *are* afraid. You are terrified of everything. That is why you stayed on your parents' farm. For selfish reasons. Not because you wanted to help them, that was purely a convenient lie! You delayed starting your life because you were frightened."

Nessa grew even paler and took a step back, so Elise advanced and kept speaking. "And that is why you are not seeing what has grown between us. That is why you call it 'just friendship.' Just travelling together. Just sharing a room to save coin. Just bedplay. That is oxen-shit and you know it! You know there is more between us. You know there is more to me than some rich, spoiled brat who wants to play with you."

Elise heard her voice break and how weak it made her sound, but carried on. "I liked you because you knew that! I connected with you because you looked at me and saw the real me, not some pretty lass to sleep with or some rebel to go on adventures with, like others do. You saw more in me. I felt it. Now who is telling the other one that they are imagining things? Who is muddling the other's mind, huh?"

The veins corded on Nessa's neck. "I can't believe you would say that. I can't believe you would call me selfish and a liar. And then put that in the same sentence where you tell me what I saw in you and what I felt. I'll tell you what, Lady Falk. If you are such an expert on what I'm thinking and feeling, perhaps I do not even need to be here for this."

There was a knock on the door. They didn't acknowledge it. Didn't break eye contact.

Both of them ignored it for a few knocks more. But there was no way back into the conversation. The distraction was too big and the enormity of what had just been said made it hard to carry on.

After a while, Elise gave up. Ignoring propriety, she wrapped a blanket around herself and opened the door. Nessa quickly jumped behind the opening door, shielding her naked-ness from their visitor.

It was a young girl. Wordlessly, she handed a small package over to Elise. It was wrapped in paper dyed midnight blue and took up most of Elise's hand. No white ribbon this time. The girl ran away and Elise closed the door.

They both looked at the package in Elise's palm.

"There you go. You have a new diversion now," Nessa snarled. "You won't need me for a while, then." She started getting dressed. "I'll take my selfish, lying arse to work. Know this: if I see your face today, I'm walking in the opposite direction. And if you follow me to the hot shop, I'll have one of my masters throw you out." She pulled her mussed hair into a ponytail, grabbed her coat, and stepped into her boots. "Have a productive day, *your ladyship*."

She stormed out, leaving Elise wearing her blanket, and clutching the package. Squeezing it tight to keep herself from crying uncontrollably.

Moments ticked by. Elise felt like a mirror with cracks that were slowly growing and threatening to splinter her off into millions of pieces.

She dealt with what she could. The little things. Mechanically, she got dressed, put some sugar pumpkin oil on, combed her hair. Only when she tried to get it curl inwards towards her jaw, did she remember the small package.

Distantly, as if she was watching another person do it, she opened the package and looked at what was inside.

At first she couldn't figure out what it was. Then it dawned on her. It was a firesteel. Elise looked at it as her mind slowly put it into context. She placed it on the bed and fetched the other two things. A piece of flint. Some char cloth. And, finally, a firesteel.

With shallow breaths, Elise stared at the three pieces. She knew what they were now and what they would become if she assembled them, added a couple of other things if she wanted to be fancy, and placed them in a metal tin. They'd make a tinderbox. How had she not known? How did she not guess? She shivered, suddenly icy cold.

These were the pieces of a *tinderbox*.

She looked at herself in the mirror. Her face looked

drained of all blood. She knew she couldn't stay here staring at the pieces. But she couldn't go tell Nessa what was happening either. Not anymore. Still, time was still on her side. These weren't all the pieces, there would no doubt be a fancy box coming next. Unless Elise was mistaken *she* would not make her move until Elise had received all the pieces. They should be safe for now. Well, no matter what happened, Nessa should be safe. Elise just wasn't sure what would happen to herself.

She looked around the room, lost for a course of action. Panic tainted every part of her mind and body. Her eyes landed on one of her inky handkerchiefs.

"Work. Yes. That is where I should go. Yes. That is what Nessa would do. A solution might come to me there," she muttered to herself. Nodding mechanically. The ache in her gut made it painfully obvious that she didn't believe her own words.

The winter-white afternoon light streamed in through the window, distracting Elise and making her squint. Not that she hadn't been distracted before. She had been making mistakes, not hearing Archibald when he spoke to her, and even been rude to the delivery boy. How could she focus on work? Her mind was on the pieces of the tinderbox at home and her heart was busy beating forlornly for an angry woman in a workshop on the other side of town.

Elise blinked against the all-too-bright light and missed the lever for the printer which was straight in front of her. She walked into it, smashing it into her shoulder with a loud thud.

"What in the names of all the gods do you think you are doing, girl?"

Elise steeled herself. "I am sorry, Mr Richards. As I

explained this morning, I have had bad news from home and so am a bit distracted today."

She saw a muscle in his jaw twitch. "Distracted was when you arrived half an hour late. Distracted was when you handed me the wrong types. Distracted was when you twice disobeyed my very clear instructions. Distracted, and the last case of it I was going to forgive, was when you took the paper out of the printer too soon. Now this, this was not distraction –this was the last straw." He adjusted his glasses, jaw still twitching. "I can get any young worker in Nightport to help me with this project. They might not be as eloquent or as well-read as you, but right now I would settle for someone who isn't... *distracted.*"

Elise resisted the urge to wring her hands. "What are you saying?"

"I am saying, Miss Aelin, that I am cutting your time in my employment short. I have had enough of your capricious mood and your tendency to treat this job as a hobby. Do you know how many people in the city do not work? Do you know how many would come to work early and leave late for such a comfortable and esteemed job as this one? Do you know how many people would ignore even their own mothers dying to make sure that they kept it?"

There was a myriad of replies that popped up in Elise's head. None of them were appropriate for civil society and some would probably have gotten her thrown out by the city guards.

She was aware that she would only have had a couple of more weeks working for Archibald anyway. What is more, now that she knew the city better, she could easily use her wits to get another job. Still, this defeat, on top of her shattered relationship with Nessa and the looming threat of the tinderbox, was almost too much to bear. She didn't argue. She merely gave a curt nod. What did it matter anyway? What did anything matter anymore?

He looked extremely satisfied. Like he had expected a scene and was pleased that none was forthcoming.

"Very good, Miss Aelin. As the day soon will draw to a close, I can finish up the remaining tasks on my own. You might as well take your leave now. I probably need to venture out to find another temporary assistant anyway."

He reached for his coin purse, to pay her daily wage as he did at the end of every day. She saw him count out coins and wasn't surprised to see that there were fewer than for a full day's work. She wasn't going to quibble. Perhaps when she got herself back on her feet and sorted out the mess that her life had become, she would get her revenge. If not, living well and hopefully prospering would be revenge enough on this sad little man.

She took the coins from him, gave another curt nod, gathered her coat, and walked out without a sound. She ambled, in a daze, back to the lodging house. She still didn't know what to do about the tinderbox or the person she knew must have sent those three parts.

She dragged her feet, dreading having to see the pieces laid out on the bed and having to make decisions. Even more than that, she dreaded going back to the room and not finding Nessa in it. She felt convinced that Nessa wouldn't come back there tonight. In fact, she might have already cleared out her things on her lunch break. Time that Elise had spent staring into space. There might not be a single trace of Nessa Clay in the room where they had slept, eaten, shared their secrets, made love, and fought. Just the thought of that room being empty and bare made Elise want to cry.

Do not cry. If you start, you may not be able to stop.

She took any excuse to stop and look at something, not giving anything full attention, merely delaying seeing the room she had shared with her first true love. She knew without a doubt that this was what Nessa was to her now.

Despite this she did, of course, arrive at 21 Miller Street in the end. Almost at the time she would have normally come home. She was happy to see that there was someone waiting for her. As happy as she could be, considering that the waiting person wasn't Nessa. Instead, it was Cai, soon joined by Fyhre, who walked around the corner with a piece of sugar pumpkin, clearly bought from a street vendor. It made sense that they were here. Factory workers started the day earlier than everyone else and therefore finished a little earlier, too.

Cai spotted her and shouted. "Well 'ello there, treasure! We just got here an' reckoned we'd wait for ye. Ye're home early. Did the old printer fall asleep so ye could sneak out?"

Elise laughed mirthlessly. "No. In fact, Mr Richards is very well aware that I left. He terminated my employment early. I no longer have a job."

Fyhre's mouth hung open in surprise, showing a piece of chewed sugar pumpkin. It made Elise a bit nauseous, but she was so numb that she didn't mention it.

"Ye're jokin'! On what grounds?" Cai asked.

Absentmindedly, Elise ran her fingers through her hair. Then scrunched it to make it curl in. "Would you mind awfully if we do not talk about it? I have enough woes right now."

Fyhre merely frowned so it was Cai who replied in the usual low rasp. "Of course. Fancy unburdenin' yerself of those other woes instead? We were just comin' by to share a meal with ye an' Nessa, but we're real good listeners."

Elise's throat constricted at the mention of Nessa's name. She needed a while before she could talk about her.

"Thank you but no. Where are Sanjero and Jac?"

Cai laughed. "We don't always come as a pack, mate. The boys are home, tendin' to each other. They've got their five-year anniversary today. That's why they've been all over each other lately. They'll come up for air next week or so."

Elise scraped her toes in the dust on the cobbled road. "I see. That is sweet."

She didn't look up. She didn't need to. She was sure that they were staring at her, trying to read her. Waiting for her to explain. How she hated to be watched. Like a clockwork doll. Like at court.

"I…" She cleared her throat, trying to get rid of the sadness. "I doubt Nessa will be joining us. In fact, I would not be surprised if she is busy getting ready to leave Nightport for good."

Fyhre swallowed her mouthful of sugar pumpkin loudly. "What?"

"We, well, we fought this morning. I said things which I cannot take back. Things that she will probably struggle to heal from. She rushed off."

Cai gave a scoff of exasperation. "And ye didn't go an' explain? Fetch her back an' beg her pardon?"

"I was not provided with much of a chance. She told me she that if she saw me, she would walk the other way." Elise paused to glare at Cai. "Besides, she said some deeply hurtful things, too."

Fyhre suddenly found her voice. "Aye, I'm sure. But ye're the one with a way with words an' knowledge of the world. Nessa is naïve an' insecure. Proud, too. If ye reckon she's worth the effort, then ye must take the first step towards makin' up."

Cai nodded along. "And when she sees ye, I'd wager she can't walk away. In fact, I'd wager she's dyin' to be close to you. To get an apology, ye know? To hear that it's all right and that ye care for 'er."

"We'll come with ye to find her," Fyhre said.

Elise stared at her for a moment, weighing her options.

"Don't just stand there," Fyhre insisted. "Munch down the

last of my sugar pumpkin while we go to Brownlees and find yer ladylove." There was no room for debate in her tone.

Elise took the sticky fruit she was offered and nibbled on it. Not because she was hungry, but because she knew she'd need some energy if she was going to convince Nessa to listen to her. Her feet moved on their own, following Cai and Fyhre. After what felt like an eternity, they arrived at the workshop. When asked if Nessa was there, Josiah Brownlee shook his head, arms crossed over his broad chest.

"She's not. The lass looked like a wiltin' plant, so I sent her off to get some food. I reckon she went straight for a big glass of ale instead, she looked like she was hankerin' to drown her sorrows. Bad idea, that. Newcomers drink too much and too often. Thins their blood an' poisons their stomach."

Elise covered her eyes with hand. This was pointless. They would never find Nessa.

She does not want to be found. Not by you anyway.

"Thank you muchly, Mr Brownlee," Cai said.

"Fine," Brownlee grunted and went back inside.

Both Fyhre and Cai turned to Elise. The pity on their faces made Elise's stomach sour; she was not someone to be pitied. Despite this, she found she was aching for one of them to hug her. To tell her it was going to be all right. A broken sob escaped her throat.

"Now, don't cry an' don't worry, treasure," Cai said. "We'll find her. Even if we 'ave to scour every gods-cursed tavern in Nightport. We'll start with the ones that we know she has 'eard of."

Fyhre put her arm around Elise's shoulder. Elise leaned into her. She smelled of factory smoke and was surprisingly soft for someone so muscular. Gently but firmly, Fyhre coaxed her in the direction Elise knew would bring them to the Goblin's Tavern.

CHAPTER 26
THE WHITE RAVEN

That morning, Nessa had arrived at her masters' workshop with her untidy hair barely tamed by a hair tie, face and body unwashed, and wearing clothes that were scarcely put on properly. But she had arrived. And she had knuckled down and worked. That was what she was raised to do, and she fell back on that now.

Still, the argument had left Nessa heavily preoccupied. She tried her best to work hard and pick up Josiah's teachings while his wife was down by the docks, discussing a trade deal. Nevertheless, Nessa's efforts were in vain. During her lunch hour, she had snuck out to the back of the building and cried into her juice while forcing down half a sandwich.

A short while before work was to end, Josiah sighed and said, "Ye look and act like a sack of milk-cabbage. Bugger off and get some food an' sleep. And get yer brain workin'! Ye're no use to me like this. Just don't tell Secilia that I let ye shove off early."

"Thank you. I think I might go get some… food, yes."

Nessa had hurried out of the hot shop, into the fresh air of the early evening. Or well, the air that would have been fresh, if it hadn't been a mix of factory smoke, the stink of people, and the sickly sweet scent of wilting flowers that a girl on the pavement was selling. All topped off with a hint of horse manure. Nessa had loved this city from the second she visited as child. But right now, it was too much for her. Too busy. Too smelly. Too crowded. Too foreign.

And now, here she was. Without a clue where to go or what to do. Her stomach growled.

Of course. Take your master's advice and go get some food. Things might be a bit better if you're not hungry at least. They surely can't get worse.

She picked the quietest road she could see and started down it. She ignored the bakeries. No bread. Her stomach turned at the memory of her partly eaten sandwich at lunch. She needed hot food and strong drink to wash it down with. To wash down everything that had happened.

She passed tavern after tavern, but they all seemed wrong. Too dark, too rowdy, too empty… it was all wrong. After a few roads and enough walking to make her feet hurt, Nessa was ready to give up. Maybe even go back to Ground Hollow. She leaned against a wall and closed her eyes for a moment. Everything seemed so bleak, and she didn't think it was just the hangover and hunger speaking.

"Well now, you look as depressed as a thirsty mouse drowning in saltwater."

The voice sounded close, and Nessa's eyes shot open immediately.

In front of her was a man dressed in cobalt blue from head to toe. Even the stylish top hat on his head was cobalt blue. His teeth, though, which were visible in an overdone smile, were so white he appeared to have painted them with chalk.

"Hunter? Seriously? How in the name of all the gods do you keep showing up everywhere?"

He put his hand to his chest as if offended. "How exceptionally rude. You are the one who came trudging down one of my favourite streets. I was not even looking for you tonight."

She winced. "I'm sorry. Bad day."

"Do you know what would cure that?" he asked, sounding far too cheerful for her liking.

Nessa scowled at him. "Since it's you asking, I'm assuming it's going to be frequenting a tavern and drinking far too much of their overpriced drinks."

"Oh no, sweet thing. I think you have had quite enough of that in the last few days. You look like you need some distraction. Some good old-fashioned fun."

"What I need is food."

He held his hands out, palms up. "All good fun and distraction come served with food and drink."

She grunted her agreement. A listlessness, almost a numbness, was taking over her. She had ruined the best part of her new life, her friendship with Elise. Why had she slept with her? Why could she not control herself anymore? Everything had been so easy back in Ground Hollow.

At least I was in control back then.

She was not only out of her comfort zone in this city, she was in over her head. Going back to her village seemed like the sensible option now, even if it wasn't all that tempting. At least she would be wanted and loved in Ground Hollow.

Hunter, clueless to her thoughts, rubbed his chin. "Now, where do I take a wholesome country lass for an evening of fun and distraction? And of course, some food for the beast that lives in her belly, growling and eating its way around Nightport. Hmm."

While he deliberated, Nessa was coming to a conclusion of her own. If she wanted to give up on this new life and go back to simple, predictable Ground Hollow, she should have one last big Nightport adventure. A proper farewell.

"I want to see the White Raven."

Hunter lifted the brim of his hat to see her better. "Pardon?"

"I want to go to the White Raven. I want to play cards all night and maybe watch some fighters beat the blood out of each other. And, of course, I want to get so drunk out of my skull that there is no room for my thoughts in there anymore."

"I don't reckon that's a good idea," Hunter said, worry bringing out his real accent.

"Well, I do. Why are you complaining, anyway? Don't you get a handful of coin if you bring me there? Surely you are on the payroll of the White Raven."

"No, I'm 'fraid not. The Scarlet Crow and the White Raven figured out that they don't need anyone to drum up customers no more." His voice sounded different without the midlands pretence, kinder and warmer.

Not that this calmed Nessa. She stomped her foot, like a child. "I don't care! I want to go there, with or without you."

Hunter, frowning, held up his hands. "Fine. I'll take ye there. Just go easy, let me set ye up somewhere safe. And let me order ye some sandwiches? You eat cheese and shroom sandwiches, right? Nightport speciality, y'know. Ye'll feel better with a full belly."

"No. Yes. Whatever, mother. Let's go," she muttered.

He looked appeased. "Does Elise know where you are?" he asked, back in his attempt at a Highmere accent. He started ambling down the street. Nessa followed this strange man in blue.

"No. But I don't think she much cares."

He clasped his hands behind his back. "Ah, so this mood is down to a lover's quarrel?"

"There is no mood. Just a change of direction. After tonight, I'm leaving. I've realised that I am not Nightport material."

Hunter's eyebrows rose up his forehead. "Really? You

EMMA STERNER-RADLEY

seemed so enamoured with the city and exceedingly happy to be out of your little pocket of a village! And what about your future as a glassblower?"

Nessa chuckled wryly, looking up at the sky. It was perfectly cloudless with the beautiful beginnings of a rosy sunset. How awful. "What's the point in all of that?"

Hunter caught her gaze and held it as they walked on. "What do you mean? I thought it was your dream?"

"It was. Well, my number one dream was always escape. Leaving Ground Hollow for somewhere I could fit in. I thought that might be achievable, but deep down I wasn't sure I'd ever take the step and actually leave. There would always have been a reason to stay just one more day, one more week. For my parents, for Layden, or for any other excuse I could conjure up. Then Elise swept in, took my hand and off we went. Easy as that. Like it was an everyday thing, like choosing between goat's milk or cow's milk."

Hunter adjusted his top hat. "That *is* an easy option. Cow's milk if it's available. Goat's milk if it's not. Or if you are saving your coin."

She glared at him, and he pinched his lips closed with his index finger and thumb, signifying that he would shut up.

Nessa shoved her hands in her pockets. "My second dream was glassblowing. I suppose it was a secret one as I barely admitted it to myself. But I admitted it to her. She sort of drew it out of me. Then she...simply made it happen. We traipsed all over this foul-smelling city until she found me a glassblower who would apprentice me. She wouldn't give up until I had everything I hadn't dared to think I could achieve."

"She's persistent. You have to give her that," Hunter said.

Nessa didn't reply. She was too busy sorting her thoughts. Talking about this hurt, but she had to make him understand. Make herself understand.

"Then my dreams... shifted. I still wanted to be in Nightport and I still wanted to be a glassblower. But something else became more important. She became more important. Waking up with her in the morning, eating my meals with her, hearing how her day went, you know? Trying to impress her was suddenly more important than anything else. But she's... so beyond me. As angry as I am with her, I have to admit that. Elise is confident, beautiful, sophisticated, different, charming. I'm all dusty and damaged, and she is glimmering and bright like the sun. She doesn't want me."

Hunter made a noise like a rusty gate. "Well, I wouldn't say that."

"No. She doesn't want me the way I want her. Whether she knows it or not, she just wants me as a conquest. As a diversion, I think. I don't know. The argument we had made it all so confusing. I do know that she thinks we can be friends and casual lovers but it doesn't work that way. Life is not a game. It's serious, and she doesn't see that. I can never be enough for her, not in the long run."

Nessa kicked a stone that had the audacity to be in her way. It was a little too big to kick, and it hurt even through her boot. The physical pain somehow soothed her.

Hunter was throwing her quick glances. "How will you know that if you do not stay?"

"I can't stay here. Everything here reminds me of her. Everything here is hers. It's immense, fascinating, and ever-changing. I'm not. I'm only Nessa Clay from Ground Hollow. If I stay I'll be angry at everything and everyone all the time. Like I am now. Or I'll shrink into nothingness, just be shy and not talk to anyone."

Hunter pulled at his earlobe. "Are you sure that is not your current mood talking? Should you not think this through?"

Nessa kicked the ground again. This time there was no stone to take her wrath. "I don't know. I'm tired of thinking. If I have to think anymore I'll punch something! I don't want to talk about this anymore. Or anything else for that matter. Everything is gods-cursed oxen shit."

He opened his mouth as if to ask further questions, but then settled for, "Ah, my first impression was right, then. You are in desperate need of distraction."

"Yes. Now let's stop talking and just get there," she snapped.

They walked in silence along Nightport's dusty streets. Hunter strutted in his usual peacock way while Nessa dragged her feet, worrying that no distraction would be strong enough to mute her dire thoughts. A beggar severely insulted her after she only gave him one copper, and she didn't even flinch. Her limbs were heavy, and her stomach hurt.

They passed a small tavern. Outside it stood a group of young people, mainly men. They were all powdered, rouged at the cheek, and had eyes lined with kohl. Their clothing was elegant but in bright colours and showing far too much skin to be considered proper. Pleasure sellers. They were so beautiful that they managed to distract Nessa from her gloom for a moment.

Why did people buy such beauty? Surely it would be a bigger prize to try to win their affection and admiration. Or was it because the buyers couldn't find a lover any other way? She tried to gauge the people who approached the pleasure sellers, but they all looked sane and healthy enough. Nessa would probably never have her questions answered. The pleasure sellers here were seen as a natural part of society, but they tended to keep to themselves. Nessa had learned that from Secilia Brownlee. She had proudly told Nessa that her father had been a pleasure seller, the best in the city in his day, apparently.

Nessa's shoulders slumped. This was all yet another sign of how foreign and confusing this city was to her. Back in Ground

Hollow, there had been a young lady who was a pleasure seller. She had not stood on the street, but had customers come to her house. Usually they were men. It had always bothered Nessa that the townsfolk had whispered and giggled behind the woman's back. She had been seen as a necessary evil, fulfilling needs in a practical and fast way so that people could get back to work. However, Nessa had still heard people whisper ugly things like *harlot* behind her back. That had always struck Nessa as particularly unfair. It intimated that the pleasure seller was the one who could not get enough of bedplay, who wasn't strong enough to resist the pull of carnal needs. The truth was that she was simply trying to make a living, since her parents had lost their farm and her schooling had not gone very well. After all that, was being a harlot really a bad thing? Nessa wasn't sure. She wasn't sure of much right now.

She stopped in her tracks for a moment. Perhaps things weren't as simple back in Ground Hollow as she had always thought. She looked at a painted, barely grown lad flirting with an old man in front of her, and decided that things certainly weren't simple here either. Did Nightport's pleasure sellers enjoy their work? They were clearly respected and had other options to survive, unlike pleasure sellers in rural parts of Arclid. She sighed at her own ignorance and confusion.

Fatigue washed over her. She wanted it all to crumble into dust. Or maybe she just wanted her feelings to crumble and vanish. She scuffed at the ground again, achieving nothing more than stirring up dust from the cobbles.

She had come to Nightport because she wanted more than she could find in Ground Hollow. She wanted more than what was promised her there: early mornings and early nights and back-breaking work in between. The same faces every day. Quick rolls in the hay after too much ale. Then settling down with a partner and stagnating. She knew that wasn't fair —

they probably didn't stagnate at all, but she would if she tried that life.

Where in the name of all the gods do I fit in?

Hunter must have noticed she had stopped because he turned back. He was next to her now, watching her look at the pretty pleasure sellers.

"Ah, looks like you might have found your own distraction. Would you like me to enquire about the price?"

Nessa jerked to attention. "No!"

He smirked. "No, I suppose not. You do not want a professional. All you want is a pretty wild child who fights like a beast and speaks like a lady."

"She does not fight like a beast," Nessa muttered. She knew that she should have argued with his assumption that Elise was what she wanted. But what would be the point? "Anyway, I don't stand a chance with that 'pretty wild child' any more. She's furious with me."

"Oh, I am sure you could make amends. Arguments happen and then you make up. I prescribe some flowers, some sweet words, and that charming, broad smile of yours," he said confidently.

Nessa swallowed the lump in her throat. "The flowers and the smile I can manage. But I have no idea what words might help. Or if they would even reach her. We are so different and I think we speak at cross purposes most of the time. I don't care right now. I just want some distraction. Something dark. Something primal. Somewhere where she won't come looking for me."

"And you believe that is the White Raven?"

Nessa shrugged. "It's worth a shot."

He still looked sceptical. "As you wish. I was on my way to do some rounding up of customers for the Goblin's Tavern tonight, so I would prefer if we took a shortcut to save some time?"

"Sure. Doesn't matter to me."

"Splendid. Follow me," he said, picking up the pace.

Nessa followed dutifully, never one to keep anyone from their work. Hunter made a swift turn and began walking down a dark alley.

Nessa squinted into the passageway. As far as she could make out, it contained nothing but bricked-up windows flanking the dark emptiness, with a mangy-looking rat running towards them for good measure. And yet, Hunter strutted down it as if taking a stroll in a lovely park. She followed, wishing she was still out on the street. There might be drunkards and beggars out there, but at least she could see where she was putting her feet. Without warning, Hunter stopped and performed a move she couldn't quite make out. Whatever he did illuminated the alley with a shaft of light, bringing the noise of chatter, music, and clinking glasses with it. It all came from a small door that Hunter somehow managed to locate in the thick darkness.

"How in the names of all the gods did you manage to find that?" Nessa whispered as she cast glances around the darkness. She wasn't sure why she was whispering.

Hunter closed the door again, banishing the only source of light. That was when Nessa saw what was right at eye level. How had she missed it? Next to the door was a white, strangely luminescent picture of a bird. It was a little bigger than a coin and shone in the darkness as if it had been lit by flame or gas. But looking closer, it was only painted on the stone wall.

Nessa stared at it. "What lights it up? Some sort of magic?"

Hunter sniggered. It annoyed Nessa more than it should.

"No, little country mouse. You know there is no such thing as magic. It lights up thanks to a chemical compound in the paint. It was created by the landlord's wife who happens to be Nightport's finest chemical expert. She also makes some of the… less than legal powders you can purchase inside. I suggest you do not try any of them. They will alter your mind for the night, and if you are not careful, you will crave that alteration every night."

Nessa crossed her arms over her chest. "I'm not the type to use powders."

She thought she caught him smirking in the darkness. "No, I suppose that is true, Miss Clay. Anyway, welcome to the backdoor to the White Raven. I can proudly say that very few know about this entrance."

He opened the door again, and Nessa was blinded by the light. She blinked a few times until her eyes adjusted. Then it was her ears' turn to suffer, as a wall of sound hit her. She could hear a band playing over the din of countless voices.

Wait. Was that someone screaming? No, must have been a woman with a shrieking laugh. Right?

She took a step forward, but pulled back again. "So, are there really white ravens in there? Do they actually exist?" she squeaked.

Now she saw Hunter smile, his chalk-white teeth gleaming in the light. It was a kind, reassuring smile. "Yes, there are three of them in there. Living in a large cage behind the bar, all in love, all mating in a happy three-bird relationship. Now stop stalling. Come on, I will make sure you are safe."

He opened the door wider and stepped in. Nessa followed him one hesitant step at a time.

Nessa blinked repeatedly, still getting used to the light, even if it was quite dim. Only a few sconces on the walls illuminated the scrubbed white walls that Jac had mentioned. Everything else was coloured in mottled reds and faded blacks. The place was uncomfortably cramped. It was with great difficulty that the waitress moved between the tightly packed tables. As Nessa's eyes became used to the low light, she could make out what was happening in this loud room.

Some people at the tables were simply drinking, chatting, smoking pipes, and by the looks of it, flirting. Others were looking around furtively as they rubbed something against their gums. Most of them, however, seemed to be occupied with card games. Quite a few tables played only with a deck, while others had stacks of coin they pushed to the middle of the table as they placed their bets. Nessa saw one table where three women had a kind of honeycomb-like, wooden structure on the table. They took turns placing their playing cards into it in an intricate pattern. She squinted at it through the smoke in the room, trying to decipher the pattern of their game but failed. Just as she was about to ask Hunter what it was they were playing, she was distracted by the music changing to include singing.

Turning to her side, Nessa spotted a singer holding court on a small stage. Quite a few people got up from their tables to stand and gaze reverentially at her. Nessa doubted it was because the singer had a particularly unique voice; in fact, Nessa couldn't help but think that Elise sang better. It was her beauty. Even at a distance, Nessa could see liquid movements, generous curves, and gleaming skin so richly dark brown it appeared black. All this in a tightly fitted, blood-red dress accompanied by a black shawl, which didn't seem to cover as much as drape over her body. Nessa considered getting closer to get a view of the woman's face, but decided against it. She didn't want to be obviously ogling the singer. With a nauseous feeling in the pit of her stomach, she realised that Elise would have been fascinated by this woman.

The singer played to her crowd of adoring listeners. The band behind her clearly pouring their hearts and souls into the music. The song was slow, dark, and sensual in a way which felt wrong to Nessa. The lyrics were about a man who cheated at cards all night and stole from his richer playing companions when the night became morning. Nessa picked up a few words describing what they did to the card sharp when he was found with his stolen goods.

The bloodiness of the description made Nessa scrunch up her nose. The seductive tone in the singer's voice as she sang about the gore and blood made it so much worse. She looked around and saw people grinning and nodding along to the music. Some even miming along to words about knives being plunged into the man's private parts. Nessa swallowed her disgust and tried to tune the lyrics out. Leaving the slow back-beat, the teasing melody of the violins, and the deep tones of the bass to be the background to her walk across the floor of the White Raven.

There was a bar running all along the short end of the room. Behind it stood a handful of men and women, all busy pouring concoctions into glasses or surreptitiously selling little vials. Nessa saw a man walk past her with one of the vials he had just purchased. It was filled with a light grey powder. He took some out and brushed it against his gums. Behind the busy barkeeps was a cage. Even at this distance, Nessa could see the flutter of white wings in there.

She looked to her side, making sure that Hunter was still with her. He smiled at her and pointed to an archway into a pitch-black adjoining room. Next to the archway, on the eerily white wall, the words "FIGHT ROOM" were written in black. There was a chalkboard underneath which had what looked like two names and a time on it.

She swallowed and nodded to him, trying to look unmoved. In truth, the idea of seeing an arranged fight made her skin crawl.

The White Raven smelled of stale alcohol, something chemical and pipe smoke. All mingled with the sweat and perfumes of the big crowd. Above it was a permeating stink of iron.

Is that blood? No, can't be. Must be part of the chemical smell that those powders leave when they get poured into the vials. Yes, that's it. Calm down, Nessa.

It was overwhelming, making her head spin. She turned to Hunter, and saw him smile and nod at people he clearly knew. This was a mistake. This place was too wild, too crowded, too outlandish, too… dark for Nessa. She desperately wished Elise was here. Elise would help her make sense of this. Nessa's whole body was tense, her shoulders creeping up towards her ears.

Hunter was staring at her. "Nessa? Are you sure you want to be here? Should I take you home?"

He sounded mothering again. Like she was a vulnerable child. Like she wasn't brave or street smart enough for this place. Like she was too addicted to safety to be able to be without it even for a night.

Nessa planted her feet and straightened her back. "Yes. This is exactly where I want to be. I want a tall drink and a card game."

He gave her a long look. "All right. If you are sure. I will come with you to order a drink. Then I will set you up at a table where the stakes are not too high and the players are not too murderous."

They walked over to the bar. Hunter began speaking familiarly with one of the barkeeps, a big burly man with a beard. The smell of alcohol was stronger here, but there was also an overwhelming sweet smell. It seemed to emanate from the glass that a short, blonde, and busty barkeep was filling. She looked up at Nessa and winked.

Nessa smiled shyly and looked back down at the drink. "W-what's that you are making? Sorry if it's obvious. I'm not very good with drinks."

"Don't fret, pretty. I made it up, an' I call it Sunset Burn. Ye'll know why when ye see an' taste it. It starts with unsweetened winterberry juice, tart as ye like. Then some

283

winterberry brandy an' a dash of sunberry essence. Followed by a healthy helpin' of a strong, imported booze from Storsund by the name of vodka. Then I top the whole thing with lots of sugared sunberries. Sweet, tart, an' packs a punch. Like me."

She winked again, and Nessa felt her cheeks grow hot.

"I'd like one of those, please," Nessa said in a choked squeak.

"Aye. Let me finish up this one, an' then I'll get started on one for ye, tall beauty."

Nessa liked being the tall one, up until it made her think of Elise usually having that role. "Sure. Thanks," she muttered, looking down at the sticky floor.

Hunter tapped her on the shoulder. "Sounds like you found a drink. Good. I have asked my friend Svein here for a cheese and shroom sandwich for you and a suitable table you can join. He reckons that the big round table in the corner over there is playing Four of a Kind. The blokes are apparently hassle-free and have been asking for players. I would suggest you join them when you get your drink."

He looked at her appraisingly. She returned his gaze and straightened her back. After all, it was merely some drinks and a card game. She had handled bar brawls and drunk, pushy men. She could look after herself.

Are you sure about that? This isn't Ground Hollow. These aren't the neighbouring boys with more brawn than brains.

She ignored the treacherous worry creeping in. "Yes, that's fine. Thank you for your help. Now run along to the Goblin's Tavern. I've got it from here."

Hunter frowned. "If you say so. If you get into trouble, signal Svein here. Get the short blondie to fetch him or something. I have asked him to lend you a hand if you need it."

"I'm sure I won't. But thank you again."

He squeezed her shoulder. "Please do not end up being

careless because you have a broken heart. You've nothing to prove, love."

He bowed to her and then pranced out. As if he hadn't a care in the world, poured full of all the confidence that could fit into a man. Oh, how she envied that self-assurance. Even if it wasn't completely genuine.

Nessa turned back to the bar. The short barkeep handed her a sandwich which Nessa ate slowly while her drink was being made. As the ingredients were being poured into a glass, which almost looked clean, Nessa pulled her gaze over to the white ravens. Their cage spanned the entire wall behind the bar. As she chewed, she mused that the tavern could have been a lot larger if so much of it was not taken up by the cage. The novelty of the birds must be worth it.

One of them flapped its wings and then took flight, leaving its two cage mates on their perch. It flew to the other side of the cage, giving Nessa a closer view. It looked odd. Ravens were meant to be black, ominous, and brooding. Strangely, these birds' white colour didn't make them look any less eerie. In fact, it made them look unnatural, like their colour had been bled out of their feathers. Their pallid beaks appeared to melt into the white.

Nessa met the bird's gaze. Its eyes, milky with a little dark centre, stood out, like they were pieces of enamel glued to the bird. It tilted its head as it stared at her, as if it was trying to tell her something. Something she should know. Judging her. Calling her dumb, prideful. Self-harming.

Nessa looked away, focusing on the glass that now contained liquids the colours of a sunset bleeding into each other. As the barkeep took out a bowl of dried sunberries and slowly plunged her fingers into it, she gave Nessa a suggestive smile. Nessa understood all too clearly what the gesture was a euphemism for. Did the barkeep flirt like this with everyone or had she just taken a liking to Nessa? If the latter was the case, Nessa could have revenge on Elise by bedding this attractive blonde. But of course, she didn't want to.

Once more she was struck by her own disinterest in bedplay outside of a relationship. It seemed like such an empty, overly complicated way to deal with a physical need. A need that could be resisted, like she usually did. Or if you couldn't resist, a need which was easily handled with your own hands or the corner of a pillow. Others clearly saw a point in it, but it was lost on her. At least it had been. Then last night happened. It was different. What exactly was last night?

Everything.

It had shaken her to the core. Almost made her cry, and not because she had been drunk. The knowledge that to Elise it had purely been bedplay for fun nearly smothered her. During the fight, what had Elise said about it? Nessa had been so hurt and confused that she hadn't taken the words in.

She shook her head, trying to shake the puzzlement and aching out of it.

"There ye go, tall beauty. Here's yer Sunset Burn. That'll be three coppers."

Nessa took the coin purse out of her pocket, trying not to wince at the steep price. When she went to put the copper coins in the barkeep's outstretched hand, she felt the blonde use her fingers to caress her wrist. Nessa hastily smiled, thanked her, and took her drink. She turned before the barkeep could reply and headed for the table that Hunter had pointed out to her.

There were three men there. One was shuffling the cards while another drank deep from a glass of ale. The third was holding court, telling a story which had the other two laughing, making the drinking one almost choke on his ale.

There was a hard lump of discomfort in her belly. She was standing by the table now. They all turned to look at her. She was relieved to see their faces were expectant, not unwelcoming.

"Good evening, gentlemen. The barkeep, the big bearded one, said that you were looking for a fourth player?"

The man who had been telling tales looked about Nessa's age. He was plainly going for the handsome scoundrel type, and pulling it off with his glittering eyes and a dimple in his badly shaven chin, He smiled, flashing teeth as chalk-white as Hunter's. How did they get their teeth so white? Elise had bought some sort of alcoholic herbal tonic that she rinsed with each night, and yes, Nessa had picked up that habit too. Mainly to make sure that her breath smelled nice as they went to sleep. But even Elise's clever tonic could not make teeth white. Did they actually paint them?

I'll have to ask Elise. No wait. Ah, oxen shit.

While his teeth were white, the shirt that covered his broad chest and had probably been white once, was now a mottled mix of cream and grey. Including dark brown, drop-shaped stains on his collar. Nessa had no doubt it was blood. She could only hope that he had cut himself shaving.

Looking at his chin, he hasn't shaved for a while, though. And this is the safe *table?*

The handsome man wore braces to keep his brown, leather trousers up, he hooked his thumbs into them as he smiled at her. Puffing his chest out.

The ale-drinking man, who was sitting very close to him, was shorter and less handsome. Ghost-white skin, gaunt cheeks, and yellow buckteeth. He snorted at the handsome man's puffed out chest and pulled one of the braces, snapping it back on his friend's thumb. Then he went back to his ale. He wore the light grey uniform of a factory worker, but he had crimson and cobalt stains everywhere, marking him out as someone employed in the dye works.

She briefly wondered if he had manufactured the dye

which had been used for the midnight blue wrapping paper that their strange packages arrived in. Now she might never know the mystery of those packages.

The third man was older, tawny-skinned, and had a large scar across his forehead and down towards his dark brown eyes. He was bald but was sporting a large, oiled moustache. The moustache oil smelled of something sweet, maybe figs? The cloying scent hung heavy around the man. Too heavy. Nessa took a step away from him and towards a chair closer to the others.

The handsome one gave her a broad smile. "Of course, we'd welcome a fourth player. Especially a pretty one, like ye. We're bleedin' bored to the teeth of each other's company. Some new blood sure would be welcome. Do ye play Four of a Kind?"

Nessa had played it a number of times. Her father had taught her when she got tired of simpler games like Fool the Angel. However, playing it with her father or with the other children at school was different than playing it here for coin. Still, she knew she betted sensibly and that she was ready to lose a lot today. What would she spend her coin on back in Ground Hollow anyway? She needed the thrill and distraction right now. No thoughts or feelings, just risk and the chance to overcome her worries.

She sat down and got comfortable, leaning back as if she owned the place. "Sure. Deal the cards."

She didn't introduce herself. This didn't seem like the sort of place where you made friends. She simply took a long drink of her Sunset Burn. As promised, it was fiery with alcohol and tasted a confusing mix between sweet and tart. She took another swig and relished the alcohol burning its way into her stomach.

Soon the cards were dealt. Nessa looked at the four that had been counted out for her. She hoped that when she picked them up, she would find at least two, preferably three, or, in a perfect world, four of a kind. Then it was all about betting and the next four cards she was dealt. After that she would have to play the hand she'd been dealt and hope that within those eight cards was at least one set of four.

She picked up her cards and saw the six of rubies and the six of onyx. Two of a kind. That was a start. And it was something to bet on. She squared her shoulders and returned the smile the handsome man was still bestowing on her. She saw the corners of his mouth twitch a little, the smile faltering for an instant, like he suddenly wasn't so sure of what she might do next. Neither, she realised, was Nessa.

CHAPTER 27
SEARCHING FOR NESSA CLAY

Elise, Fyhre, and Cai walked into the tavern where she and Nessa had bought Layden a tart before he returned to Ground Hollow. Gods, how Elise hoped Nessa hadn't followed in his footsteps. What if she wasn't in Nightport anymore, but trudging back to the village where Elise's words all but sent her? Why had she hurt Nessa like that? She blamed her quick temper, she blamed her unrequited love, she blamed the hangover, she blamed her sharp tongue. She blamed herself so much that she wanted to hurt herself.

Cai clapped her on the back. "Well, that ain't a good face. Less down in the dumps, more fightin' spirit, please. We're findin' yer woman an' then ye can sweet-talk her an' win her back."

Elise scoffed listlessly. "I am not so certain. Certainly not in here, the place appears all but deserted."

"Too early in the evenin' for punters. I'm a' look around anyway," Fyhre muttered and marched off.

"What happened 'tween you two?" Cai asked, glancing around the tavern.

Elise sighed, taking a few steps into the room. "We ended up making love last night."

"Hey! Nice goin' for a posh lass. Why is she not speakin' to ye today? Did ye do it wrong?"

Elise turned to glare. "No, I did not! We fought this morning. I wanted to talk about what had happened and explain that it meant a lot to me. That I had fallen for her. I wanted us to stay home from work and discuss our future —"

Cai interrupted. "Nessa Clay skip work? Never."

"Yes. That is basically what she said. She was so nonchalant and evasive. It got my dander up. Well, that and being frightened that she would reject me. Of course, having just woken up and being hungry did not help in the slightest."

"Don't forget hungover."

"Thank you, Cai. Yes. That, too," Elise said acerbically, while checking if the tavern had a basement. It didn't.

Cai nodded to a bored barkeep and then looked back to Elise. "Was that it? All this bleedin' fuss over that?"

"Well, no. We both got more upset than we should, and we started saying hurtful things to each other. We lanced the wound, and all sorts of poison spilled out. I gather she thought I was only bedding her for fun, as a conquest. If she meant that. She said an awful lot of things. I hope she did not mean them all," Elise said quietly.

"Why would she reckon that?"

"She..." Elise hesitated. "Might not have thought that love was an option with me. When we met, I told her that I did not engage in bedplay for love, only for fun. Still, it has been obvious that I have fallen in love with her this past fortnight, has it not?"

Cai hummed. "Aye. To us. But Nessa's different."

"Yes. I need to talk to her. I will be so patient and calm this time. I will grovel and explain that the things I said were only to hurt her, to defend myself, and that they were dumb.

But what if she is gone? Or refuses to speak to me? She is the best thing in my life. I look at her and I see my future, the only future I want. If she does not want me, I will accept that. If she stays away because of a misunderstanding, however... I cannot bear the thought."

Cai started to say something but stopped, instead opting for clapping Elise on the back again. There really wasn't anything to say, was there? Elise had found the most marvellous person in the world and somehow won her trust and affection. Then she and her stupid mouth had burned it all to the ground. Perhaps she should simply pick up the pieces of the tinderbox and go willingly to their sender. To *her*.

Fyhre walked back to them. "Unless she disguised 'erself as a bunch of fishermen with long beards, she ain't here."

Elise screamed and punched the wall hard, immediately regretting it as the pain seared in her knuckles and saw her companions jolt.

Cai sought her gaze. "Look. If she's in Nightport, ye'll find her. If she went back to her little piss pot village, ye'll find her. If she's the only future you want, ye'll keep lookin' for as long as it takes. When ye find her, just be honest an' calm. She loves ye back. I'm willin' to bet my shirt on it."

"Don't. The factory owns it," Fyhre muttered and opened the door for them.

Cai chuckled that deep, hoarse laugh. Elise tried to at least smile, for their sake, but her face appeared to have forgotten how that worked.

CHAPTER 28
GAME CHANGER

An hour later, Nessa and the three men were all warmed up and well into their game. Nessa had won a fair few hands, mainly because she had been lucky with the cards and bet steadily but aggressively. However, a few times it was because she had bluffed successfully. Bluffing was not usually her thing, and clearly her appearance showed it, as the men had not expected it. A lever in Nessa's mind had been pulled. Why shouldn't she bluff? What did she have to lose? She was probably going to go home to Ground Hollow tomorrow. Maybe even tonight. She'd help her parents at the farm and take it over one day, settling down with some nice woman or man from the village. She took another long pull of her drink.

Nessa won more and more, while the handsome man was right behind her on the winning streak. The man from the dye works, however, had lost almost all his coin. He was cursing under his breath and gulping down his third glass of ale.

The blonde barkeep came over for the third time, asking if they wanted something else. As per the other times, they all said yes. She took their orders and left.

The handsome man turned to Nessa. "Well now, we don't usually get such speedy service. What 'ave ye done to, or with, the lovely Leighla to make 'er rush over 'ere every eye blink?"

He waggled his eyebrows. She was about to reply, but realised she didn't care if he thought she was bedding the barkeep. She merely shrugged.

The barkeep — Leighla was it? — soon came back with their drinks. She put another winterberry brandy in front of Nessa and leaned in close to ask, "Do ye need anythin' else, pretty? Some dammon nuts, maybe?"

She placed her hand on Nessa's shoulder. The feel of the hand, even through Nessa's shirt, felt so intimate. It was all wrong. Her hand was too warm and too big. Not like Elise's at all. Nessa's heart thudded. She wanted Elise with her so badly, like a child wants its security blanket. She needed her. Could there be a way that Elise might love her?

No. No one truly falls in love with you. They love you as a friend, family member, or a pet. Or they fall in love with their idea of you, thinking that dependable Nessa will make a good wife.

That had been the case in her long-term relationships, she knew that now. She didn't blame them, she didn't much see what she had to offer to anyone.

She was growing maudlin. The self-pity and loathing disgusted her. Perhaps she had had too many drinks. She didn't care; she ordered another glass of brandy and said yes to the dammon nuts.

The barkeep removed her hand from Nessa's shoulder, seeming disappointed to not have gotten more than a muttered order.

When asked if he wanted another drink after his shot of vodka, the dye-works man huffed and stood up. He swallowed the shot down in one go and put some coins for it in Leighla's hand. Rubbing his bloodshot eyes with dye-stained fingers, he said, "No. Bugger this for a start. I'm bloody tired of losin' me coin an' just tired. I'm goin' home to bed an' the better 'alf."

He took his few remaining coins and stumbled towards the door. The moustachioed man rubbed his bald head and looked at his handsome friend, who was shuffling the cards.

"It's lookin' like we're down one player, Jayk. Reckon the three of us should carry on? Or rifle aroun' for a fourth?"

The handsome man, apparently called Jayk, looked around the room. Nessa joined him. Quite a few of the people who had been standing around chatting or flirting seemed to have dropped off. Left were the hard-core players and the hard-core drinkers.

Jayk clicked his tongue. "Seems to be some folk around that have lost their playin' mates. We should be able to get a fourth, I reckon."

Nessa saw that his gaze had stopped surveying and was fixed on one person. A tall, slim woman in a dark purple dress, who was walking from table to table seemingly looking for a card game to join. The woman was impressive in her stature and the elegant way she moved. Confidence and poise dripped off her, and Nessa swallowed a quick bite of envy.

In a quick move, Jayk was on his feet. He sauntered over to her and, with two fingers, lightly tapped her shoulder. Nessa couldn't help but notice that he had tapped exactly where the dress had stopped and the shoulder was bare. Nessa rolled her eyes. *Cheeky ape.*

The woman turned unhurriedly and looked at him with the kind of inquisitive air one would give a new breed of animal. Nessa could see him give his swindler smile and stand to full height, jutting out his chest and planting his feet wide. Trying so hard to impress, while this woman didn't even need to try. Nessa saw him speak to the woman, her give a regal nod, then they walked together back to the table. The woman in purple sat down next to Jayk.

Nessa took another drink of her brandy, wondering when her next glass and the nuts were arriving. Still with his eyes on the newcomer, Jayk explained what they were playing. Once more the impressive woman merely nodded, while taking stacks of coins out of a small bag that matched her dress. Nessa wondered if the woman was mute or just didn't think them worthy of hearing her speak.

Jayk picked up the deck again and shuffled the cards once more for good measure. Then he dealt them. Nessa picked up her cards and was thrilled to see that she was starting off with three of a kind in eights. All she needed was the eight of sapphires and she'd have four of a kind. She kept her face blank, making sure not to show how lucky she had been.

When it was time to place their bets, the woman in purple pushed a stack of silver coins to the middle of the table.

"We're bettin' smaller amounts than that, lady. Coppers. Not silvers," said the bald man.

"Well," said the newcomer slowly, "then that should change. The night is wearing on, and none of us are getting any younger. It is time to bet like adults and set this game alight."

Her voice was melodic, in a way that spoke of years of practice more than a natural ability. The accent sounded High-mere and Noble in every syllable. It was so much like the accent that Elise had been failing to hide ever since they came to Nightport that Nessa felt yet another stab of longing.

Nessa found the woman watching her. She wasn't surprised. When the newcomer sat down, she had surveyed first Jayk, then the bald man, and now it was clearly Nessa's turn. She stared right back, trying to learn what she could from her new opponent.

She had plenty of time while the bald man toyed with his moustache and grumbled while counting his coins, taking his time placing his bet. Jayk was busy drinking down his half-brandy, half-vodka mix. So, Nessa indulged her curiosity, not even caring if the woman caught her. The Nessa who left Ground Hollow almost two weeks ago would have worried about that, but the Nessa who would return there soon didn't care at all.

The newcomer's dress was lavish, fitted like a second skin, and the deepest purple imaginable. The woman wearing it was pale, in fact she had the whitest skin Nessa had ever seen. It should have made the woman look ill, pallid. Instead, she looked like she was made of porcelain.

Out of respect, for the woman and strangely enough for Elise, Nessa tried not to look too much at the woman's slender body. Instead she focused on the face. This lady wasn't exactly beautiful, but she had a daunting — almost commanding — face with a straight, slim nose; such high and protruding cheekbones that they could cut someone; and a heart-shaped mouth with purple-tinted lips that she kept tightly shut when not speaking. Her eyes were big and dark with kohl-black lashes so long they seemed to brush the tops of her cheekbones. Nessa wondered if such eyelashes could be real or somehow manufactured.

As she watched, the woman cocked her head, birdlike. Those tightly pressed lips briefly quirked into a smile. Her eyes widened, looking strangely eerie. For a moment, she reminded Nessa of the white raven she had exchanged looks with at the bar.

Finally, the bald man pushed a stack of coins into the middle of the table. Jayk didn't hesitate. With a flourish of his hand, which Nessa now noticed had a small tattoo of a skull, he pushed a tower of coins to join the other two.

Nessa looked back at her three eights, counted out the coins, and pushed her own stack onto the table.

Why not? Most of the coin I have now, I won tonight, anyway.

They were dealt another four cards, and Nessa didn't get her fourth eight. No matter, three of a kind got you quite far in this game. The bald man who had been playing with his moustache now rubbed his face, leaving streaks of moustache oil on his dark skin.

"This is oxen-shit. I'm out," he muttered and dropped his cards on the table.

The tall lady in purple made no comment. Instead, she pushed another stack of coins to the middle of the table. Jayk did the same with a smile and a wink in the lady's direction. Nessa barely kept herself from laughing at him. She matched their bets, still confident in her eights.

Now it was time for the reveal. Jayk, unsurprisingly, offered to go first. He put his hand down, showing a pair of tens. Nessa sighed in relief. If it had been three tens, they would have beaten her eights. The rules stated that the bigger number would always win.

The tall lady reached out a hand towards Nessa in a gesture that offered her to go next.

Nessa put her cards down. It was gratifying to see Jayk run his hand through his unruly hair at the sight of the three eights.

"Ah. Bugger. I thought you were bluffin', country girl," he said under his breath.

Nessa looked at the other woman who, while keeping eye contact, placed her cards on the table. She had separated them. The first four had no match, but Nessa did see that one of them was her missing eight of sapphire. The lady's other four cards were laying snugly against each other and happened to be the two of sapphires, the two of rubies, the two of onyx, and finally, almost hidden by the other three, the two of emeralds. Four of a kind.

Jayk groaned, but Nessa gifted a generous smile to the winner.

"Well done, milady," she said, waiting to see if the woman would deny the title.

The woman's purple-painted lips twitched into a smirk. "Shall we chalk it up to beginner's luck as this is my first hand with you?"

Nessa was going to reply but found herself strangely tongue-tied. Something about this woman made her feel like a skitter-beetle in the presence of a grand ice bear. Perhaps it was the way that she looked at Nessa, as if she could see right past her skin, muscles, her whole body in fact, and into her every deepest thought and dream.

This is what Hunter aims to be like. I'm glad he doesn't quite manage it.

The bald man replied instead. "Aye, let's do that. Now deal another bleedin' hand before I sober up."

The cards were dealt. Inwardly frowning, Nessa looked down at the one of onyx, the queen of sapphire, and the seven and eight of emeralds. No hope there. Normally she would bet a little just to see her next four cards and if she could make anything of them. But as she watched the lady in purple push another stack of silver coins to the pot, that choice faded away. The game had changed to an all-or-nothing approach. Nessa folded and so did the bald man. Only Jayk matched her bet with a look of determination on his face. Nessa had a gut feeling he was about to lose again.

A while later, the fortunes had changed. Nessa and Jayk were no longer the clear winners. In fact, Jayk had lost most of his coin. Nessa was faring better as she had folded quite a few of her hands, only playing the cards that were safe bets. The bald man was at the same mid-level coinage he had been all night.

The woman in purple was winning big. And to Jayk's chagrin, the one who now had most of his coin.

Another hand was dealt. Nessa took a sip of her drink to hide her excitement when she saw her cards.

Through some stroke of luck, close to divine intervention, Nessa saw the knaves of onyx, sapphires, and emeralds looking up at her. All she needed was the knave of rubies and she'd not only have four of a kind, she'd have a *high* four of a kind. One that could only be beaten by four queens or four kings.

This was the hand she had been waiting for.

The lady in purple placed her bet. It was as high as ever. That was no surprise, everything about this woman dripped wealth. Nessa matched the bet but didn't go any higher. There was no way she was going to tip off this woman about her great hand. She ate some dammon nuts and watched the bald man twirl his moustache and then fold with a sigh. Jayk looked like he was in physical pain. Gone was the swindler smile and the flirty gleam in his eye. He slapped the cards down on table without a word.

"There we are. Looks like the gentlemen are out. It is just you and I now," the lady said with amusement.

Her gaze bored into Nessa, as if she could see the cards if she looked deeply enough into Nessa's eyes.

Nessa gave her a smile which she hoped was vague enough. She sat forward a bit and suddenly her inebriation popped up to remind her how many drinks she had enjoyed. She wasn't flat-out drunk, but she certainly wasn't sober either.

"Then let's have our next four cards and see what the gods have given us to play with," Nessa said.

The lady in purple gave a brief nod and dealt the cards. Nessa picked hers up.

There he was, the knave of rubies. She also had two fives, which could be used to split the winnings if her opponent had a foursome higher than her own but no side pairing. All in all,

Nessa was in an exceedingly comfortable position here. This was the hand to bet it all on. If she, against all odds, did lose, she would weigh up just how dangerous it would be to walk back to Ground Hollow tonight. If she won, she would have another couple of drinks and go find herself a room for the night. One that didn't contain the ebony-haired beauty who haunted her heart.

The lady in purple gave a theatrical sigh. "Well? Are you going to place your bet or sit there ogling your cards? They are not going to improve by you staring at them, cherished."

Her voice sounded bored and condescending. That helped clear Nessa's preoccupied, drunken mind. She hadn't even noticed that the lady had placed her bet. Unsurprisingly, it was high again. What was surprising was *how* high it was. Almost double the usual amount. Either this lady had an astounding hand or she thought Nessa a good victim for a big bluff.

Nessa scoffed. "Oh, I'm sorry. I just wanted to drag out the suspense a little. Make you wait to lose," she drawled.

She counted out enough coins to not merely match her opponent's bet but to surpass it. She expected the lady in purple to put up enough coins to match the raised bet. Then they would reveal their cards. To Nessa's surprise, her opponent gave a chilling, far too high-pitched giggle instead. Right before pushing all the coins she had stacked up in front of her into the pot.

The bald man gasped. Jayk mumbled, "I didn't see that comin', mate."

Nessa measured out her own response and decided on a casual shrug. She didn't even have to fake the nonchalance. All her feelings and thoughts seemed to reach her through a fog of numbness. Everything about this evening felt surreal, like it was happening somewhere else. To someone else. The stacks of coin in front of her hadn't been hers at the beginning of the evening. She had walked in here with no more than a few silvers and coppers. What did it matter if she spent these strangers' coins? She didn't even bother to count them, she simply tried to match the size of the opponent's stacks, and pushed them into the middle of the table.

Jayk sat up. "Careful there, country lass. Ye sure ye want to do that? She seems to 'ave the coin to burn, ye do not."

Nessa arranged her face in a snarl, hoping it looked more scary than silly. "What do you know about what I have? What do you know about me, you prancing cock? Stay out of this. I make my own choices, and I say that no stakes are too high tonight."

It wasn't Jayk who replied but the over-the-top voice which belonged to the lady in purple. She tittered and said, "What delightful news! In that case, how about higher stakes than mere coin? How about we bet for who gets to spend the night in Elisandrine Falk's bed? Would that be acceptable, Nessa Clay?"

Suddenly the surreal, numb feeling shifted. Like a landslide. Everything was wrong now. Like seeing through a cracked window. Confused as she was, Nessa felt instantly sober. She stared open-mouthed at the woman in purple.

The lady just laughed as if they were sharing a joke.

"Do you still not know who I am, farm girl? I am your queen, and I want my toy back. Now then. Where is Elisandrine?"

CHAPTER 29

MAKING THE WORLD A
TINDERBOX

The next place Elise, Cai, and Fyhre searched was the Scarlet Crow. Only after having scoured it from top to bottom did Fyhre point to the black door leading down to the basement. Down to the White Raven.

Elise didn't think Nessa would go there, but as they were already in the tavern, it didn't hurt to have a quick look. Cai opened the door, and they walked down the narrow stairs, Elise praying to gods that she didn't believe in.

Now she found, in this musty room with white-washed walls, the woman who held her heart. Nessa was standing by a table. She was facing a handsome man in braces and a woman in purple. There was a familiar scent lingering in the air, under the smoke, liquor, and powder-stench. Elise breathed it in deep to fathom it out. It was a mix of lavender and purified alcohol, a perfume that Elise hadn't smelled in a while.

Except... I have. That night on Core Street. Was she following me that night? Has she been one step behind me this entire time?

As Elise got closer, she heard the man in braces say, "The gods-cursed Queen? Ye can't be. Ye don't have the royal paint on yer face."

The woman in purple sniggered. "Oh, silly boy. The royal make-up is put on when I am officially the Queen and ready to rule. If I am incognito in Nightport to fetch my favourite toy home, then I obviously would not put it on. Especially not if I take the night off to gamble and drink your disgusting, cheap brandy."

Elise knew that voice as well as she did her own. Just like she knew the lavender and alcohol scented perfume. She didn't need that woman to be wearing the royal mask of blue, grey, and white to recognise her. It was the Queen all right. And she knew that *she* was the toy the Queen was talking about.

Elise stepped forward. "Get away from her."

The haughty, imperial woman turned on her heels. It was such an unnatural move that she looked like an automaton. That fitted her well. All cogs and clockwork instead of nerves and heart.

"Mm. My beautiful Elisandrine. Well now. I have been talking about you and then you saunter in. I should have known that this farm girl of yours would act as a flame to a moth. I suppose she is a somewhat fetching flame, in an unassuming way. Albeit, not all that clever, it would seem," she drawled.

Unbidden, Elise's lips drew back into a snarl. "Do not dare make comments about Nessa! She is more intelligent than you, with your limited imagination, could ever fathom and much more than 'somewhat fetching.' You are here for me. Leave her alone."

The Queen looked unperturbed. "As you wish, my little tinderbox maker."

Tinderbox maker.

If she hadn't been convinced before, she was now. It had been the Queen's men asking about her and Nessa. They had just been disguised to not raise suspicion. When they found the runaway and her travel companion, they had reported back to the Queen. Who had begun to send mystery packages. There was only one question left to answer.

"My Queen," Elise began, "as you are answering questions honestly for once, can I get a real answer before we start playing games again? Why did you start sending me tinderbox parts? Why did you not simply barge into our room and demand I come with you to marry your brother? Or whatever it is you want with me?"

The Queen tutted and shook her head. "Oh, you know nothing of what I want, little fire-starter."

Elise ground her foot into the sticky floor. "Answer the question."

Her former mistress held her hands up in surrender. "I wanted some fun, Elise. You know how regimented my life is. For once, I had time to hunt and play, and I took it. Arclid is at peace, no wars and none of those pesky revolts. Oh, and one of my other ladies of court has been chosen to be Macray's wife. Remember Kelene? White hair, thin as a rake? No child-bearing hips, but I am certain she can squeeze a Royal brat or two out for my brother. Then they can both start mounting villagers to their hearts' content. Everything is under control right now, so I took some time to play with my prey."

The Queen's face lit up with cruel glee. "By the way, my guards found your hidden satchel on the path to the city. With your family crest? You really should have burned it. Would you like it back? There was a hair clip in it which you can have back, too. Although I see you no longer need that. I like your hair shorter. Suits you. Is it still long enough for a lover to pull? I think it might be. Should I come over there and try?"

Discomfort filled Elise's belly. Both at how much she didn't want this woman to touch her now and how much she'd enjoyed it at times. Often against her better judgement. She refused to show any of it. "Never mind that. If you do not require me to come back to marry Macray, then start explaining what you do want with me. And why your 'play time' had to be so elaborate."

Her Royal Highness strode closer, her long dress hiding the heeled boots that clicked menacingly on the black stone floor. She reached out a hand and ran her finger along Elise's left cheekbone. Her hand was cold, but that wasn't why Elise shivered.

The Queen spoke slowly and precisely. "Remember what I used to say about you, my sweet Lady Falk? You make the whole world…"

"…into a tinderbox," Elise finished quietly.

"Exactly. You would, without meaning to, make any place in the world a proverbial tinderbox. Even the most peaceful, calm, and boring place would become 'flammable' when you arrived. All turned into a huge tinderbox, just waiting for your next action or your next word to start a fight, a small war, or a slew of broken hearts – setting it all ablaze."

The Queen paused to laugh. "The others at court hated it, wanted me to get rid of you. I stood my ground and said that you were needed, that your light eyes proved that we had diversity at court and such nonsense. The truth was that your fire-starting was entertaining. We would visit somewhere and, in the blink of an eye, you would have enraged the lord of the manor. We would do a tour of my grounds and, in no time, you would have caused trouble with some pretty milkmaid. You rush into situations and make them… interesting. I wanted to keep that."

Elise frowned. "Keep that? What do you mean?"

"I mean that I wanted you to marry my dull brother so that I could keep you around. Ladies of court come and go whenever alliances need to be made. It was only a matter of time before you were sent out to pasture, married off to someone in the highlands or something. Making you my sister-in-law would keep you within my grasp. I could visit you on my trips south and share your bed if I liked. After all, you are notoriously talented between the sheets, little fire-starter. If I got bored in Highmere, I could send for you and make you accompany me on my trips around Arclid. Well, all around the Orb. I know you would love to see the other continents. So far you have only seen this one and Obeha, correct?"

Elise waved the question off. "Yes, but that is not relevant. You called me a toy, this sounds more like a pet. A pet you plan to bed. I am quite sure that is illegal in Arclid, Your Majesty. Especially as it would not be consensual. I never wish to see you again, much less touch your pasty, bony body."

The Queen beamed. "Ah, tempestuous as always. Imagine speaking like that to your Queen. The gall! The absolute nerve! Excellent. Where my Elise goes, drama and trouble are never far behind. So wonderful to see you again, little fire-starter. And you brought friends. Do not be rude, introduce us."

Elise tried for a calming breath. "This is Cai and Fyhre, I am afraid I have never learned their surnames." She held out her hands towards the Queen as she addressed her friends. "And this is our sovereign. In all her manipulative and mentally unstable glory."

The Queen merely laughed. Then she turned to Fyhre. "Did Elise say your name was Fire?"

Fyhre squared her shoulders. "Uh. Aye, it's pronounced fire. But spelled F-Y-H-R-E, your Majesty. I'm Fyhre Stockton an' this is Cai Weybourne."

The Queen didn't look like she was listening. She seemed busy raking her eyes over Fyhre's body. "I see. My, you are a well built one. You look like you could carry me all the way to bed and not even be the least fatigued when we got there."

Fyhre blushed, and Cai reached out a hand to place it protectively around her waist.

The Queen jeered. "Oh, do not look so flustered. I am not here to bed factory workers. I came here to have some fun with the escaped Lady Falk and bring her home." She returned her gaze to Elise. "If you will not be my sister-in-law and the powers at court refuse to allow you to be a lady in waiting, then I shall have to keep you as something else. Shan't I?"

Elise rubbed her forehead. "I am predicting that you do not mean a groomsman or a cook."

The Queen's giggle was condescending. "We both know I will have you as one of my mistresses. It will shame your family, of course, but you are bound to find new friends amongst the women and men lucky enough to be my lovers. Most of them are quite like you — carnal, hot-blooded troublemakers. Exactly my type. I will have them introduce you to the job thoroughly one night."

The Queen smiled wolfishly, her meaning all too clear to Elise.

Suddenly, Nessa's clear voice rang out. "That's it!" She shoved her way to the front of the throng. "I was going to stay out of this because I felt this was between you and Elise. But I won't let you talk about her like that. She's not a toy, not a pet, not some bed slave for you to throw to your other bed slaves to break in. She's not your little fire-starter, tinderbox maker, and certainly not your prey. She's a human. A strong, sweet, intelligent, and generous one."

Nessa stomped her foot hard before continuing. "If you think that you can own her because of your past together, your status, or because Elise's parents gifted her to you, you're wrong. She belongs to herself and will do whatever she wants."

The Queen paced towards Nessa, making every step ring out in the much too quiet room. Every person there – brawler to barkeep – looked on in stunned silence. When the Queen stood in front of Nessa, she towered over her.

"You are incorrect. Lady Falk belongs to me. She forgot that and ran off. Probably because some little country wench convinced her to," she retorted, each word clipped with regal rage.

Nessa's open face was the picture of defiance. "No one had to convince her of anything. You sent her off to marry your brother. She didn't want to. She was sure no one would miss her if she left, so she ran off. I had nothing to do with that."

"Well, she was mistaken. I miss her," the Queen said, a snakelike smile playing on her purple-painted lips.

Nessa shook her head. "As a toy, as a possession to laugh at and to mount at will. That. Doesn't. Count. I would rather die than let you take her away against her will. And I will never let you convince her she is nothing more than someone whose quick temper and erotic drive can be *entertaining*. She's the real queen here. You? You're just a spoiled, heartless child."

The Queen's smile dissolved. "I am your Queen. I can kill you. Kill your family. Burn that ugly little village of yours to the ground."

Nessa snorted. "Really?"

She looked around the room, addressing the people sitting slack-jawed at tables or standing wide-eyed by the bar. "Let it be known that if anything happens to the village of Ground Hollow, or to Jon and Carryanne Clay, that it was the Queen who did it. It was only a generation ago the people of Arclid last rebelled because these Royals thought they could do whatever they wanted. If she burns down an innocent village – one that supplies you with the grain for your bread, and the fruit for your alcohol, I might add – then revolt again. Start by spreading the fact that those deaths happened because the Queen desired to enslave a woman who simply wanted to be free."

The silent crowd was stirring. People moved in their seats, fists clenching, arms crossing over chests. Shocked faces were turning to scowls.

Elise wanted to shout with glee. Nessa was right: the

people of Arclid were docile up until rumours of abuse of power and attempted slavery started to fly. Especially slavery for sexual purpose, which had been the reason for the last sizable revolt. The Queen could not risk it. Her reign was already on thin ice as she had yet to choose a husband and have children.

Elise stepped closer to the Queen, looking away from Nessa and back to her former mistress. Somehow, the Queen looked less formidable now.

Elise tilted her chin up. "She is right. Nessa is always right. You know she has you now. It was our luck that you happened to be here tonight. You ran into us in a situation that you did not set up, that you cannot control. Look at all these witnesses. Look at these tough, salt-of-the-earth people. They will not bow to you and look the other way, not like the slime at court. Tell me, did you recognise Nessa right away?"

The Queen adjusted her sleeve, feigning indifference. "It was a few hands into the game when I realised that I had seen her before. I had seen her with you, stumbling home after a night in a tavern. Walking arm in arm down these filthy streets. Saying farewell to you in the morning, before you went to that ridiculous printing job. I recognised the dull, dowdy farm girl you were playing house with. You turned down being a princess for this? Pathetic."

There was a fire burning in Elise's chest now. "Stop it! She is anything but dull and dowdy, and you know it. I see the way you look at her. You know she is everything you can never be. Honest, kind, loving, loyal, conscientious, unselfish. Not to mention that she is the most interesting person to ever walk the Orb. You simply cannot stand that I would choose her over you, even if it meant death for me. So, out of jealousy and spite you decided to win all her coin and toy with her a bit? Was that it?"

"Does it matter, fire-starter? Make this easy on all of us,

come with me and discuss this at court like civilised people. I can pay you handsomely. Perhaps even find you a more legitimate position at court than mistress. The royal theatre might have a vacancy?"

Elise shook her head in disbelief. "You simply cannot grasp this, can you? I do not want to be your diversion, your toy, your lover. I want nothing more to do with court or Highmere. No more schemes, no more games." She stopped to take a breath, she had to remember to breathe. "I wish to be my own person. To get by through hard work and newly learnt skills. I wish to – what was it you called it? – 'play house' with Nessa. She is my everything, and if I am lucky enough that she will still have me, I want to spend the rest of my life by her side. She has earned my love, respect, and admiration — something you could never do."

She and the Queen stared at each other in silence. Those cold, dark, regal eyes didn't blink. Her purple lips twisted, making her look like she had tasted something sour. Elise forced herself to stand tall and maintain eye contact. Her brain was frantically trying to figure out what to do next but coming up with nothing.

"That makes it all clear, doesn't it? Elise is leavin' here with us, an' ye will let her go," a voice said, sounding like it was stating the obvious.

The Queen, Nessa, and Elise all turned to the speaker. It was Fyhre. Her features were a mask of grim determination, her feet planted, and her bulky biceps contracting under the tight shirtsleeves as her hands balled into fists.

The Queen raised her eyebrows, a smile now twitching at the corners of her mouth. "Oh, really? Will I? And where would be the fun in that?"

Cai butted in. "Honestly, Your Queenliness. Wouldn't it be easier an' more fun to scurry off an' find a new toy? Then, if ye got bored with him or her, ye can start chasin' Elise again. Just leave everyone else out of it. Leave Ground Hollow an' Nessa's parents in peace. An' stop ruinin' everyone here's night. There's a bleedin' fight scheduled tonight. Jhones against Calder. An' because of ye, there hasn't even been any bettin'!"

All of a sudden, there was a roar of displeasure from the crowd. Clearly these people took their fights seriously and disliked that the unpopular Nobles had waltzed in and interrupted their fun.

Elise watched as the Queen looked around. She could almost see the cogs moving in her sharp, twisted, sovereign brain. So many witnesses. People who didn't like the royalty or the rich on a good day. Ones that were now drunk and angry. Ones that probably had knives and brass-knuckles.

Elise smiled to herself. *Regretting that you did not bring your guards, Your Majesty?*

The Queen sniffed. "Fine. Conceivably, it might be more fun to find someone new. Someone younger and with actual curves. I shall take that into consideration."

"Consider it swiftly. Because I and my friends are leaving," Elise said, loud and clear.

She grabbed Nessa's hand and headed for the door, trusting Cai and Fyhre to know when it was time to scurry away. Their footfalls behind her confirmed her assumption.

The door seemed so very far away. Every step she took, Elise was terrified that she'd hear the loud clicks of the Queen's heels. Or hear her shriek out an order to "seize them" to some hidden guard or hired muscle. Elise just wanted to be outside, where she could run without looking like a frightened field mouse.

"Go left," Nessa whispered. "There's a secret backdoor that Hunter showed me." Elise obeyed without question.

Finally, they were all out the door and in an unfamiliar alley. It was pitch dark, and Elise's frightened mind saw guards and hired assassins everywhere. The door slammed close, and

Elise wasted no time in running towards the distant light of streetlights.

Are the others with me? Yes, you idiot. You are the only one with heeled boots and the one in the worst physical condition. If you can keep this pace, they certainly can.

They got out of the dark alley and kept running. Their steps pounded the streets of Nightport, and soon Elise realised that she didn't know where she was leading them. She was just running away.

"Where should we go?" she panted to the two locals.

"Let's find Hunter," Cai shouted back. "He'll know where to hide ye. Jus' in case her Queenliness comes after ye."

"Fine. Where would he be?" Elise replied breathlessly.

"He said something about rounding people up for the Goblin's Tavern tonight. He might still be there," Nessa replied, annoyingly not the least out of breath.

"There's a shortcut," Fyhre said and took off running to the right.

They all followed without question. Elise was doing a lot of that tonight. As she ran, she realised that she couldn't ignore the smell of lavender and purified alcohol which, real or imaginary, still clung to her nose. It was threatening her more efficiently than words ever could. She ran faster.

CHAPTER 30

MAD HEART

As they saw the sign for the Goblin's Tavern, fires and all, Nessa was relieved to spot a glimpse of cobalt. Thank the gods for Hunter's unique style. She headed for the man head-to-toe in blue.

"Hunter! You have to help us," Elise panted as she almost ran into him.

He took a step back and surveyed them. "I... I... what now? What in the name of the gods has happened to you four?"

"We had to run," Fyhre said.

Hunter put his hands on his hips and glared at her. "Sweetest heart, I can see *that*. But why?"

Nessa grabbed his elbow to get his attention. "That harmless table you led me to? It didn't stay harmless for long. A new player joined, and it turned out that she was the gods-forsaken Queen."

Hunter scrunched up his nose. "The queen of what?"

"Of Arclid, you imbecile," Elise snapped.

His eyes grew big. "What?"

Cai chuckled while pointing to Elise. "Seems our mate 'ere

is secretly a big deal. Close to the bleedin' Queen. Even underneath the Queen some nights, it seems."

Elise groaned. "Thank you for adding that last bit, Cai. Yes, I am afraid I have lied a little, Hunter. The truth is that I was a lady-in-waiting before being shipped off to marry Prince Macray. Neither he nor I approved. I came across Nessa, through a long story which involved her climbing to my window, and we both wanted to leave. So, we travelled here together. My real name is Lady Elisandrine Falk. I am so terribly sorry for deceiving all of you."

Fyhre and Cai looked shocked but said nothing.

Hunter smiled widely. "Aha! I know you had a juicy secret. How splendid! A real Noble in the flesh. Hmm, but you said you were born in Silverton? Not Highmere? Was that a lie, too?"

Elise put her hands on her hips. "We are not all gathered in Highmere, as if under some form of house arrest, you know. There are Nobles in quite a few of the towns scattered around Arclid, actually. Newhaven, Chislehurst, Crawley, and of course Silverton, to mention a few."

"Can we get back to the main story here and stop reeling off facts about Noble life?" Nessa muttered.

Hunter shook himself alert. "Yes, of course. I wish you would have confided in me, but no matter. So, am I to understand that the Queen came to fetch you back tonight?"

Elise looked down at the ground. "In a manner of speaking, yes. She has in fact been here for quite a while, it seems. She has been incognito while toying with me. Trying to confuse and scare me before swooping down and picking me up in her long talons to take me back to Highmere."

Hunter made a sound, half scoff and half hum. "Well, this is not Highmere. This is Nightport. Here we see Royalty as a necessary evil at best and a disruptive, power-hungry nuisance at worst. You, however, have become one of us. At least that is the way I see it. And Nightport looks after its own. Like a harsh but loyal parent."

He stared into space before shaking himself out of his reverie. "We need to hide you deep in the city until she tires of playing with you and goes back to court. Or transport you somewhere further into the lowlands or the highlands, by carriage or ship. What will it be, heartling?"

"No. Further away. In case the Queen hunts 'er," Fyhre said.

Elise nodded. "Fyhre is right, I need to get far away. I doubt the Queen will chase me, but tonight has shown that I cannot predict her behaviour. I should leave Arclid. However, leaving for one of the other continents... means that visiting will be hard," she said, facing Nessa.

She looked so terrified and little that Nessa had to take her hand. "It's all right. My parents will understand. When it comes to Layden, well, I bet he'll wish to take his family for a trip at some point. He could visit us then."

Elise's mouth opened a little but no sound came. She closed it, swallowed, and in a small voice said, "I meant it would be hard for *you* to visit *me*. Do you mean that you will come with me? Even after our fight this morning? Even after all I said?"

Nessa nodded, hoping that her face showed her resolve and affection. "Yes. We've got issues to discuss. But the argument was based on the fact that we didn't understand the depth of the other's feelings. You thought I didn't love you, right? Well, I thought you only wanted to be my friend and bedfellow. The things you said to the Queen about me makes me think that I was wrong and that I'm forgiven. So, unless you meant the things you said this morning, and those things keep you from wanting to be with me, I'd like to stay with you."

Elise gripped her hand tight. "I did certainly not mean those things, my cherished. I was hurt, and I thought you refused to let yourself love me because you found me unworthy. I lost my temper. As per usual. There will be plenty of time for explaining later. Just know that I adore you, hope you forgive me, and that I will do anything to keep you with me."

"Us, however, ye'll have to leave 'ere," Cai said. "Sorry to interrupt an' sorry to 'ave to say goodbye, but I reckon it makes sense for us to split up now. Me an' Fyhre can double back an' try to confuse anyone who might be lookin' for ye. Ye need to find a place to lay low while ye pick yer way out of the city. An' speakin' as a born survivor, the less details I know, the less I can be forced to tell anyone chasin' ye. That goes for Royal guards and the city guards alike."

Nessa looked from Fyhre to Cai. She hadn't known them for long, but they already felt like close friends. "Hunter will know where we go. Come visit us one day?" she asked.

"Aye. An' one day ye'll come back to Nightport," Fyhre stated in her succinct way.

"Absolutely," Elise replied. "Thank you both for your assistance tonight. It was vital, and I adore you for it." Then she tossed herself at Fyhre, hugging her so tight that the larger woman nearly toppled backwards.

Cai laughed and joined the hug, making it an Elise sandwich. Nessa watched through the haze of tear-brimmed eyes. When Elise had released them, it was Nessa's turn for a more sober embrace from each.

"Please pass on our goodbyes to Sanjero and Jac. Give them hugs from us. Tell them that they have to come with you when you visit," Nessa croaked.

"Aye. Will do," Cai said, patting Nessa's shoulder. "Take care, heartlings. May the gods be kind to ye, an' may the Queen catch the fuck-pox."

They shared one last laugh, all except Elise who was choking on the description of the bedding disease. Fyhre and

Cai left with heavy steps, walking back towards the White Raven by the looks of it.

They watched them for a heartbeat or two until Hunter cleared his throat. "We need to find you a ship, then?"

Nessa took Elise's hand before answering. "Yes. Will there be one tonight, do you think?"

He shook his head. "It is far too late now. Morning is a good time for ships travelling to the other continents."

"Then Cai was right, we should lay low tonight. Somewhere close to the harbour, perhaps?" Elise asked.

Hunter looked at her as if she had been naughty. "It is a port. But yes."

Elise rolled her eyes. "Port, harbour, whatever it is. *Wherever* it is. At the end of Core Street, is it not?"

"Wait, you have not visited it?" he asked, incredulous.

"No. We were warned that it was rough and smelly, so it was not exactly a priority for us. Does that matter right now?" Elise asked.

He wrinkled his nose. "I suppose not. But, but… it is the heart of this city. Night*port*, remember?"

Nessa's patience was draining. "Yes, yes. Enough of the tourist notes. We need a place to stay, we need some of our belongings, and then we need a ship as soon as humanly possible. I don't want us anywhere near that Queenly pain in the arse when she starts scheming again."

Hunter gave a brisk nod. "Right. Let us start walking in that direction and we will nail down more details as we go."

With that, he began to stroll down the street. Nessa was about to ask him to speed up until she realised how innocent he looked at his leisurely pace. She fell into step with him and soon felt Elise's presence by her side. Four chilly fingers slid against her palm and a thumb brushed the back of her hand. Nessa took the hand and squeezed it, hearing Elise breathe out a shaky breath.

Hunter turned to them, carefree as ever. "So, you actually played cards with the Queen, Nessa. Who won?"

"I think I did. That doesn't much matter now, does it?" Nessa snapped.

He shrugged. "I guess not. I merely wondered what happened to the coin you played for."

"I would assume the Queen took it. It is probably being spent on a slew of mercenaries to hunt us down," Elise said in a chipper tone so forced it almost shattered.

Hunter smiled at her pityingly. "Right. Anyway, as you need more distance between you and her Royal Highness, you require a sea voyage to one of the other continents. So far, we are all agreed, yes?"

Both women nodded as they walked along.

He clapped his hands. "Good. Luckily, from Nightport, there are ships to all three. However, I fear the steamships to the Western Isles and Obeha will be filled. Autumn is growing colder, and people want to travel to the warm continents. However, if there is a ship across Whistler's Sea to somewhere in Storsund tomorrow, I can get you on board."

Elise scrunched up her nose. "Storsund? But that is so far north, worse than Arclid's highlands. I was taught that it was a huge barren place with snow, dangerous trains, and dirty coal mines. That is why the Queen dreaded visiting there."

Hunter chuckled. "Do not underestimate it. It is not barren simply because it is cold and big. In fact, it is thriving. You are both better schooled than me, so you must know that the steam engine was invented there. And the locomotive. Well, rail tracks are being laid all over the continent now, making their industry flourish, their trade thrive, and their economy grow accordingly. And, they have frost fairs every winter on the River Orla. Huge marketplaces and circuses all on the thick ice. Marvellous!"

"You've been there?" Nessa asked.

"A few times. To the two harbour cities you can sail to from here. I worked as a rope boy on the sail ships as a young lad. You wanted adventure, Miss Clay, if that is your real name. Well, Storsund is full of adventure. Dark forests, big cities, and more history and folklore than you can shake a stick at. Lovely vodka to keep you warm as well."

"Well, at least I can see what their architecture looks like. My father would have liked that notion," Elise said quietly.

There was a shout of "You there!" behind them, and as if on command, they all took off running.

"Probably not for us, but better safe than sorry, eh?" Hunter said as he ran, his cobalt coat slapping against his legs.

They ran until Nessa's lungs ached in the cold air. Then, her feet were on a more yielding surface. Wooden planks covered what must be the port. There were none of Nightport's gaslit streetlights here. The only illumination came from lanterns with block candles in them attached to some of the buildings and gas lit lamps dotted on the edges of the dock, marking out the drop to the sea. They all stopped and tried to catch their breath. Poor Elise was doubled over, gasping. Nessa filled her aching lungs with air that smelled of the salty sea and wet wood. Rotting fish guts spilled on the planks, provided an unwelcome undertone.

Hunter held out his arms like he was offering the vista to them. "Welcome to the port of Nightport," he huffed.

"You know, the 'port' bit is obvious. But the 'night' part has always confused me," Elise admitted in rasping pants.

Hunter took a deep breath. Then another. Not wanting to sound breathy as he broke in to his theatrical tour guide bit, Nessa assumed.

"Well, some say it was the dark deeds that took place in the city, usually after nightfall. Others say it was because the wood smoke and fog made the city look dark from the vantage point of sailors out on their ships. The truth is that no one remembers anymore. Sad really," he said.

"And irrelevant right now," Nessa snapped.

The other two looked at her strangely, but didn't argue. Nessa's blood was rushing so hard she could see the veins on the backs of her hands bulging. Maybe Elise's quick temper was contagious. Maybe it was just fear. All Nessa knew was that they had to find somewhere safe. Immediately.

"There is a long line of warehouses down here. Filled with lumber and grains to go across the sea. I know of one where I have sometimes gone to lay low for a while. Or where I have suggested visitors wanting some release sneak in with a lover or two," Hunter said mischievously.

"Will it be safe for us to spend the night there?" Elise asked, slightly less out of breath now.

Hunter inclined his head. "It should be, yes. It is further away from the others and not much to look at, so it does not normally attract attention."

Elise darted in another question. "And while we hide in there, can you try to get us tickets for one of the steamships?"

He dusted off his cuffs. "I shall do more than try; I shall get them for you. The taverns down here are where all the captains and ship crews drink. I will find the right people to ask."

"Thank you, Hunter. For that and for taking time away from your work to aid two hunted nobodies," Nessa said.

"No need to even mention it. You have become my friends, and I am low on those. Furthermore, you are not nobodies. The Queen herself hunts you. You are famous! I can live long on the tales I can regale Nightport visitors with about this night. I will tell them of your adventures while I lead them to an expensive tavern and keep embellishing until they are out of coin. Earning me a nice pay-out, indeed."

Nessa elbowed him in the side, while Elise merely laughed. It felt nice to have a moment of calm and banter.

"Oh, and I will return to 21 Miller Street and fetch a few things for you. I cannot take all that much, though. It might look suspicious if I come out of your rooms with large bags stuffed with frilly dresses and jewellery."

Nessa held up her hand. "We won't require that. Mainly it's our coin we'll be needing. Especially to pay for the tickets you will get us. We can use Arclid coins in Storsund, right?"

"Of course. We share a currency with them and Obeha. Only the Western Isles insist on their strange tin coins. I have a pencil and some paper in my coat pocket. I will make a list when we are inside. No need to pay for the tickets, by the way. Most captains around here owe me a favour. I make sure of it. Your payment can be offering me a home to visit in Storsund."

"So, then we will be owing you a favour, too. Why am I not surprised?" Elise teased.

Hunter winked at Elise, closing both eyes as he did so.

Nessa rolled her eyes. *Why can't these people wink properly?*

"Are we almost there?" she asked.

"Almost," Hunter said, picking up the pace.

He took them further down the dock until they came to a scruffy-looking warehouse, smaller than its neighbours. It had lanterns on the wall, too, but they were unlit, making it look abandoned. To the left of the door there was a collection of rocks on the ground. He picked up an ordinary-looking stone. Under it was a rusty key. He took it and unlocked the sizable warehouse doors. They opened with a creak that must have been heard all the way back to the White Raven.

Hunter hurried over to the right-hand side of the unlit building, where there seemed to be a table of some kind. He lit a gas lamp, and the warehouse was illuminated by a frail light, struggling against the thick darkness. Nessa wished it was summer, so they could have some warming sunlight soon. Alas, the safety of daylight was hours and hours away.

She looked around and saw stack after huge stack of timber. "Don't they have trees in Storsund?" she asked in a whisper, which was more due to the impressive vastness of the warehouse than the fact that they were hiding.

Hunter laughed. "They have plenty of it. This timber is going to the Western Isles, where the trees have slender stems of yielding wood. Our sturdy timber delivered, the ships come back to us loaded with sunberries and spices. Import and export. You have something we want, and we have something you need."

He bent down and grabbed a bundle that was wedged under the rickety table holding the lamp. "Speaking of needing, you will require these. They are blankets I keep for the amorous visitors I direct here. It gets a tad cold as the night goes on. Although the warehouse should apparently be insulated to not damage the timber. The cold draughts makes the wood shrink. Or is it expand? I was not properly listening to the owner, she tends to babble on."

He must have spotted the impatience on Nessa's face, because he threw the bundle at her. She deftly caught it and he carried on speaking. "No pillows or mattresses, sadly. You will make up for it when you get to Storsund, plenty of cosy luxury to be had there. Simply ask anyone for nice hotels and rented rooms. Did I mention that most of them speak our language? You should be able to make yourself understood. At least if you stay in the big cities. The countryside I know nothing about."

Nessa scoffed. "Oh, don't I know it."

He made a face at her which improved her mood enough for her to chuckle. Looking pleased with that, he took a crumpled piece of paper and a pencil stump out of his coat pocket. "So. What is it you want me to fetch from your room?"

Elise took a step forward. "The book that Nessa gave me, which is on the night stand next to the bed. It has a bright cover, you cannot miss it. On the dressing table is a hairbrush, please pack that and a couple of hair ties for Nessa. Also, the two jars of sugar pumpkin oil that Nessa's mother sent us. You will find them on top of the dresser. And of course, our stash of coin, which you will find in a plain wooden box hidden behind our shoes in the wardrobe."

"It's covered with an old shirt, too. Lift that and you'll see the box," Nessa added.

He nodded at her before writing that down. She could only hope he wouldn't be fool enough to lose that piece of paper.

Hunter looked back up at her. "Anything you want from the room, Nessa?"

"I suppose a full change of clean clothes would be too bulky," she mumbled. He agreed, and they all fell silent while Nessa pondered.

"I think I'd like some writing paper and a pencil. I need to write a farewell letter to my parents and Layden." Even Nessa could hear how her voice wavered. She cursed her weakness; neither of her parents would appreciate this sentimentality.

Hunter smiled reassuringly. "Of course. And I will make sure it gets delivered to them. In fact, I might venture there myself. I have never been to Ground Hollow. I might get to see a man marry a cow."

She sneered at his attempt to cheer her up by baiting her. "What you might see is a boot kicking you out for being rude. People are raised properly in Ground Hollow."

He laughed but then brought the attention back to the crumpled piece of paper in his hand. "Anything else to go on the list?"

Nessa and Elise looked at each other, both shaking their heads. Neither of them had brought much with them to

Nightport, and it looked like they would leave in the same way.

"Splendid. I shall pick those things up. As you did not ask for much, I can probably fit in some clean underthings and maybe a shirt or two. I have no idea what underthings ladies wear, but I trust I will find some smaller objects of clothing tucked away in the dresser?"

Elise smiled kindly at him. "Yes. The top drawer has the undershirts, socks and nether coverings. Thank you. Bring as much as you can fit in the satchel, which hangs on a hook by the door. And in the carpet bag I bought to carry food in, that will come in handy now. I think it is by the foot of the bed."

"I shall do exactly that. I will try to pick up something to eat and drink as well. You two have a long night ahead and a lengthy journey awaiting you tomorrow."

He bowed and left. When the door closed on him and the chilly ocean air, Nessa glanced over at Elise. She was fretting with her scarf, loosening and tightening it at her throat. Nessa had to look away, staring at her feet seemed a good choice right now.

Moments ticked by until Elise broke the silence. "So... the things that were sent to us in the midnight blue wrapping paper. They were parts of a tinderbox."

"I gathered that from your talk with the Queen."

"Silly really. I should have guessed that right away. I just..." Elise wrapped her arms around herself. "I did not believe the Queen cared enough about me to pursue me. I thought I was merely one of many diversions, forgotten the second I was out of view."

"Clearly you're more memorable and loveable than you think," Nessa mumbled.

"Yes. It would seem that I am suffering from your usual problem."

Nessa felt her ire prickle up. "Excuse me?"

Elise's eyes widened, and she held her hands out. "Oh, I meant no harm. I only meant that you constantly underestimate what people feel for you. You missed that Isobel had taken a liking to you and you did not notice that I had... fallen for you."

Nessa swallowed, feeling as if there was something jagged in her throat. "Did you mean those nice things you said about me to the Queen?" she croaked out.

Elise took a small step closer to her. "You know I did. I meant all those things. Unlike the things I said this morning. Gods, was it only this morning? This day has taken an age."

Nessa scuffed her boot against the dusty floorboards. "There seemed to be a lot of truth in those things you said."

The tug of war in Nessa threatened to rip her apart. Pain and pride on one side, her need for Elise on the other.

Elise wrapped her arms back around herself. Was it to ward out the cold or to comfort herself?

"There is a peculiarity to the truth coming out," she said. "It can help you or it can hurt you. This morning, I said some things that I do *not* believe to be true. But yes, I also said some truths. However, I made them sound worse than they are and chose the ones that would hurt you. Because you hurt me." Elise took a shaky breath before continuing. "I thought we were finally taking the step towards being together. Truly together, lovers not solely for the night but for life. I have never been that vulnerable and open with someone. I have never fallen this deeply before, never been so completely at someone's mercy."

"So, the way I was this morning..." Nessa trailed off.

"Hurt like being trampled by marrow-oxen, yes. I expect that was why I hurt you back. I apologise for that," Elise said, voice breaking.

Nessa tried to catch her eye. "I apologise, too. I said plenty of horrible things about you. And you were right, you know. I do see more in you than others do. I see more than the rich, chatty, wild child. I see more than someone who is fun to run around with or to bed. And I adore all that I see. I just didn't think you could commit to a relationship." Nessa heard how that sounded and quickly held a finger up in the air, asking for patience. "Not because there is something wrong with you; it's me. I'm not in your league. I know I can be boring, overly practical, and naïve. Additionally, as you rightly pointed out, I'm scared. I'm constantly worrying and completely addicted to being safe. Maybe that *was* why I stayed in Ground Hollow."

Suddenly Elise looked stern. "Nessa, I do not know if fear was part of your reasoning or not. But I know that the main reason for you to stay was that you wanted to help your family. You did not lie regarding that – I did. I lied to hurt you back. To unsteady you, to make you listen to me. It was childish, unfair, and cruel."

Elise reached out as if to touch Nessa but let her hand fall. Instead she added, "One of the many things I love about you is how you help others. You even climb up castle walls to help others. You agreed to be chased by Royal guards and to barely have time to say goodbye to your family just to help others. To help me. There is not a single selfish bone in your body."

Nessa stepped closer. "I-I'm so glad you see me like that. Your opinion of me matters so much. I'm sorry that I hurt you and pushed you away this morning. I truly do believe that we could make a good couple. If you really d-do want me by your side, it will work. I feel it every time my heart thuds when you smile. It has chosen you. And it seems that your heart has chosen me, too. I'm sorry that I underestimated your feelings."

Nessa bit her lip, trying to push back tears. "I'm also sorry I called you those things. You can't help being born rich and raised in Noble circles. And bedplay and pretty distractions are not the only things you want; that was a ridiculous statement.

However, there is nothing wrong with how much and how often you enjoy bedplay. In fact, your appetite for everything in life is one of the most wonderful things about you. I'm so angry at myself for making you feel bad about that."

Elise's eyes found hers, and they glistened as wetly as her own probably did. The tip of Elise's nose was growing pink. Nessa couldn't help but marvel at the adorableness of it.

"As we are apologising for everything we said," Elise said softly, "I will add that I'm sorry to have made you doubt that you belong out in the world. You definitely do. You were so brave to leave your safe village and to come to vast, dark Nightport with a stranger in tow and no certain prospects. You have quickly grown, acclimatised, and even prospered in a way that few could."

The space between their bodies seemed warmer than the rest of the warehouse. Nessa was very aware of how close they were and how easily they could be holding each other. But there was still unspoken words, or perhaps unspoken emotions, standing between them and the physical reassurance that Nessa hungered for.

"Is it t-true that everyone saw how we felt about each other but me?" she asked, putting her hands in her pockets.

"Well, yes. That part was true. Layden quickly noticed it. Fyhre and Cai saw it, so did Jac and Sanjero. Not to mention Hunter, who picked up on it before I was aware of it myself, I think."

Nessa sighed and then chuckled. "That's me all over, isn't it? Even more clueless when it comes to love than everything else."

"Well, Layden did say that you had missed that his wife was so negative towards you because she had an unrequited infatuation. She thought you had ignored her and her broken heart. But he knew, and I have learnt, that you simply do not notice these things. You do not understand that you are such a

328

wonderful creature that people can easily fall head over heels in love with you. Real, long-lasting love. Like mine."

They smiled at each other. Their smiles fragile and unsure.

Nessa scuffed the coarse floorboards with the toe of her boot. "Do you think we stand a chance at being together, then?"

"I think we might. I will do whatever it takes to make it work. And you, well, you have made your stance obvious. Especially with your actions, you seem to be uprooting your life completely. Leaving your family, friends, and your safe haven of Ground Hollow behind for us. I would venture to say that you are betting a lot that we will be able to make it work."

Both of their smiles grew stronger, more confident. "I only bet big when it's prudent. As that Queen of yours found out tonight."

Elise clasped her hands in front of her. "Well, there you go then. It must be a prudent bet. Unless you are having second thoughts? I would understand if you are. I am not an easy person to live with. And Storsund is a long way away. It would be hard and expensive to visit your family."

Nessa gave that thought a moment to settle. Her pulse was up, making her unbutton her coat while she searched her mind for doubt, finding plenty.

"It's crazy. There is nothing safe about escaping to a foreign continent like this. Probably hunted by an all-powerful, spiteful monarch. The only person with me being one I have only known for about a fortnight. A woman who is famous for being impulsive and getting into trouble wherever she goes. A woman who has the power to make me feel my best, but also my worst. The sensible thing would be to put you on that ship tomorrow and go back to Ground Hollow."

Elise looked down and nodded. Nessa reached for her, whispering, "But love isn't sensible." She caressed her cheek, then threaded her fingers through windblown hair, giving it a little scrunch to make it curl around Elise's face. A gesture she had seen Elise do countless times.

"Thank you," Elise whispered. Somehow Nessa didn't think she meant for adjusting her hair.

"I thought I left Ground Hollow to see something new. Because I was bored and uncomfortable with everyone knowing me. You have shown me that there was more to it than that. Being with you has revealed that what I wanted deep down was to challenge myself. To grow and to let go of my fears. You make me take risks. And so far, while it has put me in danger, it has taught me who I want to be. I want to stay someone who knows when to bet or fold, yes. But I want to become someone who always gambles on a good hand. As far as I can see, you're the perfect hand for me, so bugger being sensible. Let's have our next adventure."

Elise looked at her, tears trickling out of golden eyes. "Even with the Queen chasing us?"

"Oh, we don't know she will. I'm sure it would hurt her pride to admit that she wanted you back enough to risk her people's anger. Or to spend all that time and coin chasing you. I think it's more likely that she'll try to find another tinderbox-maker to pet."

Elise hummed her agreement. "Nevertheless, what if she does decide to chase us?"

Nessa's hand found its way back to Elise's hair. This time it went below the pitch-black tresses to caress the nape of her neck. "Then she'll have to be fast and clever. And tenacious. Which doesn't seem to be her strong suit."

Elise sniffed and wiped her wet cheeks. "Hmm, no. She has even less patience than me."

"There you go then," Nessa said simply.

Elise retrieved the hand resting on her neck and kissed it.

Something fell into place. Nessa no longer had the feeling of something unspoken between them. There were still things to discuss, but they were on the same line now. They were a set again. As she looked at Elise, she felt her whole body growing weak while her heart grew stronger. Her love grew stronger. That reddening nose, those wet eyes, and those tear-stained cheeks — Nessa wanted nothing more than to kiss every drop of pain away from the woman in front of her. First, she had to say those words. But how?

Nessa rubbed the back of her neck. "We h-have spoken about love. And our feelings. About falling for each other and a-adoring each other. But we... we haven't..." She trailed off.

Elise dried her cheeks again. Then, in a low but certain tone, she voiced their thoughts. "We have not said 'I love you' yet. I think I may have spoken of love, but I am not certain I said the words clear and simple. Well, there will be no more misunderstandings. No more underestimating each other's feelings. I love you, Nessa Clay. With all that I am and all that you inspire me to be."

Nessa heard a croaking sound leave her lips. She hurried to clear her throat and say, "I love you, too. More than I knew I could love someone."

Elise took her hand and pulled Nessa towards her. They collided in a clumsy kiss, her nose stabbing Elise's cheek. Neither cared. They kissed. And kissed. And kissed. Elise placed Nessa's arms around her waist. Nessa couldn't hold her close enough but did a valiant attempt to actually meld their bodies into one through the medium of embracing.

After a while, Elise broke away, staring starry-eyed at Nessa. She stared back in heart-pounding wonder. Everything suddenly felt so bright in that dark, dank warehouse.

Elise shook her head gently and began laughing, and Nessa quickly joined her. She rested her forehead against Nessa's. "So. We go to Storsund, then. How long do we stay?"

"I don't know. We shall see, I guess. It'll be an adventure where I won't have the safety net of my parents and Layden close by. Which is good. It means I won't give up and recede back into my old life. However, there will come a time where I'll miss them too much, I think."

"When that happens, we will return to Arclid. I will buy us tickets right away. The Queen be damned," Elise said.

"Thank you." The words left Nessa's mouth in a croaked whisper.

"No. Thank you. For gambling on me. On us. Oh, and another promise I will make you. I will find you another apprenticeship with a glassblower. You will learn the craft and get to work with your beloved glass."

Nessa took her hand. It felt cold, and she rubbed it a little to bring her warmth. It was the least she could do. No one had ever made her feel the way Elise did. So wanted. So understood. So loved. Not having the words, she let her body tell Elise how she felt. She pulled her close again and kissed her gently.

Elise grabbed onto her waist, her hands tightening almost painfully. Nessa's breath left her chest as Elise deepened the kiss, claiming her mouth and making it feel like it was the most natural thing in the world. As if everything was wrong unless their bodies were connected at some point. Nessa revelled in the kiss, trying to convey everything with the touch of her lips and her tongue.

Part of her wanted to take this further. To make love to Elise and involve her whole body in this wordless pact of affection and belonging. But she was so bone tired. Late nights of drinking and the emotional turmoil of the last couple of days had taken their toll. She felt Elise sway a little on her feet. Reluctantly, she extricated herself.

"Should I take your unsteadiness as a sign of my kissing talent or are you exhausted, too?" Nessa whispered.

Elise hummed happily. "Both." Her hands were caressing Nessa's back.

"Would you like to rest?" Nessa said, closing her eyes to keep her resolve. To keep from melting into one big puddle of affection and desire.

Elise leaned in, nuzzling at her throat. "Only if I can hold you. I hope to never let you go again. Gods only know what you might get up to if I do."

Nessa chuckled. "Me? I thought you were meant to be the troublemaker?"

"Well yes, but I think you are superseding me. After all, we had a fight and my reaction was to be so distracted at work that I lost my position. Rather prosaic and dull. You on the other hand, went to the most dangerous gambling den in Nightport and played high-stakes cards with the Queen herself. Then you nearly got your entire village killed and started a revolt against the monarchy. One that might still take place, I hasten to add. I would say you outdid me tonight."

They laughed but stopped when the urge to kiss got too strong. Elise's hands were pushing their way under Nessa's coat, waistcoat, shirt, and finally her undershirt. For once, they weren't cold but pulsing with welcome heat. Even Elise's mouth felt deliciously warm, and Nessa had to force herself to stop kissing it long enough to say, "I guess I'm picking up your habits."

Elise quirked an eyebrow. "And you chose that one? Trou-blemaking?"

"You seem to think that I'm in control here. I'm just a slave to my heart, and that little creature is mad with love. Not to be trusted to make any decisions."

"Ah, it is lucky that you will be travelling with me, then. I can keep an eye on you and that mad heart of yours," Elise said softly.

Nessa kissed the tip of her nose, which now that the crying had stopped, had gone back to its normal sandy colour. "Very good indeed."

Elise let go of her, stretched, and yawned. It was conta-gious enough for Nessa to have to yawn as well. Elise smoothed out one of Hunter's blankets on the ground and then took off her scarf, rolling it up into a ball.

"There. A mattress, a pillow, and the other blanket to cover us. Does that sound suitable to you, madam?" Elise asked.

Nessa immediately laid down on the blanket. She opened her ox-leather coat, and Elise wordlessly crept into Nessa's embrace. She pulled the other blanket over them, cocooning them safely. Everything was now warm and smelled of timber, the sea, and of course of Elise, who cuddled close to her, as usual. Nessa wondered if a heart could implode with joy. She gently rubbed Elise's back and let her mind relax away from fights, being hunted, and important life decisions. Her mind wandered in time with her hands moving on Elise's back.

"Maybe I should cut my hair, like you have. Combing and braiding it each morning takes a lot of time. And strands of hair constantly escape the braid, you know that better than anyone, you're always tucking them behind my ears. Oh, and this coat is pretty warm, but do you think it will be warm enough for Storsund? We don't have proper winter clothing and I…" Nessa trailed off as she heard Elise snuffle a little.

Her heartling was clearly asleep. She kissed Elise's hair and let her own eyes close. Discussions about outfits for their new life could wait. Right now, she was warm enough, tired enough, and loved enough to solely focus on getting some sleep.

She and Elise had fallen in love while sharing a bed. Every deep breath, every brush of sleeping limbs, every dream, bonding them tighter to each other. It seemed that their sleeping bodies and minds had fallen for each other and then their waking selves had followed. Sleeping in each other's arms had been their starting point, and Nessa guessed it would remain the touching stone of their relationship. Her eyes closed and her breathing slowed to match Elise's.

~

A little later, Nessa woke up to a hand slipping inside her clothes, sliding tentatively against her naked skin. Soon it cupped her breast, very gently.

"Is that all right?" Elise whispered.

Nessa hummed happily. "Yes. What a lovely way to wake up."

"Oh sorry. I thought you were already awake. Considering what you were doing."

Stopping in the middle of a stretch, Nessa asked, "Doing? What do you mean?"

Elise gave a her a crooked smile. "You were asleep then. Perhaps I should not tell you."

Nessa swatted her on the backside. "Tell me!"

"Fine. You were... moving your hips in an interesting way."

"Interesting, how?" Nessa asked, guessing the answer.

"Well, I would never use the word 'humping' in regards to a lady," Elise said with a smirk.

"Uh-huh. How about a woman raised on a farm?"

Elise pretended to think, rubbing her chin theatrically. "I suppose 'humping' would work in that instance, yes. It is a good thing you are underneath me and not above. Otherwise I would have been ground into the floor."

Nessa sighed. "Oh, come on. It can't have been that bad."

"How about I show you what it was like?" Elise whispered, seduction in every syllable.

She began rolling her hips down against Nessa's. Suddenly, Nessa became very aware of Elise's leg between hers. Had that thigh been pressed so tightly against her core the entire nap? No wonder she had begun grinding against it.

Nessa couldn't help but moan. Elise's face livened at the sound. The gaslight threw shadows across her beautiful features, making her look more dangerous than usual. More wanton. It was such a contrast to the sweetness of their resting together. It seemed to raise the heat between Nessa's thighs now. She claimed Elise's soft lips with her own. This time, the moan came from Elise and was muffled into their shared kiss.

All of a sudden, there was an almighty creak, and they both broke apart to look at the door.

Standing there was Hunter Smith. He had their satchel over his shoulder and the carpetbag in his right hand. His left hand seemed occupied with struggling to hold both a paper bag and the door key.

His slim nose twitched. "No. Still not seeing the allure in all that carnal stuff. But at least you seem to have made up. Good for you. I have procured your tickets and found out that the passage to Storsund will take around six weeks. And I only packed that one book for you, so you will need something else to fill the time. I trust that…" Here he pointed at their bodies, "…grinding stuff should keep you busy all the way to Charlottenberg. Which is where you'll alight: the less than attractively named Hangman's Dock which is the port in the more beautifully named city of Charlottenberg."

He paused to put the bags down. "Then I recommend getting on one of their famed trains and heading to Skarhult. It is bigger and a less obvious place to hide than a harbour city. If I recall correctly, it is known for its delectable pastries. Speaking of food, here are some cheese and shroom sandwiches. I picked up a bottle of honeyed winterberry juice too."

He held out the paper bag Nessa had spotted in his hand earlier.

Elise slowly extricated herself from Nessa and got up.

Nessa was amused at how her body complained at the loss, her arms almost reaching out to pull Elise back down.

Yes, we'll be able to stay busy during the sea voyage. As long as we have a room and some food, we should be happily occupied with talking, cuddling, and… coupling. I wonder if I'll be able to climax every time or if my issues with that will return. It doesn't matter. I'm sure Elise won't mind if we have to try a few extra times.

Nessa watched Elise stretch languidly.

Look at that magnificent woman. I want to try for that climax right now. Nessa Clay, stop thinking about that and pay attention!

Nessa quickly stood up, wiping off the dust from the blanket and the floor. She couldn't wait for her next long bath. "Thank you again, Hunter. You have been such a good friend to us."

"No need to thank me. As I said before, get settled in Storsund and make sure you have a home with an extra bed, and enough coin to buy me a meal, as I have a feeling that I will be visiting you soon."

Elise took the paper bag from him. "Really?"

He sighed. "Yes. My employers no longer seem to believe my lies about my sexual conquests. I was a mere lad when I last sailed to Storsund, but I am willing to wager that they would be more understanding of a man being an ambitious rogue, despite not being a lover. Besides, I am constantly upsetting the rougher denizens of Nightport one way or another. And now, well, sooner or later our Queen is bound to find out that I helped you."

"Surely, she will have given up on me long before then," Elise said.

Nessa shook her head. "Don't be so sure. As I've said, you are simply not easy to give up."

Elise gave her smile, one that was strangely shy and

demure for Lady Elisandrine Falk. Thinking about the name reminded Nessa. "Oh, we'll need new names. And if you are to come and find us, Hunter, you'll need to know them."

He shrugged. "I would stick with Nessa and Elise if I were you. They are common names and changing your first name can be very confusing — trust me, I've tried. I would suggest you both pick the same surname and pose as a married couple. That should confuse things if the Queen does come looking for you. Come up with a surname now and on the ship's manifesto tomorrow it will say Elise and Nessa…"

"Glass," Elise replied immediately. She beamed at Nessa.

She remembers my little speech about my love for glass. Of course she does.

Nessa took her hand as she nodded her consent to the name.

Hunter's shapely eyebrows raised and his lips pursed. "As you wish. That sounds a bit prosaic to me, but then my name is Smith so I cannot comment. I promised Captain Levi of the good ship *Fairlight* that he would have another cabin filled. Now, I simply need to tell him to make out two common class tickets for Mrs E and Mrs N Glass for the 8.15 departure for Storsund."

"Are you certain you do not want payment?" Elise asked.

"Positive. I went into the closest tavern, and within mere moments, I had two captains telling me they needed passenger numbers to prove to their financiers that their route is needed. They both said they would gladly use this occasion to clear their debt to me. Both were sailing for the beautiful, icy plains of Storsund. The *Fairlight* left the earliest so she will be your vessel. You should be some of the few people on the ship."

He snapped his fingers. "Which reminds me, there are usually people on these ships who have used their last coins to buy the ticket. They need currency for when they reach Charlottenberg. Ask around, searching out people who have several changes of warm clothes with them, then buy what they can spare. I could only pack clean underthings and one shirt for Nessa and one dress for you, Elise. You will arrive cold and smelly unless you buy more clothes from your fellow travellers."

Nessa squeezed his arm, the way he had done with her before, assuming it was a form of physical affection he felt comfortable with. "You think of everything. Thank you, Hunter. You're a far better man than I think anyone sees."

"Shh. Not so loud, I have a reputation to maintain. Now that I have the names that will go on the tickets, I shall go fetch them from Captain Levi and return shortly. After we have said our goodbyes, you can get back to your animal activities while I return to the city centre and start spreading the rumour that you left to go back to Ground Hollow. Perhaps muddy the waters by saying that you wanted to travel to the highlands after that."

He left without waiting for a response. Nessa wondered if his speed was for his own sake or theirs.

Elise leaned closer to her. "Not much for goodbyes, is he? Did you see him writhe and grimace when we said goodbye to Cai and Fyhre?"

"No, I can't say I did."

"Well, he looked awfully uncomfortable. I think we should keep our goodbye short and unemotional. We owe him a lot, and I would hate to make him feel out of sorts."

Nessa put her arm around Elise's waist. "Of course. Very wise, Mrs Glass."

Elise rushed her, enveloping her in a kiss which took Nessa's breath away. As the kiss deepened and she felt their chests connecting, she stopped it.

"Heartling, don't. Or we'll end up being naughty in those blankets again. And we are not to make Hunter uncomfortable, remember?"

"Right. Yes. Of course, We will merely sit and eat our sandwiches. Platonically," Elise answered, slightly out of breath.

Nessa's eyes were drawn to Elise's lips and she forced herself to look away. "Eating... sandwiches. Platonically. Yes."

Elise brought the bag over to the blankets and sat down while peering into it. She unpacked the sandwiches and the large bottle of juice, which Nessa took a deep swig out of when she sat down next to her.

Elise surveyed her sandwich. "You know. This is actually one thing I shall not miss about this city. I have not dared to tell anyone, but I genuinely dislike shrooms."

Nessa leaned in and replied conspiratorially, "Me too. Far too slimy. And this is my second one tonight. Ick. Still, let's not tell anyone or we'll never be welcome back here."

They shared a smile before tucking into their sandwiches. Slimy or not, the food was welcome after their eventful day. When the sandwiches were gone, they passed the bottle of juice back and forth, making sure their fingers touched every time they did so.

After that Nessa began writing her farewell letters. The one for her parents was easy. They tended to be direct, to-the-point people. She wrote that she loved them and missed them. Thanked them for everything and pointed out that she had been lucky to grow up in a safe, sweet village with a mother and a father who were happily married and successful at farming. She explained that, while that was an incredible life, it wasn't for her. Nightport had shown her that she was built for cities and new experiences. So, she was going to take her friend, Lady Falk, with her and try out a city or two in Storsund. She promised to write them often and to visit when she could. And to stay safe.

Layden's letter was trickier. She didn't know how honest to be. She should probably keep that one short as well. She was too exhausted to tell all. Besides, Hunter would be back soon.

She sat back against a stack of timber and sighed. Elise was resting on the blanket next to her. Nessa tapped her pen on the paper to the beat of her lover's breaths. Then she copied the main points from her letter to her parents, thanking him for being a wonderful companion and confidant through their lives. Trying to make it sound less like a 'goodbye forever' than it felt. Then she added a few lines stating that she was in love with Elise. That he had been right about that. And that this time, she was sure she had found the one.

She needed him to be convinced.

He's still going to worry. Because he knows how different I and Elise are. Because he knows we haven't known each other for long. Because none of my previous relationships have lasted. There's nothing I can say that will change that.

She promised him that she'd keep an eye out for apothecaries in Storsund and see what the competition was doing. Hoping this would in some small way make up for losing his best friend to another continent. She signed the letters, folded them, and stuck them in her coat pocket for now. Nessa slumped, staring into space. When would she next see all of them?

Then that telltale creak of the door was heard again. Nessa's heart leapt in her chest. She knew it was probably Hunter, but there was a chance that someone had found them. Or that someone was coming in here to use this hideout as a place for a tryst. Perhaps just to sleep off the brandy.

The sight of cobalt velvet calmed her nerves.

"Hello ladies," Hunter said.

They got up, and Nessa reached out to take the two pieces of card he handed them. They were tickets for the 8.15 departure of the *Fairlight*, printed in sharp blue ink. At the bottom, handwritten, were their names. 'Mrs Nessa Glass and Mrs

Elise Glass.' It made Nessa's breath hitch to see their new names. And to see them written as if they were married.

Elise was looking over her shoulder. "Elise Glass. I like that. Short and sweet."

"Sweet as you, milady," Hunter said with his charm-offensive grin. "Now, you will be offered three basic meals and drinks a day aboard. Anything additional, you must purchase and pay for in the Noble section. Everything there will be expensive. However, it is the only place on board to get drinks that are stronger than watered-down wine."

"I think we have had enough strong drink for a while," Elise said with a snort.

Nessa took her hand. "Agreed. We should stick to alcohol-free drinks and drama-free socialising. Mainly just the two of us, I think. We both need time to recover and adjust. Six weeks at sea should do that nicely."

Hunter clasped his hands behind his back. "In that case, I shall leave you to start your sober seclusion right away. Get some sleep. At sunlight, which will be in a handful of hours, there will be the sound of an ear-piercing siren. It signals the start of the workday at the docks. I suggest you get up and ready to leave the moment you hear that signal. The workers in these humbler warehouses are always late, knowing they can keep their own hours as long as everything gets loaded and unloaded on time. But you should still hurry, just in case."

Nessa tried to pour all her gratitude into her smile. "All right. Thank you for the warning. How will we know where the *Fairlight* is docked?"

"What? Oh. Did I forget to tell you about that? Sorry, it has been a long day for all of us. Captain Levi said it is three berths away in the direction we came. The *Fairlight* is a huge steamship, you cannot miss her."

"It seems I keep repeating 'thank you,' but I do not know what else to say," Elise admitted with a smile.

Hunter inclined his head towards her. "Then simply say goodnight and that you shall see me when I visit the Glass family in Skarhult."

"Very well," Elise replied. "Come see us as soon as you can."

She went towards him with outstretched arms, but stopped herself. Instead, she clearly decided to take Nessa's queue and clapped him on the shoulder, giving it a bit of a squeeze before she let go.

Nessa went for variety and held her hand out. He shook it sombrely. She smiled and said, "Keep Nightport safe for us, mate. We'll want to return some day. Speaking of returning to Arclid, here are the letters for my parents and my best friend, Layden. Are you still willing to deliver them?"

"Absolutely. I shall do it tomorrow when I have finished my shift at the day job."

Nessa moved closer to him. "Thank you. Just ask anyone you meet in Ground Hollow, and they'll tell you where to find the Clays and Layden Amani. Farewell, Hunter."

"Farewell, ladies. Be careful with each other. Next time, you shan't have Fyhre and Cai to help reunite the both of you."

With laughter in her voice, Elise promised while Nessa nodded her agreement.

He walked out, with a little less strutting than usual. Nessa watched him go with a lump in her throat. The door closed behind him. She waited a few heartbeats until she turned to Elise with a naughty grin. "So. What do we do now?"

CHAPTER 31
UNDER THE WATCH OF THE MOON GODDESS

"So, what do we do now?"

That was what Nessa had asked.

Elise's mind came up with only two options. Sleep and lovemaking.

She tried for a neutral voice. "That depends, heartling. How tired are you?"

"Exhausted," Nessa replied on an exhale.

"Well, then. We should probably sleep."

Nessa put her hands in her coat pockets. "Yes. Yes, we should. We need to be rested tomorrow. Ready for a long trip."

"And we need to not be too exhausted to be woken by that siren. We have to be out of here before the warehouse workers catch us trespassing," Elise pointed out.

Nessa pushed back her shoulders. "Exactly."

Elise took a deep breath. Then another. After that, she threw herself at Nessa, tearing her coat off while kissing her. Nessa responded with the same fervour, tugging at Elise's clothes like an impatient, hungry child craving its dinner. She actually growled when she finally got Elise's wool coat off.

Elise felt a strident tug deep inside her belly, shooting

down between her legs and turning into liquid heat. Her knees wobbled a little. Sleep was no longer an option. It had never been an option. Too many nights had been spent sleeping in this woman's arms. Praying for the possibility of a kiss. Of an intimate touch. To hear a moan from those soft lips. To feel the touch of those strong, pretty hands. All over her. All the way into her.

Now it was hers to have. And a part of her doubted she'd ever be able to go to sleep without trying to get another dose of Nessa. If she would ever stop trying to make up for lost time. For all those moments of longing and need.

She felt Nessa roughly kiss her neck and nearly sobbed with the pleasure of it.

They manoeuvred themselves onto the blankets. Elise took what she had needed for so long and felt her heart soar when Nessa so happily gave her everything over and over again. Tonight, Nessa had no struggle climaxing, emotion seemingly driving away all over-thinking. Their cries and moans were hopefully lost in the shrieks of night owls or the distant bustle of Core Street.

When they finished devouring each other and decided on sleep, it felt like Elise had passed through the state of tiredness and gone straight into a new state of being. Some form of love-drunk sleepwalking. She nestled into Nessa's body, as close as she could get, and tried to remember who to thank for all of this.

"Heartling," she whispered.

"Yes?" Nessa replied drowsily.

"What was the name of that moon goddess you favour?"

Nessa tucked her arm under her head. "Ioene?"

"Yes. That is the one. You know, it is a full moon tonight."

Another sleepy mumble. "Yes, I believe it is."

"If I was the type to pray, I would thank Ioene."

Nessa softly cleared her throat. "For the moonlight tonight? You can't even see it."

"No. For you. For us. That this worked out. I never dared to believe it would," Elise said, stricken by the truth of it.

"It did. And it will continue to," Nessa said. "I'll pray to Ioene for the both of us. She'll watch over us. Keep us safe from enemies and keep our relationship strong and blissful."

"She can do whatever she pleases as long as *you* are watching over us, too," Elise added.

"Of course I am, and so are you. My parents taught me that love needs loyalty, empathy, and honesty. But most of all, it needs the people involved to be willing to work to make it last. Father said that a relationship is easy the first few years, but after that it requires patience and effort. And to take solace in that, the patience and effort will be rewarded a thousand-fold. We're going to work for this, and be rewarded with decades of love."

Relief washed over Elise. "Yes, we are. Goodnight, my cherished."

"Goodnight, love of my life."

Elise's senses were filled with Nessa. Nessa's warm skin, Nessa's sweet scent, Nessa's taste on her tongue, Nessa's gentle breathing, and her beautiful, resting face.

Elise had never felt so safe or been so satisfied. And sleep had never felt so alluring. She gave in to it, happily.

CHAPTER 32
DOES MAGIC EXIST?

Hunter had been right about the loud siren. Luckily, he had also been right about the warehouse workers not showing up on time. When Nessa and Elise had gotten up, smoothed down rumpled clothes and hair, they grabbed their bags and hurried out, with no one in sight.

The rest of the docks, however, were swarming with what Nessa assumed were sailors, dock workers, and assorted staff for the ships. Women filling out paperwork boarded and left ships at breakneck speeds. Others, mainly men, carried boxes on while their counterparts offloaded other cargo. The air filled with shouted orders and people wishing each other good morning.

Nessa and Elise walked past a man eating a sandwich while he carried a crate under one arm. Nessa smelled the fresh bread and had to stop the impulse to ask him for half.

"Gods, I'm starving," she whined.

Elise took her hand. "We are sure to be fed as soon as we leave dock. Look, here is the *Fairlight*. She is enormous!"

Nessa followed Elise's gaze and saw an imposing creature of

green and white metal. The *Fairlight* did indeed look colossal, but then, to Nessa, all ships looked huge and impressive.

"You know, I've only ever been on canal boats."

Elise looked at her. "Really?"

"Yes, I used to be go with Father to Little Hollow to barter grains and fruit for meat and fish. We'd get our ox to pull the boat along the canal. But that's my only experience with travel on water."

"Well, I am convinced you will love it. There is something magical about looking out and seeing nothing but water. I have only done it a handful of times. When the Queen visited Obeha, usually. She wanted me with her. I thought it was because she enjoyed my company, but it seems she simply wanted to be amused by what trouble I would cause."

Nessa pulled a face. "Oh, she's got shrooms for brains. Besides, I bet she did like your company. You're very charming, you know."

Elise gave her hand a grateful squeeze. Then she approached a woman with a clipboard and a white and green uniform.

"Boarding the *Fairlight* headed for Charlottenberg, Storsund?" the woman asked.

"Yes, here are our tickets," Elise said, handing them over.

The woman looked at the tickets and smiled up at her. "Thank you, Mrs Glass. You'll find your double bed cabin on the right side of the ship. Number eight. The porter here'll take your luggage to your cabin so you can relax and enjoy the view before we leave dock. There is an on-board library, and there'll be games played on the deck. Until it gets too cold, of course. May Thrale be with us on this journey."

"Thank you," Nessa said, both to the woman and to the runt of a porter who hurried their bags aboard.

As they walked after him, Elise whispered, "Did you hear that? She had a Ground Hollow accent."

"No. Appledore, two villages over."

Elise chuckled. "I still have much to learn," she said as she linked her arm with Nessa's.

They stepped onto the deck and found a place to watch Whistler's Sea, which lay ahead of them in huge swathes of darkest greyish-blue.

Nessa shivered in the sea breeze. The morning was cold and she was very well aware that things were only going to get colder as their journey progressed. She watched Elise pull her coat tighter around herself and asked her, "Why couldn't we have gotten passage to the Western Isles or Obeha again?"

Elise scowled at her. It almost didn't break into a smile. Almost. "Because beggars cannot be choosers, my cherished. Besides, the Queen is less likely to guess that we would go to Storsund in autumn. If she is going to look for us, she will probably scour all the ships to warmer climes."

Nessa put her arm around Elise's waist and pulled her close. "Well. At least the cold is a good reason to cuddle close. Any excuse to hold you."

"The day you need an excuse for that will never come, Nessa Clay."

"Ah, no. It's Nessa Glass, remember?" she said, tracing Elise's jawline with her index finger.

Elise smiled before dipping her head to kiss the fingertip. "Yes, of course, Mrs Glass. My apologies."

"Thank you, Mrs Glass."

They turned their back on the harbour, looking back out at sea.

Nessa breathed in the salty, cold air. "You know what? I actually can't wait until we leave. I'm barely even frightened by the enormity of it all. I came to love Nightport, but I also came to love seeing new things. The vast ocean and then Storsund, there's so much to see. Still, I'm glad you have some experience with being at sea. As always, travelling with you makes the risks seem so much smaller."

Elise hummed. She looked pensive, staring at the dark, cold water. She blew out a long breath. "Sea travel with you will be a lot nicer than sailing with the Queen. She complains about everything and likes to make the crew's life a misery."

"I'm not surprised," Nessa said with a chuckle. Then her mirth died. Now was the time to ask. "Um, while we are on the topic of you being with the Queen. I never dared to ask. Did I understand her correctly? Did she say that the two of you had... gone to bed with each other in the past?"

Elise frowned, gazing out at sea with even greater deliberation. "Occasionally, yes."

Nessa hated herself for asking but couldn't help it. "I see. Do you p-prefer doing... that with me compared to doing that with her?"

For the first time since the conversation started, Elise looked at Nessa. "Of course. Not just because you are a better lover, much more considerate and passionate, but because I love you."

Nessa felt her cheeks burn. She fake-coughed. "I'm sorry I didn't hear that last part. What were those last three words?"

Elise's forehead furrowed deeply. "I love you?"

Nessa felt joy buzzing in her belly. "Hmm. No. Didn't make it out this time either. It must be all the noise from the port. Or perhaps the ocean winds snatched the words away. Say again, please?"

Elise smirked at her, wise to her game now. "I love you so much. I love you with everything that I am and everything that I have. I love the very breath of you, Nessa Cl... Nessa Glass."

Nessa felt her entire face grow warm now. She hoped her blush wasn't too unattractive. "You do, don't you? I still can't believe it. And yet, thinking back, there were so many times where your actions proved it. I can't believe I missed it for so long."

"Neither can I. You are a silly, little thing."

Nessa laughed. "Takes one to know one! Anyway, I won't make that mistake again. And I will never make the mistake of not letting you know that I love you, too. Everything about you. Even the way you make every place a tinderbox. Do you know why?"

Elise crossed her arms over her chest. "No. Why?"

"Because it lights up even the darkest places. And I get the great fortune of basking in the light and the warmth of the fire that you bring. The passion. The fascination with life. The excitement that radiates through you. The Queen saw only the trouble you caused. I see the joy you bring. I hope that you'll let me continue to see it. Continue to adore it."

Elise smirked. "Well. You are coming with me to the great, vast North. You are not going to get rid of me now. We will both be following the fires I make. For better or for worse."

"Great. I can't wait for our next adventure."

Elise tilted her head and her gaze looked suddenly unfocused. "Adventure? Hmm. That reminds me. See if there is something in your right-side coat pocket."

Nessa did as she asked and found a piece of paper. It took her a moment to remember what it was. "The prediction from the fortune teller on Core Street," she said quietly.

They looked at each other for a while, remembering what the fortune had said. The confrontation with a black-hearted person, avoiding the colour purple, the faraway adventure.

Elise spoke first. "Well, that must have been a strange coincidence, right?"

"Yes. Because there is no such thing as real fortunes, are there?" Nessa asked.

"No, that would be… Well, that would be magic, would it not? Magic is not real."

There was a moment of silence.

A seagull cried above them, making them both jump. Nessa cleared her throat. "The only magic I believe in is the power of your beautiful eyes. And possibly the effects of a good, hearty breakfast."

Elise laughed. "Well, I cannot take my eyes off of you, so you will have any perceived magic of my eyes every day. Oh, and the next thing on our schedule should be to find where and when this ship serves breakfast."

Nessa sighed happily. "You really are the perfect woman for me, Mrs Glass."

Published by Heartsome Publishing
Staffordshire
United Kingdom
www.heartsomebooks.com

Also available in paperback.
ISBN: 9781999702953

First Heartsome edition: October 2017

GLOSSARY

LOCATIONS

The Orb
The planet on which our story takes place in. (Like our "earth" but smaller.)

Arclid
Where our story starts. The smallest continent on the Orb.
Arclid is divided into the highlands, midlands, and lowlands.

Obeha
A big continent, to the south-east of Arclid

Western isles
A mass of islands making up a continent southwest of Arclid.

Storsund
A continent north of Arclid

Ground Hollow
A small farming village, based inland in the lowlands. Its only fame is that it borders Silver Hollow Castle. Home of
Nessa Clay.

Silver Hollow Castle
The only royal castle in the lowlands. Old and not well main-

tained. Residence of Prince Macray (next in line to the throne after his sister, the Queen.)

Little Hollow

Tiny, farming village neighbouring Ground Hollow. The two villages are connected through a man-made canal.

Nightport

The biggest city in Arclid's lowlands. A harbour city with a bad reputation. At the time of our story, Nightport is experiencing a renaissance due to the invention of steam power and industrialism.

Silverton

Affluent town mainly inhabited by Nobles. It borders the midlands and highlands. Surrounded by a lake. This is where Elisandrine Falk was born.

Highmere

Capital of Arclid. The Queen's castle is in the centre of Highmere and the city is mainly based around the royal court. Inhabited by Nobles as well as some commoners who are servants or soldiers.

FLORA AND FAUNA

Lux beetles

Large insects that glow in the dark. Their appearance is somewhere between our butterfly and our firefly.

Marrow-oxen

Similar to our bovine creatures but slightly larger and more muscular. Often used in rural areas.

Skitter beetle

Fast, black beetles with wide backs and many small legs. Sometimes has white markings on the back, especially on the females.

Sunberry

Big, sweet, yellow berries. The flavour is similar to a mix of our strawberries and cloudberries. Together with water and honey, it makes Sunberry juice. Frequently used in the making of various kinds of alcohol.

Winterberry

Small, tart, red berries. Tastes like a mix of our cranberries and blackcurrants. Often used to make brandy but also mixed with water and honey to make juice.

Sugar pumpkins

A sort of small pumpkin that is incredibly sweet. Indigenous to Arclid. Multiple uses, for example – in cold sauce for desserts, to make dessert wine and to create scents for oils and candles. Often used instead of honey or sugar in food, as it is cheaper and more readily available (especially compared to the very rare sugar which is imported to Arclid.)

Dammon nuts

Small, sweet, and oily nuts. Tastes like almonds but are softer, thereby easier to smash for food and to make oils. Common all over Arclid.

Yellowfish

The most common fish in Arclid. Looks and tastes a bit like cod, but has a creamy yellow colour.

Milk cabbage

A sort of flavourless but very nutritious white cabbage that is common in the midlands and exported to the rest of Arclid.

Shrooms

Small, flavourful mushrooms. Very common in Arclid, especially in the lowlands.

GODS

Thrale

One of Arclid's main three deities. God of the sea. Usually depicted as an old, strong, weathered man with white skin and a blue beard. Traits: Indifferent to human suffering but will listen to the prayers of those who live a wholesome and healthy life. Wise and with a sense of humour.

Harmana

One of Arclid's main three deities. Goddess of the land (the ground/the soil). Usually depicted as a voluptuous, brown-skinned, large woman of great beauty with green eyes. Traits: patient, promiscuous, quiet and caring.

Aeonh

One of Arclid's main three deities. God of the sky. Depicted as a handsome, gaunt, tall man. Skin tone varies with times of day. Traits: Usually kind, unless he becomes jealous or suffers unrequited love.

Ioene

A minor Arclidian goddess. Goddess of the moon. In love with the goddess Sarine but forced apart from her by Aeonh. Usually depicted as a small, pale, timid but beautiful woman.

Sarine

A minor Arclidian goddess. Goddess of the sun. In love with the goddess Ioene but forced apart from her by Aeonh. Usually depicted as a yellow-skinned, curvy, radiant woman.

Sauq

A minor Arclidian god/goddess. God/goddess of death. Has no gender. Usually depicted as a pitch-black cat-like creature but much larger than any human or any of the other gods.

OTHER

Noble

The richest and most influential people (after the royal family) in Arclid. Based in a few cities, mainly in the north. Forced to marry and publicly live heterosexually.

Nether coverings

Underwear for lower part of body. Gender neutral. Can be anything from knee-length to very small.

Centurian marble

Marble, expensive building material known for its pink striation in white stone

New Dawning

Architecture style invented by royal architects in Highmere, created to make the villages around Arclid have a coherent, impressive style. Not very practical.

Leaf tea

Tea made with whatever herbs and edible leaves are around. Common on the countryside where other drinks are not readily available.

Sunberry essence

The strongest and most expensive alcohol in Arclid. Made with sunberries and aged for many years.

Cheese and shroom sandwiches

Rye sandwiches topped with a mix of chopped shrooms and soft cheese. Nightport speciality which the city is known for.

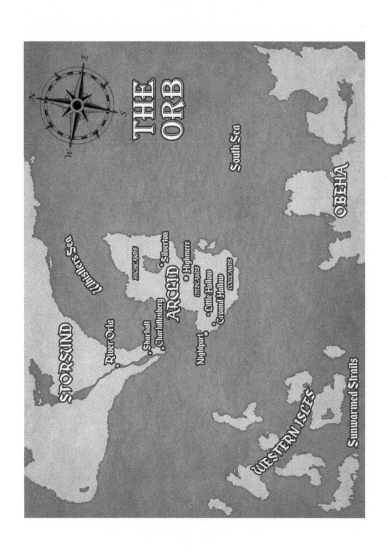

COMING SOON

Tinderbox Under Winter Stars, the second part of The
Tinderbox Tales will be available Spring 2018.

Emma Sterner-Radley spent far too much time hopping from subject to subject at university, back in her native country of Sweden. One day, she finally emerged with a degree in Library and Information Science. She thought libraries was her thing, because she wanted to work with books, and being an author was just an impossible dream, right? Wrong. She's now a writer and a publisher. (But still a librarian at heart, too.)

She lives with her wife and two cats in England. There is no point in saying which city, as they move about once a year. She spends her free time writing, reading, daydreaming, working out, and watching whichever television show has the most lesbian subtext at the time.

Her tastes in most things usually lean towards the quirky and she loves genres like urban fantasy, magic realism, and steampunk.

Emma is also a hopeless sap for any small chubby creature with tiny legs, and can often be found making heart-eyes at things like guinea pigs, wombats, marmots, and human toddlers.

Connect with Emma
www.writingradleys.com

LIFE PUSHES YOU ALONG

The unchallenging and dull life of an assistant in a small London bookshop is where Zoe Achidi feels safe.

Frequent customer, Rebecca Clare, makes Zoe's days a little brighter. But the beautiful, and impressive businesswoman in her forties seems unobtainable.

Zoe's brother and her best friend are convinced that she is stuck in a rut. When they decide to meddle in Zoe's life, they manage to bring Zoe and Rebecca together.

As they find the bravery and resolve to allow life to push them along, the question soon becomes - will it push them together or apart?

HUNTRESS *by* A.E. Radley

Amy is stuck in a rut. After graduating, she never left her temporary job at the motorway service station. Daily visits from a mysterious woman are the highlight of her days.

Until one day, when the mystery woman vanishes.

Amy investigates the disappearance and makes a shocking discovery. Suddenly, she's being framed and no-nonsense Claudia McAllister is being sent to arrest her. Will Amy's unique approach to evading capture prove successful?

AVAILABLE NOW FROM
HEARTSOME

MERGERS & ACQUISITIONS *by* A.E. Radley

Kate Kennedy prides herself on running the very best advertising agency in Europe.
One day her top client asks her to work on a lucrative project with the notoriously fastidious Georgina Masters, of the American agency Mastery.
The temporary merger causes a fiery clash of cultures and personalities. Especially when Georgina sets her romantic sights on Kate's young intern, Sophie.

HEARTSOMEBOOKS**.COM**

AVAILABLE NOW FROM
HEARTSOME

THE LOUDEST SILENCE *by* OLIVIA JANAE

Kate, an up and coming cellist, is new to Chicago and the
'Windy City Chamber Ensemble'. During her first rehearsal,
she is surprised and intrigued to meet Vivian Kensington, the
formidable by reputation board president who also happens to
be…deaf.

Slowly Kate develops a tentative friendship with the cold-
hearted woman and as she does, she finds a kindness and a
warmth that she never expected.

As their friendship begins to grow into something more, Kate
wonders, is it possible for two women, one from a world of
sound and one a world of silence, to truly understand one
another?

HEARTSOMEBOOKS.COM

CPSIA information can be obtained
at www.ICGtesting.com
Printed in the USA
BVHW042131150522
637098BV00003B/11